OF MURDER AND MADNESS

SPECIAL OFFER!

Dear Reader,

Thank you for choosing Of Murder and Madness as your thrilling journey into a world of mystery and suspense. As a token of my appreciation, I want to give you a FREE digital copy of this book!

Join my mailing list by using the exclusive weblink located in the back of this book to receive:

Free Digital Download: Journey into darkness with your complimentary Of Murder and Madness ebook copy!

Exclusive Offers: Promotions and special discounts you can't get anywhere else!

Thrilling Updates: Prepare for even more thriller stories with sneak peeks and first looks into future releases!

Don't miss out on this limited-time opportunity to receive your FREE Of Murder and Madness digital copy and join a community of thriller fanatics!

Thank you again for choosing Of Murder and Madness. I hope you enjoy the dark twists and turns that await you within these pages.

Sincerely,

Myles Schulman

OF MURDER AND MADNESS

A RILEY WALKER NOVEL

MYLES SCHULMAN

SCHULMAN PUBLISHING

Schulman Publishing LLC
13359 N Hwy 183 #406-1285,
Austin, TX 7875

First Edition: November 2022

The publisher is not responsible for websites (or their content) that are not owned by the publisher. If you would like to contact the author please visit www.mylesschulman.com.

ISBN 978-1-958565-00-1 (Hardback)

10 9 8 7 6 5 4 3 2 1

For my family

"Because hands were lifted up against the throne of the LORD, the LORD will be at war against the Amalekites from generation to generation."

—Exodus 17:16

OF MURDER AND MADNESS

ONE

The call came in just before midnight. Riley lifted the cell phone from her jacket pocket and cleared her throat before answering, "Detective Walker."

"We got a DB at 7200 South Wentworth," Shift Sergeant Hall said. Riley recognized his raspy voice through the phone's receiver. "They found the body in a rundown apartment complex. You know the place?"

Englewood Terrace Apartments was one of a dozen buildings on Chicago's South Side that had closed during the recession and never reopened. Now the decrepit complex housed every breed of lowlife imaginable.

"Yeah. Who phoned it in?"

"Anonymous tip. Dispatch received the call at twenty-two hundred from an unlisted number. Probably a burner."

"That's some response time."

"Hey, don't give me that," Hall said. "If you knew half of the things I've got to deal with tonight, your head would spin."

"Forensics?"

1

"Already at the scene. The coroner should be there soon to collect the stiff. I heard we caught a bad one."

"They're all bad ones. Anything else?"

"Commander Briggs wants you partnered up. The guy's name is Kurt Thompson. He's a new transfer from the El Paso County Sheriff's Office."

"I don't need some rookie screwing up my case."

"He's not a rookie. According to his file, Kurt worked several years in Vice. Major Crimes before that."

"He hasn't worked here."

"Sorry, commander's orders. I'm just the messenger."

Riley's lips tightened. There had to be some way out of this, but nothing came to mind. She took a drag of her electronic cigarette and exhaled.

"Walker, you still there?"

"Let me know if anything else comes up," she said, and hung up the phone.

Hard rain pummeled her windshield as she merged onto Interstate 94 and headed east. It had been three weeks since the Bureau of Detectives demoted her from the elite Violent Crimes Task Force to working nights on Chicago's South Side. Now the department was issuing a partner to keep her in check. She gazed down the lonely stretch of road, wondering what waited for her at the other end.

Riley exited onto Lafayette Avenue, then took West Seventy-Second Street to Wentworth. The gutters overflowed, spewing runoff into the streets. She glided down the road until she spotted two patrol units parked in front of a boarded-up apartment building. Its red brick walls were covered with graffiti.

She pulled up to the curb and shut off the engine. The pitter-patter of rain danced along the roof as she took one last drag, then raised her jacket's hoodie. She stepped out of her dark gray Crown Vic and popped the trunk. Her bulletproof vest had slid across the rear compartment during the drive, so Riley tethered it to the wall liner, then released the plastic clasps of her examination kit.

She retrieved a tactical flashlight, two elastic gloves, and a tube of lip balm—a ritual performed more times than she cared to remember. After tucking the items into her jacket, she looked down the road to a white van with rusted wheel wells, then shut the trunk. The front gate swayed from a single hinge. She palmed it open and hustled across the walkway to the boarded entrance.

The thick double doors sealed behind her, muffling the wailing storm. Riley tried to catch her breath, but the damp stench of urine and mold caused her to gag. A frail old man in a thrashed overcoat was kneeling beside an overstocked grocery cart. He hacked a mouthful of phlegm onto the floor and stared up at her with ghost-white eyes. "Are you an angel?"

"No," she said.

A young, baby-faced patrolman entered the lobby from behind a battered door and shined a flashlight toward her. "Officer Walker?"

Riley raised a hand to shield her eyes. "It's Detective."

He lowered his flashlight. "Sorry about that. Follow me."

The embroidered name tag over his coat read "Williams, Bureau of Patrol." He had to be a rookie. Riley could always spot new officers by how they carried themselves—still able to separate the uniform from the man. She followed Officer Williams up the narrow staircase. The cold cement steps were cracked, and the support railing's sheen had dulled from years of wear. There was a flash of concern on Williams's face as they ascended to the next floor.

"What do you have for me?" she asked.

"We think the anonymous tip came from one of the tenants in the building. Dispatch said they uncovered the body after smelling a foul odor from one of the apartments. It didn't take us long to find out which one."

Riley stepped over a pacifier resting beside a blood-speckled syringe. She wondered which of the items had been discarded first. "Tenants?"

"Squatters, junkies, lowlifes, take your pick. They come up here to get high," Williams said. Their voices echoed off the surrounding walls like a mausoleum. "From the looks of things and the smell, I'd say he's been dead a while."

"What about witnesses?"

Williams reached the third-floor platform and held the stairwell door open for her. "A couple of us cased the building, but none of the squatters are saying much of anything."

"Of course not. Everyone around here knows not to talk to cops," Riley said, and entered the doorway. Her footsteps alerted a pair of officers at the end of the hall. They spotlit her with their flashlights as she approached the taped-off apartment. Jordan Bradley was the senior lead officer, but she didn't recognize his partner. The uneasiness between them was palpable.

"It's pretty bad in there," Officer Bradley said. "You should cover up."

Riley removed the tube of lip balm from her jacket pocket and rubbed a small amount beneath her nose. The menthol aroma would mask the stench of rotting flesh. Bradley dropped his cigarette butt to the floor and extinguished it with his boot heel. "Eighteen years on the beat and I've never run into anything like this before. A fatal stabbing or shooting, sure, but this . . . this is something else."

Riley snapped the blue elastic gloves around her wrists. "You touch anything in there?"

"I already told you, no one's touched nothing," Williams said.

Bradley flashed a sneering grin beneath his thick mustache. "Don't you worry, Detective. Aside from making sure the corpse is a corpse, we left everything just as we found it."

"Good. Canvass the building again. See if you can get anything from the old man in the lobby."

"You got it," Bradley said, then signaled for the trio to move out. "Place gives me the creeps anyway."

The three patrolmen disappeared into the darkness as Riley ducked beneath the yellow police tape and entered the apartment. Stale air hung like a fog. She reached beside the doorframe and fingered the light switch, but nothing happened.

"Perfect."

The city must have cut the power to the building years ago. She removed the flashlight from her jacket and smacked it to life. The beam flickered against the cobwebbed ceiling, then steadied. She scanned her light across the room. Wallpaper buckled at the seams, revealing generations of washed-out paint and primer. A brown-stained sofa with exposed foam padding rested behind a sea of broken glass and torn carpeting. It was a modest space, even for a junkie.

Riley kneeled beside the doorframe and rubbed her thumb over the tarnished latch casing. If someone had forced their way in, there would have been damage to the wood. But everything was intact. She turned around and swung the door toward her. Multiple scrapings surrounded the edges of the keyhole.

"You picked the lock," she said.

It was possible the door had been picked long ago, but unlikely. In a place like this, why would anyone take the time when they could just kick the door in? The soles of her boots squeaked against the linoleum tile as she entered the kitchen. She dragged her index finger across the barren countertop, leaving a streak in the thin layer of dust. Her flashlight hovered over a corroded metal sink with a missing faucet, then trailed past a set of punched-in cabinet doors. She glimpsed at herself in the oven's shattered viewing glass. Her reddish-brown hair appeared black in the darkness of the room.

The floor creaked behind her. Riley turned around to find a dark figure standing beyond the police tape. She reached for her holstered pistol and raised her flashlight over a pair of hard-worn eyes.

"Who are you?" she asked.

The man pulled back his lapel, revealing a detective badge attached to his belt. "Detective Kurt Thompson. You must be Detective Walker. I've been assigned to work with you on this case."

Riley eased her grip. He was handsome in a rugged sort of way. Cropped hair, stubbled jaw, dressed in all black. She approached the doorway and stopped on the opposite side of the police tape. "I don't know what they told you, but I work alone."

He leaned in. "So do I."

There was whiskey on his breath. After sizing him up, she backed away from the door. "Gloves on. I don't need you marking up the place."

Kurt removed a pair of plastic gloves from his coat and ducked beneath the police tape. "Have you tried the lights?"

"They're out," she said, and turned away.

"Of course they are."

She entered the bathroom to find that the shower's piping was missing. Looters, no doubt. Copper pipe could go for two dollars a pound at most scrap yards—three if it was unleaded. She checked behind the door, then returned to the living room. Kurt was placing something into his inner coat pocket. "Find anything in there?"

"This place has been ransacked. Looters stripped the pipes from the fixtures and walls. Everything they could grab is gone."

"Well, now we know why our caller wanted to remain anonymous," Kurt said, tracing his flashlight across the room. "What a dump."

Riley opened the bedroom door. They shined their flashlights over a stalky man with a camera draped around his neck. His white plastic jumpsuit crinkled with every movement as he lowered the dust mask from his face. "Good, you're here. I was just about finished up."

Riley crossed through the open doorway. The bedroom was a dark abyss with the pungent stench of rotten meat permeating every inch of space. She beamed her flashlight across a set of boarded windows and broken shelving. In the center of the room, a man's corpse sat upright in a wooden chair. He was naked and facing the far wall, which revealed a message written in blood.

CAN YOU SEE

The large, oppressive letters dripped to the floor like skeletal fingers reaching out to her. She approached the corpse, avoiding the rusted nails in the floorboards. A massive wooden cross was tattooed down the center of his back. She rounded the chair and raised her flashlight over the victim's face. Bloodstains flowed from his hollow eye sockets as if he were weeping red.

"What happened to you?" she asked.

American traditional-styled tattoos covered his body: a dagger through the left bicep, a black snake coiled around the right forearm, and the letters BSMC inked across his chest.

"The tattoos look gang related," she said. "Send a copy of the photographs to the GID. See if we can get a match."

"You got it," the photographer said from the doorway.

Kurt motioned toward the wall. "That blood from the victim?"

"Most likely," she said without taking her eyes off the body. "There are multiple lacerations to the torso. We'll have to wait for the medical examiner's report to determine a cause of death. Did we find a murder weapon?"

"No, the place is clean." The photographer shrugged. "All things considered."

Riley lowered her flashlight to the purple ligature marks wrapped around the victim's wrists and ankles. She peered up at his gaping mouth. Thin cuts coated with dry saliva surrounded the edges of his lips.

"He was tortured," she said. "Bound and gagged. Whoever did this must have removed the restraints before they left."

Kurt approached the body. He aimed his flashlight at the floor beneath the chair. "No scuff marks, no blood, and no signs of a struggle. This isn't the kill site. Someone dumped him here."

She inspected the victim's hands. When skin cells die from oxygen deprivation, the hands shrink, giving the appearance of overgrown fingernails. With her thumb and index finger, she lifted the victim's wrist a few inches off the arm of the chair with ease. "He's past the state of rigor mortis. From the coloring of the skin, tissue decay, and lack of maggots, I'd put the time of death around forty-eight hours ago."

Kurt examined the body with his flashlight. "Looks like a gang feud to me. They probably tortured him for information or revenge."

Riley shook her head. "No, not this one. Gangs display their murders publicly to frighten rivals and keep their own in line. Either that, or they get rid of the evidence all together." She glanced around the room. "This is a private affair."

Officer Williams entered the doorway. "Coroners are outside. What should I tell them?"

Riley rose to her feet. She knew all she could without further inspection from the medical examiner. "We're finished. Did you get anything from the old man?"

"He's got glaucoma. Didn't see a thing," Williams said, then backed out of the room. Riley sighed. The weight of the week wore heavy on her shoulders.

Kurt gazed up at the message on the wall. "Can you see . . ." He peered around the room. "See what? There's nothing here."

She frowned. "I don't know."

Riley removed her gloves, then walked out of the apartment. Two overweight coroners in matching windbreakers wheeled a gurney topped with a black body bag down the hallway.

"Who's cutting tonight? Jamison?" she asked.

"No. Leeds," the first coroner confirmed. "But he isn't coming close to your guy. We're swamped. This is our eighth call tonight."

Riley rested her hand on the stretcher. "I need you to expedite this one."

"Didn't you hear me? I said the doc is busy. We've got bodies lining the hallways. He could get to your VIC after the weekend. Tuesday at the latest, but there's no way he's going to have time for your autopsy tonight."

The coroner tried to push away, but Riley's grip tightened over the metal frame. "Then I'll go down there and ask him myself."

He stopped. "What's the big rush?"

"I just have a bad feeling about this one. You'll understand once you see the crime scene."

"Fine. I'll ask him, but no promises. If Dr. Leeds says no, that's it. Saturdays are our busiest night, and I don't need you holding us up any longer."

Riley removed her hand. "That works."

The pair of coroners continued rolling the gurney toward the apartment. It was a long shot that Dr. Leeds would break procedure, but she couldn't afford to wait three days for a preliminary report. This was big evil. She could feel it in her bones.

Kurt followed her in lockstep down the stairwell. "No murder weapon, no witnesses, and no leads. I'd say we hit the jackpot."

"What we need to do is identify the body. The sooner we find out who the victim is, the sooner we find out why he died—and then who murdered him."

The three patrolmen hushed their laughter as they entered the lobby. Officer Williams broke from their huddled circle. "All good, detectives?"

"Put a seal on the door after they take the body. We don't need any more looters sifting through the crime scene," she said.

"A department seal won't stop anything," Bradley said, then took a drag of his cigarette. "Not in this place at least."

"Coroners are moving the victim now," Kurt said.

"Do we have a problem?" asked Bradley.

"That's up to you."

Williams retrieved a bright blue police seal from his jacket. "I've got one right here. Let's go."

Bradley flicked his cigarette at Kurt's feet, then joined his fellow officer in the stairwell. Riley raised her hoodie and pushed through the front doors. She ran across the walkway to her cruiser and slid into the driver's seat. Kurt joined her from the passenger side.

"Don't you have a car?" she asked.

"I took a cab here," he said, wiping the rain from his hair. The edge of a black tattoo peeked from his shirt collar. It was just for a moment, but the tattoo appeared to be two parallel black bars. Riley clenched her jaw, then inserted her keys into the ignition. The windshield wipers swayed across the glass, bringing clarity to the outside world. She pulled away from the curb, driving down the road. Kurt peered out the window at the passing buildings. "Have you seen anything like this before?"

"There were over seven hundred homicides in this city last year. None of them were like this."

He turned to look at her. "To take the time to remove someone's eyes like that, you'd have to be some sort of monster."

Riley took a drag, then exhaled. "The world is full of monsters, and they look like us."

TWO

"Cause of death was due to severe trauma to the brain," Dr. Leeds confirmed. His light green scrubs were stained red with the victim's blood.

Riley bowed her head over the pale, marble-like corpse resting on the slab between them. "How so?"

The doctor reached overhead and pulled a surgical light close to the victim's face. Every bruise, cut, and blemish was revealed with vivid detail. She leaned in for a closer look. Sterile fumes stung her nostrils. The body was covered in antiseptic to prevent microbial spreading.

Leeds pointed to tiny fissures of bone exposed around the ridges of the victim's eye sockets. "His frontal cortex has suffered multiple lacerations through the orbital cavities. Tissue damage was caused by a blade approximately three inches in length. Perhaps a folding knife. You see the small abrasions here and here? Those entrance wounds show signs of shearing from a jagged edge." He paused to cough into his shirt sleeve. "Excuse me. I'm still getting over this damn cold."

"Were there any prints on the body?" Riley asked.

"No."

"Why take the eyes?" Kurt inquired. He was standing beside her with his arms crossed.

Dr. Leeds turned off the surgical light and returned it overhead. "I'm sorry to say I don't know."

"Is it possible they harvested the eyes to be sold?" Riley asked.

The man rubbed his thumb through the gray hairs on his chin, then nodded. "The act itself was not surgical. The killer ruptured the victim's oblique and rectus muscles. If the goal were to preserve the eyes after enucleation, they would have used a scalpel or spoon. These eyes were stabbed with quick, deliberate thrusts." He extended his fist to demonstrate. "An attack like that must have reduced them to nothing more than mush."

She tried to repress the images from her mind. "Do you have a time of death?"

"Judging from the state of decomposition, I'd say around thirty-six to forty-eight hours."

"What about the stab wounds? How recent are they?" she asked.

Leeds surveyed the victim's abdomen. "No signs of clotting. They must have been made around the same time. It's also worth noting that the victim has three fractured knuckles on his right hand, including a break of the fifth metacarpal bone—also known as a boxer's fracture. Visible scar tissue along both of his hands tells me he's seen a lot of fights."

"A guy like that couldn't have gone down easy," Kurt said.

"You're right. He was drugged," the doctor said, then lifted his clipboard from the corner of the slab. He skimmed through the medical report and cleared his throat. "Blood test picked up traces of ketamine hydrochloride."

"What's that?" Kurt asked.

"A date rape drug," Riley said. "On the street it's called Special K. Is it possible he was unconscious when the murder took place?"

Leeds reviewed his clipboard again. "There was a sizable amount of histamine in his system, and the ligature marks on his wrists and ankles would indicate a struggle. He was awake, and he felt everything." He removed his wire-rimmed glasses and waved a hand over the victim's torso. "The placement of these stab wounds is not random. They were made to prevent exsanguination. The killer avoided every major artery, to prolong the suffering for as long as possible. Whoever did this wanted to take their time."

"Thank you, Doctor."

"My pleasure." Leeds covered the body with a white sheet. "I'll let you know as soon as we have confirmation on his ID."

Riley turned away from the slab and pushed through the vinyl-slatted doorway. Unexamined corpses in black body bags lined the hallway.

"This seems gang related to me. Why else would someone go through the trouble of torturing him?" Kurt asked.

"You don't leave a corpse in a place like that unless you want it to be found. All of this feels wrong."

"Does it ever feel right? An abandoned building is just as good of a place to dump a body as any other."

"It still doesn't explain the message," she said, then opened the door to the front lobby. The security guard glanced up at them from behind the counter, then licked his thumb and turned the page of his book. Riley and Kurt stopped in front of the entrance.

"So what, then?" he asked.

"It was an invitation. The killer wanted us to find him."

"Why?"

"I don't know," she said. This case was going cold fast, and if she didn't find a lead soon, it would become stillborn. She took a drag of her e-cigarette.

"There's no smoking in here," the security guard said.

Riley pocketed her cigarette and raised her hoodie. "Without the victim's ID, and no leads, there's nothing else we can do tonight. I'll take care of the paperwork." She pushed through the front door into the pouring rain. "Go home."

Her teeth chattered as she ran across the parking lot to the cruiser. She started the engine, but the car's heater provided no comfort—her chill was skin deep. Torn flesh, ligature marks, blood smears. Riley found that the cases she worked stayed with her like a nasty stain, an ever-present darkness haunting the back of her mind. It reminded her of a quote she once read from a German philosopher: "If you gaze long enough into an abyss, the abyss will gaze back into you."

The medical examiner's building faded in the rearview mirror as she drove west on Harrison Street toward the interstate. After a fifteen-minute commute, she dropped off her cruiser at the station, then drove her white Ford Mustang home—a one-bedroom condo in Hyde Park. She entered the front door, then heeled it closed behind her. The living room was an empty shell save for the stack of storage boxes full of case files.

Riley removed her grimy boots and slid them next to the front door. The cold hardwood floors creaked beneath her feet as she walked to the kitchen and placed her jacket over the counter. She knew better than to try to sleep while a case was weighing on her mind, so she grabbed a beer from her refrigerator and powered on her laptop. She leaned the bottle against the edge of the counter and slammed her palm down on the cap, causing it to pop off. It wasn't dinner, but it would do.

She raised the beer to her lips and took a drink. When her laptop finished booting up, she entered her password, then browsed through a series of articles from the *Chicago Wire*, a local news outlet that focused on underreported stories. On the website's homepage, she read a headline: "Kane Initiative, A New Era for Chicago." It was written by a reporter named Holly Hart. Riley double-clicked the link, and a full-page article appeared on the screen. A large man with piercing eyes stood over a miniature model of the city.

Riley continued reading.

Business mogul Robert Kane held a private gala event in the signature room of Hancock Tower late Friday night to reveal his proposal for the remodeling of Chicago's southern districts. Kane, along with several firms, has promised to begin aggressively investing in the city's most impoverished neighborhoods, then expand into the industrial regions.

"These areas have become a breeding ground for crime and violence. By tearing down these buildings, we will root out these criminal enterprises while restoring our city to its former glory." Kane said during a rousing speech.

Mayor Cox is hopeful the project will bring much-needed jobs to the city. "We're losing 1200 residences each year," he says. "This initiative will put Chicago back on the map." Newly appointed District Attorney, Matthew Locke, on the other hand, is skeptical of the impact the initiative will have on crime. "This project will bring much-needed disruption to those areas. But we don't know what the repercussions will be."

Construction for the Kane Initiative will begin next month.

The DA was right. The department's crusade against a rising crime rate had been a losing battle for years. Demolishing those buildings would force gangs to move their operations deeper into the city, and with fresh territory would come new turf wars. It would be a bloodbath.

The article left a sour taste in her mouth. Riley took another drink, then got started on the paperwork.

THREE

The Chicago Police Department Homicide Division resided on the ground floor of the building, with five rows of desks divided for each area of the city. Even at this early hour, the bullpen was teeming with detectives as Riley hustled across the outer walkway to Commander Briggs's office at the back of the room. The frosted glass window on the door showcased his name and title in bronze lettering.

Her palms were sweating with anticipation. Briggs wasn't keen on theories, and with no ID, murder weapon, or leads, speculation was all she had. Riley took a moment to compose herself, then opened the door to find the man sitting behind a wide mahogany desk. His perpetual scowl deepened as she entered.

"Detective Walker. How nice of you to show."

A three-car pileup on the interstate had added fifteen minutes to her commute, but she knew there was no point in giving an excuse.

"Sorry I'm late."

"Let's not make it a habit," Briggs said.

Riley took her seat next to Kurt in one of the traditional wrap-

16

around chairs across from the commander. He leaned forward and interlocked his fingers before resting them over the desk. "Now that we're all here, what do you have for me?"

Riley handed Briggs an unmarked manila folder. "The body was found in an abandoned apartment complex. From what we gathered, he was placed there postmortem."

Briggs pulled a copy of the victim's autopsy report from the folder and lifted a pair of dark reading glasses from his desk. "Cause of death?"

"According to the medical examiner's report, the victim was stabbed through the eyes. No weapon was recovered from the scene," Riley said.

Briggs turned the page to a close-up photograph of the victim's petrified face. "Were there any witnesses?"

"A patrol team canvassed the building, but no one admitted to seeing anything," Riley said.

Kurt shifted in his seat. "The place is crawling with junkies. Even if they knew something, none of them would snitch."

Briggs turned his attention back to the file, then proceeded to the next photograph. "Tell me about the stab wounds."

"They're superficial. ME believes they were made to cause a slow bleed," Riley said. "Ligature marks on his wrists and ankles show he was bound when it happened. Blood work found traces of incapacitating agents in his system."

Briggs furrowed his brow. "Drugged, bound, tortured, then killed. That's a hard way to go." He turned to the next photograph. "Can you see . . ."

He removed his glasses and looked up to her. "Dramatic, don't you think?"

"Not if that was their intention."

Briggs clenched his jaw. "What are you saying exactly?"

"I believe the message was for us."

"Don't you start with that. Just because some nut finger-painted the wall doesn't mean anything. I've seen all sorts of crazy in my time." The commander knuckled a finger against the desktop. "We deal in facts. Hard evidence, not theories."

"The victim was covered in tattoos. Possibly gang related," Kurt said.

Briggs considered the information with a slight nod, then closed the file. "Sounds like a promising lead. Be that as it may, Mayor Cox is up for reelection and needs our division to hit its numbers. I want the both of you to put this case in the black quickly." He leaned back in his seat. "Detective Thompson, you're dismissed. I want to have a word with Detective Walker."

Kurt stood up and exited the office without glancing at Riley. She waited until he was clear of the door before speaking. "The VIC has been dead for over twenty-four hours. I don't have time to break in the new guy while finding out who did this."

Briggs smirked. "You remind me of your father." He rose from his seat and rounded the desk. "It's useful to have someone watching your back. If not on the street, then at least in the office. Someone to keep their ear to the pavement."

"My hearing is fine."

Briggs leaned back against the front of his desk and crossed his arms. "Then it shouldn't come as a surprise that Reyes wants you out. She's looking for any excuse to remove you from the bureau. Hell, probably the whole department."

Deputy Chief Rachel Reyes was a glorified bureaucrat who cared more about the optics of the department than the cases it solved. Under her direction, the Criminal Network Group had seen sweeping policy reforms in use of force, apprehension, and interrogation—all of which made Riley's demanding job on the Violent Crimes Task Force almost impossible. Now, Reyes was going to leverage the mayor's re-election and the division's poor clearance rate to muscle her out of a job. The realization hit like a punch to the gut.

"Taking me off VC wasn't punishment enough? What does Welles think about this?" she asked.

"Agent Welles has denied your appeal to return to the Violent Crimes Task Force. Reyes will never give you another opportunity to embarrass her. I told you not to go to the press."

"Shepard was far from innocent, but he was the wrong man. If we charged him, it would have been a death sentence."

Briggs clenched his teeth and pointed at her. "And I told you, that wasn't your call to make. It was for the courts to decide."

"We both know he wouldn't have made it to a hearing. Accused kiddie rapists don't last a day in county. Is this why you partnered me up? Reyes wants me to be kept in check?" She leaned in. "Frank, what aren't you telling me?"

Briggs rose from the desk and returned to his seat. "I've put in my two weeks with the chief."

"You're retiring?"

"Year after year, I've watched this department slide. No matter what we do, things just seem to get worse. I'm tired of fighting. I've done my time. Figured it best to pass the baton. Let someone else shoulder the burden." He lifted the case file from his desk and handed it to her. "I gave you a partner, Riley, because you could use all the help you could get."

She took the file and rose from her seat. The door was six feet away, but it felt like a mile. When she exited the office, a tempered voice whispered beside her, "You've got a lot of nerve, Walker."

Detective Hank Maloney was leaning against the wall next to the doorway. He must have spotted her on the way to Briggs's office.

"What are you talking about?"

Hank teased the greasy hair from his eyes. "I've had a girl on ice for two days, and now I have to wait longer because of your special request with the ME. Do us all a favor and stick to botching your own cases."

"You don't need any help from me to do that. What's your clearance rate? Twenty percent? Twenty-five? I'm surprised IAD hasn't opened a case into which side you're playing for."

"The only thing Internal Affairs should investigate is how a rat like you is still with the department. Just stay out of my way," Hank said, then walked down the hall.

Riley met Kurt at the edge of the bullpen.

"What was that about?" he asked.

"Nothing," she said. "Did the prints come in yet?"

Kurt handed her a piece of paper. "Just came in from the DMV. Our guy's name is Johnny Stone. He's got a rap sheet like a laundry list. Aggravated assault, theft, battery, disorderly conduct, resisting arrest—he's been in and out of the system for years."

"That explains the scar tissue on his hands. Any next of kin?"

Kurt shook his head. "No. The form didn't mention any known associates either."

"They wouldn't be listed there. We'll have to wait for the Gang Investigation Division for that info."

Kurt handed her a slip of paper: a scowling mugshot of Johnny next to a long list of crimes he'd committed throughout the years. She scanned his record until she found his current residence. 6230 South Laflin Street.

"There's an address here." Riley folded the paper, then slid it into her jacket. "Let's go."

FOUR

"There's a lot of eyes on us," Kurt said.

"I know," Riley said, as a group of men in dark clothing watched them from a street corner. Although her cruiser didn't have overhead lights, it was clear they viewed her as a threat. She stopped at the intersection and glanced toward a man with gold dentures. He fashioned his hand as if he were holding a gun and aimed at her head.

"What's the address?" she asked.

Kurt lifted Johnny's identification form from the dashboard. "6230 South Laflin Street."

She eased around the turn while keeping the man's hand in her peripheral vision.

"It's like this place is living on borrowed time," Kurt said.

"Aren't we all?"

A black SUV screeched around the corner and sped toward them. Booming rap music muffled its roaring engine as it passed. Kurt pointed to a mustard-colored two-story house with a brick foundation. "There it is."

The numbers "650" were nailed to the front of the house with a discolored outline for the missing "1". She parked behind an all-black motorcycle with the Harley Davidson logo on the side of the gas tank. Several people watched her from the surrounding windows.

"We're not welcome here. Keep your eyes open," Riley said, then opened the door. She popped the trunk and prepped her gloves and flashlight, then locked her examination kit.

Kurt patted his pockets. "You got an extra pair?"

She sighed and unclasped her kit again, then handed him a pair of gloves.

"Thanks."

Riley shut the trunk and approached Johnny's house. The yard was littered with empty beer cans and broken glass. She ascended the creaky porch steps, then kneeled in front of the door handle.

"What are you doing?" Kurt asked.

"The killer used a lockpick on the apartment where we found Johnny. I'm checking for similar markings."

She shined her flashlight over the door handle. The hardware was corroded, but no scratch marks. She turned it off and stood up.

"See anything?"

"No."

A soft thud reverberated within the house. She turned to Kurt. "Did you hear that?"

"What?"

"I heard something inside. Was anyone else listed at this address?"

"No."

Riley pounded on the door three times. "CPD! Open the door!"

She listened for a response, but heard nothing. Riley knocked three more times. "Police!"

Leaning to the side of the porch, she aimed her flashlight

within the front window. The blinds were too dense to see through.

"Doesn't sound like anyone's home," Kurt said.

"I know what I heard," she said, then twisted the handle. "It's unlocked, but won't open."

"Stand aside. Let me try."

Riley stepped back to the edge of the porch. A wind chill blew her hair to the side. Kurt shouldered the door twice. "The damn thing is barricaded."

Riley peered around the neighborhood. She didn't want to attract any more unwanted attention. "Come on, let's check the back."

She stepped down from the porch and walked around the side of the house. The waist-high chain-link fence was sealed with a padlock. Kurt gripped the fence and hopped over. "Need help?"

"I got it," she said, then joined him.

A rat's nest of torn garbage bags filled the narrow passageway. Shards of beer bottles crunched beneath her boots as they trudged toward the backyard. The rear of the house was filled with rusted appliances and car parts. Riley worked her way around an old car hood, then lunged over an air-conditioning unit. A stray cat hissed at her from atop a pile of bald tires before scampering away.

They continued up the sun-faded rear staircase to the top landing. A hole had been punched through one of the four small windowpanes just above the door handle. Riley leaned in and saw scratch marks surrounding the keyhole.

"The killer was here." She pointed to the lock. "Same markings as the apartment."

Riley cupped her hands against her head and peered through the window. The glass was smeared with dirt, too difficult to see through. She twisted the handle, but the door was blocked from the other side.

"What's wrong?" Kurt asked.

"The door's locked."

"Why would the killer lock up after himself?"

"They wouldn't," Riley said, then took a step back from the door. She radioed dispatch. "5215, requesting backup at 6230 South Laflin Street. Suspect inside the building."

A low voice came in through the receiver. "5215, 10-4. Sending a unit now."

Riley drew her Glock from its holster. Kurt followed suit with a chamber check. She reached her arm through the broken window and unlocked the door. "Ready?"

He nodded, and Riley quietly opened the door. The gray sky illuminated the dark entryway, casting their long shadows over the floor.

"CPD! If anyone is in here, come out with your hands in the air!" Riley said.

She followed a set of muddy footprints into the kitchen. A swarm of flies buzzed around food-encrusted dishes in the sink. Each of the cabinets had been rummaged through with discarded food cans and spoiled condiments strewn across the counter. The stench of rotten meat wafted into her nostrils. "Ugh, you smell that?"

The odor was unmistakable—the nauseating reek of a dead body.

"I'll check upstairs," Kurt said, then ascended the rear staircase. "CPD! If anyone is in here, make yourself known now!"

Riley crossed the kitchen to the living room, where a confederate flag was nailed to a makeshift bar littered with beer bottles and cans. Each of the couch's cushions had been sliced down the center, leaving clusters of white filling scattered along a stained floor rug. Someone was here, and they'd torn the place apart looking for something. But for what? What did Johnny have that was worth his life?

She stopped at a framed photograph of Johnny standing beside an older man with a goatee. They were posing in front of a sun-bleached barn with their arms wrapped around each other. She leaned in closer to get a better look at the older man. His face was obscured by a pair of dark aviator sunglasses. Was he responsible for all of this? What was his connection to Johnny? He appeared to be in his fifties—old enough to be Johnny's father.

"Walker. I've got something up here," Kurt called from upstairs. Riley returned to the kitchen, then climbed the rear staircase to the second floor.

He was standing on the edge of the landing. "Look."

She peered down the hallway to a wide blood trail that extended from the bedroom door to the front staircase.

"CPD! If someone is in here, make yourself known!" Kurt said. There was no response. He looked back to Riley, and she nodded for him to move forward. Kurt raised his pistol and silently approached the door. If someone was in the bedroom, they wouldn't hear him coming. Riley leaned against the wall and mimicked his movements. He stopped at the edge of the doorframe, then quickly peeked inside.

"Anything?" she asked.

"I can't tell."

Kurt raised his pistol, then entered the doorway. Riley followed him inside and quickly scanned each corner of the room. They were alone. She lowered her pistol with a small sigh of relief.

Blood soaked the white carpeting surrounding the bed. The glass from the wardrobe mirror had been shattered into a million pieces.

"There was a struggle," she said.

"Looks more like a massacre. You think this is where Johnny was tortured?"

"Could be. The amount of blood looks consistent with his wounds."

Riley spotted a leather jacket draped over a chair back. She stepped over the blood pool for a closer look. A large back-patch showed an image of a snake crawling through a human skull. Above the image, it read "Black Snake Motorcycle Club."

"BSMC," she said.

"What?"

She pointed to the jacket. "BSMC. The letters on Johnny's chest. It's the name of his motorcycle club. Perhaps his death was gang related after all."

A low squeak sounded outside the bedroom. Riley placed the napkin on the chair, then retrieved her pistol. Kurt leaned against the bedroom wall to limit his exposure. "Show yourself!"

"CPD. Come out with your hands in the air!" Riley said, and aimed at the doorway. Their calls were met with silence.

"Last warning, asshole!" Kurt said.

Riley crossed the room and sidestepped into the hallway. Empty.

"Check downstairs," she said.

Kurt descended the rear staircase as she crept down the hall, avoiding the blood trail. She neared the next door and used her foot to nudge it open. The shower curtain had been pulled back from the bathtub. Liquid soaps, detergent, and other cleaning products were spread over the floor beneath an open vanity cabinet.

The smell of death grew stronger with each step down the hallway. She passed another closed door and approached the front staircase. On the last step of the landing, the floor squeaked beneath her boot—the same sound she'd heard from the bedroom. Riley froze, realizing she wasn't alone. The hallway door burst open behind her. A large man with a scar across his cheek shoved her head against the wall, then ran down the stairs.

"He's here!" Riley said.

She wiped the blood from her brow, sprinting after him down

to the front entryway. A heavyset corpse of a bald man in a BSMC jacket lay slumped against the front door. His eyeless face rested beneath a message written in blood.

CAN YOU SEE

The man darted through the living room. Kurt stepped around the corner to block his path, but was body checked into the side paneling. Drywall cracked beneath their weight. Kurt dropped his pistol and fell to the floor. The man continued through the kitchen and out the back door. Riley chased him onto the back porch and took aim. "Freeze!"

But she was too late. The man had run around the side of the house.

"Damn it," she said, then weaved through the backyard. She rounded the side of the house as the man slipped into a pile of trash. He quickly rose to his feet, then cleared the front fence. A patrol unit careened to a stop in front of the house. The man rolled off the car's hood, then continued running across the street to the next row of houses.

Riley jumped over the fence and ran into the street. "Go around! Cut him off on the other side."

The patrol unit's tires spun to a burnout against the cold pavement, then sped down the road.

Kurt leaped over Johnny's fence and joined her in the street. "Which way did he go?"

"Straight ahead."

They entered the next row of houses. A pit bull barked at them through the divider fence. Riley saw the man. He looked back and knocked over a pair of trash cans, then broke from the alleyway and entered the next cross-street. A dark sedan swerved out the way and skidded onto the sidewalk.

Riley and Kurt jumped over the trash cans and pursued him

between two brick buildings. He was halfway through the corridor when the patrol unit screeched to a stop, blocking the other end. The two officers drew their weapons and shielded themselves behind the car.

"Get on the ground!" the first officer said.

The man stopped and looked back at Riley. She took aim. "It's over. There's nowhere for you to go."

"On the ground, now!" Kurt said.

The man shook his head. "You don't know who you're up against."

He was of no use to her dead, so Riley holstered her pistol and took a step forward. "Then help me understand."

"What are you doing?" Kurt said.

"It's okay," she said, taking another step forward, "I know you were looking for something in Johnny's house. What was he hiding?"

The man gritted his teeth, then reached into his pocket. "Stay back!"

Riley took a half step back. "Okay, okay. I just want to talk."

"He's reaching," Kurt said.

"No, he's not," she said. "He had the drop on me in the house. If he had a weapon, he would have used it."

"I can't take that chance," Kurt said.

"Get on the ground now!" one of the other officers said.

"Don't shoot!" Riley said. She extended her hand toward the man. "You don't want to do this. We can talk about it. Whatever is going on, we can work it out. No one has to get hurt."

The man shook his head and looked at the officers.

"Hey! Look at me. Look at me. Don't look at them. Look at me."

The man turned his attention back to her.

"You don't have to do this. We can protect you," she said.

He shook his head. "No you can't."

Then he jerked his hand from his pocket. Kurt and the two officers open fire, shooting the man from both sides. He dropped to the pavement with a silver lighter clenched in his palm.

"Shots fired! Shots fired!" the two officers said.

"Damn it!" Riley turned away. The first officer ran over to the man and cuffed his hands behind his back. The second officer grabbed his shoulder mic. "3411, 10-1 shots fired. Suspect critical. We need EMS."

Blood pooled beneath the man and spread across the pavement. Riley leaned her back against the brick wall and slid to the ground. Kurt holstered his pistol and stood in front of her. "He didn't give us a choice."

Riley pulled out her electronic cigarette and took a drag. "I know."

FIVE

"Looks like he nicked you pretty good," the EMT said, placing a bandage over Riley's forehead.

"Will it need stitches?" she asked.

"It's not that deep. With some ointment, the gash should heal pretty quickly."

The EMT removed a penlight from his shirt pocket and held it in front of Riley's face.

"What are you doing?"

"I'm checking to see if you have a concussion. Just follow the pen with your eyes." He waved the pen from side to side and up and down. Then he turned on the flashlight. "Just look forward."

He shined the penlight into each of her eyes, then clicked it off and on. "Looks good."

"Can I go now?" she asked.

"Just a few more questions. What's your name?"

"Riley Walker."

"Age?"

"Twenty-nine."

"Where are we?"

"South Side."

"And your partner's name?"

"Asshole. Are we done?"

The EMT tucked the penlight back into his shirt pocket. "Yeah, it looks like you're good to go. Just take an aspirin if you start to feel a headache."

Riley slid from the bench seat and left the rear of the ambulance. A crowd of spectators had formed around the yellow police tape surrounding Johnny's house. It wouldn't be long before the press arrived. They always sniffed out these situations like bloodhounds. Dead bikers, an officer shooting—she could almost write the headline herself.

Commander Briggs joined her on the sidewalk. "The officers' body cams got the whole thing on tape. COPA sent their review to the state's attorney's office. They're recommending the OIS was in self-defense. Full exoneration."

The Civilian Office of Police Accountability kept a short leash on the department by investigating instances of misconduct. But over the years, it had been weaponized to impose directives, turning that short leash into a noose. Hearing that COPA had signed off on the officer-involved shooting allowed her to breathe a little easier.

"Good. Well, at least the department's stellar reputation will stay intact. I'm fine, by the way."

"Wish I could say the same for your suspect. They took him to Provident Hospital."

St. Bernard Hospital was closer, but Provident had a larger staff and a more equipped trauma facility that could give the man a better chance of survival. It was a smart decision—Riley just hoped the time difference wasn't fatal. "Is he going to make it?"

"Last I heard, he was breathing when they took him into surgery. You think he's our man?"

"He might be, but it's too soon to tell."

A pair of coroners walked through the house, carrying a body-bag-covered corpse on a stretcher. The journalists began taking photos of them descending the front steps.

"House of horror. The press will eat this up. What the hell happened in there?"

"Someone broke in through the back door, killed victim number two, and kidnapped Johnny Stone. We found another message."

"Can you see?" asked Briggs.

Riley nodded. "Same as before. I don't think our suspect did this. The lock was picked on the apartment where we found Johnny. The door to Johnny's house was picked and broken into. It's not a lot, but it's enough to question."

"All right. Let's get a gag order on the messages. I don't want the phone lines getting overwhelmed with false confessions."

A man in a navy-blue windbreaker and matching baseball cap followed the coroners down the porch steps and approached Kurt in front of the house. They shook hands and started talking.

"I need to go," Riley said, and joined Kurt on the sidewalk.

"Detective Walker?" the man in the navy windbreaker asked.

"That's right."

"I'm Sergeant Berns, FSD. We found something you should see."

Riley and Kurt followed the sergeant into the house, stepping around a large bloodstain in the entryway.

"We conducted a full sweep of the house. Canine unit sniffed this out."

He stopped at an open hole in the living room, where six floorboards had been removed. Resting next to the hole was a backpack and an AR-15 rifle. The gun's magazine was loaded into the lower receiver, which appeared to be crafted from an aftermarket single piece of aluminum. Unlike the rest of the rifle—which was matte black—the lower receiver was aluminum silver.

"I haven't seen one like that before." Riley pointed. "Looks like it was a home job."

"There's a drill press in the back of the house," Berns said. "Simple way to make a gun untraceable. Just shave off the serial numbers and attach your own eighty lower receiver."

"Where did he get something like that?" Riley asked.

"Pretty much any gun shop or online hobby craft store. ATF can't do anything about it, since you're basically buying a block of aluminum. That's why it's called an eighty lower, because it's only eighty percent finished. You need to drill holes into it in order for the rest of the rifle components to function. I've seen these grow in popularity over the years. There's this kid out in Texas, one of those crypto-anarchist types. He sells kits that could mill eighty lowers for you. Just pull the specs from the internet and you got yourself an unregistered, untraceable, bona fide ghost gun."

So much for gun control.

Sergeant Berns slid on a pair of gloves, then lifted a backpack from the floor. He unzipped it and pulled out a dark green drug brick. Its plastic covering was stamped with the BSMC logo.

"Looks like the Black Snakes are in the drug trade," Riley said. "What is that?"

"It's fentanyl," Kurt asserted. "A synthetic opioid one hundred times stronger than morphine. I've seen it before. Down at the boarder they called it venom. Two milligrams of this stuff would kill you before you knew you OD'd."

"I want all of this tagged and processed," Riley said. "Call me if you find anything else."

"You got it," said Berns.

Riley entered the kitchen, where another forensic team member was dusting the back doorknob for prints. "Did you find anything?"

"Nothing yet." His voice was muffled through his face mask.

"There might be some DNA on the broken glass, but I wouldn't hold my breath."

"Get photos of the muddy footprints," she said.

Kurt entered the kitchen. "Do you have any idea how much that brick is worth? No wonder they tortured Johnny for the stash location."

"You think the Black Snakes did this?"

"I do. I think Johnny and our second victim stole the drugs from the club, but they were caught before they could fence the brick. Scarface was sent to get it back."

"Why leave the message?" Riley asked.

"To throw us off. Make their murders look like they were about something else, to protect the club."

Riley nodded. "It's possible."

"Judging from the look of that brick, I'd say we have bigger problems. This doesn't happen in a vacuum. There's more where that brick came from."

"Keep that to yourself. If anyone from the Gang Investigation Division hears, they'll take over this case, and I'm not willing to let that happen."

"Maybe they should. If I'm right, this is bigger than a double homicide."

Riley stepped closer to him. "I'll close this case with or without you. Just don't get in my way."

She walked through the living room and out the front door. A handful of reporters were interviewing the locals as their cameramen filmed the scene. She walked down the porch steps and crossed the front yard.

"Detective Walker!" a voice called out from behind the police line. Riley skimmed the crowd until she recognized Mason Shriner, a reporter from the *Chicago Times*. He was leaning over the police line in a flashy sport coat.

"What do you want, Shriner?"

"You never call, you never write. What's a girl gotta do to get in touch?"

"We have nothing to talk about."

"Oh, come on. We got along so well on the Shepard case."

"Did we? The report was supposed to be anonymous. Your article got me kicked from VC."

"The *Times* wouldn't go to print without a name. You told me, 'Whatever it takes.' Besides, aren't you happy you got an innocent man off? You should thank me."

Riley turned away.

"Okay, okay, you're right. I burned you. But you won't like what I have to say about this. I'm extending an olive branch. Give me a comment so you can get ahead of tomorrow's headlines. Frame this story the way you want for the public."

"You're fishing."

"I know this victim isn't the first."

She stopped. "I don't know what you're talking about."

"Drop the act. A little birdie tipped us off about your meet with the medical examiner. Mm-hmm, that's right. I know all about it."

"That's pretty good, Mason. You ever consider becoming a cop?"

"Not my style. I prefer cashmere to Kevlar. Listen, bottom line, this story can be told a million different ways, sweetheart. I'm offering you a chance to weigh in on one."

"I'm flattered," Riley said, then walked toward her cruiser. The last thing she needed was a heater case. Now that the paper had caught wind of her investigation, public pressure would mount. If she didn't bring it to a close, Deputy Chief Reyes would have plenty of justification for removing her from the department. Kurt was leaning against her cruiser with his arms crossed. "I'm not backing out."

"What?"

"I'm not backing out of this case. I'm just saying if Johnny's death is tied to a drug operation, it's going to get ugly."

"It already is," Riley said, and rounded her cruiser. "You should talk to the locals. Maybe one of them saw something that could help."

"Where are you going?"

"Provident Hospital. If our suspect is alive, I'm going to find out what he knows."

Kurt glanced around at the sizable crowd. "Why do I have to do the legwork?"

"Because I didn't shoot our only suspect," she said, then entered her cruiser. A patrolman lifted the yellow tape and waved her through. She eased through the crowd of spectators, then drove out of the neighborhood.

SIX

Riley turned up the radio and nodded to the blues music. She considered Kurt's theory about Johnny stealing the drugs. It didn't sit right with her. Why would he steal from his own club? And better yet, why didn't he leave town? Johnny must have known they would come for him. It would have been suicide to stay.

And then there was the second victim. What was his role in this? Both of the victims' eyes were removed. Each had the same message written next to his body. Maybe they were partners in a drug deal that went south? There were too many missing pieces for a clear picture. Her phone buzzed in her jacket pocket. She reached inside and answered it. "Detective Walker."

"Riley, it's Roy, I just heard what happened. Are you all right?"

It was no surprise that word of the shooting had reached the Gang Investigation Division so quickly. News spread through the department like a fever.

"I'm fine. Just got grazed is all. COPA signed off on the OIS, but the press had already caught wind of it. No telling what's coming down the pike."

"The department will answer to the public. Not you."

"We'll see. I'm on already thin ice with the deputy chief. If things go south . . ."

"Hey, if COPA approved the shooting, you have nothing to worry about." Roy said. "Listen, there's something else I wanted to ask you. Word is there were drugs at the scene, a lot of them. Do you want to talk about it?"

"I think it's best to keep things to myself for now. See how things play out."

"All right. Well, if you change your mind, I'm here."

"Thanks, Roy. I'll see you later."

"Maybe tonight?"

"Maybe. I'll let you know," Riley said, then hung up the phone.

She parked in the front lot of Provident Hospital and entered through the double sliding doors. She followed a sign that pointed to the critical care unit at the end of the hall. Riley peered into each of the open curtains, looking for her suspect.

"Excuse me," a soft voice interrupted. She turned to find the unit manager with a laminated badge clipped to her blue scrubs. "You can't be here."

Riley flashed her badge. "Detective Walker, CPD. I had a suspect that was brought in earlier today."

"Name?"

"I don't have a name. He was shot several times in the torso."

"Be more specific. Black, white, male, female?"

"He's white. Dark hair. Large build, with a scar across his cheek."

The unit manager looked over to a nurse. "Deborah, did you see a white male with multiple GSWs to the abdomen come through this morning? Scar on the cheek?"

"Yeah, I remember the face," Deborah said. "After we stabilized him, he was prepped for surgery in the ICU on the fourth floor. Ask for Dr. Hubbard. Elevator is down the hall."

"Do you know if he's alive?"

Three nurses rushed into the room with a young blond woman on a gurney. She was unconscious, with infected track marks down her arms.

"Draw up one cc of Narcan!" a nurse said. "She's not breathing."

"Sorry, I don't," the unit manager said to Riley, then joined the nurses. She removed a needleless syringe from a medical cart, then inserted it into the woman's left nostril.

Riley walked down the hall and took the elevator to the fourth floor. The intensive care unit was bustling with nurses and medical staff. She found an information desk, where a woman in flower-print scrubs was typing on a computer.

Riley leaned over the counter. "Excuse me."

"Yes?"

"Is Dr. Hubbard around?"

She pointed to a curly-haired man in a white smock. "Right over there."

"Thank you," Riley said, then approached him. "Dr. Hubbard?"

He looked up from his clipboard. "Yes. How can I help you?"

Riley flashed her badge. "I'm Detective Walker, CPD. I was told you operated on a gunshot victim earlier today?"

"Yes, right this way." Dr. Hubbard waved for her to follow. They walked through a pair of double doors and continued down the hallway.

"Is he alive?" she asked.

"Yes, but his white blood cell count is really low from the blood loss. We're administering a heavy dose of antibiotics into his system. If one of his wounds gets infected, he could go into septic shock."

Dr. Hubbard opened a door to a recovery room. An EKG

beeped at a slow, rhythmic pace. "His name is Sam Hyde. We have his wallet in storage."

Riley walked to the edge of the hospital bed. Sam rested faceup with a respirator down his throat.

"How long will he be out?"

"Until tomorrow. We had to remove one of his lungs. When he wakes, it will be difficult for him to communicate. He'll have shortness of breath, and his throat will be sore from the respirator."

Riley leaned over the bed. The man's hospital gown revealed tattooed sleeves over both of his arms. Spiderwebs on each elbow, a "1%" surrounded by barbwire on the left bicep, and a black snake on his neck.

"He's a suspect in a double homicide with gang ties. I want him secured to the bed, and a guard posted outside his door at all times."

"You'll have to arrange that with the desk outside," Dr. Hubbard said. "Even though an escape is unlikely, given his condition."

"I'm more worried about who will come for him." Riley handed him her card. "Call me if his condition changes. I want to speak with him as soon as he wakes up."

The doctor pocketed her card. "Of course."

She walked out of the room and returned to the information desk. "Excuse me."

The woman in floral scrubs looked up to her. "Yes?"

Riley flashed her badge. "I have a homicide suspect in that room behind me, would you—"

Her cell phone rang.

"Sorry, I'll be right back." Riley turned away from the desk and answered it, "Detective Walker."

"Walker, it's Hall. IAD wants you to come in and discuss the shooting."

"It was already cleared by COPA."

"I know, but they want your account. Union rep is under a lot of pressure to make a statement before the story breaks. We got word from our media sources that they're going to run the piece with a police brutality angle since the victim was unarmed."

"Victim? He attacked me. He's a homicide suspect."

"If it bleeds, it leads. You know the drill. Just stop whatever you're doing and come in right now."

Riley hung up her phone and called Kurt.

"Detective Thompson."

"Hey, it's Riley. Did you get anything from the neighbors?"

"Not much," Kurt said. "Most of them wouldn't answer the door. Those that did only had two words to say. I'll let you guess which ones."

Riley wasn't surprised. "Snitches get stitches" was a common expression in neighborhoods like Johnny's. Except on the South Side, stitches would be the least of their worries.

"An old widow at the police line who said she saw Johnny the night he was murdered. She said he arrived home at 11 p.m."

"How does she know the time?"

"His motorcycle wakes up the neighborhood. She couldn't ignore him if she tried."

"Well, at least that gives us a timeframe. Did she say if Johnny was with anyone?"

"He was alone," said Kurt. "Why?"

"We only recovered Johnny's motorcycle from the crime scene. That means our second victim arrived either by foot or drop-off. He was probably already inside the house when they came for Johnny."

"I think he was an accomplice. Both victims belonged to the club. Same wounds, same messages next to their bodies."

"It's possible," Riley mused.

"Is our suspect still alive?" asked Kurt.

"Barely. The doctor said he might succumb to an infection. We won't be able to question him until tomorrow." She looked to the end of the hall. A man with a goatee and a dark bomber jacket stared at her. He looked familiar, but Riley couldn't place him. "Our suspect's name is Sam Hyde. Run a search and see what you can dig up on him."

The man turned toward the elevator and pressed the service button. The letters BSMC were tattooed across his knuckles.

"I have to go," she said, then pocketed her phone. "Hey! Stop!"

The man entered the elevator as she ran down the hall. She pushed through a pair of nurses, then ran around a gurney. She entered the corridor just as the elevator doors slid to a close.

"Damn it!" Riley pressed the service button, but the elevator had already begun descending to the ground floor. She pushed through the stairwell door and ran down four flights of stairs to the lobby. A cluster of families and hospital personnel roamed the entrance hall. She looked in every direction, but he was nowhere to be found.

Riley cut to the front of the twelve-person line and leaned over the front desk. "Have you seen a man with a goatee and dark jacket walk through here?"

"Yeah, about every fifteen minutes." The receptionist smirked. "If you want help, you need to take a number like everyone else."

Riley turned around and ran through the front sliding doors. The parking lot was full of vehicles. He could be anywhere. She ran into the lot and looked in both directions. A dark motorcycle barreled toward her at top speed. She leaped out of the way. The man with the goatee roared passed her and out of the parking lot. Riley lifted herself off of the pavement and watched him speed down the road.

SEVEN

"Run us through it again," Sergeant Mendoza requested, then took a sip of coffee. His partner, Sergeant Barnes, glared at Riley from across the table. "We want to make sure you left nothing out."

"Do you two get off on this? I told you what happened five times," Riley said.

"What were you thinking? Entering the house without back-up," Barnes said. "Do you know how many funerals I've been to because an officer played Dirty Harry?"

"No wonder she was dropped from the Violent Crimes Task Force," Mendoza added.

"As I told you before, I wasn't alone, and I called for backup before entering the house."

"Because you heard something." Barnes leaned in. "What was that again? I want to be sure we're clear for the record."

They were using the PEACE method to pinpoint flaws in her story. The more she talked, the more information Barnes and Mendoza had to trap her with. They were good at it too. Disparaging her career to rile her up almost worked.

"I heard movement," she said.

"You entered the house without a warrant," Barnes accused. "Making everything we found today inadmissible."

Mendoza smirked. "Not good."

Riley took a moment to think about her response, knowing it could be used against her. She decided to stick to the facts and give them nothing else. "We were investigating the home of a homicide victim. After knocking on the front door, I heard movement from within. We walked around the back of the house and found signs of a break-in through the rear door. I called for backup, then entered the house. We had more than enough reasonable suspicion." She stood up. "What is this? What are we talking about here?"

"We're establishing a baseline of events leading up to the shooting," Mendoza said.

"You have them. I've gone over it plenty of times. You're both keeping me from my investigation."

Mendoza glanced at his wristwatch. "We've only been here four and a half hours. What's the rush? We've got all night."

"I don't," she said, and walked toward the door. "Some of us have actual police work to do."

Mendoza shifted in his seat. "Where do you think you're going?"

"Am I being detained?"

"Not yet," Barnes said.

"Then we're done. If you want any more details, you can get them from the other officers at the scene."

"You know what your problem is, Walker?" Barnes said. "You may work for this department, but you're not one of us. You're an outsider, and it's always only a matter of time before outsiders get cleaved from the herd."

Riley shut the door behind her and walked down the hall of interview rooms. The meeting was a farce. She was annoyed at herself for not seeing it before. No doubt Deputy Chief Reyes was behind this—using Internal Affairs to catch her in a procedural slip-up. The meeting had cost her the afternoon, and she would not waste another minute dwelling on it. She entered the bullpen and collided shoulders with Detective Maloney.

"Watch it, Walker," he said.

She rubbed her shoulder and continued down the aisle. Kurt was searching through a list of gang profiles on his desktop computer.

"Anything come in on the Black Snakes?" she asked.

"We got a message from forensics. The GID's database had nothing on Johnny's tattoos or the Snakes. It's like they don't exist. At first I thought they might be a new club, but that brick couldn't have come from your run-of-the-mill basement drug lab. Something of that quantity must be tied to a much larger operation, so now I think they're just new to Chicago. I'm checking the VICAP federal database as well." Kurt handed Riley an intake form. "I followed up on Sam Hyde as well. He's been arrested several times for drug possession. Not much else."

"No surprise there," she said, and placed a pixelated photograph of the goateed man on Kurt's desk. "While I was at the hospital, I saw another member of the club. A security camera caught a glimpse of him."

Kurt examined the image. "What happened?"

"Nothing. He got away before I could get close. I had the hospital add round-the-clock security to Johnny's room until we can take him into custody."

"If they're making mistakes like that, then they must be getting desperate."

She rounded her desk to find a pair of brown storage boxes resting in front of her computer. "Are these from Johnny's house?"

"Bagged and tagged. I requested a review of the evidence before it goes into lockup."

She removed the lids to find the boxes full of marked evidence bags. The culmination of Johnny's life packed within a few cubic feet of space. Not so different from her own, she imagined. Riley removed the items one by one and placed them on her desk. A bronze flip lighter, a tarnished silver money clip, and a pair of brass knuckles with the letters BSMC over the faceplate. She rummaged through the rest of his possessions. There were no photographs of loved ones, no inkling of lifestyle interests or hobbies. It was clear the club was all Johnny had in life, which made it difficult to believe he would ever steal from them.

"Damn, it doesn't look like the Black Snakes are listed on VICAP either." Kurt leaned back in his chair. "It's like they don't exist."

Riley pulled out Johnny's leather jacket and laid it flat across her desk. She looked for labels, anything that could indicate where the jacket came from. She flipped it over to the front side and opened the lapel. A bright white piece of paper caught her eye from the inside pocket. Reaching within, she retrieved a cocktail napkin that read "Thirsty." The red, embossed lettering show-cased a beer bottle instead of the letter I. Riley knew of the place —a trucker bar on the outskirts of the city. It didn't seem like something Johnny would keep on his person. She turned the napkin over to find a phone number written in purple ink.

Riley held it up for Kurt to see. "Look at this."

"What's that?"

"A cocktail napkin. There's a phone number written on the back." She returned the jacket to the box and set it on the floor.

"What are you doing?" he asked.

Riley logged on to her computer. "I'm checking Whitepages." She entered the phone number into the search bar. The results page came back blank. "It's not listed."

"We could get a warrant for a trace," Kurt said.

"No chance. Even a sympathetic judge wouldn't approve a

warrant without proof the number is directly involved with Johnny's murder."

"You found it in his jacket."

"It's circumstantial. We have nothing to tie it to the crime." She leaned back and combed her fingers through her hair. The case was careening toward a dead end, and there was nothing she could do about it.

"Can your phone record audio?" Kurt asked.

She stared back at him, not liking where this was going.

"You said it yourself, our suspect may not survive the night. The Black Snakes aren't listed on any gang registry. This phone number may be the only chance we get of finding out who's behind this."

As much as she didn't like the plan, he was right. Calling the number was the only play they had left.

"All right," she said, then took a photo of the napkin with her phone. After they returned the evidence boxes to storage, Riley and Kurt went to one of the empty interview rooms. She placed her phone on the table and opened a recording app. "What are you going to say?"

"If the number belongs to another member of the club, they'll be most concerned with recovering the drugs. I'll impersonate Sam and give them a false location to the stash."

"They know he's in the hospital."

"But they don't know his condition. I'll tell them it's my one phone call. If they want their drugs back, they won't have a choice."

"Where will you send them?"

"I'll tell them the drugs are still under Johnny's floorboards. By the time they arrive, we'll be waiting."

It was a solid plan. They had nothing to lose, and if the club believed him, it wouldn't take much time to organize a small sting operation. They wouldn't need more than a couple backup units to secure an area. Riley pressed the red record button on her phone's screen. "Call from a blocked number. Something unrecognizable might spook them."

Kurt started dialing. He put his phone on speaker and placed it beside hers on the table. It rang.

"Come on," Kurt said.

The phone rang a second time, and he leaned in. It rang a third time, then clicked. A woman's voice came through the other side of the line. "We're sorry, but the number you have dialed is no longer in service. Goodbye."

Kurt ended the call. "It's a burner. They ditched the phone once they found out Scarface was taken to the hospital. Damn, that was our one shot."

Riley pulled her phone off of the table and closed the recording app, leaving the image of the cocktail napkin on the screen. She double-tapped the image to zoom in. The phone number was written in purple ink with neat, symmetrical lines. Not at all what she would expect from a guy like Johnny, especially when he had several fractured knuckles.

"Maybe not," she said.

"What do you mean?"

Riley showed Kurt the photo. "This was written by someone else. Johnny was meeting someone at the bar. Grab your coat—we're going to find out who."

EIGHT

Riley drove her cruiser East on I-94 toward Indiana. The windshield fogged against the cool night air. She turned on the defroster, then took a drag.

"I just can't figure it out," Kurt said. "It doesn't make sense why the Black Snakes wouldn't show up on any gang registry."

"Perhaps they're not as big as you think."

"Or maybe they're just well connected. It's possible they have a backer with deep pockets. Someone with the means to keep them off the radar."

"You learn that in Vice?"

"Something like that."

He was deflecting, and she wanted to know why. "There's a million places you could have transferred to. Why Chicago?"

"I figured I could do some good. Same as you, I imagine."

"Why did you leave El Paso?"

Kurt seemed hesitant to respond. "There was nothing for me there."

"What do you mean?"

"Most people believe the United States shares a border with

49

Mexico, but they're wrong. The cartels own every inch of that land. What we were doing down there wasn't protecting the public, it was damage control."

Riley pulled off Interstate 94 for East 130th Street toward Indiana Ave. "You make it sound like a lost cause."

"Some things are."

She glided down the road. Thirsty was a single-story brick building with barred windows and black double doors. Big rigs, tractor trailers, and auto-transport vehicles filled the surrounding parking lot beneath its neon sign.

"Looks more like a truck stop than a biker bar. Why would a guy like Johnny come all the way out here?" Kurt asked, looking out the passenger window.

"High traffic volume, low visibility, plenty of escape routes— it's a good place for a drug exchange." Riley parked the cruiser and scanned her surroundings. "Any of these trucks could be loaded and we wouldn't think twice."

They stepped out of her cruiser and past a pair of bearded men smoking cigarettes near their eighteen-wheelers. Riley spotted a security camera mounted above the door as they made their way through the front entrance.

Moody blues music and low lighting gave the bar an air of quiet desperation. Road-weary truckers sat with elbows propped against the bar and glasses to their lips. A handful of young women in tight, skimpy dresses were seated throughout the room. Working girls, she figured. It wouldn't be difficult to find a lonely John in a place like this.

Riley flagged the bartender with a wink and a nod. He finished wiping a spill, then tossed the rag over his shoulder. She quickly searched for gang tattoos as he lay both palms against the edge of the bar. They were clean.

"What can I get you?" The bartender grinned.

Riley flashed her badge. "Information."

His smile faded fast. "What kind of information?"

She retrieved her phone and pulled up a photo of Johnny's mugshot. "Someone who might have visited the bar."

"Many people come through here. I can't make any promises."

Riley showed him the screen. "Look."

He leaned in and winced. "Yeah, I've seen his ugly mug before. Sat in a booth down at the end over there. Didn't talk much. Just drank his beer in silence. It's not too often we get biker types in here. Just truckers, and the occasional couple that gets turned around on the interstate."

"Was he with anyone?"

The bartender shrugged. "Not that I saw."

"You sure?" Kurt stressed.

The man crossed his arms. "Hey, I just serve the drinks. Besides, he wasn't the kind of people you want around."

Kurt nodded toward a group of young girls at the end of the bar. One of them smiled with a full rack of braces. "Are they the kind of people you want around?"

The bartender leaned in. "You've got to understand, they have nowhere else to go. Most of them come from abusive homes. Turning tricks is an easy way for them to get by. I don't want any trouble."

"Then stop lying to us," Kurt pressed.

He bowed his head. "Fine. If you must know, he spent time with company."

"What company?" Riley asked. "One of the regulars?"

"No. This woman wasn't from around here."

"Describe her," Kurt said.

The bartender rubbed his chin. "She had brown hair, dark glasses, a blue blazer, and gloves."

"How tall was she?" Riley asked.

"About your size. The only time I got close to her was when she was sitting down."

"Come on, that could be anyone," Kurt said.

"I don't know what else to say. She looked like she was from some sort of law firm or something."

"How old would you say she was?" asked Riley.

"Early thirties. Good face."

"When was the last time you saw them together?"

"Couple of nights ago."

"On my way in, I saw a security camera mounted above the entrance. I would like to see the footage of that night."

"That old thing has been broken for months. We keep it up as a deterrent. Not that there's much in here to steal."

"How many times have you seen her with the biker?" she pressed.

"About four or five. He would sit over there in the same booth and babysit his drink until she arrived. Then they would talk."

"About what?" Kurt asked.

"I don't know. I try to stay out of other people's business."

"Then what happens? Did they ever leave together?" asked Riley.

"No. She always left first. He would stay in the booth for another ten minutes and finish his drink alone."

"How long were their conversations?"

"I don't know, I didn't time them."

"Give us an estimate," Kurt said.

"About fifteen minutes. Maybe longer."

Riley pocketed her phone. "Thanks for your help. We'll be back if I have any more questions."

"No. Thank you," the bartender fumed, then helped another customer.

"You think the woman was a contact? Maybe a go-between for the club and another party?" Kurt asked, his voice low.

"Perhaps a buyer." It made sense why Johnny would come

here. The bar was far from the city, and the clientele was always passing through. It was the perfect place to disappear.

"We should split up. I'll talk to that group at the end of the bar," Kurt said.

Riley peered across the room and spotted three young women sitting in a booth. "Good idea."

The two blondes sitting next to each other looked like sisters. The third was a brunette in a short denim skirt and cowboy boots. Riley approached the group and stood at the end of the table.

"Evening," she said, noticing the six empty beers between them. "Slow night?"

The first blonde flipped her hair and tilted her head to the side. "Oh sugar, you're barking up the wrong tree. We don't roll that way."

"Speak for yourself," the brunette flirted. "I could eat her up."

Riley pulled back her jacket lapel, revealing the detective badge attached to her belt. "Mind if I join you?"

"Shit," the second blonde said. "We didn't do nothing."

Riley took a seat, blocking in the brunette.

"I'm not here to bust you, I just have a couple of questions." She placed her phone on the table and pulled up Johnny's mugshot. "Do any of you recognize him?"

All three leaned in and looked at the phone.

"I've seen him a couple times. Strong, silent type. Kept to himself," the second blonde said.

"Did you see anyone with him?"

The blondes shook their heads. The brunette stared at the photo with a blank expression.

"What about you? Does he look familiar?"

She looked down and shook her head. "No. Sorry."

Riley looked across the table. "You two give us a minute."

The blondes slid out of the booth and adjusted their skirts. "We'll be at the bar."

The remaining woman avoided eye contact by taking a slug of beer. Riley stared at her, wielding the silence like a club.

"What do you want? I already told you I don't know him."

"We both know that's not true."

The brunette went silent and picked at the beer label with her fake fingernail.

"I'm not here to bust you, I just need some information." Riley slid her phone in front of her. "Tell me what you know about the man in the photograph."

She averted her eyes and took another slug of beer. Beneath her casual indifference, Riley sensed a grueling fear of Johnny. "What did he do to you?"

The woman finished her drink. "He's more trouble than you're worth."

"Whatever it is you're afraid of, I can help you."

"I've done nothing wrong, nothing you can prove. Take me in if you have to, but I'm not saying a thing. Now, if you'll excuse me."

Riley stood up. "You're making a mistake."

The brunette grabbed her purse and slid out of the booth. "No one stays around here for long. Faces come and go. I have a kid to take care of. A little girl. I don't intend to be one of them."

Riley watched as she joined her friends at the bar, then walked away with a sigh. Kurt was waiting by the entrance. "I struck out. You?"

"One of the girls knows something, but she's too afraid to speak." Riley walked toward the door. "Come on, I have an idea."

Kurt fidgeted in the passenger seat. "I'm freezing my balls off."

"If I turn on the heater, the car's exhaust will give us away."

"We're wasting time."

Riley rubbed her hands together for warmth, then turned up

the car's radio. The host of a talk station appeared through the static. "The Kane Initiative will bring much-needed jobs to the city. Construction workers, electricians, plumbers, the little guys who've been trampled by our weak economy."

"You mean lining the pockets of those at the top," the guest speaker said.

"What are they jawing about?" Kurt asked.

Riley turned the radio to a music station. Deep, resonant blues guitar played through the car's speakers. "Nothing."

Kurt nodded to the rhythm. "Now, this. This reminds me a bit of home."

"Where's that?"

"Galveston. Now, I've got a place in Bronzeville. You?"

"Hyde Park."

"Well, what do you know? Guess that makes us neighbors."

Riley's phone buzzed in her pocket. It was a text from Roy Dunn, a detective with the Gang Investigation Division, a specialized unit created to suppress organized crime within the city. She and Roy had shared a graduating class at the police academy and joined the department at the same time.

You free?, he asked. Riley didn't know how late she would be out on observation and didn't want him to wait for her.

Not tonight, she texted, and pocketed her phone.

Across the parking lot, the brunette stumbled out of the bar holding hands with a man in ripped jeans and a baseball cap. She watched as the man led her to a dented sedan with aftermarket rims.

"I'm going to get a cup of coffee," Kurt said.

Riley turned off the radio. "Wait, that's her."

The couple entered the back seat of the man's sedan.

"Well, I'll be damned," Kurt said.

Riley turned on the car's engine and stealthily glided across the lot, parking behind them. The sedan's rear windshield had already started to fog. Riley and Kurt stepped out of the cruiser and rounded each side of the sedan. Riley opened the door. The shirtless brunette shrieked. The man looked up at her. "Who the f–"

Kurt opened the door behind him and yanked the man out of the car by the collar.

"Hey—hey! I didn't touch her!" the man said, as Kurt manhandled him against the hood of the car and cuffed his wrists.

"Shut up," Kurt said.

The brunette slipped her shirt on and sat up.

"What's your name?" Riley asked.

"Roxy." The brunette quivered. "Roxy Taylor."

"That your real name?"

She nodded. "Yes."

Riley leaned in. "I spent six years in Cook County Children's Home. Do you know what happens to little girls in the system?"

Roxy looked down. "I'll tell you anything you want to know, just leave my girl alone."

"Tell me everything," Riley said.

"His name is Johnny. At least, that's what he told me his name was. We just hooked up twice."

"What happened?"

"I saw him sitting alone in a booth. His breath already smelled of booze, so I knew he would be an easy catch. He had on one of those motorcycle jackets. You know, the ones with the big patches sewn onto the back. I gave him a quickie. My usual routine. He didn't want anything fancy. The first time was fine, but the second time was rough. He got violent. I could see it in his face like a switch got flipped."

"Have you seen him with anyone else?"

"I'm not the only girl he got with, if that's what you mean."

"No, not a working girl. Someone else that he met with regularly. Another woman you weren't familiar with."

"Well, I saw him meet with this one woman a few times. I thought she might have been a relative of his or something."

"What did they do?"

"Nothing, they just talked."

"Did he talk about anything with you?" Riley asked.

Roxy went quiet. She seemed hesitant to speak. After a moment, she looked up. "There are bad people who will come for me if they found out I was telling you this."

Riley kneeled down to Roxy's eye level. "They won't. Just tell me who they are."

"Okay, but you didn't hear this from me. Johnny is part of a motorcycle gang called the Black Snakes. They're drug traffickers."

"Who are they trafficking for?"

Roxy shook her head. "I never asked, because I didn't want to know. One night, Johnny mentioned something about a farm."

"A farm?"

"Yeah, he complained that he was tired because he had to work on the farm all day."

"Does the farm have a name? Did he say where it was?"

Roxy shook her head. Riley placed a hand over her shoulder. "Roxy, I need to know where it is."

Tears ran down her cheeks. "I don't know. He never said where it was. That's all I know, I swear."

Riley stood up and glanced around the parking lot. A couple of drunk truckers staggered out of the bar with the blondes under their arms. She looked down at the smeared mascara running down Roxy's cheeks and felt a terrible ache in her heart. "I believe you. Let me see your cell phone."

Roxy dug into her purse and handed Riley her phone. She

flipped it open to a background image of a young girl with pink ribbons in her hair. "Is this your daughter?"

Roxy nodded. "Penelope. She's four years old."

"Cute," she said, and dialed. Riley's phone rang in her pocket. She ended the call and added Roxy's name into her contacts list. Then she entered her own name into Roxy's phone. "I want you to be my eyes and ears out here. You now have my personal number. If anything happens that you think I should know about, or if you're ever in trouble, I want you to call me."

"Thank you," Roxy said.

"I'm not finished. In the future, I may need some information." Riley handed Roxy her phone back. "Don't ignore my call."

She clutched her purse and rose from the back seat. "Am I going to need to worry about Johnny?"

Riley shook her head. "No."

Roxy half-smirked, then crossed her arms and wandered back to the bar.

Kurt pulled the man off of the car's hood. "What do you want to do with him?" he asked.

"Let him go."

Kurt removed the handcuffs. "Looks like your lucky night, pal."

The man turned around and spit in Kurt's face. "Pigs."

Kurt punched him in the jaw. The man staggered back against his side mirror, snapping it off the car as he fell to the ground.

"That's enough!" Riley said.

Kurt kneeled beside the man, took out his wallet, and dropped two bills on the ground. "Look at me."

The man wiped the blood from his lip as his eyes drifted up to Kurt.

"If I catch you out here again, I'll stomp your neck. Understand?"

"Y-yes. I understand." The man trembled.

Kurt stood up. "Get the hell out of here."

The man collected the bills and the side mirror off the ground, then entered his car and drove away.

"You were right. This is bigger than I thought," Riley said, then took a drag.

"What did the girl say?"

"Johnny told her he worked on a farm. I'm assuming that's where the drugs came from."

"Did she say where?"

"No, but it's a start. We can pick things up again tomorrow morning."

"Sounds good," Kurt said, then opened the cruiser's passenger door.

"One more thing." Riley turned to him. "That guy had it coming, but don't expect me to look away again."

"Wouldn't dream of it," he said, and entered the cruiser. She took another drag and looked around the parking lot. She tried to imagine what it must be like to raise a child in these dire straits. To come here night after night just to get by. The thoughts caused her to shiver with deep loneliness. She pulled out her phone and called Roy. He answered on the second ring.

"Change your mind?" he asked.

"I don't want to be alone tonight."

"Then I'll be waiting."

"See you soon," she said, then hung up the phone.

NINE

An ear-piercing bang jolted Riley from sleep. She sat up in bed and heard two more bangs outside her bedroom window. Her mother burst into the room, clutching her infant brother in her arms. "Riley, get out of bed."

"What's happening, Mommy?" she asked.

"I need you to get up—now." Her mother yanked the covers from her legs and grabbed her wrist.

"You're hurting me!"

She rushed Riley to the closet and placed Michael in her arms. "Take your brother and wait here until I come back. Hold him close. Don't let go."

"But I—"

"Shh, listen to Mommy. Stay here and take care of your brother."

She kissed Riley on the head, then stood up and shut the door. The closet was pitch-black. Riley had never seen her mother so scared before. Was it the noise? Why hadn't she taken them with her? Michael cooed, a soft murmur in her arms. She rocked him back and forth. "It's okay, Michael. It's okay. I'm—"

Her mother's bloodcurdling scream left her speechless. It was followed by another bang, then silence. Riley's heart pounded against her chest. She needed to get out, but she was too petrified to stand up.

Riley opened her eyes.

Roy was lying beside her, shaking her shoulder. "Hey, you all right?"

She sat up in the bed, sweaty and sore. "Yeah. I must have dozed off."

"Sounded like a bad one."

"What time is it?"

"It's late. You sure you're okay?"

She leaned over and lifted her underwear from the floor. "I'm fine. It's just been a busy couple of days."

He looked up at her with his big green eyes. "You know, you could stay. You don't have to leave every time."

"Reyes has my neck on the chopping block. I need to be sharp tomorrow."

"Got any leads?"

That was a question she'd been hoping to avoid. She didn't want to lie to Roy, but she also didn't want to divulge anything that could get her case taken over by the Gang Investigation Division or the FBI's joint Gang Task Force. When the feds got involved, investigations turned into negotiations, and justice became a means of catching the biggest fish at the cost of everyone else.

"A few," she said, and rose from the bed.

"Well, if you ever need help, you can call me."

"Thanks Roy," she said, and buttoned her shirt. She noticed a framed photograph of Roy with his arms wrapped around a beautiful woman and a young girl. "Is that your wife?"

"Ex-wife. Yeah."

"I'm sorry."

Roy opened the nightstand drawer and pulled out a bottle of eye drops. The black anchor tattoo on his forearm shone in the moonlight. "Don't be. We separated years ago."

"What happened?"

He dripped the solution into each of his eyes. "In short, the job."

It was an all-too-familiar story. Divorce rates for law enforcement were well above the national average. The long hours alone could put a strain on the strongest of relationships.

Roy capped the bottle, then leaned across the bed. "Are you sure you need to go?"

"There are a few things I want to follow up with at the department." Riley slid on her jacket, then leaned over and kissed him. "I'll see you later."

TEN

"Hey," a voice called out.

Riley raised her head off her desk. "What is it?"

Kurt dropped a copy of the *Chicago Times* in front of her. "We got bumped to page four."

She rubbed the sleep from her eye. "Is it bad?"

"Could've been worse. It looks like they softened the piece since the bastard is still alive."

Riley turned to page four and found the article below the fold. The caption read "CHICAGO POLICE SHOOT UNARMED MAN IN BACK ALLEY." Beneath the headline was a picture of police units sectioning off the alleyway. Riley was in the background providing her account of the events to two COPA representatives. Mason had been right. She didn't like what he had to say, but the police brutality angle was something the department could manage, and it kept the heat off her investigation. It was the type of article she expected from the press. Focusing on the "what" at the cost of the "why." No context, no background information, just vapid narratives and catchy headlines. Objective journalism was dead, she thought, if it had ever existed at all.

She tossed the newspaper into the trash bin. "I'll read it later."

Kurt looked over the business listings scattered over her desk, the culmination of her all-night search for the Black Snakes' drug farm. "What's all of this?"

"There are dozens of farms within a hundred-mile radius of Thirsty. After researching each business's ownership and history, I narrowed the list down to three."

"You were here all night?"

"It's nothing. I couldn't sleep anyway." She opened her desk drawer and grabbed a half-empty bottle of mouthwash. She unscrewed the cap and swirled the contents around her mouth before spitting into an empty coffee mug.

"Look at this." Riley logged on to her computer and accessed a map of Chicago. "Farmland is restricted to agricultural zones west of the city." She entered the addresses into the search bar and watched three red pins drop over the map. Then she hovered her mouse cursor over each of the businesses. "Stalwart Farms near Bolingbrook, Plainfield Farms just one town over, and the Hewitt Farm in Shorewood, farther south."

"We have a witness at Provident Hospital. I'm not going to waste time based on the word of some whore."

"I believe her," said Riley.

"She told you what you wanted to hear."

"It's our only lead, and the doctor said we won't be able to question him until he wakes up." She turned toward Kurt. "The Black Snakes know they're exposed. Their drugs are missing, two of their members are dead, and one is in police custody. Unless you want to stay here and fill out paperwork, I suggest we go out there and find them before they disappear for good."

Kurt grunted and pointed to the screen. His knuckles were scabbed and inflamed. "I figure it'd be best to begin with the Shorewood farm and work our way back. We don't want to be caught in the middle of nowhere with a gang of bikers after dark. Better print the map too."

"My phone has GPS."

"Not if you lose service out there. Come on, we're losing daylight."

She printed a copy of the map and pulled her jacket off the back of her chair. Riley and Kurt exited through the rear department parking lot and took Interstate 55 south toward Shorewood. The interstate was congested with people on their morning commutes, but it opened up once they were clear of the city and surrounded by trees and open plains.

"What branch were you in? Army?" she asked.

"What?"

"Last night. You learned to throw a punch like that from somewhere."

Kurt rubbed his knuckles. "I enlisted on my eighteenth birthday, after the towers fell, but I never made it through bootcamp."

"Why not?"

"I wasn't too good at following orders." He looked over at her. "From what I hear, neither are you."

"What have you heard?"

"That it's a long way down from the elite Violent Crimes Task Force to the graveyard shift. You must have pissed off the wrong people."

"It's complicated."

"Yeah, well ain't it always." Kurt shrugged and looked out the window. "Pull into that gas station."

"Why?"

"It's the only one I've seen for miles. If the MC rides through here often, chances are someone has seen 'em."

Riley glided into the lot and shut off the engine. "Don't be long—we've got a lot of ground to cover."

He nodded with a subtle grunt before walking across the

parking lot. Riley sank deeper into her seat and watched the clouds darken overhead. The gray sky stretched to the horizon above the open plains. It was remarkable how quiet things became once she was outside the city. No bustling traffic or sirens, just silence. The solitude made her question if people were meant to live in cities. If all the crime and suffering she had witnessed throughout her life could be attributed to man's proximity to one another. She took a drag of her e-cigarette, but nothing happened. The light on the end-tip flashed red. It was out of juice.

"Damn."

She considered reaching beneath her seat for the emergency cigarette carton, but decided against it. Instead, she opened the driver's door and walked past the gas pumps to the convenience store. Kurt met her in front of the entrance.

"What did they say?"

"Not much. The clerk at the checkout stand didn't recognize the Black Snakes' logo or Johnny's mugshot."

"And you believe him?"

"I don't see any reason for them to lie."

"I'll meet you in the car. I just need to pick something up."

She entered the store, two aisles full of snacks and soft drinks. An elderly clerk at the checkout stand was watching a baseball game on a small television behind the counter.

"Got any e-cigs?" she asked.

"We only sell the one-and-done disposables," he said, eyes peeled to the game. "That alright?"

"Yeah."

The clerk swiveled in his stool and picked a palm-sized rectangular box from the shelf. "Nineteen ninety-five."

She slid a twenty-dollar bill across the counter. "Who's playing?"

"Cubbies rerun. I tape all the games," he said, taking the bill.

"Keep the change."

66

"Receipt?"

"Yes."

She glanced through the storefront window and saw Kurt take a swig from an aluminum flask. He wiped his mouth, then stuffed it into his coat pocket. The clerk closed the cash register and handed her the receipt. "Are you just passing through?"

"Something like that. How long have you been here?"

"Oh, it'd be just about twenty-three years this November." The clerk gleamed with pride. Probably the owner of the station, she figured. Riley removed the e-cigarette from the packaging. "That's a long time. You ever have any trouble out here?"

"What kind of trouble?"

"Any suspicious characters?"

The clerk smirked. "As I told the other guy, no. I don't get bikers often, and certainly not the type you're looking for."

She handed him the empty carton. "You sure about that?"

"This is a fine community. People around here would take notice of that sort of thing."

"Of course. Thank you."

"Have a nice day," the clerk said as she walked out of the store.

A young woman was leaning against the front wall, thumbing a white Bic lighter. "Hey, you got a light?"

Riley stopped and held up her e-cigarette.

"Trying to quit, huh? I tried a couple times—it didn't last, though. I got too nauseous. Withdrawals suck. How are those working for you?"

Riley took a drag. "Could be worse."

"I'm dying over here. Mind if I bum a puff?"

Riley offered the e-cigarette. The young woman took it, revealing a pink burn scar on the back of her hand. She inhaled, then blew a steady cloud of vapor. "You look familiar. Have we met before?"

"I don't think so."

The woman took another drag and stared at her skeptically. "I never forget a face."

"You must have me confused with someone else."

She snapped her fingers. "You were in today's paper. The detective from the alley shooting." She smirked and leaned back against the wall. "The article never explained why you shot him."

Riley held out her hand. "I didn't shoot him, and I can't discuss an ongoing investigation."

The young woman smiled and handed back the e-cigarette. "Was it related to Johnny Stone's murder?"

Riley tried to hide her surprise. Victims' identities were never disclosed to the public. "What's your name again?"

The young woman placed a cigarette between her lips, then pulled a silver flip lighter from her blazer pocket. She cupped her hand around the flame as she lit her cigarette. "I never said."

"Who are you?" Riley sneered.

The woman took a drag, then exhaled. "Holly Hart, *Chicago Wire*. You're a long way from the city, Detective Walker."

"So are you."

"I go where the story takes me."

"There's no story here."

"That's what my editor said after the first college girl was uncovered from the Third Street Ripper killings. You don't remember me, but I followed that investigation through all seven murders."

"That was a bad one."

"Yes, it was, and catching that professor earned you a spot on the Violent Crimes squad. My gut was right then, and I know it is now. The question is, are you going to tell me what you're doing out here, or will I have to ask the cashier inside?"

"You're wasting your time."

"Johnny's death is gang related, isn't it?"

"I already told you. No comment," Riley said, and turned away.

"See you around, Detective."

Riley walked back to her cruiser. The last thing she needed was a member of the press looking into her case. Holly must have connected Johnny's death to the unidentified body recovered from his home. She couldn't have known they discovered Johnny's mutilated corpse in an abandoned building the previous night.

"Who's your friend?" Kurt asked.

She opened the driver's door. "We're not friends. Let's go."

ELEVEN

Shorewood was a small community in the Troy Township, forty miles west of the city. Riley glided across a low bridge over the DuPage River, then turned off of West Black Road to an unpaved pathway. She followed it to a modest, country-style home with sun-faded white paint and missing side paneling. A man in a denim jacket pushed through the screen door and stood over the edge of the porch.

With Kurt alongside her, she approached the front of the house. "Mr. Hewitt? Are you the owner of the farm?"

The man spat a mouthful of dip onto the ground. "Last I checked." His eyes narrowed. "Unless the bank foreclosed on the property?"

"We're not from the bank. I'm Detective Walker. This is Detective Thompson. We're investigating a homicide, and I believe a suspect may have been in the area. Would you mind if I ask you a few questions? I don't want to take up too much of your time." Riley retrieved a picture of Johnny Stone on her phone and held it up to him. "Have you ever seen this man before?"

Mr. Hewitt shook his head. "I wouldn't forget that ugly mug. No, I can't say that I have."

"Do you get many bikers around the area?" Kurt asked.

"Bikers?"

"Yeah, motorcyclists. Black leather jackets, big patches with skulls on the back."

"No. If there's one thing the people around here enjoy, it's peace and quiet. If there were a group of rowdy bikers, the towns-folk would complain."

A young woman with a black eye stepped through the screen door, holding a child. "Everything all right?"

"It's fine," Mr. Hewitt said. "Go back inside."

She bowed her head and retreated into the house.

"Are you two the only ones that work on the farm?" Riley asked.

"There were three of us, but my brother Lucas died of cancer a while back. This is a family-run farmstead. Been that way for generations."

"How'd she get that shiner?" Kurt asked.

"Who, Jess? She's a clumsy one. Slipped in the kitchen. Hit her head on the table."

Kurt placed his hands on his hips. "Uh-huh. Let's see what she has to say about it."

Mr. Hewitt crossed his arms. "Jess is putting Junior to sleep right now."

"Thank you for your time," Riley said, then grabbed Kurt's arm and leaned into him. "Let's go—we'll just make it worse for her."

"It ain't right. That son of a bitch—"

"I know. But we're not here for her. Let it go."

Kurt glared at Mr. Hewitt, then turned away.

They returned to the cruiser, and Kurt slammed his door shut. "We should talk to her. She has a child."

"You saw her face. She's terrified of him. She won't talk, even if she wants to. And what do you think he'll do to her the second we leave?" Riley started the engine and pulled away from the house. "If she wants help, she'll reach out."

Kurt clenched his fist against his mouth. His leg shook in agitation.

"It's personal for you, isn't it?" she asked.

"It's complicated."

The entrance to Plainfield Farms was blocked by a chain-link fence with an aluminum sign zip-tied to the gate:

NOTICE:

THIS PROPERTY IS

CLOSED TO THE PUBLIC

Riley looked past the barrier to a disheveled home with charred windows and a caved-in roof. A rusted sea-foam green tractor rested next to the blackened remnants in a field of over-grown weeds.

She returned to the driver's seat. "The owners are long gone. It doesn't look like anyone's been here for a while."

"We should head back to the station. This is a waste of time."

"If the Black Snakes are out here, I need to know for sure." She started the engine. "Besides, we only have one farm left."

After a twenty-minute drive northeast, she exited the inter-state on Weber Road, then took Rodeo Drive to Stalwart Farms. The property extended for miles with endless barren fields of dirt. She drove through the entrance and followed a narrow road to a tin-roofed barn that housed tractors, plows, and other farming equipment. A group of eight men were prepping the machines and pouring sacks of seed into large containers.

Riley exited the cruiser and looked around the property. An old two-story house rested next to an office trailer. A white pickup truck drove past four grain silos, then pulled up beside her. The driver, a narrow-faced man with a slick combover, stared at her through the windshield. He stepped out of the truck wearing a jacket with a GHC logo over the left breast pocket. He didn't look like a farmer, more white collar than blue.

"Can I help you?" he asked.

"I'm Detective Walker. I need to ask you some questions regarding a homicide that occurred earlier this week."

"A homicide?" the man asked. "What homicide?"

"Are you the owner of the property?"

The man retrieved a business card from his back pocket and handed it to her. "George King. I'm the manager here at the Green Harvest Corporation."

"I'm sorry, I thought this was Stalwart Farms."

"It used to be," George said. "The property was acquired by the GHC a couple of years ago."

"I see." Riley accessed a photograph of Johnny Stone on her cell phone and held it up. "Can you identify the man in the photograph?"

George leaned in and squinted at the image, then shook his head. "No. Never seen him before."

"Any bikers pass through here recently?" Kurt asked.

"Not that I've seen. The only people who use this road are shuttling crops or cattle."

"How many people work on the farm?" Riley asked.

"We have about eleven men at any given time. Fifteen on a busy day. I'm not understanding how we're involved in . . . whatever this is?"

Riley tucked George's business card away. "Would you mind if we speak to them?"

"Not without a warrant."

Kurt stepped forward. "You sure that's how you want to play this, chief?"

George crossed his arms. "We run a tight ship around here. Talking to the workers will cost us time and money, both of which are in short supply. We have a strict schedule to maintain, and the rains have already pushed us behind for planting season. I can't have you two disrupting our operations any further. Until you have a warrant, I'm going to have to ask you to leave."

Riley handed George her card. "If you see or hear anything, call me."

They returned to the cruiser and backed out of the property.

"You think he's hiding something?" Kurt asked.

"Not a chance. This farm doesn't look like a place that's hosting a large-scale drug operation."

"What makes you so sure?"

"All of the tire tracks are in pairs of two. No signs of motorcycles. George is telling the truth."

Riley drove away from the farm and continued down the road. Kurt grabbed the map and looked it over. "Maybe Roxy misheard Johnny when he complained about working on a farm."

"No, she was sure of what she heard." Riley took a drag and thought about where the farm could be. Virtually all the ones she'd researched were incorporated and highly regulated by the state. She doubted any of them could maintain a covert drug operation while avoiding surprise inspections and on-site reviews. Her only option was the few remaining local farms, which weren't held to such high scrutiny. "Maybe I need to expand the search. There could be more farms—"

Kurt crumpled the map and tossed it against the dashboard.

She pulled over on the side of the road and stopped. "What's your problem?"

"We have a suspect at the hospital who can give us everything! We should try questioning him, or look for other leads, instead of chasing ghosts."

"Maybe I just realize there are better ways than a fist or a bullet."

"You don't know me," Kurt said.

"I don't, huh? Why don't you have another drink to take the edge off?"

Kurt rose from the cruiser and slammed his door. Riley turned off the engine and peered out the windshield to the open plains. The Black Snakes' farm had to be out there somewhere. But where? It didn't make sense. She reached over the dashboard and unraveled the paper map. A hole had been torn through the center of the page, leaving a dark circle on the border of the green agricultural zone. She stared at the vacant hole. "Chasing ghosts . . ."

Opening the cruiser door, she joined Kurt outside. He was leaning against the trunk with his arms crossed.

Riley rounded the cruiser and stood beside him. With a sigh, she began to speak.

"My team was tasked with apprehending a kiddie rapist who strangled five boys and dumped their bodies in back alleys all over the city. We didn't get the case until the son of a governor's aide went missing. Turns out missing children aren't a high priority when they're from the inner city. The press had a field day, and the department came under a lot of pressure. From the killer's MO, we knew we had three days to find the boy, so we worked day and night to find a connection between the victims. We didn't have any leads until one of the parents mentioned in passing that all of them attended the same church.

"We interviewed the entire congregation, including the priest, the janitor, even the choir boys. Out of a handful of suspects, only one fit the profile, John Shepard. He was a registered sex offender and addict. Once we brought Shepard into custody, someone in the department leaked his name to the press, and Deputy Chief Reyes was forced to respond. She assured the public that justice would be swift and that the sixth boy should be reunited with his family soon. Shepard failed to give us any alibis for the nights the boys were taken, and we found carpet fibers on the victims that could be tied to the floor of his van. The problem is, each of the victims were strangled by someone who was right-hand dominant, and Shepard was left-handed. I brought this up to the deputy chief and the DA, but they wanted to go through with the prosecution. So I leaked it to the press."

"Then what happened?" Kurt asked.

"The sixth victim was found the next morning, and Shepard was released."

"I'm sorry."

"So am I." She raised the map and pointed toward the hole. "You're right. We are chasing ghosts."

"What do you mean?"

"No one in the area has seen any bikers. These maps are updated annually. They don't include businesses that have closed down. We can't find the farm, because it no longer exists on any map. We need to look for farms that have closed down like the one in Plainfield. I knew in my gut I was right about Shepard, and I know I'm right about this."

Kurt took the map and looked it over. "It would explain how the Black Snakes have operated under the radar for so long." He handed it back to her. "All right, I'll go with you a little longer, but if nothing comes of this, we need to change our approach."

"That's fair."

Riley and Kurt returned to their seats. "So where can we get our hands on these old property records?" he asked.

She started the engine and shifted into drive. "City Hall."

TWELVE

City Hall was a massive stone building with large windows and Greek columns. Riley and Kurt entered through a revolving door and walked down the grand entryway. The large bronze lanterns hanging overhead gave the marble interior a warm yellow hue. They entered the service center and approached the reception desk. An elderly woman with wool-like hair and wearing a purple cardigan looked up at them through her thick-framed glasses.

"May I help you?"

"Detective Walker, CPD. I would like to speak with the deed commissioner."

"I'll be right back," the clerk said, and disappeared into a back office. A moment later, she returned, followed by a man in a gray sweater-vest who sported a combover. His name tag read Damon Serling.

Damon leaned over the counter and grinned. "Hello, detectives. How may I help you?"

"I need to look through your available property records," Riley said.

"That information can be accessed online at the city of Chicago's website or at a public library."

"We know that already," Kurt grumbled. "Why do you think we're here?"

Damon's eyebrows rose. "Excuse me?"

"The business we're looking for may have closed down years ago. We need to compare older property records to today's listings."

"How far back do you need?"

"A decade, maybe more," she said.

Damon let out a sigh. "In that case, you'll need to search our storage room. Please, walk around the side and follow me." He walked to the edge of the counter and lifted a wooden panel for Riley and Kurt to enter, then rested a hand on the receptionist's shoulder. "Marilyn, I'll be in the back if you need anything."

"Okay, thank you," she said.

Damon removed a set of keys from his belt and unlocked a door.

"Watch your step," he said, entering the doorway. Riley and Kurt followed him down a back stairwell to the lower level, then along an underground hallway. Damon stopped at the fourth door on the right and unlocked it.

"Right this way, detectives," he said before stepping into the pitch-black room.

Riley felt a chill down her spine as she followed Damon's voice inside. The space was cold and damp. She could sense that the room was large from the echoes of her footsteps against the cement floor.

"Everything okay?" she asked into the darkness.

There was no response. Riley looked back at Kurt's silhouette in the doorway. He shrugged and called into the room, "Hey, you get lost in there?"

A row of fluorescent bulbs sprang to light across the ceiling.

Damon was standing next to a switch on the side wall. "Sorry about that."

The enclosed concrete room was divided by rows of metal shelves. Damon put on his reading glasses and weaved through them one by one.

Kurt leaned against a table and crossed his arms. "Having trouble?"

"Just a second. It's not often that I come down here." Damon dragged a stepladder across the floor and used it to reach the upper shelves. He leaned close to read the identification markers. "Now let's see. I'm pretty sure the property deeds should be right around . . ." Damon raised his arm and pulled a large cardboard file box off of the top shelf. "Here they are."

He descended the stepladder and handed the box to Riley. "You may look at them on the table over there."

"Thank you."

The corners of the box were worn with age. Riley removed the lid to find the box full of files. The ones near the rear were yellowed and had a musty odor. Many of the files had stiffened and stuck together, though they appeared to be categorized by year. She needed to be careful not to miss anything.

"These files go all the way back to the sixties?" she asked.

"Some of the older ones were not stored properly for many years. The humidity may have caused some damage."

"Don't you have digital copies?" Kurt asked.

"We did, but last week we were scheduled to transfer the catalogue to a new platform, and during the update our files became corrupted. IT is still trying to recover the assets. This is all we have for now."

Riley removed a stack of folders from the box and handed it to Kurt. "These go back twenty years. I'll look through the last ten. Compare your list to the most recent. The farm we're looking for doesn't exist on the current property list. It should give us a timeline for how long the Black Snakes have been in operation."

She placed the property lists next to each other for a side-by-side comparison. Skimming them, she looked for inconsistencies.

"Nothing here," Kurt said, closing a file and replacing it with another.

Riley finished looking through one as well and placed it back into the box. They continued this research process of scanning property records and returning the completed files eight more times each.

"Find anything yet?" Riley finally asked.

"Nothing," Kurt responded. "A couple farms were established, but they still exist today. You?"

"I'm not seeing anything either."

She continued skimming through the documents line by line. It was a tedious process, but she had the scent. With every completed sheet, she felt she was getting closer to the truth.

"I'm running out of files here," Kurt said.

"Keep going—it needs to be here somewhere." Riley looked to Damon. "Are you sure this is all of it?"

"That's right. That's all the records we have."

Riley combed through the ninth folder in her pile and returned it to the box. She glanced over at Kurt's stack, then opened her final folder and traced her finger down the property listings until one caught her eye. She compared it to the current list of farms and found it wasn't there. "Got one."

Kurt drew closer to her. "What is it?"

"Sturgeon Farms. Keep looking through your folders to make sure there aren't any others."

She dragged her finger across the listing to the address. "It's less than ten miles away from Thirsty."

"Sounds promising," Kurt said. "Who's the owner?"

Riley looked at the end of the listing line. "Kane Capital Investments."

"Kane? As in Robert Kane?"

Her mind raced in a million directions. What was the link between Kane and the Black Snakes? Was he their partner? A member? There were too many missing pieces for her to see the whole picture.

"Did you finish looking through your files?"

Kurt put his second-to-last folder back into the box. "Not yet."

Riley dug into the box and pulled the property file from eleven years ago. How long was Sturgeon Farms in operation before it closed? She skimmed through the listings and didn't see any mention of it, then did a double-check just to be sure.

Kurt finished looking through the tenth folder and put it back into the box. "Nothing."

"Damn, I was hoping you would find another. It looks like Sturgeon Farms was only open for one year. That means that the Black Snakes could have been operating from there for the last ten."

"Did you find what you were looking for?" Damon asked. "I have to get back to the front desk."

"We did. Thank you for your help," she said.

"You got the address?" Kurt asked.

"Yeah, I got it," she said. Placing the final file back into the box, she handed it to Damon.

Riley and Kurt walked out of the archive room and up the stairwell. As they reached the top of the stairs, her phone chirped.

"What is it?" Kurt asked.

She looked at her screen. "Voicemail. Basement must have blocked the signal."

Riley continued walking out of the service center as she raised her phone to her ear to listen to the message.

"Hello Detective Walker, this is Watch Commander Hall. I

wanted to let you know that the set of prints you requested yesterday came in from the lab. They'll be here for you when you come back to the station."

She hung up her phone and pocketed it. "Prints came in for our second victim. We'll have to look at them later."

"The MC might expect us. There's a chance we could be walking into an ambush."

"Then we'll just have to be careful."

THIRTEEN

Riley took Interstate 94 East to the 57 South and exited onto 147th Street. She was unfamiliar with the area, as it extended beyond the South Side. The farther she drove, the more trees appeared within the glow of her headlights. Raindrops trickled down her windshield. It was going to be a chilly night. She regretted not packing her overcoat.

"Turn left here," Kurt said. "We're getting close. We should find a place to park."

"The cruiser is unmarked," she said.

"It's too risky. They might be looking for it. Last thing we want is for them to know we're coming." Kurt pointed to an alcove of trees off the side of the road. "Over there."

Riley checked her rearview mirror to make sure she was the only one on the road, then took her foot off the gas pedal and glided off the shoulder between the groups of trees. Plenty of cover from prying eyes. She parked her cruiser and killed the engine.

Riley pushed open the driver door and rounded the cruiser to pop the trunk. She reached inside and grabbed her flashlight and bulletproof vest. Kurt grabbed a second gun magazine and stuffed it into his pant pocket.

"There's no telling how many of them are out here. Maybe we should call for backup?"

Riley handed him a second vest. "I don't plan on getting close."

Kurt laid his coat on the roof of the car and slid the bulletproof vest over his head.

Riley raised her jacket's hoodie, then locked the car. "You ready?"

He joined her at the top of the alcove. Riley looked down the road in both directions, then crossed the street. The road leading to the farm was empty, but she decided it would be better if they stayed out of sight. She stepped off the road and entered the dense woodland. Each step she took plopped over the muddy ground. They walked through thick underbrush and pushed past contorted branches. After a ten-minute trudge through the woods, the edge of a cross street came into view.

"There's a clearing up ahead," she said.

"Stay low," Kurt said.

They inched their way to the edge of the tree line. Riley peeked across the street toward the farm's entrance. A metal barrier between two cemented polls blocked the path forward. It was wrapped in a rusted chain and sealed with a padlock.

"It looks like it hasn't been opened for years."

"Doesn't mean they're not inside," Kurt said. "There must be another way in."

The woods on either side of the barrier were dark and motionless. She walked into the middle of the empty crossroads. "I think you're right. There must be another opening."

She continued along the leaf-covered path, following the tree line of the farm. Her boots were soaking wet, and her fingers were feeling numb. Riley crossed her arms for warmth as she walked. She kept her eye on the woods, looking for a break in the trees.

Kurt pointed to a five-foot gap between two trunks. "There."

Riley wiped the rain from her brow. There were several tire tracks leading into the woods. She could tell the trail had been used many times over the years given the lack of vegetation surrounding it. It was too narrow for any car to pass through, but a motorcycle could thread the gap easily. "You're right. This is it."

She glanced at Kurt, who nodded back at her. It was an acknowledgment of the potential danger they were heading into. She needed to be certain that he would cross the barrier with her.

"Let's stay off of the trail. Follow it from a distance," Kurt said.

She walked another ten feet along the edge of the property, then entered the woods. Rainwater pooled along an embankment, forming a stream across her path. She slipped into the stream and fell to her knees. Kurt approached and extended a hand. "You all right?"

Riley ignored the gesture and scrambled back up. "I'm fine." Through the sound of the rain, a low rumble echoed in the distance. "Do you hear that?"

"What?" Kurt asked.

"Listen. It's like some kind of motor."

Kurt stood still. "Yeah, I hear it. We must be close."

Riley and Kurt climbed over the slope and weaved between the crooked trees until a clearing came into view, an open circular space surrounded by dense woodland. Across the clearing stood a rickety brown house and barn surrounded by a field of weeds. A single dirt pathway led from the front of the house to the barricaded entrance. She peered to each of the house's darkened windows for signs of movement. "Looks like nobody's home."

"Sounds like the noise is coming from the barn," Kurt said.

"What do you think it is?"

"I don't know. Sounds like a generator."

A large man in a black leather jacket stepped out of the barn, holding a pistol. Riley and Kurt ducked out of sight. They watched as the thug rounded the side, revealing the Black Snakes Motorcycle Club patch sewn onto the back of his leather jacket.

"Looks like the girl was telling the truth," Kurt said.

"Yes, it does."

"What is he doing?"

"Making sure there aren't any trespassers."

After the thug finished circling the barn, he looked around the perimeter of the property, then opened the barn door and went back inside.

"We should go. Now that we know they're here, we can take it to the DA. Let's get a warrant."

"It's not enough." Riley frowned.

"Not enough? What more do you need? We have the farm, the gang, and a girl who can testify to the drug smuggling."

"It's all circumstantial. A group of bikers hanging out in the woods and the word of a working girl won't be enough for a warrant, let alone to convince a jury. We need more. I need to see what's in that barn."

"Are you crazy? If they see you, they'll shoot on sight. You don't need to do this—we can find another way. Come back later after dark."

"There might not be another opportunity. For all we know, they're prepping to move the entire operation now that the police seized the drugs from Johnny's house."

"I don't like it," Kurt said. "What if they spot you?"

"Go back to the road and call for backup. Don't wait for me," she said, then broke from the tree line.

"Like hell," Kurt said, following her into the field. They slowly crept through the weeds toward the barn. The mechanical whirling became deafening as they approached. Riley pressed herself against the side of the barn and found a crack between two swollen planks. A bright light shone from within. She looked inside, but her view was obstructed by a wooden crate.

"Can you see anything?" Kurt asked.

"No, my sight's blocked."

Kurt pressed his hands against the barn wall until one plank came loose. "Got it."

He slid the board an inch to the side and held it in place. "Quick. Look."

Riley peered into the barn. Two industrial light posts were linked to a gas generator. She tilted her head for a better look. Twelve bikers in matching leather jackets stood on each side of a long wooden table in the center of the barn. Massive stacks of fentanyl bricks, identical to the one she'd recovered from Johnny's house, rested on the table. The men were cutting them open, weighing the drugs on electric scales, then packaging the contents into hundreds of little plastic bags for distribution.

She backed away from the barn wall.

"You good?" Kurt asked.

She nodded and kneeled through the field back to the tree line. She didn't stop until the farm was out of sight.

"What did you see in there?" Kurt asked.

"The Black Snakes are using the barn as a distribution center. They were breaking down drug bricks into small plastic bags. It was like an assembly line."

"Same bricks as before?"

Riley nodded. "Same kind of packaging we found at Johnny's house."

"How many?"

"Fifteen, maybe more. All I could see was what was on the table."

"Do you realize how much money that is?"

"We can't let them bring it into the city," she said.

Riley and Kurt trudged through the dense woodland back to

the cruiser. They tossed her wet jackets onto the back seat and removed their bulletproof vests. Riley turned up the heater and rubbed her hands together.

"No small-time dealer can push that much product. Even a gang of that size would take months to sell it. For something this big, you need an extensive distribution network," Kurt said. "My guess is the club is connected to a cartel."

"So what then, the Black Snakes are just the middlemen?"

"Yeah, I don't think they're running things. They just move the product."

"What makes you say that?"

"Remember, we couldn't find the Black Snakes on any local or federal police database? That tells me either they're the luckiest sons of bitches alive, or they're not the ones dealing on the street."

Riley backed the cruiser out of the alcove, then took off down the road. "Roxy mentioned Johnny would occasionally meet with a woman at the bar. She said the woman looked like a lawyer. Not the type of person Johnny would associate with. Now, I think she might have been a contact."

"A buyer," Kurt said.

"Maybe." Riley took a drag, then exhaled. "It's time to take this case to the DA."

FOURTEEN

The next morning, Riley and Kurt walked to Commander Briggs's office in the back of the department. They had worked deep into the night documenting their account of the Black Snakes' drug farm and the sequential steps that led them to it. They couldn't afford to leave out any details. Their report needed to be ironclad if they were going to convince a judge to sign off on a warrant.

Riley stopped in front of the commander's office. The door was shut, but she could hear a muffled conversation from within. She knocked twice. The talking stopped, and the Briggs's booming voice came through the door. "Come in."

They entered the office to find him sitting behind his desk. "Detectives, what do you have for me?"

It was odd that Briggs addressed them by title instead of by name. It wasn't until she noticed the woman sitting across from him that it became clear why. Deputy Chief Rachel Reyes turned around in her seat, staring at Riley with cold, piercing eyes. She was clad in full uniform with her hair pulled back tight in a bun.

"Am I interrupting?" Riley asked.

"Nonsense," Briggs said. "Deputy Chief Reyes was just leaving."

"Actually, I would like to hear what Detective Walker has to say." Reyes waved her hand, motioning for Riley to take a seat. "After all, her investigation has stirred some interest with the press, and that can be problematic for the department."

Riley ignored the gesture, standing in defiance. "It's a non-starter. COPA concluded that the OIS was in self-defense."

"But the situation should have never escalated to that point. If only you followed procedure and waited for backup before entering the house, we could have avoided this spectacle altogether," Reyes said.

"I was trying to stop a killer. I don't have the luxury of calling shots from behind a desk."

"Why don't we stick to the case at hand," Briggs said. "I have already discussed the matter at length with Detective Walker."

Riley and Reyes glared at each other.

"Detective." Briggs cleared his throat. "What do you have for me?"

Riley opened her case file and placed a crime scene photograph of Johnny's corpse on the desk. "We believe Johnny's death was gang related." She pointed to the BSMC tattoo across the chest. "Johnny Stone, our first victim." Then she removed a second photograph of the biker slumped against Johnny's front door. She pointed to the matching tattoo across the biker's knuckles. "Ezekiel Rivers, goes by Zeke—the second victim we found in Johnny's house."

"What do the letters mean?" Briggs asked.

"BSMC stands for Black Snake Motorcycle Club. We believe Johnny and Zeke stole the fentanyl brick from the club, but the Black Snakes found out before they could fence the drugs and skip town. The gang killed Zeke and tortured Johnny for the location of the stash."

"And our suspect in the hospital was sent to collect? That right?" Briggs said.

"That's right."

"Why didn't you bring this to the Gang Investigation Division? They could have aided your case," Reyes cut in.

Riley paused, unsure how to answer.

"Because until today, our theory was just that, a theory," Kurt defended.

"What do you mean?" Reyes asked.

"The Black Snakes aren't listed on any local or federal registry. We checked the GID and VICAP databases—they're ghosts."

"So how did you find them?" Briggs asked.

"We got a tip from a working girl that Johnny knew."

Reyes tilted her head. "Snitching on a gang like that can be deadly. How did you get her to talk?"

"I was very convincing," Riley said. "The club is operating out of an old farm. They're using the barn as a distribution center. Last night, I saw a dozen more fentanyl bricks like the one we recovered from Johnny's house." Riley placed a map on Briggs's desk. She had circled the area around Sturgeon Farms with red marker. "The area is shielded by dense woodland. The club uses their motorcycles to weave through the trees down an unmarked footpath."

"How many members did you see on the farm?" Reyes asked.

"Twelve, maybe thirteen. They were armed."

"How could something like this happen and no one know about it?" Reyes asked.

"Because no one would care to look. The farm hasn't been in operation for a decade. It was purchased by a holding company, then closed down the same year."

Reyes leaned in. "What was the name of the holding company?"

Riley reached into her file, savoring the moment. She placed the property tax record onto the desk. "Kane Capital Investments."

Briggs's eyes widened. "As in Robert Kane?"

"Let me see that." Reyes took the document, read it over, then looked up to Riley. "Who else knows about this?"

"No one. I brought it to you first."

"Kane's hands are in a lot of pockets. Politicians, CEOs, land developers. If you go after him, you're going to make a lot of powerful people hurt," Briggs said.

"He contributed to the mayor's last campaign, for God's sake. We need to discuss this privately." Reyes stood up. "You can leave your report with us."

"That's fine. I have copies," Riley said. She wanted to make it clear that this wasn't a case the Reyes could bury. "We need to bring this to the DA quickly. There's no telling how long we have before the Black Snakes bring those drugs into the city."

"Keep your phone on you," Briggs said. "We'll be in touch."

Riley walked out of the commander's office and shut the door behind her.

"Looks like Kane's reach goes further than we thought," Kurt said.

"I wouldn't be surprised if he pushed to have the area rezoned."

"Detective Walker," a voice called out.

Riley looked down the walkway to see Roy. She turned to Kurt. "Go on, I'll catch up."

"Uh-huh," Kurt said, and continued into the bullpen.

Riley walked over to Roy. "Hey, what's going on?"

"I hate how we left things last night, and I just wanted to come by and apologize. I'm not used to talking about my ex-wife, and sometimes I just get caught up in my own self-pity."

"You don't have to explain anything, Roy. It's fine."

"You sure? It seemed I upset you before you left."

"No, we're good."

"Alright then." He crossed his arms and leaned his shoulder against the wall, nodding to Briggs's office. "So what's going on with the commander? You staying out of trouble?"

She glanced at the door, then back to Roy. Now that she'd presented her report, there was nothing they could do to pull it from her. "I have a big case coming to a head soon."

"How big are we talking?"

"If all goes well, big enough to get me reinstated onto the Violent Crimes Task Force."

Roy let out a low whistle. "When are they taking the case to the DA?"

"I don't know. Whenever Reyes is involved, it's always politics before justice. She's probably figuring an angle to present herself in the best light."

Roy leaned in. "Maybe once it's over, you and I can celebrate."

"Yeah," she said, almost blushing. "I'd like that."

"Good, because—"

Riley's cell phone rang in her jacket pocket. "Sorry, I've got to take this. I'll see you around."

"Good luck," Roy said, and walked down the hall.

She answered her phone. "Detective Walker."

"Hello Detective, this is Dr. Hubbard at Provident Hospital. You asked me to call if there were any changes to the patient's condition."

"Yes, I remember. What happened?"

"He's awake."

"Thank you for letting me know. I'll be over to question him as soon as I can."

Riley hung up and returned to the bullpen.

"What was that about?" Kurt asked.

"Nothing," she said. "Grab your coat—Sam is awake."

FIFTEEN

Riley and Kurt stepped off the elevator in Provident Hospital and walked down the hallway.

"How soon do you think we'll hear from the commander?" Kurt asked.

"It shouldn't be long. A case this pressing must shoot to the top of the DA's priority list," she said.

"They won't go down easy," Kurt said. "Guys like these have nothing to lose."

"What makes you so sure?"

"I just know."

They approached the receptionist's desk. A woman in pink scrubs and matching pink-framed glasses looked up at them. "Can I help you?"

Riley flashed her badge. "I'm Detective Walker. Is Dr. Hubbard around?"

The receptionist rose from her seat. "He's currently with a patient. I'll let him know you're here."

She crossed the hallway and stuck her head into one of the treatment rooms.

"I hate hospitals," Kurt said. "They always smell like disinfectant."

The woman returned to her seat. "Dr. Hubbard will be with you in just a moment."

"Thank you," Riley said. She pulled out her phone and prepped the voice recorder app. "He might be more cooperative if I do the talking."

Kurt crossed his arms. "Fine with me."

Dr. Hubbard soon joined them in the hallway. "Sorry about that, I was just finishing up with another patient."

"What is Sam's condition?" Riley asked.

Dr. Hubbard led them to his room. "He is conscious and able to speak, but like I told you before, he will have difficulty communicating. It takes time for the body to adjust to having one lung. He will be out of breath, and his throat will be sore from the intubation."

"I understand," Riley said, and flashed her badge to the police officer sitting next to Sam's door. He tipped his cap, and they entered the room. Sam was lying propped up on the bed with his wrist cuffed to the side railing. His tired eyes followed her as she walked across the room to the side of his bed. Kurt stood at the edge of the room with his arms crossed.

"Hello Sam, I'm Detective Walker." She pressed the record button on her phone and read from a credit-card-sized laminated copy of the Miranda warning she kept within the sleeve behind her badge.

"You should have killed me," Sam grumbled. His voice was a low whisper.

"I prefer you in a six-by-nine cell in a maximum security prison," she said. Sam's gaze went inward as he seemed to think about his options, but Riley wanted to shut them down quickly. "You fled the scene of a homicide with two counts of aggravated battery against a police officer and resisted arrest. With your

95

record, I'd say the question isn't if you're going to prison, but for how long. You're looking at a minimum of ten to fifteen years. I couldn't care less if you rot in there, but I need to know who killed Johnny Stone. Work with us and I will convince the judge to go easy. You might make parole in six to eight."

"I ain't no snitch," Sam croaked.

Riley didn't want to reveal her hand, but if she was going to gain a confession, she needed to use all the leverage she had. "We found the drugs in Johnny's house. We know about the club and the farm. It's over. There's nothing for you to protect."

Sam shook his head. "You have no idea who you're dealing with."

"Last chance," she said. "The moment I walk out that door, my offer goes with me."

Sam didn't flinch. He stared at her with a stone-cold expression. Riley stopped the recording and pocketed her phone. "Fine, I'll see you in court."

She walked toward the door. Sam took a deep breath. "Do you have a family, Detective Walker? Someone you care about?"

She stopped and looked at him.

"We will find them," Sam said.

Riley continued out of the room. Kurt followed her outside and closed the door. "Like I told you. Nothing to lose."

"It doesn't matter—soon enough, we'll bring them all down," she said as they walked down the hall. She thought about the loyalty it would take to throw away fifteen years of her life. Sam's unflinching allegiance to the Black Snakes was a perverse reflection of her own devotion to law and order. They were two sides of the same coin. A sobering reminder of what she was up against.

Kurt was right. These people had nothing to lose, because for them it was about principles toward an outlaw way of life. And she respected that.

On the way to the elevator, her cell phone rang. "Detective Walker."

"If you screw me on this, it'll be the last thing you do in this department," Reyes said. "No ceremonial goodbyes, no pension, no future. Understand?"

"Wouldn't dream of it."

"The DA wants to see you. Head over to his office now."

The line went dead. Reyes had hung up on her. Riley pocketed her phone.

"Was that the call?" Kurt asked.

Riley nodded. "The DA wants to see us."

The Cook County State's Attorney's Office was a time-warp of modern offices retrofitted within a century-old building. Riley and Kurt crossed the lobby and took the elevator to the third floor. The pair walked to the end of the carpeted hallway and approached a secretary just outside his office door. She stopped typing on her desktop computer and greeted them.

"Hello, do you have an appointment?"

"I'm not sure," Riley said. "Do you have something for Detective Walker?"

The secretary glanced at her computer. "I'm sorry, I'm not seeing you on the schedule."

The office door opened, and District Attorney John Locke stepped out to greet them in a blue, pinstriped suit that matched his eyes. "That won't be necessary, Dolores. This meeting is off the record."

His gold owl signet ring reflected the overhead lights as he waved them inside. "Come on in, detectives."

Locke motioned for the pair to take a seat on the sofa across from Deputy Chief Reyes. His office was a large mahogany room with dark leather furniture. The floor-to-ceiling windows behind his desk illuminated shelves full of law books and framed photographs of Locke glad-handing Chicago's top echelon.

"Would you like a drink?" Locke offered.

"Yes," Kurt said.

"No thanks. We're on the clock," Riley said.

"Of course," Locke acknowledged. He turned to the alcohol cart on the side of the room and poured himself a double shot of bourbon into a crystal tumbler. "Tell me, you're the detective from the Ripper case, correct?"

"That's right."

"Now, the deputy chief tells me we have snakes in the garden." Locke unbuttoned his blazer and sat in the armchair across from Riley. "I'm going to be frank with you. The crime rate has steadily risen over the past decade. Gang activity has hit an all-time high. You may have just found the silver bullet we need to shift the tide in our favor. I just need you both to understand that you're about to embark on a path few dare to tread."

"You mean retaliation?" Riley asked.

Locke nodded. "These are dangerous men. I can't predict how they'll react to this, and I can't guarantee your safety when this gets out."

Riley looked to Kurt, and he nodded. It was an acknowledgement of consequences, for good or worse.

"We understand. How soon can we move?" she asked.

"I'll get your warrant, but first I need you to sign an affidavit." Locke turned his attention to Reyes. "How soon can you assemble a raid team?"

"We already have funds allocated for situations like these. The team will only need a few hours to prep. We can take the farm tonight under the cover of darkness," Reyes said.

"What about Kane?" asked Riley.

"We will arrest him at the same time we raid the farm," Locke said. "We know Kane will be in attendance for the unveiling of the

John Martin exhibit at the Art Institute of Chicago tonight." The district attorney finished his glass and rose from his chair. "This city may have a brighter future yet, Detective."

Riley rose from the sofa and shook Locke's hand. "Thank you."

Locke smiled a million-dollar grin. "No. Thank you."

SIXTEEN

"Pay attention, because I only have time to say this once," Sergeant Bryant said in front of a projected map of Sturgeon Farms.

He turned toward the image, revealing the large yellow police letters on the back of his windbreaker jacket. "There are two buildings on the property. A farmhouse and a barn. Alpha team, led by Officer Harris, will approach from the north and enter the farmhouse through the rear. If anyone attempts to flee through the front of the house, Delta team, led by Officer Connelly, will approach from the south and stop them. Once the house is clear, both teams will converge on the barn." He eyed Riley and Kurt in the back of the room. "According to our sources, this is where the drugs are held."

Deputy Chief Reyes leaned over to Riley. "You better be right about this."

"I am."

Sergeant Bryant traced his finger across the map. "We will take two vehicles and split up at—"

The conference room door opened, causing the hallway lights

to wash out the colors of the projection screen. The disturbance made the eight sergeants shift in their seats.

Detective Maloney stood alone in the doorway.

"This is a closed meeting," Sergeant Bryant said. "Operations personnel only."

"Sorry, I thought this room was empty," Maloney said, then backed out the door.

"As I was saying," Bryant said. "We split at 147th Street. I want all vehicles to go lights out. These men are armed and dangerous. The last thing we want is for them to see us coming." Sergeant Bryant stepped away from the screen, his eyes fixated on the group. "The name of the game is control. Control the movement, control the outcome. Set your radios to channel nine. No one goes in without my say-so. Questions?"

"You buying the first round when it's over?" Connelly asked.

All the officers chuckled.

"You can buy your own drink, you cheap bastard. Anyone else?" The sergeant looked around the room. "Good, let's move out."

The officers rose from their seats.

"What about Kane?" Riley asked Reyes.

"We have a separate unit on their way to the museum now."

"Just one unit?" Kurt asked.

"With the amount of press covering the event, Kane will be on his best behavior. Just make sure you get the proof we need to put him away for good."

Riley and Kurt followed the group of officers through the department to the rear parking lot, where two unmarked black SUVs lined the curb.

"Detectives," Sergeant Bryant called out. "We're with the second group. Follow our vehicle."

Riley entered her cruiser. The edge of her bulletproof vest dug against her ribs. She pulled her jacket lapel aside to loosen it.

Kurt opened the passenger door and slid into his seat. "That's not going to help. You're wearing it too low."

Riley loosened the Velcro strap. "The department doesn't have a budget for new equipment. When officers retire, their gear is passed down to new recruits. This vest was made for a guy."

She finished adjusting the vest, then followed the two SUVs out of the parking lot.

"We need more men for this," Kurt said. "The Black Snakes are ride-or-die. I wouldn't push my chips on them going quietly."

"We're lucky to have this many. Besides, Sergeant Bryant knows what he's doing."

"Let's hope. Have you been on a raid before?"

"No. You?"

"Once," he admitted after an uncomfortable hesitation. "It didn't end well."

The two SUVs went lights out a quarter mile from Sturgeon Farms and diverted paths at 147th Street, just as the sergeant had planned. Riley followed the second vehicle and eased off the gas pedal as they neared the farm's entrance.

"This is it," she said.

With one smooth maneuver, the SUV pulled over to the side of the road and parked on the dirt. Four officers exited the vehicle armed with AR-15 rifles, leg-holstered pistols, and flashbang grenades mole-clipped to their tactical vests. The officers huddled together and tethered earpiece receivers to their radios before covering their heads with balaclava masks. The group looked more like an insurgent militia than law enforcement.

Riley and Kurt stepped out of the cruiser and joined them just as Sergeant Bryant opened the SUV's passenger door and raised his handheld radio to his mouth. "Comms check. Can everyone read me?"

The group gave him a unanimous thumbs up.

"Alpha team in position?" Bryant said into his radio.

"Affirmative," Harris responded through the receiver.

"Someone's coming." A masked officer pointed.

A silver Chrysler sedan pulled off the side of the road and parked beside Riley's cruiser.

"Stand by. Wait for my signal," Bryant said into his radio. "What the hell is this?"

The sedan idled motionless, steam rising from its rear exhaust pipe.

"Engine's hot," Connelly noted.

"Anyone you know?" Bryant asked Riley.

The windshield was too dark to see inside. It was an unmarked sedan, but the civilian license plate told her it couldn't be an undercover unit. "They're not with us."

The sedan blinded the group with its high beams. Riley used her arm to block the light. The four officers raised their rifles and flanked each side of the vehicle.

"Get out of the car!" Connelly said. "Hands where I can see them!"

The driver's door cracked open. Connelly lowered his rifle and pulled the driver from the vehicle.

"Don't shoot, I'm press," Holly Hart said with her hands raised.

"Bring her to me," Sergeant Bryant said.

Holly yanked her arm away from Connelly's grasp and walked toward Sergeant Bryant. "The public has the right to know what's going on here."

"You're impeding our investigation. Leave now or I'll have you arrested for obstruction."

"I'm not going anywhere. You need cause to remove me. Anything short of that won't play well for you."

"What are you doing here?" Riley asked.

"I told you, I go where the story takes me. After I got Sam Hyde's name from Provident Hospital, I paid a visit to the Cook

County jail. Their records showed that he and Johnny Stone were cellmates for two years."

Riley looked at the ground and felt a thickness in her throat. How could she have missed that?

"Oh. You didn't know?" Holly smirked. "I had a hunch Johnny's death was gang related, but I didn't know for sure until I saw you at the gas station yesterday. I knew you'd lead me to the Black Snakes if I followed you for long enough."

"How did you get your hands on prison records?" Kurt asked.

"It helps if you say please."

Kurt looked at Riley. "We don't have time for this."

"What do you want?" Riley asked Holly.

"If you want me to leave, then I'll need an exclusive."

There was nothing the woman could do to damage her investigation. If tonight's plan was successful, they'd have all the evidence they needed to bring down the club and Kane.

"Done," Riley said. "Now go."

"I'll be in touch." Holly walked back to her Chrysler sedan. Sergeant Bryant waved his hand, gesturing for Delta team to advance into the woods. The four officers raised their rifles, then entered the tree line in a staggered formation. Riley, Kurt, and Sergeant Bryant followed the men into the woods. The surrounding trees were towering shadows in the moonlit sky. She strained to keep sight of the four sergeants as they weaved through the trees. Their silhouettes faded in and out of the surrounding darkness.

"If the Black Snakes recruit members through the prison system, it would explain why there was no record of the club on any local or federal gang registry," Kurt said.

"How's that?" Riley asked.

"Prison gangs keep their affiliations hidden. Otherwise, the guards would separate them from gen pop. Johnny was a violent criminal. Someone like that would be an asset for the club."

"Until they become a liability," she said.

The low hum of the generators became audible through the trees.

"You hear that?" Kurt said.

"I do. We're close."

As they approached the edge of the property, each of the officers took cover behind the nearest tree. Bright lights radiated through the cracks of the barn's paneling.

"They're here," she said, and kneeled beside Kurt.

Sergeant Bryant raised his radio. "Alpha team, you have the green light. Move in now."

A group of four officers broke from the trees across the field like a line of shadows. They approached the rear of the farmhouse and disappeared from view. Through the front windows, four flashlights flipped on inside the house. The lights methodically moved from room to room, starting with the first floor and then the second. Once the last room was checked, all the flashlights turned off simultaneously, and the house became dark again.

A static buzz came through Sergeant Bryant's radio. "The house is clear."

"Take the barn," he responded.

With that command, Delta team silently advanced into the field with their rifles elevated in all directions. Alpha team exited through the front of the farmhouse and joined them. The officers were well trained, all moving as a unit. As they neared the barn, Riley realized something was missing, and her heart pounded against her chest.

"Where's the guard?" she asked.

"What are you talking about?" Bryant said.

"The guard we saw earlier is gone. No one is protecting the barn."

"And that mistake will cost them."

"It's not a mistake, Sergeant. Tell your men to stand down. They're walking into a trap."

"That's not your call to make." He scowled.

She looked back to the field. The officers were twenty yards from the barn.

"You could be wrong," Kurt said.

"Would you leave that amount of product unguarded?"

Before Kurt could answer, Riley sprinted into the field. "Stop!"

"Come back here!" Sergeant Bryant shouted.

Riley ignored him and continued running toward the barn, "Stop!"

The deafening rumble of the generators stifled her cries. She needed to get closer if the officers were going to hear her.

"Stop! Don't go in the barn!"

She considered discharging her pistol, but feared the gunshot would cause them to storm the barn. The only thing she could do was scream.

"Stop! It's a trap!"

The officers lined themselves against one side of the large barn door, their rifles aimed toward the entrance. She fought against the constriction of her bulletproof vest and waved her arms above her head, hoping to catch their attention. "Stop! Don't open the barn!"

An officer in the back of the line slung his rifle over his shoulder and hustled to the barn door.

"Don't!" Riley said.

The officer placed both hands over the metal handle and pulled.

The barn exploded into a violent burst of flame. Thousands of wood fragments soared into the air. Riley stopped dead in her tracks, feeling the heatwave against her face. She wanted to scream again, but all she could muster was a low whimper.

"No."

Kurt and Bryant sprinted past her, disappearing into the plume of smoke.

"We need fire and emergency medical services! Now!" the sergeant said into his radio, then dropped it in the dirt.

The blaze illuminated the surrounding area, casting everything in a bright orange hue. Riley caught her breath and scanned the property for signs of movement. If this was an ambush, now would be the time to strike. She gripped her holstered pistol, looking around in all directions. She saw hundreds of barren trees, but no people. If members of the BSMC had been around before, they were long gone now.

Kurt returned through the field, dragging an unconscious officer by the vest. He was followed by Bryant and the rest of the sergeants hobbling to the tree line. Their uniforms were scorched and bloody. Riley propped an officer's arm over her shoulder and guided him back to the forest. The group reeked of burned rubber. Kurt rested the officer against a tree trunk and pulled off his balaclava mask. Officer Harris was unconscious and bleeding from both ears.

"Harris, wake up! Harris! Harris!" Sergeant Bryant said. He kneeled beside the man and patted both of his cheeks. After a moment, Harris's eyes opened, and he looked around in a daze. "Wha ... What ..."

"Harris, are you all right?"

He opened and closed his mouth.

"Damn it, do you understand me?"

Harris looked around. "There's ringing in my head." He opened and closed his mouth again. "What's happening?"

Bryant rested a hand on his shoulder. "Relax, you have a concussion. Just sit tight." He rose to his feet, "Is everyone else okay?"

Officer Connelly removed his mask and took a knee. The left

side of his face was singed red, with thin cuts across his cheek and a bloodshot eye. "We're in one piece."

"Medics are on their way," Bryant announced. "Won't be long now."

"What the hell happened?" an officer asked him.

"The plan went to shit. That's what happened. The barn was rigged to blow."

Riley walked back into the field. Flaming wood planks had landed on the neighboring farmhouse, causing the roof to catch fire. She watched as the blaze consumed everything. A festering rage boiled within her, black and formless, like a tar pit. She'd been counting on this raid to take down the club, and now she had nothing. No drugs, no gang, and no evidence to speak of.

Kurt joined her in the field. "You think the leak came from one of us?"

"I don't know." She frowned. "It could have also been someone in the DA's office. We may never know."

"Damn," Kurt fumed.

Riley took a deep breath and looked up to an ocean of stars. She couldn't remember the last time she'd seen so many. In the depths of the city, the most she would ever see was the pale moon against a great black emptiness, maybe a few scattered pinpricks of light. But out here, in the darkest of places, she found more stars than she'd ever imagined. She took another deep breath and felt her head clear. "That amount of product is worth too much to go to waste. They must have moved it before we arrived." She pulled out her flashlight and uncovered multiple tire tracks leading away from the barn.

Kurt kneeled down and rubbed his hand across the loose dirt. "You're right. These tracks are fresh. We must have just missed them."

She swayed her flashlight back and forth across the trail.

"They definitely left in a hurry. Their tracks kicked up a lot of dirt."

Ambulance sirens echoed in the distance. It wouldn't be long before they arrived. Riley looked back to the tree line and saw the group of officers picking each other off the ground and hobbling into the woods.

Kurt rose to his feet. "Nothing else we can do here without forensics. At least they'll be able to tell us what caused the explosion."

Riley's cell phone rang. She pulled it out from her jacket pocket. "Detective Walker."

"Hello Detective, this is Shift Sergeant Hall. I'm calling to let you know we have Robert Kane in custody."

"I'll be right over," she said, and hung up the phone.

"What is it?"

"Kane is at the station."

SEVENTEEN

Riley opened the door to viewing room five. Deputy Chief Reyes was waiting against the back wall with her arms crossed. "What the hell happened out there?"

"They knew we were coming," Riley said, then set her case file on the side table. "Someone talked."

"That's enough," Reyes said. "Make one more allegation against this department and I'll have your badge. Tonight was a disaster. The mayor is furious, and every major news outlet wants to know why we just detained one of the city's biggest investors. I'm giving you both one shot at making something stick, otherwise Kane walks."

"Walks?" Kurt asked.

"We can't let him go," Riley said. "Kane is our only lead to the club."

"You're lucky I don't cut him loose right now." Reyes took a step closer to Riley. "Make him talk, or it's over."

There was no arguing with the deputy chief on this. Her decision was final. Riley turned to look at Kane through the two-way viewing glass. He was seated at the interview table in a black tuxedo with platinum cufflinks and slicked-back hair. The room was a claustrophobic space, with white-painted brick walls and a single florescent light overhead.

"How long has he been in there?" she asked.

"About an hour."

Kurt leaned closer to the viewing glass. "Has he said anything?"

"Not a word. He hasn't even asked for a lawyer."

Riley lifted her case file from the side table and walked toward the door.

"Walker," Reyes called out, then held up a finger. "One shot."

Riley walked out of the viewing room and into the hallway.

Kurt followed behind her. "You know he's playing us. People like Kane never expose themselves like this."

"I do," she said, then entered the interview room.

She dropped her case file onto the table and took her seat across from Kane. Kurt leaned his shoulder against the side wall, staying within the man's peripheral vision.

"Mr. Kane, I'm Detective Walker. This session is being recorded, and anything you say can and will be used against you in a court of law."

She could feel Deputy Chief Reyes watching her from behind the two-way mirror. This needed to be done by the book—no room for mistakes. "I understand that you have been read your rights and you have not requested a lawyer." She paused for a beat to let him confirm, but he said nothing. "I'm going to ask you a series of questions, and it will be in your best interest to comply."

She waited for Kane's response, but he remained silent. The lack of reciprocation gave her pause. She had conducted dozens of interviews before, but none were like this. Kane was stone cold. He stared at her with a dull, unflinching gaze. He had sized her up and was not impressed. She decided to lay into him by getting down to brass tacks.

Riley opened her case file and slid the Sturgeon Farms property deed across the table. "Kane Capital Investments, your company, owns a farm that is being used as a drug distribution hub for a gang called the Black Snake Motorcycle Club."

Kane stared at her, emotionless. He didn't respond. He didn't even move a muscle. Riley's lips tightened. "What is your involvement with the club?"

Again, Kane didn't respond. It was like she was talking to a statue. She glanced over to Kurt, who shrugged his shoulders. If she didn't get this man to open up about his involvement, her case would be over. She looked back to Kane and leaned in. "I can assure you, refusing to talk with me is not going to help your case." She pointed to the deed. "This does not look good for you. Cooperate, and maybe I can help convince the judge to give you a lesser sentence."

Kane didn't say a word.

Kurt pushed off the side wall and leaned over Kane's shoulder. "I don't know what kind of game you're playing here pal, but this isn't going away. You're looking at multiple felonies. Drug trafficking, racketeering, and that's before we comb through your business affairs. Who knows what else we'll find when that happens? If you don't talk to us right here and right now, there's no communication after that. The moment we walk out that door, we're done. You Understand?"

"Last chance," she warned.

Kane remained silent.

Riley placed the property deed back into her case file, then rose from her seat. If Kane didn't speak to her, there was nothing else she could do. He had stonewalled them from extracting any more information that could strengthen their case.

"If you're not going to talk, then we're done." She walked across the interview room and opened the door.

"Is that all?" Kane asked.

She stopped in the doorway.

"Tell me, Detective Walker, what do you hope will come of this?"

Riley returned to her seat. "Justice."

"Justice," Kane mused. "Justice is a farce, dictated by whoever is in power."

"From where I'm sitting, you're not the authority." She rested her hand over the case file. "We have you on this."

"That farm has been abandoned for years. I own dozens of properties like it all over the city. Warehouses, depots, every kind of place a gang like the Black Snakes would take advantage of." He leaned forward. "You have nothing."

His words stung more than she was willing to show. At this point, it would be impossible for a prosecutor to link Kane's involvement with the club since the barn had burned to the ground along with any evidence. She decided to bluff him.

"We took down the Black Snakes at the same time we brought you in. We have everything. The club, the fentanyl, all of it." She examined Kane's face for an involuntary response. There were seven universal micro-expressions one could emote: fear, happiness, disgust, anger, contempt, sadness, and surprise. From hours spent in interrogations, Riley had become skilled in detecting these silent admissions. The raise of an eyebrow, the tensing of a jaw, the subtle change in breathing. Anyone could tell a lie, but no one could hide their inner feelings.

The corner of Kane's mouth tightened and raised a millimeter in an act of pure contempt. He didn't like what she had told him, but what concerned her was what he didn't show—neither fear nor surprise. This could only mean that he didn't believe her, or worse, he already knew the truth.

Kane chuckled to himself and leaned back in his seat. "If that were true, we wouldn't be talking. It must be exhausting running all over the city. Answers that only lead to more questions. I'm sure everyone will have questions for you as well, in time."

He was right. Reyes would push for his release as soon as media pressure mounted against the department. Kane's connection to the Black Snakes was tenuous, and with no farm, no drugs, and no gang to speak of, there was only one thing left for her to do. She grabbed her case file off of the table and rose from her seat. "I'm detaining you for twenty-four hours. If I were you, I would get used to the view."

"Tick-tock, Detective."

She exited the interview room. Deputy Chief Reyes joined her in the hall. "What do you think you're doing? I told you to make him talk, or he walks."

"I heard you, and I'm holding him anyway. You can tell the press whatever you want, say he's helping the investigation for all I care, but as long as this is my case, he stays."

"If this remains your case," Reyes said.

"If you do that, then you'll have a bigger problem on your hands."

"What's that?"

"Me. I'll make sure everyone knows who's to blame for letting illegal drugs flow freely on their streets. You'll become a household name by the time I'm through."

Reyes gritted her teeth. "I'm not resting my neck on the chopping block for this. As I told you before, if things go south, if you're wrong about Kane, it'll be the last thing you do in this department."

"You know, that's the difference between you and me. I'm trying to protect this city, and all you want to do is protect yourself."

"Get out of my face," Reyes said.

Riley and Kurt walked down the long hall of interview rooms toward the bullpen.

"There's a chance the club moved the drugs to one of Kane's other properties. If we can find out which one, we can bring an end to the entire operation," Kurt said.

"Just keep your cards close to the vest from here on out. I don't know who to trust."

When they reached the bullpen, she felt a churning in her stomach that made her shudder.

"You all right?"

"I'm fine. I'll be right back," she said, then walked into the bathroom. Her legs became heavy. A heatwave washed over her as she entered the nearest stall, dropped to her knees, and retched into the toilet bowl. Her head throbbed like a jackhammer between heaves. When she was finished, she wiped her mouth and lifted the case file from the floor.

Riley flushed the toilet with her boot heel, then checked beneath the other stalls to make sure she was alone. She washed out her mouth in the sink, splashing water over her face. The cool liquid soothed her pounding temples. She looked in the mirror at the healing cut above her brow. It had been a rough few days, and the case was weighing on her.

Taking a deep breath to center herself, Riley returned to the bullpen. Kurt was searching through Kane's property records on his desktop computer.

"I'm going to turn in for the night," she said. "My nerves are shot. I won't be good to anyone like this. You got this?"

"There's a full pot of coffee on the burner. I'll manage."

She handed Kurt her case file. "Here. I'll see you first thing tomorrow."

"Thanks," he said, and placed it on his desk. Riley nodded, then headed toward the rear parking lot.

"Hey," Kurt called to her. She stopped and turned to face him.

"We came close tonight. It's not over yet."

"We'll see," she said, then exited through the rear of the department.

Riley entered her Ford Mustang and drove out of the station and onto the interstate. She wondered if there was anything she could have done differently. Perhaps she should have pressed Kane harder about the farm. It would have been difficult for him to explain why he would continue to own a farm that was no longer in use. But she concluded that no matter what she did, Kane wouldn't provide any information that could be used against him.

She merged into the middle lane as several memories surfaced to the forefront of her mind. The ear-piercing bang of the barn explosion. Agent Connelly's singed red face. The smell of burnt rubber. Her thoughts were shaken by a bright light reflecting in her side mirror. A man on a dark motorcycle pulled up beside her, matching her speed. She looked out the driver's window. His face was obscured by a helmet visor, but she could tell he was looking back. The biker roamed over the divider line between them.

Riley engaged her right turn signal, but was cut off by another biker on her passenger side. The second biker's black hoodie flapped in the wind, and a bandana covered the lower half of his face. The motorcycles hugged both sides of her Mustang. This was no coincidence. The Black Snakes must have followed her from the station. Three more single high beams blinded her rearview mirror as the men barreled toward her.

She floored the gas pedal, jolting her tachometer to the red line. Her engine roared to ninety miles per hour, but the two bikers matched her speed—never straying more than a few feet away. Riley clenched her teeth. They were too fast to outrun. She looked to the passenger window. The man in the bandana took his hand off the handle bars and pulled a gun from his belt. Riley turned to ram into him, but he veered away, cutting off two lanes.

The surrounding vehicles skidded across the asphalt, blaring their horns.

Riley drove through the opening then weaved through traffic. The five club members gave chase, serpentining behind her. Muzzle flashes sparked in her rearview as cracks of a gunfire rang out. She white-knuckled the steering wheel and lowered her head. The rear windshield of the neighboring sedan shattered into a spiderweb of broken glass. It swerved in front of her. Riley pulled the steering wheel in the other direction to avoid a collision. Her mustang passed the sedan with only inches to spare. Two of the following club members crashed into it and fell to the pavement. The accident caused several other vehicles to pile up.

She sped across several lanes and took the next exit ramp off the interstate. Once the highway was out of sight, she looked into her rearview mirror to make sure she hadn't been followed, then called Kurt. He picked up on the second ring.

"Detective Thompson."

"It's me. Listen, a handful of club members ambushed me on the highway."

"You all right?"

"Yeah," she said, checking the rearview mirror again. "They're gone now. I think they followed me from the station. Check to see if any plates were caught on the cameras surrounding the building."

"Will do."

"Thanks. I'll let you know if anything else comes up," she said, then hung up the phone. Riley took her time navigating the side streets back to her apartment building. Although they hadn't recovered any evidence from the farm, the raid must have been a serious disruption to ongoing operations. And with Kane in custody, they became desperate. Desperate enough to attack her in public. She stopped at the red light before her apartment building and peered down the road. All five club members were watching her from the parking garage entrance.

She lifted her pistol from its holster and waited. The streetlight turned green, but she didn't drive forward. A car pulled up behind her and honked twice before driving around. The streetlight turned yellow, then red again. The Black Snakes revved their motorcycles.

She was in a vulnerable position and needed to act fast. Riley put her car in park, stepped outside behind her door, and took aim. The club members spun their motorcycles around in a burnout before speeding away. Their engines echoed into the distance. She glanced around to make sure all of them had fled before returning to her car. The message from the club was clear. If you come after us, we'll come after you. Anytime, anywhere.

After returning to her apartment, Riley left her boots by the door, then entered her bedroom to remove her gun and badge. She thought about keeping her Glock in the gun safe on her nightstand, but after the night's events, decided to keep it in her bed.

She lifted her pillow to find a black snake coiled on her mattress. It hissed and lunged at her arm. Riley fell back to the floor, and it slithered from her bed and down the hall. She rose to her feet and followed it to the living room.

Leaning over the kitchen counter, she grabbed a butcher knife from the drawer. The snake moved toward her stack of case files in the back of the room. Riley raised the knife and swung as close to the snake's head as possible, severing its torso in two.

She leaned back against the wall and slid to the floor. Blood filled the cracks in the wooden floor where the knife stood upright on its edge. The lower half of the snake thrashed in a death rattle along the floor while its head remained motionless.

Riley felt violated. She lifted her phone and scrolled. Roy answered on the third ring. "Riley? It's the middle of the night. You okay?"

She watched as the lower half of the snake slowed to stillness.

"Yeah, I'm fine. I just wanted to hear your voice."

"Where are you? Did you close your case?"

"I'm at home, and no, I didn't. There were complications. You'll probably hear about it tomorrow."

"Happens to the best of us. Don't worry about it. You'll bounce back."

"Thanks, Roy."

There was a momentary silence on the line.

"Do you want me to come over?" he asked.

"No, I'm fine."

"You sure?"

"Yes."

"All right then. Have a good night."

"You too," she said, and pocketed her phone. The club had broken into her home and planted the snake to kill her in her sleep. She needed to make sure they would never get a second chance.

EIGHTEEN

The next morning, a horde of reporters occupied the front steps of the station. News of the botched raid attempt had spread through the department like wildfire. Every detective Riley walked past refused to look her in the eye. She had less than twenty-four hours to prove Kane's involvement with the Black Snakes, otherwise Reyes would bring her investigation—and career—to a swift end.

She entered the bullpen to find Kurt's seat empty. His desk was a cluttered mess of stray papers, notepads, and binders, topped with an empty coffee pot that needed to be returned to the break room. Riley removed her jacket, then checked her desk to see if he had left her any notes, but her tabletop was clear. She rounded Kurt's desk and opened the top drawer. A half-empty bottle of Jack Daniels rested on a pile of folders and office supplies.

Her phone rang in her jacket pocket. She closed the drawer and answered it. "Detective Walker."

"I want my exclusive," Holly said. "Rumor has it Robert Kane was taken into custody. Can you confirm?"

"How did you get this number?" Riley asked.

"Don't dodge the question. You promised an exclusive into your investigation. What happened last night?"

Before she could respond, a voice called out to her from across the room.

"Walker!"

She rose from behind Kurt's desk to find Briggs waving her over.

"The investigation is ongoing. Don't call this number again," Riley said, then hung up the phone. She walked out of the bullpen to the commander's office.

"Shut the door behind you," he said.

Kurt was sitting in one of the wooden chairs on this side of Briggs's desk, wearing the same wrinkled clothes as yesterday.

"You good?" she asked.

"Uh-huh," Kurt said, but his demeanor and bloodshot eyes told her otherwise. She knew the look. Kurt must have stayed up the entire night researching Kane's properties.

Briggs took his seat behind his desk. "The deputy chief tells me the raid was a bust and now you're on the clock. I hope you two have a Plan B in mind."

Kurt placed two documents side by side on Briggs's desk—a highlighted list of properties owned by Kane Capital Investments next to an overhead map of Chicago. The map was marked with multiple red dots.

"I spent the night tracking down all the properties owned by Kane's firm. We'll need to amend the search warrant to cover these properties."

"How many?" Briggs asked.

"Eighteen," Kurt said.

Briggs lifted the map from his desk and looked it over. "Eighteen?"

"Yeah, eighteen," Kurt said.

Briggs set the map back down. "You want to search eighteen properties in less than twelve hours?"

"We found fresh tire tracks at the farm. The club moved the drugs in a hurry. This is our best chance at finding them."

"What makes you so sure?" Briggs asked. "They could have moved the drugs anywhere."

"Would you let that amount of product out of your grasp?"

Briggs frowned and leaned back in his plush leather chair. "I can't do it. We don't have the resources for something like this. Especially on such short notice."

"We have less than a day to bring charges, or else Kane walks," Kurt said. "Reyes made that clear last night."

Riley wished she had spoken with Kurt before this meeting. "We might be able to narrow down the list."

"I did narrow it down," Kurt said. "They're at one of these properties. I'm telling you."

"I'm sorry," Briggs said. "But you'll need to find another way."

"This is bullshit!" Kurt darted up from his seat and stormed out of the office.

"This won't end with Kane," Riley said to Briggs once he was gone.

"What do you mean?"

"The club planted a snake in my apartment."

The commander's eyes widened. "Are you serious?"

"It was in my bed. This case will only end in one of two ways." She slid the documents from the desk and walked across the office. She paused at the door to look back at him. "You said you're retiring because no matter what we do, things seem to get worse. I'm beginning to think you're right."

She left the office and returned to the bullpen. Kurt was seated at his desk, his leg shaking with agitation.

"Has Kane asked for a lawyer?" she asked.

"Kept to himself all night."

"And the farm?"

"The barn and house burned to the ground. There was nothing left to recover. Forensics determined the barn door was rigged to blow, but they're still trying to determine the compound that was used for the explosion."

Riley placed the documents on her desk and reviewed them. "Are you sure these are all of Kane's properties?"

"All that I could find," Kurt said.

She looked them over one by one. A meatpacking plant, a textile mill, apartment complexes and small business properties. All abandoned within the last two decades. Then she compared Kurt's selection to the master property list.

"I see other abandoned properties here. How did you narrow it down to these?" she asked.

"Kane isn't looking to draw attention. That's why he went to such great lengths to conceal the farm. Those properties are secluded from the public."

Riley reviewed the list again and again for something that could suggest the club's whereabouts. After a third attempt, she felt a painful lump in her throat.

"We'll never search these properties in time," she admitted. "Even with the manpower, there are too many. And we still have a leak."

Kurt leaned across his desk and lowered his voice. "Yeah, about that. Last night, I got to thinking about those tire treads we found outside the barn."

"What about them?"

"The club left in a hurry, right? For all we know, we just missed them. Maybe by a few minutes."

"What's your point?"

"Well, that tells me that the tip probably didn't come from the DA's office, since they knew about the raid yesterday afternoon. If someone from their office had warned the club, they would have had plenty of time to move everything from the farm. Which means whoever notified the club only learned about it last night."

"I don't follow?"

"How many people knew about the raid other than the DA's office?"

Riley thought for a moment. "Reyes, Briggs, the raid unit, and us."

"No, there's one more you're forgetting." Kurt nodded to the desk at the end of the next row. Riley looked over to see Detective Hank Maloney talking on his cell phone.

"He barged into Agent Bryant's meeting, remember? That would have given him just enough time to warn the club we were coming."

Detective Maloney locked eyes with Riley, pausing his conversation. He rose from his desk, then walked toward the rear parking lot to finish his call.

Riley rose from her desk. "You're right. Come on."

She began walking down the row of desks, following Hank to the back of the room. "Hank was my superior when I first became a detective."

"He was your partner?"

"It didn't last long."

"Why not?"

"Hank always said that within the CPD, you need to go along to get along. Let's just say we didn't."

Riley and Kurt pushed through the rear door to the parking lot. Detective Maloney was on his cell phone, walking toward his cruiser. He opened the driver's door and Kurt pushed it shut.

"I'll call you back," Maloney said, then hung up the phone. "You've got a lot of nerve, pal."

"Last night, you entered a meeting you shouldn't have. Why?" Kurt asked.

"You serious?" He looked over Kurt's shoulder to Riley. "You better put a leash on your dog before something bad happens to him."

"Answer the question, Hank," Riley said.

"I don't have to explain anything to you two." Maloney opened the door again. "You're holding me up."

Kurt shoved it closed and grabbed Hank by the lapels. "You need to do better than that. A lot of people got hurt."

"Everything all right over there?" an officer called out from three parking spaces away. He had been watching the exchange with his partner.

Kurt released Hank and took a step back. "Yeah, everything's fine."

Hank put a hand on the car. "I've seen your kind before. Reckless, angry. You're falling down a dark hole just hoping to hit the bottom. I don't know what it is you're searching for, kid, but I can tell you I don't have it. If you ever lay a hand on me again, I'll put you down."

Hank entered his cruiser, then drove out of the parking lot.

Kurt ran his fingers through his hair. "We should follow him. He can lead us to the club."

"Hank is too smart for that. He won't go anywhere near the club, especially now."

"The farm burned to the ground, along with any evidence. We have no drugs, no club, and no time to search through all of Kane's properties. Hank is the only one who can tell us where the club is hiding."

"No, he's not," Riley said as she walked toward her cruiser.

"Where are you going?"

She opened her car door. "Provident Hospital. You coming?"

NINETEEN

Riley and Kurt took the elevator to the fourth floor at Provident Hospital. The intensive care unit was crowded with doctors and nurses roaming between patient rooms. The detectives walked through a pair of double doors and continued down the hall to Sam's room. Through the window, Riley could see Sam lying in the hospital bed, watching TV.

The guard posted at the doorway was playing a video game on his cell phone. After a moment, he sensed Riley and Kurt standing over him.

"Yes?" the guard said, pocketing his phone.

Riley revealed her badge. "Riley Walker, CPD." She nodded to the room. "Has he been any trouble?"

"We caught him trying to remove his handcuffs, so we put extra restrains on his wrists and ankles. Other than that, not a peep," the guard said.

"Why don't you get yourself a cup of coffee," Kurt said, handing the guard a five-dollar bill.

"Thanks." The guard smirked and rose from his seat. "I'll be back in five."

"Make it ten," Kurt said.

They entered the recovery room and shut the door.

Sam turned his head against the pillow to look at them. "You two pigs again? I already told you, I ain't no snitch."

"Yes, you are," Riley said. "We raided the farm last night. We have the fentanyl, we have your MC, and we'll make sure all of them know it was you who gave us the info."

"You bitch!" Sam said, thrashing. His movements were limited by the restraints. After a moment, he fell back and tried to catch his breath.

Riley walked around the bed and stood over him. "We don't want you, Sam. We want your boss," she said. "If you cooperate, we can get you into protective custody."

Sam said nothing.

"How long do you think you'll last in the pen? A day? Maybe two? The first chance they get, they're going to cut you up just like they did to your old cellmate Johnny."

"You don't know anything about that," he said.

"I know there's no going back to the club after this. Even if you convince them to let you live, they'll never trust you again. Your days with the club are over."

Sam looked up at her. "That's a nasty cut on your head. Looks like it's going to scar."

"Last chance," Riley said.

Sam spit in her face. "I'll talk to the devil before I talk to you."

She stepped back and wiped away the saliva.

Kurt extended the privacy curtain from the wall and grabbed a roll of surgical gauze from the medical table. He shoved the gauze into Sam's mouth, then covered it with his hand. "I'm sorry you feel that way, because when I'm through, you're going to wish you were dead." Kurt pressed his knuckles against a bullet wound in Sam's ribs. The man wailed in pain through the bandages.

"You're going to give us everything," Kurt said, twisting his wrist deeper into the wound. "Your shot caller, your club, and every place they're hiding drugs."

Sam convulsed against the restraints.

"Stop!" Riley said.

Kurt only pressed harder. Riley rounded the bed and pushed him away. "I said stop!"

Sam expelled the cloth from his mouth. "You're going to pay for this! You're dead. There's nowhere you can run where we won't find you!"

Riley and Kurt left the room as Sam continued his belligerent threats. "Dead! Do you hear me? You're both dead!"

They could still hear his tirade through the door as Kurt shut it behind them.

"You two sure riled him up something nasty," the guard said, taking a sip of fresh coffee.

"Make sure a nurse looks at his side. I think a few of his stitches came loose," Riley said.

"Uh-huh," the guard said, and took another sip.

Riley walked down the hallway, clenching her fists. Kurt was putting her entire investigation in jeopardy. Any criminal defense lawyer could get her case thrown out if she got any information while Sam was being coerced.

Kurt caught up to her. "Would you slow down?"

Riley stopped walking and turned to face him. "What the hell do you think you were doing back there? If word of that got back to Reyes, Kane would walk."

"Sam knows where the club is hiding, and we're out of time. I was doing what needed to be done."

Riley pointed toward Sam's room. "That makes us no better than them."

"There's no other way!"

"There is," she said, and continued toward the elevator. "And Sam just gave it to us."

. . .

Clusters of students, tourists, and art critics gazed in fascination at each painting within the John Martin exhibit at the Art Institute of Chicago. The surreal apocalyptic imagery depicted lone figures standing among vast, cataclysmic landscapes. The more Riley looked, the more details she could discern within the shadows of the scenes.

Holly Hart walked in through the single entryway and joined Riley on the wooden bench near the center of the room. She removed the messenger bag from her shoulder and set it on the ground next to her. "I understand why you wouldn't want to meet at the office, but don't you think this is a little public?"

"Have you ever heard of the detective's dilemma? Sometimes, the hardest things to find are hiding in plain sight."

Holly pressed the record button on her phone and held it up between them. "You want to do this here or somewhere else?"

Riley looked at the eight-foot-wide painting hanging on the wall across from them. The image depicted an enormous banquet hall of massive stone columns and crowds of Babylonians draped in different-colored robes. The open sky revealed an ominous tower hidden amid a sea of dark clouds.

"That one is called 'Belshazzar's Feast.'"

"What?"

"The painting," Riley said. "The placard says it's a scene from the Book of Daniel about the fall of Babylon."

Holly lowered her phone. "I'm here for a different story."

"No, I don't think you are."

"What's that supposed to mean?"

"It means you haven't been honest about anything since the moment we met."

"What are you talking about?" Holly asked.

"At the farm, you mentioned Johnny's club by name. At first, I thought you got it from Sam Hyde at Provident Hospital, but it's clear to me now that Sam is a true one-percenter. He would rather die than give them up."

Holly's eyes widened.

"There is no way you could have known Johnny was part of the club, unless you knew him personally."

Riley held up a grainy still of Holly taken from a dashboard camera the night of the farm raid. "A bartender at Thirsty identified you meeting with him on multiple occasions."

Holly rose from the bench. "I don't have to sit here and listen to this." She turned to leave, but Kurt stepped into the entryway, blocking her escape. The woman looked around the room for another exit. There was none.

"Sit," Riley said.

Holly turned back to her and crossed her arms. "You can't prove anything."

"You know I can, and I have plenty to bury you with. You'll only make things worse for yourself. Now sit."

Holly returned to the bench.

"The one thing I don't understand is why? Johnny must have known it would be suicide to betray the club. There's no place he could have gone where they wouldn't find him."

Holly took a moment to let the question sink in. "In a word . . . conscience. The club started selling drugs to minors, and that didn't sit right with Johnny. He said when you sell drugs to children, you're not only taking their money, you're taking their souls. He made it clear that if there was one decent thing he could do with his life, it would be to end the club."

Riley recalled the crucifix tattooed on Johnny's back. Betraying the club must have been an act of penitence for a life full of sin.

"So he contacted you?"

"That's right. He read my other work and knew I had the stomach for it."

"Your other work?"

"District voter fraud, sex trafficking of undocumented immigrants, and an exposé on gang violence in the city, to name a few. We met at Thirsty a few times and planned how to bring the whole thing down. The problem is, if you're going to go after a powerful man like Kane, you need proof."

"You needed the brick of fentanyl."

Holly nodded. "Accusations alone wouldn't be enough, especially from a felon like Johnny. There isn't a prosecutor in this state who would bring a case against Kane unless it was a certainty. When Johnny didn't show up to the meet, I knew the club had gotten to him. I've been on the move ever since, trying not to stay in one place for too long."

"At the gas station, you weren't looking for a comment on Johnny's murder, you were trying to gauge how much danger you were in," Riley said. "Why didn't you go to the police?"

"You really have to ask? It wasn't long ago that I did a piece on the Homan Square black site your department was running. As far as I'm concerned, the only difference between the police and the violent thugs they lock up are the badges."

Riley didn't want to get into an argument. She was on the clock and needed to act if Kane was going to remain behind bars.

"You're right," she said. "There's a leak in the department. The club rigged the barn to blow before we arrived. Several officers were injured, and everything burned to the ground. We have Kane in custody, but if he's going to stay that way, we need more evidence." Riley leaned closer. "I need to find the club tonight."

A silence fell between them. Divulging this information was risky. A sensational story like this would make national news, but Holly was her last hope of finding the Black Snakes.

"Why are you telling me this?" the reporter asked.

"Because if Kane walks, the club will disappear, and Johnny's death would be for nothing."

After a moment, Holly reached inside her bag and retrieved a manila envelope. "The club is smuggling drugs through a train yard near the Calumet River."

"Who is their supplier?"

"I don't know. Johnny said the club compartmentalizes information like that in case any of their members get arrested. That way they wouldn't have anything to trade for a lesser sentence."

"What do they smuggle the drugs in?" she asked.

"Car parts, electronics, whatever ships in large containers. They cycle through different products to avoid suspicion."

This aligned with what Riley had seen in the barn. The Black Snakes were removing the drug bricks from wooden crates before preparing them for distribution. Holly slid several documents from the envelope and handed them to Riley. On the top page was a detailed map of Chicago's South Side.

"What is this?"

"You heard about Kane's initiative to clean up the city? Look at the slice of land he carved out for himself."

Riley looked down at a large dotted outline showing where the Kane Initiative would take place. Within it was a smaller section of land circled in red ink. Riley's heart skipped a beat. "He wants his own train port."

Holly nodded. "With the amount of product he'll be able to move, Kane will make millions."

"Did Johnny ever mention other places the club occupied besides the farm?"

Holly reached over and flipped through the pages until she stopped on a property deed. "Just one. The abandoned Goodman Equipment Plant. It's where they conduct club business. Kane purchased the plant through a shell corporation years ago."

Riley skimmed through the document. It listed that the plant had been purchased by Rush Street Investments LLC. "How did you find out about this?"

"Johnny gave me the location. I did the rest. If the club torched the farm, then this is where you'll find them."

Riley tucked the documents beneath her arm and rose from the bench. "You need to go someplace safe. Stay with a friend or get out of town. Wait until you hear from me."

"And if I don't?"

Riley looked down at Holly. "Not all police are as bad as you think. Some of us are trying to do the right thing."

She walked across the exhibit to Kurt, who was leaning his shoulder against the entryway. "You got it?"

"I got it," she said, then called Commander Briggs's office. "Frank, it's me. I have a lead on the Black Snakes. You need to hold Kane for as long as possible."

"What do you have?"

"There's no time to explain, just hold him until you hear from me."

"Reyes is going to be pissed," Briggs said, "but I'll try. Just don't do anything stupid. If you need backup, call us."

"I will."

TWENTY

After leaving the Art Institute of Chicago, Riley made a quick stop at the station to switch vehicles. Her mustang would provide much-needed cover during her surveillance of the Goodman Equipment Plant. She coasted down South Halsted Street, which acted as a border between sprawling manufacturing plants and compacted neighborhoods.

"It should be coming up on the right."

Kurt had been silent most of the ride. His elbow was propped against the door with his chin buried in his knuckles. "Slow down," he continued. "We won't be able to get away with multiple rounds. I want to see as much as possible."

Riley checked the rearview mirror for any following vehicles, then let her foot off the gas. Her mustang glided passed Forty-Eighth Street and continued along a warped chain-link fence intertwined with tree brush. From what she could see, the five-story brick building stood on the far side of a vacant lot. It looked like it had been through a war zone. Most of the windows were shattered, with chunks of the exterior wall missing or dangling on exposed steel rebar. Much of the first floor had been boarded up.

"Do you see anything?" she asked.

"Not much from here. Too many trees in the way." Kurt pointed. "Looks like there's a container depot on the hill behind the building. We might get a better view from up there."

She drove to the end of the block and turned right onto West Forty-Ninth Place. They passed a car wash, two warehouses, and a pallet yard before turning right onto Morgan Street. The entrance to the container depot was a dirt road with stacks of shipping containers on all sides. Riley parked next to a flatbed and exited. A German Shepherd barked at her from a cage, which was attached to a shanty bungalow with a tin roof and metal bars over the windows. A man with beady eyes and white stubble stepped out of the bungalow and hit the cage with his cane. "Quiet, you!"

The dog whimpered and retreated to the back of the cage.

The man shuffled toward them in a pair of loafers. "We're closed"

"Riley Walker, CPD," she said.

"You don't look like police," he said, nodding to her Mustang.

Riley removed her badge from her waist and held it up for him to see. "We would like to surveil the warehouse next to your lot."

"What for?"

"That's our business," Kurt said.

The man rubbed his chin. "I'll need to check with my manager. See what he says. I'll be right back." He turned around and went back into the bungalow.

"It's getting dark," Kurt said. "We won't be able to see anything soon." He pointed to the back of the lot. "We might see them from over there."

Riley tossed him her car keys. "I have a pair of binoculars in the trunk."

The man came out of the bungalow again. "I can't get my manager on the phone. Don't you need a warrant to be here?"

"We're not here to search this property," Riley deflected. "Like I said, we want to surveil the building behind your lot."

"You should go. I don't want no part in whatever this is."

"We will only be here for an hour. When we're finished, it'll be like we were never here."

The man rubbed his chin again. "I still think you need a warrant to be here."

"I can get one within the hour, but it will be very inconvenient for me."

"That's not my problem." The man shrugged.

Riley looked at the man's loafers, then met his gaze. "What's your name?"

"John Faulks. What's this have to do with me?"

"You said you're closed for the day. Your manager is clearly gone. So why are you still here?"

"I watch the yard overnight. Keep the trespassers and thieves away."

"You get a lot of those? People stealing two-ton empty shipping containers?"

John didn't respond.

Riley stepped forward. "You know, John, it's illegal to be living in a non-residential zone. If I have to get a warrant, it could become very inconvenient for you too."

John groaned and turned back to the bungalow. "Just do what you gotta do, then get the hell out of here."

Riley joined Kurt at her car. He handed her the keys and binoculars. "Got it."

They walked down a dirt pathway between rows of shipping containers stacked over thirty feet high.

"It's right over there." Kurt pointed to an open space that extended to the edge of the hillside.

"That's too close," Riley warned. "They might see us. Let's find a spot farther away."

"But if you go much farther, we won't be able to see anything."

Riley held up her binoculars.

"Good point."

They continued deeper into the lot, passing three more rows of containers, then approached the hillside. Riley stepped over a collection of empty beer bottles, then peeked around the edge of the container. At the bottom of the plateau, a club member guarded the entrance of the building. His dark gray jeans were ripped, and his leather jacket had multiple patches sewn into the arms.

"What do you see?" Kurt asked.

"One guard near the entrance. It looks like he's alone."

"Is he armed?"

Riley took another look at the guard's hands. He didn't appear to be holding anything. She raised her binoculars to her eyes and brought them into focus. The guard was leaning against the column with his arms crossed. She looked to the side of his hip for signs of a holster. By the way he was standing, it was too difficult to judge.

"He's leaning. I can't tell." Riley continued scanning the rest of the building. She didn't detect motion from any of the windows. "My guess is there are other members inside, I don't see anything on the other levels."

"You only see the one guard? No one else?"

"Looks that way."

"Is the entrance opened or closed?"

She shifted her focus to the double doors behind the guard. "Closed. I don't see any vehicles either."

"You sure it's a member of the club? That journalist could have been lying."

"No, she wasn't. This is it. This is where the club is hiding."

Kurt stepped behind her. "Let me see."

"Stay back," she said as Kurt kicked the glass bottles, shattering them against the side of the shipping container. The guard looked up toward her. She darted back out of sight.

"You think he saw?" Kurt asked.

"I don't know."

Riley concentrated on the sounds coming from the building. She listened for movement, but heard nothing. After a moment, she peeked around the shipping container again. The guard had moved off of the column, but he was still near the entrance. She pulled away. "I think we're good."

Kurt breathed a sigh of relief. "Yeah?"

Riley stepped aside and handed him the binoculars. "Take a look."

Dropping to one knee, he leaned around the side of the container. Riley looked to the sky. She was running out of daylight.

"There's a van," Kurt said. "Just pulled up."

Riley stood over him and inched herself around the side of the container. An unmarked matte-black van rounded the side of the building and backed in toward the entrance. The guard turned around, propping the doors open with a pair of bricks. Three more club members exited the building, including the goateed man she'd seen at Provident Hospital.

"That's them," she said.

"It looks like they're getting ready to move. Time to call it in."

The sound of gravel crunched behind her. Riley turned to see a dark figure swinging something at her head.

TWENTY-ONE

"Is everyone here?" a raspy voice asked.

"Yeah, all six."

"Good. This place is blown. Pack everything into the van and split."

Riley opened her eyes. She was lying sideways, with her right ear against a plastic tarp. The ground was cold and hard, like cement. She tried to recall how she got here, but the throbbing pain along her left temple was all she could focus on.

"All of it?" another voice asked.

"Did I stutter? More will come after they're gone. Get everything in the van now."

She looked ahead to see five pairs of black boots—two had red laces, one had blue. From her time as a beat cop, she knew colored laces held significance for street gangs and white supremacist groups. Red laces indicated that the wearer had shed blood against an enemy, while blue laces meant the slaying of law enforcement. Earning colored laces, or "lacing up," was a badge of honor for the depraved.

Her shoulder was numb from lying on it. She had been here a

while. Her mouth was gagged, and her wrists were fastened tight behind her back. Riley rotated her hands back and forth to loosen the restraints and regain sensation in her fingers.

"Dom, look who's awake."

"Pull her up," the raspy voice said.

Two of the men raised her to her knees. With her head off the ground, Riley could get a sense of where she was—a makeshift enclosure with four tarp walls draped over pipe fixtures. Portable construction lights illuminated the space within the Goodman Equipment Plant.

Kurt was kneeling beside her with his hands zip-tied behind his back and a bandana tied around his mouth. His right eye was swollen shut with bruising around his cheek. Beyond him was John Faulks. He too was bound and gagged and hunched over at the waist, mumbling a prayer to himself. She looked ahead at the five club members on the other side of the enclosure. The last of them was blue laces—a hulking thug clad in a gas mask, rubber apron, and gloves. He was pouring gallons of chemicals into three blue plastic drum barrels.

Dom, the man with the goatee, approached her and kneeled so he could look her in the eye. He snapped his fingers. "Hey, are you all there?" He slapped her across the face. She looked away and saw her gun and phone on a side table next to Kurt's. Dom grabbed her by the jaw and turned her head to face him. "I want to make sure they didn't knock the sense out of you."

She gritted her teeth over the gag and struggled to break free from the bindings.

"There you are." Dom grinned, then stood up. "You've caused us a lot of problems, Detective Walker. Now, I have some questions, and if you don't tell me what I want to know, these last minutes are going to be very painful." The guard with the patches sewn into the jacket handed Dom a pair of brass knuckles. He slid them onto his fingers, then removed her gag. "Who else knows about us?"

Riley straightened her back and looked up at him in defiance. She refused to give him anything.

"Have it your way then," Dom said, then bashed his fist across Kurt's face. The sharp cracking of metal against flesh sent a shiver down Riley's spine. Kurt fell back to the floor with a moan. Dom raised him by the collar and struck him again. The powerful blow left bloodstains over the brass knuckles. Kurt's nose was broken and bleeding into his gag. He squirmed, as if trying to avoid being picked up again.

"Where do you think you're going?" Dom said, then kicked him in the stomach. Kurt collapsed in on himself, gasping.

"Stop!" Riley shrieked.

Dom lifted Kurt by the collar. His head dangled limp in the air.

"No one knows! It's just us!" she said.

The man dropped Kurt to the floor and combed his bloody fingers through his hair, teasing it back into place. Then he stood over Riley. "Where's Kane?"

She looked over at Kurt, who was lying motionless on the ground. "He's been detained on twenty-four-hour hold. He should be released tonight."

Dom looked back at the other club members. They nodded in agreement. The thug finished pouring the last of the chemicals into the drum barrels. "Ready."

He turned away and handed the brass knuckles back to the guard. "You three finish loading the van." Removing a stainless Kimber 1911 pistol from the back of his pants, he handed it to the blue-laced thug in the gas mask. "Finish them."

Dom and three other club members walked out of the enclosure as the thug rounded the drum barrels and racked the slide. Riley reached her arms back and fished the folding knife from her boot. She thumbed open the blade from the handle, then wedged it beneath her zip-ties. The blade moved up and down against her bindings, causing the tip to cut into her arm. She fought past the pain, biting harder against her gag. John stopped praying to himself and lifted his head to see the thug approaching. He wailed through his own gag, pleading for his life.

The thug lifted the gun's muzzle against John's forehead and pulled the trigger. The ear-shattering bang was followed by a spray of blood and brain matter against the rear tarp wall. John's corpse fell to the ground, forming a pool of blood around his head. The thug took a step to the left to avoid getting blood on his boots.

Riley struggled as hard as she could against her restraints. Kurt turned his head to look up at the thug with his good eye. He didn't utter a word. No amount of bargaining or pleading would stop what was coming. The thug aimed the pistol at Kurt's head and pulled the trigger. The gun's hammer clicked against the barrel, but didn't fire.

The thug looked at the pistol in disbelief. He cocked the gun, ejecting the lame bullet and catching it in midair. He inspected the back of the cartridge, then dropped it to the ground before taking aim at Kurt's head again.

Riley broke free from her restraints just then, and thrust the blade deep into the thug's leg. He fired the gun at Kurt's shoulder, but stumbled backward and fell to the ground.

Riley lunged for the gun and tried to pry it from his grasp. They struggled on the floor, thrashing in the pool of blood. He was much stronger than her. Even with both of her hands on the gun, the thug was able to pull it between them. She used her weight to keep it in place, but could feel her grip wavering.

He inched the tip of the barrel toward her head. A few more seconds and he'd blow her brains out. She kneed the blade deeper into his leg. The thug groaned through his gas mask, and she felt his strength give way. Riley pushed the barrel under his chin and pulled the trigger. The gun fired, spraying blood across the tarp. Gun smoke filled the eyelids of the thug's gas mask.

Riley collapsed over his chest, exhausted. The high-pitched ringing in her ears matched the adrenaline coursing through her veins. She rolled onto her back and removed her gag. When the ringing subsided and her heightened senses returned to normal, she let out a nervous, half-suppressed laugh. Tears welled up in her eyes. She had witnessed the tragic end to countless lives, hundreds of petrified faces staring into that dark, dark abyss. The pain and elation of being alive was overwhelming.

Kurt rose to his knees with a grunt. She wiped her tears, then pulled her knife from the thug's leg. She crawled across the tarp and used it to cut through Kurt's restraints. He removed the bandana from his mouth and checked his shoulder.

"How bad is it?" she asked.

"Just a graze."

"Can you lift it?"

Kurt shrugged. "Yeah."

She lifted herself from the floor and grabbed her gun and radio from the table, calling dispatch. "5215, 10-1, officer down. Need backup and EMS at 4834 South Halsted Street. Multiple gunmen onsite."

The dispatcher buzzed through the receiver. "5215, 10-4. All units in area one and citywide. Officers need assistance 10-1, shot fired. 4834 South Halsted Street. Gunmen onsite."

Kurt removed a flask from his inside coat pocket and took a drink. Then he poured some against the wound on his shoulder.

"They're coming," she said.

"Not soon enough. The club will be long gone before backup arrives." He took another sip from his flask, then lifted the lame bullet from the floor and inspected it. She saw the indentation where the firing pin had struck the back of the cartridge, which meant the bullet was filled with bad primer or the gun had a light strike.

"Not if I can help it," she said.

Kurt pocketed the bullet. "Don't be stupid. We should both be dead." He tried to rise to his feet, but stumbled back to the ground.

"Try not to move. You might have a concussion." She handed Kurt his pistol and cell phone. "It won't be long. Stay here and rest."

Kurt nodded. "Just don't do anything that I would."

She walked to the edge of the enclosure and peeked through the tarp. The factory floor of the Goodmen Equipment Plant was covered with concrete debris, broken machinery, and rows of steel pillars. She crept from pillar to pillar to the other side of the floor, where five club members had removed drug bricks from wooden crates and stored them in the back of the unmarked van. Portable construction lights left the surrounding area in darkness.

Riley crouched through the tarp and snuck forward until she was twenty yards from the group. The area surrounding the entrance was filled with wooden crates stacked on top of each other. Only a few remained unopened. She needed to delay them long enough for backup to arrive.

Peering ahead, Riley saw the club members loading the drugs into the back of the van.

Dom opened the driver's door. "Get out and help us move these." The driver slid out of his seat and joined the others.

If she could get close, she could puncture one of the van's tires. Riley charted a path around the perimeter of the empty crate stacks. It would be risky, but if she could sneak across three stacks of crates, she would be within ten feet of the van. Moving around the pillar, she snuck behind the first pile of empty crates. The club members were loading the van in sequence. She waited until all of them were distracted, then darted across the six-foot gap to the next stack. She waited to see if she had been spotted. The sounds of continuous movement signaled that she was undetected.

"That's the last of it," a club member said.

"Check 'em again. Make sure we didn't miss anything," Dom said.

Riley listened to a pair of footsteps approaching. They stopped just beyond the edge of her stack. Her grip tightened over her pistol. A crate lid fell to the floor in front of her.

"Looks like we got 'em all," the club member said.

"Check around back."

Riley stepped back and crouched around the side of the crate just as the club member rounded the back end of the stack. "Nothing back here."

"All right then, let's pack it up and get the hell out of here," Dom said.

Riley breathed a sigh of relief. She moved to return behind the crate, but was cut off by a pair of black boots. Looking up, she saw the guard staring down at her.

"You," he said, reaching for his pistol.

A pair of arms wrapped around his neck from behind, then pulled him to the ground. Kurt had the guard in a chokehold. He tried to pull Kurt's arms away, but his grip was too tight. As the guard reached for his gun, Riley pinned his arm to the ground. She held it in place until he went limp.

Kurt pushed the unconscious club member off of him, then fastened a pair of handcuffs behind his back, leaning him against the back of the crate. "He'll be out for a while."

"You get lost back there?" Dom called out.

Kurt removed his pistol from his holster. "Get the hell out of here. I'll hold them off."

"Lou, stop messing around," Dom said.

"No chance," she said.

Riley and Kurt stepped from cover and took aim. "Get away from the van!"

"Hands up!" Kurt ordered.

The six remaining club members stopped loading the drugs.

"You've made a grave mistake, detectives," Dom said, turning around to face them. "You should have left when you had the chance."

Everyone grabbed for their pistols.

"Stop!" Riley said.

"Kill them."

Riley and Kurt leaped behind the nearest crates as they opened fire. A flurry of bullets splintered chunks of wood and concrete into the air. Bullets ricocheted off the steel beams, causing sparks to ignite. The deafening gunfire echoed in all directions. She looked across the aisle to Kurt, who was huddled behind a crate. Red and blue lights pulsated through the factory windows.

"We've got company!" one of the club members shouted.

The shooting stopped all at once.

"Cover the entrance," Dom said.

"This is the police!" a man spoke through a megaphone outside. "We have the building surrounded. Lay down your weapons and come outside with your hands in the air."

Riley peeked through one of the bullet holes in the crate. The driver reached into the van and pulled out a pair of AR-15 rifles with homemade aluminum lower receivers. The same ghost weapons found in Johnny's home. Her heart pounded in her chest. The driver handed one rifle to another member, and they ran to each side of the entrance. The other three took cover behind steel beams and wooden crates.

"This is your final warning," the officer said. "Come out with your hands in the air."

The two club members leaned past the entrance and fired

their rifles at the squad cars. Riley rose from her crate to help but was surprised by another, who fired at her from behind a steel beam. Bullets whizzed past her head as she returned to cover.

"I can't get a clean shot," she said.

Kurt leaned over the side of his crate and fired toward the steel beam. The man there retreated for cover, then returned fire. Kurt ducked out of the way. Riley looked through the bullet hole in her crate again. Dom shut the back doors to the van and climbed into the driver's seat.

"He's trying to get away!" she said.

Riley rose from cover and took aim, but the same man fired at her again. She crouched out of view. Kurt leaned to the side of his crate and shot him twice in the chest. He fell back to the ground.

"He's down!" Kurt said.

Riley rose from cover and fired at the van's rear left tire. It deflated with a hiss. Dom put the van in reverse and sped toward her. She shot at the back doors before diving out of the way. The van smashed through the stack of crates and collided into a steel beam. Dom jumped out, then ran into the stairwell. Riley rose from the floor, palms stinging with cuts. One rifleman took notice of the crash and turned from the entrance to face her. She reached for her gun, but it had skidded across the ground several feet away. The rifleman grinned and took aim. She was exposed, with no cover to hide behind.

A bullet struck the rifleman in the back of the head, and he collapsed to the ground. A second bullet hit the final club member in the chest. He fell backward.

Riley grabbed her gun off the floor and ran into the stairwell. She ascended the steps to the second floor while keeping her gun aimed ahead of her. The door on the second-floor landing was sealed shut. The farther she climbed, the darker the stairwell became. She slowed her movements to avoid tripping on the steps. Concrete and steel debris blocked the entrance to the third floor.

As she stepped over the rubble, she heard a door open overhead. Riley leaned over the center of the stairwell and looked up. The door two flights up was closing. She rushed up the stairs to the roof and kicked it back open, scanning her surroundings for signs of movement. Dom was standing on the edge of the roof, looking toward the horizon, where the bright Chicago skyline clashed against the surrounding darkness.

"Put your hands up!" she said.

Dom ignored her request and cupped his hand to light a cigarette.

"I said put your hands up!"

He took a drag. "Johnny turned, didn't he? That's how you found us."

"Yes."

He took another drag. "I never had a son. When I found Johnny, he was some punk kid living on the streets. His parents were addicts, too high to realize he ran away. I took him in. Raised him as my own. He was the closest thing I've ever had to family."

"Why are you telling me this?"

"Because men like me aren't meant to live in a cage," Dom said. He raised his hands in the air and turned around to face her. "Please, find who killed him."

Dom leaned back and fell over the ledge, plummeting to his death.

TWENTY-TWO

Numerous police units, forensic teams, EMTs, and coroners had descended upon the Goodman Equipment Plant, moving in and out of the building like a colony of ants. The smell of spent brass casings and gunfire lingered in the air.

Riley checked the time on her phone's screen. It was the middle of the night, but from the dozens of portable forensic lights, she could have sworn it was daytime. After giving her statement and taking her photo, one of the EMTs handed her a towel to wipe the blood from her hands, face, and hair. She craved a cigarette in the worst way. She wanted it even more than a shower.

Commander Briggs broke from the crowd of officers and joined her against the hood of the police cruiser. "How are you holding up?"

"I'm fine," she said.

"And Kurt?"

"He's still getting stitched up. I think they have to reset his nose."

"Tough break."

"Could have been worse—much worse."

"Why didn't you call it in before you came here?"

"After the raid on the farm, I couldn't risk another leak."

"You still think Kane has someone on the payroll?"

"I do. There were only a handful of us that knew about the raid. Someone from the department tipped off the club."

"I'd keep that to yourself. We can't be throwing around accusations without evidence. If that changes, let me know and we can have IA look into it."

"Where's Reyes? I'm surprised she's not here staking her claim."

"She's at her office, coordinating with the proper channels. A bust this big, no doubt she's already drafting a statement for the press."

"Never let a narrative go to waste. I'm sure this will do wonders for her career. She'll probably take credit for the whole thing."

"Hey, you did some real good here. People won't forget that."

"I don't care who gets the commendations, that's their game. I just want to make sure they don't interfere with the case."

"The DA's office has already been notified. Locke is going to meet with Kane first thing in the morning. Don't worry, he's going down for this. All of them are."

His words were comforting. For the first time since taking on the case, Riley felt she could breathe. "Let's hope."

"You kidding? A bust this big can't be ignored. Not only did you save your career, you might have just gotten yourself back into Reyes's good graces. She might even give you a second chance on the Violent Crimes Task Force if you still want it."

"More than anything."

Across the lot near the entrance of the building, Sergeant Berns walked out of the plant and waved for them to enter.

"Looks like they're ready for us," Briggs said. "If you don't want to go back in there, I'd understand."

"No, I'm okay. Really."

"Alright then. Just let me know if you need a minute."

They walked through the crowd of officers and ducked beneath the police tape surrounding the Goodman Equipment Plant. Six black cadaver bags rested near the foot of the entrance, each sealed with a zipper. She walked past the bags and entered through the doors. The forensic team had placed hundreds of plastic evidence markers on the ground, signifying bullet casings, drug residue, and human carnage.

"Nice to see you again, Detective," said the sergeant. "Although I wish it were under different circumstances."

"Don't worry about it. What do you have for us?"

They followed Berns to the bullet-riddled van, which was still crumpled around the steel beam. The forensic team had removed the drug bricks from the vehicle and stacked them into neat, even piles on a clear plastic tarp next to a food scale.

"Each of the bricks weighs in at a little over two pounds. Street value for something like that clears a quarter of a million easy."

"How many bricks?"

"Four hundred. That means all together, this is worth—"

"One hundred million dollars," Briggs said in awe. "What about the van?"

"According to the VIN, the van belongs to a Dominic Doré."

"Dom," Riley said. "He was their leader. What about the crates? Did you get any shipping IDs for where they came from?"

"Unfortunately, no. All the crates are unmarked. There's no way to tell where they came from or where they were headed."

"This was their last destination. The club has been smuggling drugs through a train yard and taken here to be broken down for distribution. Before this place, they were using the farm."

"What about the guns? Can you tell me anything about them?" she asked.

"They're the same rifles we collected from the previous house. No serial numbers, eighty percent lowers, completely untraceable. These guys were smart. You don't see this level of discretion among street gangs often." The sergeant rested his hand on her shoulder. "They took every precaution to remain invisible. Hell, if it weren't for you, Detective, we'd probably still be in the dark."

He was trying to lift her spirits, but the praise came off as flirtatious. She was used to being hit on by her male colleagues. Even in the grimmest of circumstances, it was never beneath them to make a pass. She removed his hand. "Thank you, Sergeant. What can you tell me about the barrels?"

Berns's cheeks flushed red. "I—uh, sure. The barrels are filled with hydrochloric acid. They could liquify a full-grown human body in a matter of days. You'd be nothing more than brown, gooey sludge. Judging from the gas mask and the plastic barrels, they knew what they were doing. Hydrochloric acid is extremely corrosive against most metals, and if the fumes get into your lungs, it can be fatal."

"So they've done this before?" she asked.

"Most likely. I recommend getting an excavation team out here to search the grounds for more barrels."

"We'll look into that," Briggs said.

"There's one more thing I need to show you," said Berns. "Follow me."

Riley and Briggs walked around the tarp to an evidence table covered with items collected from the scene. There were dozens of plastic bags filled with wallets, knives, lighters, cigarettes, gun magazines, brass knuckles, drug paraphernalia, necklaces, and more. Berns pointed to a row of six identical yellow-and-black plastic flip-phones. Some were speckled with blood.

"We snagged these from each of the bodies, including that

one you arrested. It looks like they were using these to communicate with one another."

"They're burner phones." Riley said. "Did you look through the contacts?"

"We did. No names, just the same ten phone numbers listed on each. Six of them are lying here now."

"So, four are missing?" Briggs asked.

"That's right."

"No, only one is missing," Riley objected. "Six phones are here, plus Johnny, Zeke, and Sam. That's nine."

"Sam didn't have a cell phone when we arrested him," Briggs contended. "Neither did the other two victims."

"Johnny and Zeke's phones could have been taken after they were killed. Sam could have given his to the club before he went to Johnny's house."

"It could be Kane," Briggs speculated.

"I doubt it. Kane is too careful to leave a trace like that."

"Then who?"

Riley looked at Briggs, keeping her informant theory to herself. "I'm going to find out."

She turned away and walked passed the line of dead bodies and out of the building. Waving through the crowd of officers to one of the SUVs, she opened the rear door. The guard with the patches sewn into his jacket was sitting in the back seat with his hands cuffed behind his back and his forehead against the rear divider.

"What do you want?" he asked.

"Dom is dead. Your crew is finished, and you're looking at forty-five to life as an accessory to murder. Are we going to talk?"

"Depends. What's in it for me?"

"Can't say for sure, but it couldn't hurt your chances with the judge if you help us."

The guard nodded his head and grunted. "Uh-huh."

"Is that a yes?"

"Yeah, I'll talk."

Riley unclipped her badge from her belt and pulled a laminated, business-card-sized copy of the Miranda warning from the back sleeve. She read him his rights, and he agreed to be interviewed.

"What's your name?" she asked.

"Phil."

"Phil what?"

"Phillip Edward."

"Okay Phil, how long have you been with the club?"

"I don't know, eight years maybe? Something like that."

"Someone warned your club that we were coming to raid the farm. Tell me who it is."

"I don't know what you're talking about."

"Well, you better start remembering, because I'm about to walk."

He started shaking his head and grunting. "I'm trying."

"Okay, we're done here," she said, and slammed the door. Phil started yelling. His muffled screams sounded like "Stop! Stop!" She opened the door again.

"It's a cop! It's a cop. I remember Dom telling us that his friend in blue came through with the tip and to pack everything on the farm."

"That's good, Phil. Did he say a name?"

"No. He never mentioned anything other than that."

"What's the last thing you heard about Johnny?"

"That he never showed up for his post. We all took turns guarding the farm, day and night. Johnny was never late. We thought he might've been pinched, so we called Zeke. Johnny was always with him. They were tight since they were cellmates from back in the day. When Zeke didn't answer his calls either, we knew something was up. That's when Dom sent Sam to Johnny's house. And I guess you know the rest."

"So Johnny never showed up, and Sam was sent to his house the next day, is that right?"

Phil thought for a moment, then nodded. "That's right."

When Riley had uncovered Johnny's body, he'd been dead for forty-eight hours, which meant whoever tortured and killed him had had a full day to do it.

"How long have you been working with Kane?"

Phil nodded his head. "I don't know. Like I said, Dom never spoke about things like that."

"How long have you been bringing drugs into the city?"

"Since I joined. They were already bringing it in from the farm. I don't know where it comes from. I just help move it from one place to another. That's all I know, I swear."

Riley grabbed the car door. "Okay, that's all I have for now. Sit tight."

"Wait, are you going to help me out?"

She slammed the door in his face. Phil's muffled cursing could be heard through the door as she walked to the end of the cluster of vehicles, where a white ambulance was sandwiched between two coroners vans. She approached the back doors of the ambulance to check on Kurt. The doors were open, and she peered within.

An EMT was adding the finishing stitches to Kurt's shoulder. His head was propped up by a couple pillows on the gurney. He had a butterfly band-aid above his swollen eye and across the bridge of his nose.

"Hey, is he going to be okay?"

The EMT looked back at her. "We gave him a pain reliever and an anti-inflammatory for the swelling. He'll be fine in a couple of days. He was lucky. The bullet just grazed his shoulder."

"What about the nose?"

"He has a nasal fracture. We're going to take him to the hospital to run some neurological examinations."

She climbed up onto the rear platform and entered the back of the ambulance. Kurt's unbuttoned shirt was hanging off of his left shoulder. His body was covered in tattoos, including two black SS bolts on his neck, a Nazi war eagle gripping a swastika across his chest, and a confederate flag pole crossed with a scythe on his ribs. She averted her gaze and stepped back out of the ambulance. Kurt leaned up from the gurney, reaching his arm out to her. "Wait!"

The EMT placed a hand on his shoulder. "Sir, you need to lie back and rest."

Kurt pushed the EMT's hand away. "It's not what you think."

Riley crossed her arms and walked across the lot toward her Mustang. She heard Kurt call out to her several times, but she didn't care. She wanted to be as far away from this place as possible.

Kurt grabbed her arm from behind. "Stop. Let me explain."

"Let you explain? We almost died tonight, and I don't even know who you are! You've been lying to me this whole time. How can I trust another word that comes out of your mouth?"

"Because you'll hate what I have to say."

Riley crossed her arms and waited.

He took his time to search for the words. "I was undercover for two years on vice, and somewhere along the way . . . I lost myself. I've done horrible things. Things that will haunt me for the rest of my life. I try to forget, but whenever I rest my head on a pillow or look out a window or have any moment of peace, they come back. Those twisted memories haunt me. Most days, I can't even look at myself in the mirror."

Tears welled up in his eyes, and he collected himself. "I know I don't deserve mercy. But I'm trying. I'm trying really hard, to find my way back."

Riley rested her hand on his shoulder. "I believe you. Go, get some rest. I'll take it from here."

Kurt wiped the tears from his cheek and walked back to the ambulance. Briggs approached her.

"Did you know?" she asked.

"Yes. I got in contact with his commanding officer when the transfer paperwork came in. I don't care who you are. If you spend enough time surrounded by hate, it rubs off. And if we can't forgive, then we're no better than them." He shook his head. "Did you get anything from our suspect?"

"He confirmed that we have a leak in the department."

"Did he give a name?"

"No, but he said Dom received a tip the night of the raid. He said it was from a cop."

Briggs looked at her. "Are you sure?"

"I don't see why he would lie."

"Maybe he's just trying to save his skin. Guys like that would say anything for a lesser sentence."

"Maybe, but it doesn't mean he's wrong. Someone told the club we were coming. The club has been in operation for at least ten years. How many vans like this have we missed? How many lives have been lost?"

Briggs's cell phone rang.

"You can't think like that," he said. "It won't do you any good. We got them now. That's all that matters. Excuse me, I need to take this." He answered his phone and walked back toward the crowd of officers. That reminded her to make a call of her own. She pulled out her phone and dialed.

"Hello?" Holly answered in a groggy slump. The call must have awoken her from sleep.

"It's over," Riley said. "The club is finished."

"Were they at the plant?"

"Yes, along with the fentanyl. We got it all."

"What about Kane?"

"He's still in custody. The DA should bring charges tomorrow morning. I just thought you should know Johnny's death wasn't in vain."

"Thanks, that means a lot. Did any of them confess to his murder?"

She hesitated, not knowing how to respond. "Not yet. We still need to bring them in for questioning."

"Would you let me know if that changes?"

"I will," Riley said, then pocketed her phone.

The EMT shut the back doors to the ambulance, then drove out of the lot. Riley slid her hands into her jacket and started walking back to the plant. The department had one chance to bring a case against Kane. As the lead detective on the case, she was going to make sure they did it right.

TWENTY-THREE

District Attorney John Locke held up his phone's screen so Kane could see the top article on the *Chicago Wire* website: "KANE CORRUPTION EXPOSED."

"You know, I always like to say there's no such thing as bad press, but this is pretty damning." He placed both hands on the table and looked at Kane and his two lawyers in the seats across from him. "You're facing a class X felony, Mr. Kane. You know what that means? In your case, thirty to sixty years in the state pen. We both know there's enough evidence to put you away for good. Hell, I could probably convince the jury to indict before lunch. Set a new world record for quickest kick in the ass. Personally, I'd love nothing more, but the powers that be want to save themselves a lot of embarrassment with a public trial during an election year. Sign the confession, and we'll settle for the minimum sentence, thirty years plus a million-dollar fine. Don't sign, and we'll recommend the full sixty without parole—that's life."

Both of Kane's lawyers drew close to him and whispered in his ears. Kane leaned back in his chair without taking his eyes off of Locke. His stone-faced glare matched his unshakeable posture.

Riley crossed her arms within the darkness of the observation room. Locke had presented a case that would cause even the most hardened criminal to squirm in their seat, but Kane's demeanor through the two-way mirror appeared unfazed.

"Something's not right. Is that the look of a man whose facing life in prison?"

"I don't care what he looks like," Reyes said, raising her chin. "There's a mountain of evidence against him. Kane would be a fool not to take the deal. Even if he fights this to his last cent, there's no outcome where he doesn't end up behind bars."

Riley leaned closer to the mirror. "We'll see."

One of Kane's lawyers stopped whispering and looked across the table. "My client respectfully declines your offer."

"What are you, nuts?" Locke asked. "Take the deal."

"Instead, we propose a trade of information for full exoneration of all crimes alleged against my client."

"Thank you for your time. I'll see you in court," Locke said, and walked to the door.

"I promise this would be of great value to the city's justice department and its presiding elected officials," the lawyer said.

Locke stopped in his tracks, then returned to the table. He sat in the chair across from them. "Okay, let's say I play ball. What could you possibly have to offer?"

"The heads of all five major gangs in Chicago," Kane said.

Locke clasped his hands together and raised his fists to his mouth. "You're going to need to be more specific."

Kane sat up in his chair and tugged on the lapels of his blazer. "You may think of me as a gangster, but I'm just a businessman. I make deals with everyone. The cost of blood is worth its weight in gold. Why fight when you can be rich? Right now, there is a tenuous truce between the Big Five, and as long as they keep the peace, they can remain part of the arrangement." Kane leaned in. "You see, there are those that run the streets, and there are those that run ... everything."

"I understand," Locke said, and stood up from his chair. "Sit tight. I'll have to confer with my partners." He walked across the interview room and pounded on the door with his fist. The guard in the hallway let him out of the room.

Kane looked at the two-way mirror and smiled at Riley as if he could see through the glass. It was right in front of her this whole time. No single drug dealer could push the amount of product recovered from the Goodman Equipment Plant. To do that would require an army.

"If Kane is the sole supplier of fentanyl to all five major gangs, that would make him the most powerful man in Chicago."

"And our best hope of turning the tide against organized crime," Reyes said.

"You're not seriously considering his offer?"

"This is bigger than anything we could have imagined. Do you know what this could do for us? For the city?"

"He's a criminal. He belongs in a cell."

"Look at the big picture. We've never had an opportunity like this before. It could change everything."

Riley's cell phone rang.

"People are dead because of him. I could have died."

"And think of how many more we could save. These gangs are a cancer that have been growing for years. This could be our one shot at removing them from the streets."

Riley turned away and answered her phone. "Detective Walker."

"Hello, Detective." The man cleared his throat. "This is Sergeant Berns, FSD. The excavation team ran a GPR probe in the lot surrounding the Goodman Plant. We found more barrels."

"How many?"

"Fourteen and counting. We're still digging them out of the ground, but I alerted the DNA Processing Unit to come over and take samples. I thought you should know."

"I'll be over as soon as I can," she said, and hung up the phone. "FSD found more bodies at the plant."

Locke entered the observation room with his cell phone in hand. "I just spoke with the mayor. We're taking the deal. He wants us to go public with the bust as soon as possible. When can your media relations group put a press conference together?"

"We can schedule one for tonight. I already have a statement prepped for the Bureau Chief. What about Kane? The press have been eager to hear from us since we brought him into custody."

"Just keep the focus on the gang and the drugs for now, and emphasize the amount we collected. It'll make a great headline."

"You're making a mistake," Riley said.

"Detective Walker," Reyes said, "need I remind you this isn't your decision to make?"

"It's okay," Locke said. "I understand you're frustrated, but this isn't the time to get emotional."

She walked up to Locke and looked him in the eye. "Is this justice?"

"No," Locke said. "This is how we win."

He walked out of the room and left her staring at the door with a quiver in her stomach and a cold sweat across her neck.

"This is for the best," Reyes said. "You'll see."

Locke entered the interview room and sat at the table across from Kane. He clasped his hands together and laid them on the table. "We accept your offer. If you can deliver the heads of each of the five gangs, we will let you walk. No charges."

"That's wonderful news," Kane's lawyer said. "Of course, we would need this agreement in writing."

"We'll have it ready by tomorrow. Until then, Kane will remain in police custody."

Riley turned away and walked toward the door. She grabbed the handle.

"Detective," Reyes called out.

Riley stopped.

"I hope you can see the value of what something like this can do for your career, and how foolish it would be to throw it away."

She turned. "What are you saying?"

Reyes walked toward her. "You think you're the only one here that's trying to do good? You're dead wrong. It's people like me that hold the line. That have to make the tough calls to maintain law and order. Deep down, you know you need people like me, otherwise there would be nothing but chaos. I'm offering you a second chance to return to the Violent Crimes Task Force, but I'll be damned if I'm going to stand here and let you sabotage this department again. If you talk to the press or try to sink this deal, not only will I rescind my offer, it'll be the last thing you do in the department. Do I make myself clear?"

"Yes," Riley said.

"Good. You're dismissed."

Riley turned away and left the observation room. The whole situation left a foul taste in her mouth. She continued down the hall and walked to her desk in the bullpen. She grabbed her black bomber jacket off the back of her chair. Her other jacket was drenched with blood from the previous night and had been taken into evidence by the department.

"Walker," Briggs called out. He was standing in front of his office door with a novelty coffee mug that read "I see guilty people."

"Where are you headed?" he asked.

She slid her arms into the jacket's sleeves and walked through the bullpen toward him. "FSD found something at the plant. I'm heading back to check it out."

He lowered his voice. "And what happened with Kane?"

"He made a deal with the DA. Reyes will give you the details."

"You don't seem too pleased about it."

"If we start compromising with criminals like Kane, when will we stop?"

"We have to work with the world as it is, not as we'd like it to be."

"Maybe, but at what cost?"

Briggs clenched his jaw, then took a sip of coffee. She turned and walked to the rear doorway. An icy wind blew around her as she pushed through the door and entered the parking lot. She zipped up her jacket and buried her hands in her pockets.

Something hard rubbed up against her knuckles.

Riley pulled an e-cigarette from her pocket and rubbed the lint from the end. She took a couple puffs to see if it worked. The vapor dissipated in the frosty morning air. She entered her cruiser and drove out of the parking lot.

TWENTY-FOUR

A parade of news vans from every major network lined the sidewalk outside the Goodman Equipment Plant. Reporters stood against the warped fence so their cameramen could show the decrepit building and the horde of police vehicles in the background. Riley drove around the lot to the entrance, which was sectioned off by two young boots standing in front of a patrol unit. She pulled up to them and parked. One officer approached her vehicle and asked her to roll down her window.

"I'm sorry, no one is allowed beyond this point."

Riley offered her credentials and badge number to the officer, then was allowed to proceed into the plant.

"Just park your vehicle in line with the others," the young boot said. He waved his arm, signaling for the patrol unit to move out of the way. "And try not to step on any of the red flags."

She glided into the lot to find that all the police vehicles had been rearranged against the street to prevent the news reporters from peering within. She parked her cruiser as instructed and took a drag of her e-cigarette. Her forearms ached. She rolled up her sleeve and rubbed her thumb over a bandage. It was sensitive to the touch. Exiting her vehicle, she opened the trunk and collected a pair of plastic gloves from her examination kit.

Riley walked across the lot. Dozens of wire flag markers had been placed in front of the building's entrance. She stayed clear of the area, taking the long way around the perimeter toward the three portable canopy tents on the opposite side of the lot. A group of men in coveralls shoveled dirt from a knee-high trench beneath the tents, exposing the lids to seven blue plastic drum barrels. Sergeant Berns was at the end of the tent, overseeing the excavation.

"Sergeant," she said.

"Can you believe this? It's like a graveyard out here."

"How many have you found?"

"The probe detected forty-eight anomalies in the soil. We've marked the spots with flags. Part of the team is surveying the rest of the building, but we're still waiting on the DNA processing unit to arrive."

"When did the press get here?"

"About half an hour ago. Someone must have reported the shooting from last night."

"How much do you think they know?"

"Other than what was released in this morning's paper? Not much. But it doesn't take a rocket scientist to connect the dots. The drugs and bodies were removed before they arrived, so all they got to work with is hearsay and speculation."

"Good, then let's keep a tight lid on things until the department gives a statement to the press."

A white van pulled into the lot and parked next to her cruiser. A team of two analysts opened the doors and stepped out of the vehicle, each holding a duffel bag.

"Looks like the DPU is here," Berns said.

"How long will it take your team to dig up the rest of these spots?" she asked.

"Hard to say for sure. We might be able to uncover them by tomorrow if we work in double shifts. The problem is we can't use heavy machinery. The probe can tell us if there's something underground, but not how deep. We don't want to destroy any of the evidence."

The DNA Processing Unit walked around the field of red flags and set their duffel bags near the edge of the tent.

"Sergeant Berns?" the analyst asked, extending his hand. "I'm Dr. Rolland, and this is my assistant, Dr. Chu."

Berns shook his hand. "Nice to meet you. This is Detective Riley Walker. She's running point on this investigation."

"Well, what do you have for us?"

Berns led the two analysts to the trench and pointed out the eight drum barrels. "Until last night, this place was under gang occupation. We believe each of these barrels may hold at least one victim in some state of decay."

"Why do you say that?" Dr. Chu asked.

"Because I was supposed to be one of them," Riley said. "The barrels should be filled with hydrochloric acid. Do you think you'll be able to gather DNA from the contents?"

Dr. Rolland kneeled down and unzipped his duffel bag. He retrieved a pair of thick purple gloves. "It depends on a few factors. The concentration, what other chemicals are being used, and how long the bodies have been stewing. HCl is very corrosive, and its pH level can cause DNA denaturation."

"Meaning?" Riley asked.

"Irreparable damage."

Dr. Rolland pulled a plastic box out of the duffel and handed it to Dr. Chu. "I'll need to take samples as soon as possible. Sergeant, tell your men to stand back."

Berns turned to the excavation team. "All right guys, take ten. Clear the area."

Each of the men dropped their shovels and climbed out of the trench. Rolland put on a pair of protective goggles and a face mask, then stepped down into the trench. He kneeled beside the closest drum barrel and loosened the surrounding clasp. Looking up to Dr. Chu, he said, "Get the vials ready."

She opened the kit and removed the first plastic vial from the rack. Rolland twisted the lid until it popped off the barrel, then set it aside. Riley cupped her hand over her nose and mouth and leaned over the edge for a better look. The dark liquid contents within looked like oil. Rolland sealed the lid back into place, then stepped over to the next barrel. He loosened the clasp and removed the lid.

The contents appeared identical to the previous container. He continued this process six more times, then climbed out the other side of the trench. He removed his mask and gloves. "These bodies have completely disintegrated, along with any traces of DNA we could have collected. I'm sorry, there's nothing more we could do."

Riley turned away and looked at the field of red flags scattered across the lot—the mass grave of forty-eight unknown souls that would be lost until the end of time. "So am I."

Riley stepped off the elevator on the third floor of John H. Stroger, Jr. Hospital. The hallway was quiet, with a stuffy smell of worn sheets and plastic dinner trays. She walked down the hall, peering into each room through the open doorways until she found Kurt. He was lying in bed with a white butterfly bandage across his nose and above his left eyelid. He had two black eyes, but the swelling in his face was gone.

She knocked twice against the doorframe. "Hey, how are you holding up?"

Kurt turned his head over the pillow to look at her. "I feel like I picked a fight with a brick wall, and the wall won. Other than that, I'm still in one piece. The doctor said I can be released tonight, once my test results come back."

"That's good." She walked over to his bed and placed a brown paper bag on his lap and sat in the plastic bedside chair. "I picked you up some fast food. I didn't know if you preferred a burger or chicken strips, so I got both."

He sat up in the bed. "Ah, thank you. You didn't have to do that."

"Yes, I did. Hospital food is the worst."

Kurt reached into the bag and grabbed a burger. He unwrapped the wax paper covering and took a large bite. "What's the word at the department?"

"There's going to be a press conference tonight about the drug bust. The Black Snakes are finished, and so is their operation. FSD found more barrels buried in the lot surrounding the building, but the bodies within are too far gone."

"How many?"

"Looks like forty-eight."

Kurt dropped his chin. "What about Kane?"

"I wanted you to hear it from me first," Riley said. "Kane has made a deal with the DA."

"What deal? What are you talking about?"

"Kane is the sole supplier of fentanyl to the top five largest gangs in the city. He made a deal with the DA to help us bring them down."

"In exchange for what?"

"Kane walks."

"That's bullshit!"

"I know, but it's not our call to make. The DA is going to draft the contract tonight."

"So, that's it then? The case is over?"

"Yes, it is. Reyes also said that because of the bust, I'll be returning to the Violent Crimes Task Force."

"I see. Well, congratulations. You've earned it."

"Thank you," Riley said, and rose from the chair. "I should get back to the station. There's some final paperwork I need to complete before the press conference."

"Oh yeah, sure. I guess, I'll—uh. I'll see you around?"

"Yeah, I'll be around," she said, then walked out of the room.

"Hey," Kurt called out.

Riley came back to the doorway. "Yeah?"

"I never thanked you for saving my life. So, thank you."

She nodded, then left the room.

TWENTY-FIVE

The press room was packed from wall-to-wall with reporters sitting in their chairs with laptops, voice recorders, and notepads in hand. Riley stood against the side of the room with her arms crossed, watching the camera crews adjust their volume levels and check their network feeds. She glanced at the time on her phone. The conference was slated to begin in two minutes, and everyone was eager for Bureau Chief Avery Benedict to address the gang bust at the Goodman Equipment Plant. She gazed across the room and saw Detective Hank Maloney looking back at her.

"Looks like a full house," a voice said from behind. She turned around to find Roy Dunn leaning against the wall next to her. "It's not every day that something this big goes down."

She looked back at Hank, and he walked out of the room. "I'm just happy it's over."

"That right?", he asked. "Cause I know we could definitely use you over at GID. I can put in a word for you with the commander."

"Thanks, but it looks like Reyes is allowing me back onto the Violent Crimes Task Force."

"No kidding? Well, you've earned it. Taking down a giant like

Kane with receipts to back it up. You've probably got the biggest balls in the room."

"If only it were that simple."

"What do you mean?"

A sudden hush came over the press room. Cameras flashed in a strobe against the front wall as Bureau Chief Avery Benedict entered through a side door carrying a large three-ringed binder under his arm. He was followed by District Attorney John Locke and Deputy Chief Rachel Reyes. Without looking at the press pool, Avery climbed the platform steps and rested the binder over the wooden podium which showcased the city of Chicago's police seal. Avery's broad shoulders towered over the podium as he opened his binder and reviewed his notes. Like an orchestral conductor, he readied himself before looking out to the crowd with a steel gaze. He grasped each side of the podium, then leaned forward to speak into the microphone.

"Good evening. My name is Avery Benedict. I'm the Chief for the Bureau of Detectives within the Chicago Police Department. Before I begin, I would like to introduce some distinguished guests that are up here with me. To my left is District Attorney John Locke, and to my right is Deputy Chief Rachel Reyes. Both of whom were essential during this investigation."

Rachel raised her chin and gazed out to the crowd.

"While investigating the death of a local drug dealer, detectives identified members of a major drug trafficking organization. This organization is responsible for the illicit importation, packaging and distribution of drugs in Cook County. Utilizing various investigative techniques to gather evidence and by working closely with the District Attorney's office, the Chicago Police Department put an end to this operation. Last night, a search and seizure warrant was executed on the abandoned Goodman Equipment Plant." Avery turned the page, then continued. "The building was a base of operations for the organization's illegal activity. As a result of this search warrant, detectives located and seized: Four-hundred pounds of fentanyl opioids, six illegal firearms, approximately twelve hundred rounds of ammunition, and other illegal weapons such as knives and brass knuckles." Avery turned the page again, then continued. "We also confiscated paraphernalia that is commonly associated with drug distribution including: three measuring scales, plastic bags, and unused gelatin capsules. At the time of the search warrant's execution, six of the organization's men engaged in hostile gunfire towards our law enforcement officers. Because of this, five of the organization's men are dead and one remains in police custody. The suspect's name is Phillip Edward. He is being indicted with conspiracy of possession with intent to distribute fentanyl, and attempt of murder against law enforcement. I'm proud to say none of our officers were killed during the exchange. I would now like to welcome District Attorney John Locke to the podium."

"Well, that was quiet a story," Roy said.

"If only it were true." Reyes had done an outstanding job twisting the events to show the department in the best light possible.

Avery turned around and shook Locke's hand before stepping to the side. Locke embraced the podium and smiled at the crowd, "Today marks a turning point for our city. A critical step in our fight against illegal drugs and organized crime. For too long, the opioid epidemic has been a plague on our nation. I've sought to it that my office has done everything in its power to rid illegal drugs from our streets while charging those responsible. It hasn't been easy, but anything worth doing rarely is. Because of the collaboration between the Chicago Police Department and the District Attorney's office, I'm pleased to announce that we've seized the largest sum of fentanyl in our city's history."

Avery and Reyes began clapping behind him. Members of the press joined in, causing the entire room to erupt in applause.

Locke smiled and nodded, basking in the praise. "Let it be known that by working together we can accomplish great things in our city and our local communities. In conclusion, I would just like to once again thank Bureau Chief Avery Benedict, Deputy Chief Rachel Reyes, and the brave officers of the Chicago Police Department. Thank you very much."

Locke gave a last nod to the crowd, then stepped to the side. Deputy Chief Rachel Reyes walked up to the podium and pulled the microphone down to her mouth, "I will now take your questions."

A man from the front row raised his hand, "There have been reports of more bodies being uncovered at the Goodman Equipment Plant. Can you confirm if this is true?"

"We are still surveying the area, but no bodies have been recovered at this time."

Another man at the end of the third row asked, "Where does the fentanyl come from? Is it made in the U.S. or does it come from another country?"

"Fentanyl is clandestinely produced, but according to our DEA sources, it's primarily coming from overseas and smuggled into the United States through Mexico."

"What was the name of the organization?", a journalist asked.

"They called themselves the Black Snake Motorcycle Club, or B.S.M.C. for short."

"Robert Kane has been detained for two days. Have you brought charges against him?", a woman from the back of the room asked.

"We rather not comment on the investigation at this time since it is ongoing and has yet to be prosecuted. Anyone else?"

"Why is Kane still in custody?", the woman asked.

"I'm sorry, who is that?"

The woman stood up from the crowd of press reporters, "My name is Holly Hart. I'm with the Chicago Wire. You may have read my article this morning about Kane's involvement with the Black Snakes. I'm surprised that the Chief, nor the District Attorney, mentioned him in their statements."

"Like I said before, I will not comment on an ongoing investigation. Are there any more questions?"

The crowd remained silent.

"Thank you everyone for coming."

Chief Avery Benedict, Locke, and Reyes walked off the stage and out the side door in a single file line. Members of the press pool gathered their things and rose from their seats.

"We should celebrate. This is a big win for you," Roy said.

"Not tonight, the case isn't closed yet and I still have things to take care of."

"Oh, come on. At least let me buy you a drink."

"Thanks for the offer, but not tonight."

"All right. Some other time, then. When you're feeling up for it, call me."

"Will do," she said, and walked out of the press room. A flood of reporters congregated in the main lobby. Riley navigated her way through the crowd towards the back offices. Before she could open the door, someone grabbed her arm from behind.

"What the hell is happening?", Holly asked. "I thought Kane was supposed to be locked away for good."

Riley looked around the room for prying eyes, "Not here." She opened the door and guided Holly inside. She looked down the hallway to make sure it was empty, then shut the door behind them. "Are we off the record?"

"Off the record? Are you serious?"

"I'm not supposed to talk about this. Tell me we're off the record or else we're done."

"Fine, whatever you're off the record. Now tell me what's going on."

"Kane made a deal with the DA. He's going to flip on his partners."

"He what? What partners?"

"Kane is the sole supplier of fentanyl to the top five major gangs in the city. He's going to give up their leadership for his freedom."

"He's going to walk? You can't be serious."

Riley looked down the hall again to make sure it was clear, "I don't like it either, but the choice isn't up to me."

"Why won't you let me run with this story? It hasn't stopped you before? We both know Kane belongs behind bars."

"I won't. I'm sorry."

"Then I guess there's nothing left to discuss," Holly grabbed the door handle. "You know, I was really beginning to think that you were different from the rest of them, but I guess I was wrong."

Holly walked through the door without looking back. Riley leaned against the wall. Her limbs felt heavy, as if all of her energy had been drained. She should be happy that the Black Snakes were finished and all those drugs would be off the streets, but in her core she knew something wasn't right.

She rose from the wall and turned into the side corridor before the bullpen. A windowless brick hallway with a single reinforced door at the end. She stopped at the door and looked up at the security camera. She listened for the buzzer, then opened the door and entered the observation room for the holding cells. Reggie Smith and Tucker Watts were sitting behind the security console.

"Working late detective?", Reggie asked.

"Something like that. I need to talk to Kane."

Tucker rose from the security console and rested a plastic container over the countertop, "You know the drill. I need your gun and any other weapons you may have on you."

She removed her Glock from her holster and placed it in the

bin. Tucker's cologne smelled like a car freshener. "I can smell you from the hallway. You got a date tonight?"

"No, just a new brand I'm trying out. You like it?"

"It's strong," she said, kneeling down to her boot, but then realized her folding knife had been deposited into evidence from the night before. She rose to her feet, "That's it."

"While you're in there, stay to the left of the yellow line. Do not exchange any items with the suspect. If the suspect tries to give you something, do not accept it and report back to us. Under no circumstances are you allowed to approach the bars. Everything you say and do will be recorded on our security monitors. Do you understand?"

"I do."

"Buzz her in," Tucker said.

Reggie leaned forward and pressed a button on the console to unlock the observation room door. Riley gripped the handle and entered the cellblock. A confined tunnel with a row of six cells on the right side of the room. The concrete floor was divided in half by a yellow painted line with the words, "Do not cross" stenciled in black. In the third cell, Kane was laying in a cot which was bolted to the wall.

"Even if you make a deal with the DA, people will learn about what you've done. What you planned to do. You won't get away with this."

"Does the DA know you're here? I don't think he would appreciate this unannounced visit."

"If the people don't come after you, the gangs will. Even in witness protection, you'll be looking over your shoulder for the rest of your life."

"It must be difficult to accept that I alone can do more to stop organized crime in this city than you and your department ever could. When this is finished, I'll be a hero. As for gang retaliation, let's just say they're more afraid of what I'll do to them than anything else. Tell me, Detective, why are you here?"

Riley stepped forward onto the yellow line, "I came to tell you to your face that no matter how long it takes, I'm going to bring you down."

"Still seeking justice then?", Kane said, then rose from the cot. "You know, this cell reminds me of my childhood bedroom. Not because of the bars, but the size of it. I grew up on a modest farm. My family would spend days tending the cornfields until our hands blistered and our backs ached. One day, a group of men from the city arrived on our doorstep demanding that we pay a protection tax. My father gave them what little he could spare so they would leave us alone, but the next month they returned demanding more money. This time we didn't have enough to give, so they broke my father's leg, then fled. We went to the police for help, but they told us there was nothing they could do. The next month, the men returned, demanding even more money. My father surrendered what little savings he had left and pleaded with the men to leave us alone. They shot him in the head and burned all of our crops to the ground. It was only then that I understood the truth." Kane gripped the cell bars, "There is no justice in this world. Only those with power and the weak."

Riley crossed the yellow line, "We'll see about that."

She then walked out of the cell block.

TWENTY-SIX

An ear-piercing bang jolted Riley from sleep. She sat up in bed and heard two more bangs outside her bedroom window. Her mother burst into the room, clutching her infant brother in her arms. "Riley, get out of bed."

"What's happening, Mommy?" she asked.

"I need you to get up now." Her mother yanked the covers from her legs and grabbed her wrist.

"You're hurting me!"

She rushed Riley to the closet and placed Michael in her arms. "Take your brother and wait here until I come back. Hold him close. Don't let go."

"But I—"

"Shh, listen to Mommy. Stay here and take care of your brother."

She kissed Riley on the head, then stood up and shut the door. The closet was pitch-black. She had never seen her mother so scared before. Was it the noise? Why didn't she take them with her? Michael cooed a soft murmur in her arms. She rocked him back and forth. "It's okay, Michael. It's okay. I'm—"

Her mother's bloodcurdling scream left her speechless. It was followed by another bang, then silence. Riley's heart pounded against her chest. She needed to get out, but was too petrified to stand up. She rocked her brother until her arms became tired, then pulled a sweater from a hanger above her head to make a bed for him to lie in. Sitting in the dark felt like an eternity.

"Anyone here?" a booming voice called into the house. Michael cried. She covered his mouth with her hand. "Shh, shh-shh."

A pair of heavy footsteps ascended the stairs. Her bedroom door creaked open, illuminating a slit of light onto the closet floor. The footsteps came closer and closer and stopped outside the closet door. She lifted her arms to cover her head. The closet door swung open.

Riley rose from her bed in a cold sweat. She had instinctually pulled her Glock from the pillow beside her and was aiming into the darkness. Her cell phone buzzed against her nightstand table. She lowered her pistol with a sigh and reached over to answer it. "Hello?"

"Riley, it's Frank. Are you up?" There was panic in his voice. Frank wouldn't call her directly unless something horrible had occurred. "I am now."

"We need you to get down to the *Chicago Wire* office as soon as you can."

"What happened?"

"This morning, they received a package . . . It was a pair of eyes."

"I'm on my way," she said, and hung up the phone.

The *Chicago Wire* office resided on the fortieth floor of the Willis Tower building. After entering through the double doors, Riley was stopped by a receptionist in the foyer. "I'm sorry, Miss, but we are not allowing anyone in at this time."

She moved her jacket to the side to show her badge attached to her belt. "Riley Walker, CPD."

"Oh, sorry about that. We've been expecting you." The woman picked up the phone behind the reception desk and pressed a button on the terminal. "Hi, Roberto, the police are here. Yes, I'll let her know." She hung up the phone. "He'll be right over. You're more than welcome to take a seat."

"Who's Roberto?" Riley asked.

"He's the office manager."

The front door opened behind her. Kurt walked in with a bandage across the bridge of his nose.

"Excuse me, sir, we are not allowing anyone into the office," the receptionist said.

"It's okay," Riley said, then turned to Kurt. "I didn't expect you to come back so soon."

"I didn't expect to be back, but after the commander's call, I couldn't miss this."

The door next to the reception desk opened. A middle-aged man in a light blue sweater and khakis entered the reception room. "Is this them?"

"Yes, it is," the receptionist said.

He walked over and extended his hand. "Hi, I'm Roberto Garcia."

Kurt took it. "Detective Thompson."

Roberto shook Riley's hand as well. "Detective Walker. Has anyone been in or out of the office since the package was discovered?"

"A few staff members didn't feel safe and left. Other than that, I can't say for sure. I almost left myself. It was quite startling to see it."

"Can you take us to it?" Kurt asked.

"Of course," Roberto said. "Follow me."

He held the door open so they could enter. The office was an open-space design with exposed ventilation and steel piping across the ceiling. A wall of floor-to-ceiling windows on the north end of the office presented a cloudy view of the Chicago skyline. Rows of long desks stretched from one of end of the space to the other, separated by privacy dividers. Computer monitors, books, loose papers, and folders cluttered each desk.

They followed Roberto past four rows of desks before Riley saw it—a fist-sized brown cardboard box with a top flap that was shut but unsealed. The surrounding desks were unmanned. Clearly, no one wanted to be near it.

She entered the vacant row and put on her plastic gloves. "Whose desk is this?"

"Mine," Holly Hart said from the end of the next row. "The box was addressed to me."

"How did it arrive?"

"It was hand delivered from the mailroom. He said the package arrived in the drop this morning."

Riley lifted the top flap with her thumb. The underside of the lid had a message written in blood.

CAN YOU SEE

Riley peered into the box to find a pair of blue eyes looking up at her. They rested within a blood-soaked bandage wrap like two eggs in a nest. She leaned closer for a better look. A sharp odor stung her nostrils, and she recoiled, rubbing her nose.

"What's wrong?" Kurt asked.

"The eyes. They're coated in some kind of chemical. It's really strong." She turned to Holly. "Was there a note?"

"Why? Have you seen something like this before?"

The clacking of keyboards and low side-conversations

subsided. Riley glanced around at the room full of eavesdropping journalists. "I'm just asking."

"No. It was just the box."

A man in a CPD windbreaker entered the hallway with a camera draped around his neck and a hard-shell briefcase in hand. Kurt raised his arm. "Over here."

Riley walked over to Roberto. "We need the room, now."

"Is that really necessary? We have deadlines to meet. I'm sure you understand."

"This is a crime scene. The sooner we process this, the sooner your staff can return to work."

"How much time do you need?" he asked.

"Shouldn't be long."

"Fine." Robert clapped his hands twice. "Excuse me every-one, please stop what you're doing." All eyes looked up at him. "The police need to use the office for a bit. Please save whatever you're working on and proceed to the exit. Come back in an hour."

The room full of journalists logged off their computers, rose from their seats, and funneled toward the front entrance. The cameraman set his briefcase on the desk next to Riley. "Did anyone move it?"

"No," she said. "The only people who touched it were the mail courier and the recipient."

"Good, that should narrow down the amount of prints." He thumbed the latches of his briefcase and opened it. Then he put on a pair of plastic gloves and removed a brown paper bag. "Once I take the photos, I'll give it a good dusting then send it to the lab for bloodwork."

"Don't stick your head too close. The eyes are covered in chemicals."

"Thanks for the heads-up," he said, then raised his camera to take a photo.

Holly rose from her seat and walked toward Riley. "Why would they send it to me?"

"I don't know."

"Is it connected to the club?"

"I said I don't know."

"Well, you must know something!"

"I understand you're upset," said Riley, "but getting worked up isn't going to help anything. I need you to calm down."

"Calm down? You're not the one with the secret admirer. I thought this was over. You told me it was over!"

"I know."

Holly shook her head. "I trusted you."

"We can have a unit escort you home and stand guard for the night."

Holly crossed her arms, trembling to the point of tears. "And what about tomorrow? And the next week? And next year? I know how this ends. These people don't forget."

Riley stepped forward. "I'll find who did this. No one is going to hurt you."

"I hope so."

"Come on, Holly," Roberto said. "Let's get a cup of coffee and leave this to the detectives."

"Don't run a story about this," Kurt said. "It will only make it more difficult for us to find whoever did this."

"We won't," Roberto said, then walked with Holly down the walkway. Kurt entered the row and glanced into the box. "Could they belong to Johnny or Zeke?"

"No. Dr. Leeds said both of their eyes were stabbed out. These belong to someone else. Someone new."

"Different MO."

"Yes, but same message."

"I thought we got all the Black Snakes?" Kurt said.

Riley sighed. "There's something I need to tell you. At the

plant, before Dom threw himself off the roof, he made a last request."

"What was it?"

"To find Johnny's killer."

"No," Kurt said, shaking his head. "That doesn't make sense."

"I know, and I didn't want to believe it, but what if the club didn't kill Johnny? What if it was someone else?"

"Like who? A rival gang? I'd understand them going after Johnny, but why send the eyes to Holly?"

"I don't know."

The cameraman turned the box to take a photo of the back-side. "Hey, I've got a shipping label here. There's a return address. 69 West. Washington, Chicago, IL, 60602."

"That's the state's attorney's office," she said, looking at the eyes. "Locke's office."

TWENTY-SEVEN

Riley and Kurt stepped off the elevator and walked to the end of the carpeted hallway to Locke's office. His secretary was seated behind her desk, talking on the phone. "Thank you for letting me know. I will pass along the message."

She hung up and turned to them. "Can I help you?"

Riley showed her badge. "Riley Walker, CPD. Is Locke available to speak with us?"

"He hasn't been in the office all morning, but I can check his calendar to see if he has any availabilities."

"Do you know where he is now?" Kurt asked.

"Unfortunately, I don't. Truth be told, I've been trying to reach him all morning, but he hasn't been answering his phone. He was working late last night, so I figure he must have forgotten to turn on his alarm."

"When was the last time you saw him?"

"I take off work at 6 p.m. He was still working in his office."

"Did he say anything to you before you left? Anything unusual?"

"Nothing out of the ordinary. Why?"

"We believe he might be in danger. Can we take a look at his office?"

She rose from behind her desk. "What kind of danger is he in?"

"We don't know for certain, we're just taking precautions."

The woman opened the door to Locke's office and let them inside. The room was dark, with gray daylight coming in through the blinds behind Locke's high-back desk chair. Riley looked for movement in the room, but could only see glimmers of furniture. "Is there a light you can turn on?"

"Oh, sorry about that," said the secretary, and flipped the light switch next to the doorframe. "That's better."

The room appeared just as Riley had seen it before. Everything was in its place, with no signs of a struggle. She walked around Locke's desk and looked down at the tabletop for anything he might have left behind. A few loose papers lay across his leather desk mat, but nothing else.

"Are you looking for anything in particular?" the secretary asked.

"No, not really. I'm just checking to see if he left a note or anything that could give us some indication of his whereabouts."

"Has he ever taken off before? Disappeared for days at a time with no explanation?" Kurt asked.

"No, never." The secretary shook her head. "If anything, he comes in to the office more often than he should. Even on weekends and holidays."

Riley pushed the papers aside, then glanced at a series of framed photographs on his desk. She focused on one image of Locke with his wife and son on a boat in what she presumed was Lake Michigan. His wife radiated in the sunlight. She had a strong type of beauty, the kind that could only be refined with age—

independent from the inside out. Her pastel-pink polo matched the light-blue and yellow polos that Locke and their son were wearing. The boy with fine, beach-blond hair must have been younger than twelve years old.

"Have you been in contact with his wife?" she asked.

"No, I haven't. Nor has she called me."

"Could you get her on the phone?"

"Certainly." She walked out of the office.

"I don't like this," Kurt said, rubbing the back of his neck. "We need to take it up the chain."

"Not yet. Not until we know for sure."

Riley opened Locke's top desk drawer. An assortment of colored pens, highlighters, sticky notes, and staplers shifted around the compartment. She reached to the bottom drawer and pulled it open. A rack stuffed from end to end with manila folders. Each was tabbed with a unique name and date, a backlog of open cases yet to be adjudicated.

"Find anything?" the secretary asked from the doorway.

Riley shut the drawer and walked around the desk. "No."

The woman entered the office and handed Riley a piece of paper. "I'm sorry, Detective, but I can't reach Mrs. Locke on her home or cell. Here's his address in case you wanted to go over there."

"Thank you," Riley said. "What kind of vehicle does Locke drive?"

Riley and Kurt entered the parking garage and walked down the row of vehicles to Locke's car, a silver four-door Mercedes Benz. The space was assigned for the district attorney, with a placard bolted to the cement wall. The driver's door was ajar, causing the interior overhead light to remain on.

"You see that?" Kurt pointed out.

Locke's briefcase was lying on the pavement in front of the

driver's door. Riley stepped over the briefcase and peered into the driver's seat. The car was empty.

"Doesn't look like he's here," she said.

"Let's find out for sure," Kurt said. "Pop the trunk."

Riley put on her plastic gloves, then leaned inside the car and pressed the trunk release button. She joined Kurt at the rear. "Make sure not to touch anything with your hands."

"I won't," Kurt said, using his forearm to push open the trunk. They looked inside to find a bag of golf clubs, gym shoes, a squeegee, and a pack of jumper cables.

"Nothing here," Kurt said, then shut the trunk. Riley walked back to the driver's-side door. From this angle, she could see a dent in the rear door surrounded by tiny scratches. "Look at this."

Kurt walked over to her. "What?"

She pointed at the dent.

"Could just be a door ding."

"Maybe." She reached down to the briefcase and lifted it off the ground. The golden clasp beneath the handle had the letters MBL engraved into it. "This is Locke's briefcase." She looked at the ground next to her foot and saw a set of car keys with the Mercedes emblem resting beneath the car. She reached down and lifted them from the ground. "Dropped his keys, too."

Riley turned around and looked at the empty car space behind her. A large puddle stained the pavement. She turned back to the dent in the door. "He was taken from here."

"What?"

She pointed to the empty parking spot. "There was another vehicle sitting here for a long time with its heater on. You can see his condensation puddle from the exhaust. It was probably a van, something large that Locke could have been pulled into." She stood up and acted it out. "It's late, and Locke had just spent the last several hours working on the Kane case. He came into the garage and was about to enter his car when the van door slid open behind him and the assailant attacked. Locke was holding the briefcase in one hand and his car keys in the other, so he couldn't defend himself. He dropped both items and kicked his car door as he was pulled into the back of the van.

"If this is the same killer as before, he probably used the ketamine to knock him out. Locke probably never knew what hit him."

Riley looked around the garage ceiling and pointed. "There's a camera there and there. If we're lucky, one of them would have caught it on tape, or at least what the vehicle looks like. I need you to go down to the security office and check it out."

"What about you?"

"This killer knows his victims' routines, which means he stalks them first. I'm going to Locke's house. If his wife is home, she might have a lead we can use. If you find the vehicle on camera, have the station put out a BOLO and then call me."

"Will do," Kurt said.

Riley walked across the parking garage and pulled out her cell phone, dialing the station. "This is Detective Walker. Can you connect me to Commander Briggs's office?"

"Just a moment, Detective."

After a moment, the line rang then clicked. "Area One Detective Commander Briggs speaking."

"It's Riley. I believe District Attorney Locke has been kidnapped."

"What? Are you sure?"

"There was a return address on the box that held the eyes. It was to Locke's office. His assistant said he never showed up for work this morning. I found his vehicle abandoned in the parking garage with his keys and briefcase on the ground next to the driver's door. We're checking to see if the garage's security cameras caught anything."

"You think this is retaliation for the club?"

"I don't know what this is, but the MO is consistent with the previous murders. The eyes we found this morning have been sent to the lab for analysis. I'll let you know once we have a positive ID."

"Riley, are you telling me those eyes we found this morning might belong to Locke?"

"Yes."

There was a silence on the other end of the line.

"Call me once you know for sure."

"I will," she said.

TWENTY-EIGHT

Riley pulled up to the front gate of Locke's estate on East Division Street, a nineteenth-century three-story building with a red brick facade and black slate roof. It was nestled within a charming neighborhood just a short walk from Lake Michigan. Her phone rang in her jacket pocket.

"Walker."

"Hey, it's me," Kurt said. "I got a copy of the security footage from the garage. It caught the whole thing on tape. Locke was taken just like you said. He was pulled into a white van as he was trying to get into his car. It was parked in the next spot for hours."

"Did you get the plate?"

"Partially. One identifier was obscured by mud."

"Mud?"

"Yeah, the whole bottom of the van is covered in it. I think it might have come from a construction site or something. It has Illinois plates, so I'm checking the DMV for a match."

"What about the kidnapper?"

"Nothing. The camera didn't have the angle, but it looks like only one person took him."

"Put a BOLO on the van. Call Briggs and Reyes and tell them what's happened. I'm at Locke's house now. I'll let you know if I learn anything," she said, and pocketed her phone. There was no time to waste. Locke was in danger, and each passing minute could be his last.

Riley exited her car and pressed the call button on the junction box. After a moment of static, she heard a voice buzz through the speaker. "Yes?"

"This is Detective Walker. I'm with the Chicago Police Department. I need to speak with Mrs. Locke."

"Mrs. Locke is indisposed at the moment. May I see some credentials?"

Riley looked beyond the gate to the top corner of the front door. A security camera was pointed down at her. She pulled her badge off of her belt and held it up. "Who am I speaking with?"

"This is Lori. I'm Mrs. Locke's aide."

"Lori, it's important that I speak with Mrs. Locke. It's about her husband."

There was silence for a moment, then the gate buzzed open.

Riley pulled open the gate door and climbed the front steps.

The front door to the house opened. A rail-thin woman with tied-back hair stood at the top of the steps, her arms crossed in a thin sweater.

"Mrs. Locke?"

"No, I'm Lori. I told you over the speaker, Mrs. Locke is indisposed."

"I need to speak with her right now. Where is she?"

"Take a seat in the living room," Lori said. "I'll go get her."

Riley moved one of the throw pillows and rested on the deep-seated couch. The living room was bright, with exposed wooden support beams along the ceiling and multiple throw rugs over imported marble floor tiles. There was a hint of lavender in the air, as if someone had sprayed the room with perfume before she arrived. The grand fireplace was encased in dark stone, which contrasted with the rest of the room.

After a few moments, Mrs. Locke was helped down the stairs by Lori. She was wrapped in a blue shawl over her loose shirt and jeans. Even without makeup, she had a natural radiant beauty. Riley stood up from the couch. "Mrs. Locke? I'm sorry to disturb you. I'm Detective Walker."

"Joan, please. Call me Joan. Lori says you have some questions for me regarding my husband?"

"Yes, I'm sorry to say that last night he was kidnapped from his office."

Joan's hand flew to her chest. She shook her head in a daze. "W-where? Who? Who would do this?"

"That's what I'm hoping you can help me find out." Riley extended her hand, "Please take a seat."

Joan reached back for the club chair, and Lori helped guide her into the seat. Beads of sweat formed along her brow. "I don't understand."

"I know this is difficult to hear, but I need your help if we're going to get him back."

Joan nodded.

"I just need you to answer some things for me." Riley decided it would be more effective to start with a few basic questions, then work her way up to more pressing matters. "When was the last time you saw your husband?"

Joan thought for a moment. "It must have been yesterday before he left for work. I tried calling him this morning, but his cell phone went straight to voicemail."

"That's good, Joan, very good. What time was that?"

"Must have been around six-thirty." There was a slight twitch in her right foot that remained constant as she talked.

"Does he stay out often?"

"The thing you have to understand about John is that he's a workhorse. He's always thinking about a case, even when he's out of the office. There's something in his mind that's too stubborn to turn off. Sometimes when he's working on a big case, he'll spend the night at the office and sleep on the couch. He told me last night might be one of those times and not to stay up late waiting for him to come home. He's working on that big drug bust that was on the news. There was a press conference about it yesterday."

"What kind of vehicle does your husband drive?"

"A silver, four-door Mercedes." Joan's hand shook on the arm of the chair. She tucked it under her shawl. "Is this helpful? I don't see you writing any of this down."

"It is, Joan," Riley said. "Does your husband have any enemies? Anyone that might want to harm him?"

"He's the district attorney! What do you think?" the woman exploded.

Lori put a hand on her shoulder to calm her down. "She's only trying to help."

Joan sat back in her seat and pulled her shawl tighter across her body, "You're right. I'm sorry. It's just . . ."

"I understand," Riley said. "Have you seen anything suspicious in the past few weeks? Any strange vehicles or people you've never seen before?"

"No, nothing that I recall."

Riley looked up at Lori. "Have you?"

She shook her head. "No, nothing."

Riley glanced back down. The gray light from the window was shining into Joan's eyes, but her pupils remained dilated. "Have you seen a white van around the property?"

Joan and Lori nodded again.

"Has your husband said anything about being followed?"

"Followed?" Joan asked.

"Yes, I believe whoever took him knew where your husband would be and when. This means he's probably been followed for a while."

Joan wiped a tear from her face. "No, no, he didn't mention anything about that."

"Has your husband mentioned anything about the Black Snake Motorcycle Club?"

"The what? Is that a gang?"

"Yes, it is."

"No. He never talked about a motorcycle—" Joan wept into her hands. "I'm sorry. I just don't understand, why. Why would someone take him?"

Riley reached over and rested a hand on Joan's shoulder. She didn't know what to say. What could she say? There was no answer for what the woman was feeling. Sometimes the only thing to do was just be there.

"I'm going to do everything I can to get your husband back."

Joan wiped the tears from her eyes. "Please just bring him home. He's a good man."

"I will do everything I can." Riley looked at Lori again. "Would you excuse us for a moment?"

The assistant waited for Joan's response.

"It's okay," she said.

"I'll be in the kitchen if you need me." Lori walked into the next room.

Riley sat back on the couch so she could be at eye level with Joan. "I was in your husband's office this morning and saw a picture of your son on his desk. How old is he now?" she asked.

"Oliver? He's thirteen."

"I know this is scary, but Oliver is going to need you to be strong right now. No matter what happens, he's going to need his mother now more than ever."

OF MURDER AND MADNESS

Joan wiped away the tears and nodded. "I know."

"How long have you been using?"

"What? I don't know what you're talking about."

"Your eyes are dilated. Your hands and feet are trembling. It's room temperature, but you're sweating bullets. You're so nauseous that you couldn't even get into that chair by yourself. I can get you some help."

"I'm perfectly fine where I am. Thank you."

"Does your husband know?"

"I slipped and fell a couple months ago. John thinks I still take the medication because of a nerve issue from the injury."

"It's dangerous to go through a detox without clinical supervision. You should have someone to monitor your recovery."

"And what will everyone else say? Hmm? What will they say about the DA's drug addict wife? It will ruin John's career. My friendships. No. I won't do that to my family."

Riley's phone rang in her jacket pocket.

"I understand," she said, then stood up and reached into her jacket. She handed Joan a contact card. "Here's my number. That's my extension on the end and my cell phone on the back. If you hear anything from your husband or anyone else, call me."

Joan wiped at the tears again. "Please bring him home."

"I'll do everything I can," Riley said, then let herself out. She walked down the from steps and answered her phone. "Detective Walker."

"We got an ID on the license plate," Kurt said. "It belongs to Craig Williams. He's an officer with the CPD. His CO said he called out sick on Monday and hasn't shown up to work since. There are three units on the way to his house, including a SWAT team. Reyes is treating this as a hostage situation."

Riley thought for a moment. "Williams was one of the responding officers to Johnny's murder."

"Damn. Any idea why he would do this?"

"No," she said, and entered her cruiser. "See if you can pull his personnel file—you might find a grievance. Send me the address. I'll be over as soon as I can."

TWENTY-NINE

By the time Riley arrived at Officer Williams's home, police had taped off both ends of the street, securing the perimeter from any through traffic. Red and blue lights pulsated from the cluster of vehicles in the middle of the road while a CPD helicopter circled overhead. Riley parked at the edge of the police line, next to a huddled group of onlooking neighbors. After ducking beneath the police tape, she was intercepted by a patrolman in an oversized rain poncho. "Excuse me, Miss, you can't be here."

She flashed her badge and continued walking through the pack of vehicles to an armored van where Kurt and Reyes were huddled with a SWAT team.

"What's happening?" Riley asked Kurt.

He turned away from the group. "Officer Williams hasn't responded to any of our calls."

"We would enter through the front and back entrances simultaneously," the team leader said to Reyes. "He's covered all the windows, so we'd be going in blind."

"What about Locke?"

"Without more information, I cannot guarantee his safety. Like I said, we don't know what the situation is inside. Going in like this would put his odds of survival at fifty-fifty."

"If anything is fifty-fifty, it's whether Locke is even alive. We don't have any time to waste. Get in there now," she said.

"Yes, ma'am," he said, and turned to his nine men in full tactical gear. "Let's take 'em down."

The squad pulled down their gas masks and formed a single-file line near the entrance of the house. The leader of the group kneeled next to the front door and snaked a borescope camera beneath the front door to peer inside. He monitored the four-inch LCD screen in one hand while guiding the camera line with the other. The back five men broke from the line and continued around the house toward the rear door.

"Did you find anything in Williams's file?" Riley asked.

"No. It's clean," Kurt said. "The guy is a boy scout."

The lead SWAT officer retracted the borescope and backed away from the door as another officer breached it with a battering ram. The squad rushed inside. Everyone listened for gunfire.

"Do you see anything?" Riley asked.

"No," Kurt said.

After six minutes, the SWAT team emerged from the house unharmed. The leader took off his earpiece and approached the deputy chief. "The DA isn't here."

"What about Williams?" Reyes asked.

"He's dead. We found him in the upstairs bathtub."

She turned to Riley. "Get in there and find out what happened to him."

Riley reached into her pocket and pulled out a pair of plastic gloves. She walked past a blue Chevy sedan that was parked against the curb in front of the house and continued through the doorway. Kurt and several members of the forensic team followed her inside.

The doorknob and lock rested on the floor, surrounded by dozens of wood splinters. The SWAT team had decimated whatever evidence she could have gathered from it. It was a sparsely furnished home. A leather recliner was propped in front of a flat-screen television, an empty dinner tray over the coffee table. She glanced into the kitchen before walking upstairs. It was a clean home, but lacked any pleasantries.

"Does Williams live alone?"

"Yeah," Kurt said. "His file said he didn't have a spouse or children."

She climbed the staircase to the second floor. The acidic stench of rotting meat filled her nostrils. "Ugh."

It reeked, which told her the body had been there for a while. No matter how many crime scenes she uncovered, she would never get used to the smell of death.

Riley reached into her jacket and rubbed the menthol-scented lip balm beneath her nose.

In the guest bedroom, an elliptical machine stood next to a rack of dumbbells and an exercise bench. She continued down the hall and entered the master bedroom, where her boots squished against soggy carpet. A thin layer of water covered the entire floor. The bed wasn't made, but she didn't see any signs of a struggle. She trudged across the mushy floor to the bathroom and pushed open the door. Within the overflowing, blood-soaked bathtub was Officer Williams. His eyeless head rested back against the tiled wall, which revealed the same message as always, written in blood.

Riley entered the bathroom and leaned over the tub. Within the murky brown water, Williams was still clothed in his uniform. His boots rested beneath the running faucet, which cascaded into the overflow. She knelt beside the tub and tightened the hot-water handle until it stopped.

"I was wrong," Kurt said from the doorway. "I was wrong about everything. Johnny wasn't killed by the Black Snakes."

"Don't beat yourself up over it. Do you have a flashlight?"

"Not on me, but I could get one."

"No, that's okay," said Riley. "I'll wait for the medical examiner's report."

"What are you looking for?"

"I'm trying to determine if his eyes were stabbed out like Johnny's or removed by some other means. Do you have a copy of his file? They should have his eye color listed. The pair Holly received were blue."

"No, that's back at the station."

Riley extended her arm to the wall and touched the edge of the message. The blood was dry. Williams's corpse was bloated from water seepage and internal gases, which meant he had been stewing in the tub for at least a few days. There were bloodstains running down his cheeks, but it wasn't enough blood to turn the water so dark. His left sleeve had been rolled up to the crook of his elbow. She turned around to Kurt. "Can you go into the next room and hand me a coat hanger from the closet?"

"Sure," he said, and turned away. Riley felt a sudden light-headedness that caused her to lean against the wall. The smell must have made her nauseous. Kurt returned to the bathroom doorway and handed her a wire hanger. "Will this work?"

"Yes," she said, and dipped the edge of it into the tub. She felt around for Williams's arm, then fished his hand through the hanger, lifting it out of the water by the wrist. His putrid flesh was an oily shade of green. She looked at the inside of his arm. A thin cut had been made down the center of his left forearm from wrist to elbow.

"Look at this," she said.

Kurt stepped into the bathroom and stood behind her. "So he killed himself?"

"It looks that way, but we'll have to wait for the medical examiner report to know for sure." She lowered Williams's arm back into the bathtub as a loud thud came from downstairs.

"What was that?" she asked as Kurt turned.

"Someone call an ambulance!" a voice called out from below. Riley stood up from the bathtub and ran out of the bedroom. She peered over the landing to find that a member of the forensic team had fallen to the ground. His open equipment kit was scattered on the floor next to him.

"What happened?" Kurt asked.

Another forensic aide lowered her face mask and looked up to them. "I—I don't know. He was s-standing here, and . . . and then . . . he . . ." Her words trailed off as she collapsed onto the floor. Another forensic team member leaned against the wall, knocking over a bar cart, then dropped to the floor unconscious.

Riley ran into the guest bedroom.

"What's going on?" Kurt asked.

"There's something in the air."

She pressed against the window frame, but it didn't budge. Kurt rushed beside her to help, but the window remained sealed. She looked closer at little bits of metal embedded within the frame. "It's nailed shut!"

She felt lightheaded again, and leaned her hand against the wall to keep her balance. Kurt stepped back from the window and grabbed a dumbbell. "Stand back!"

He hurled the weight through the window, shattering the glass, then used his elbow to knock out the few remaining fragments. Riley and Kurt leaned their heads through the opening and took deep breaths. The cool, fresh air revived her.

News vans had pulled up to the police line at the end of the street. Deputy Chief Reyes pointed to the reporters, instructing the police to keep them back. Once Riley recovered, she held her breath and ran downstairs. She grabbed the female aide by the collar and dragged her out of the house. Kurt followed her, dragging the two remaining forensic team members.

Police officers met them outside and helped move the unconscious bodies into an ambulance. Once they were handed off to the paramedics, Riley placed her hands on her knees to catch her breath.

"What happened in there?" Reyes asked.

"They started dropping one after another. There's some kind of toxin in the air."

Reyes waved over the police sergeant. "Make sure no one else enters the house without a respirator. Have someone from FSD find the source of this."

Riley looked ahead to the blue Chevy sedan parked in front of the house. "Do you have the paperwork on Williams's vehicle?"

"Yeah," Kurt said, and pulled out his phone. "I got a picture of the registration."

"What's the make and model?"

Kurt reviewed his photo. "Chevy Impala. Why?"

Riley pointed to the vehicle. Its rear license plate was missing. "Williams was already dead by the time Locke was taken. The killer used his license plate on the van to lead us here. This was a trap."

"I need to let the chief know. He'll want to get in front of this," Reyes said, and pulled out her cell phone. "We'll arrange an emergency press conference tonight. The FBI will need to be notified as well."

When the feds became involved with a case, they annexed it. Total hostile takeover. Not only would it mark the end of her tenure as lead detective, it would end any affiliation she had with the case moving forward.

Reyes held her phone to her ear and walked toward a cluster of police vehicles.

"What's that mean for us?" Kurt asked.

"It means there is no more us."

She walked to the back of the ambulance and peered inside. The three members of the forensic team had regained consciousness and were sitting upright on the rear bench with non-rebreather masks.

"Are they going to be okay?" she asked.

The medic removed a blood pressure cuff from one of their arms and joined her on the street. "Depends on your definition of okay. Will they live? Yes. But it's too soon to tell what long-term effects they may have. It's a good thing you got them out of there when you did, otherwise it could have been worse. Much worse."

"What happened to them?"

The paramedic shut the rear door and walked around the ambulance. "It looks like acute carbon monoxide poisoning. The hospital will have to run a carboxyhemoglobin test to be sure, but they have all the signs. Nausea, confusion, loss of consciousness."

"What are the long-term effects?"

"Nothing good," he said, then drove away from the house.

A woman from FSD exited the house and removed her gas mask. She approached Riley and Kurt. "Where's the deputy chief?"

"She's busy," Riley said. "What did you find?"

"Someone tampered with the water heater's ventilation, causing a backdraft of carbon monoxide into the house. All of the detectors were pulled from the walls."

Keeping the warm bath water running for a week ensured a steady emission of gas would fill the house. Once again, she was one step behind, and no closer to finding Johnny's killer.

"Thank you, I'll pass along the information."

The woman nodded to Riley and Kurt, then returned to the house.

"Who the hell is this guy?" Kurt asked.

Riley took a long drag of her e-cigarette, feeling more lost than ever. "I don't know."

THIRTY

"You're lucky to have found him when you did," Dr. Leeds said, pulling Officer Williams from the cold chamber. His body rested on the steel slab covered with a sheet. "Submerged bodies decompose at a faster rate than in open air."

"How long has he been dead?" Riley asked.

"At least four days. His insides were already rotting because of the excess fluids. We had to drain him during the autopsy, so he might look a little different from when you found him." Dr. Leeds removed the sheet from Williams's head and torso. His body appeared to be skin on bone, with sections of his lower rib cage exposed.

"Was it suicide?" Kurt asked.

"That is my assessment, yes."

"How do you know he did it to himself?"

Dr. Leeds pointed to a grouping of minor cuts at the top of Williams's left forearm. "You see that? Those are hesitation marks. Very common on suicide victims. Coroners also found a razor blade at the bottom of the bathtub that is consistent with his wounds."

"Were his eyes taken postmortem?" Riley asked.

"No. The bloodstains on his cheeks tell me his heart was still pumping and the skin around the eye sockets was beginning to scab. They must have been removed at least a day before he died." Dr. Leeds leaned over the body and hovered his finger over the officer's face. "And from the looks of things, the method is different from before. His eyes weren't stabbed out. All six of his ocular muscles were severed individually. That takes time and patience."

"So our suspect has medical experience?" Riley asked.

Dr. Leeds shook his head. "I don't think so. There are several lesions where he cut too deep within the orbital cavity. A practiced surgeon wouldn't be so careless to make that kind of mistake. Enucleation is a dangerous operation. One wrong move and a patient could bleed out before the surgery is complete."

"He could have struggled?" Kurt said. "That would cause a slip."

"Not likely," Dr. Leeds said, and lifted the toxicology report from the tray table. "We found traces of ketamine in his system, just like your previous victim. There are no ligature marks on his wrists or ankles. No defensive wounds, no skin under the fingernails, and no other signs of a struggle. He was unconscious during the procedure. We did, however, find cotton fibers in his mouth, so he was gagged for a period of time."

A pair of heavyset coroners in matching black windbreakers wheeled a line of connected gurneys through the vinyl-slatted entryway. Each had a black plastic body bag strapped to the top. "We got a six-count coming in," one of the men announced. "Where do you want them?"

Dr. Leeds pointed to the corner of the room. "Over there is fine. If you don't have enough room, put the rest in the hallway outside. What happened?"

"Another drive-by in Englewood. One of the stray bullets went through a window and popped a seven-year-old boy in the head. He died at the kitchen table in front of his mother."

"I'll get Jamison on this." Dr. Leeds set his clipboard on the tray table then walked out of the room. "Excuse me for a moment."

She leaned over the slab and looked at Williams's face. There had to be a reason the killer removed the eyes. After subduing his victims, he could kill them in any manner he pleased. Why take the eyes at all?

"Poor bastard," Kurt said. "He probably never had a chance."

"Why do you suppose he takes the eyes?"

"Don't know, don't care. Crazy is crazy, you'll never know why."

Riley looked up at him. "I wouldn't dismiss him like that. Just because we don't understand it doesn't mean there isn't a coherent explanation for what he's doing."

"I've seen a lot of deranged things in my time, but nothing comes close to this. If removing people's eyes doesn't qualify you for a lifetime in the looney bin, I don't know what does."

Dr. Leeds returned to the room and walked over to the slab. "Sorry about that. Things always appear to be short-staffed around here."

"It's okay," Riley said. "You were telling us that Williams was unconscious during the procedure."

"Yes, he was."

"And his eyes were removed a day before he died?"

"Correct."

Riley looked at Kurt. "You said Williams called in sick on Monday?"

"Yeah, that was the last his CO heard from him."

"Williams was at the crime scene Saturday night," she said. "If his eyes were removed a day before he died, then the killer must have followed him home after his shift. I doubt it was Williams who called in sick. By that time, he was already dead."

Her phone rang in her jacket pocket. She pulled it out and saw an unknown number.

"Excuse me a moment," Riley said, and turned away from the table. "Detective Walker."

"Hi, this is Joan. Um, Mrs. Locke." She sounded distraught through the receiver.

"Hello, Joan, how can I help you?"

"It's horrible. I'm watching the news and they're saying my husband was being held hostage by a police officer. They're saying there was a dead body found in the house, but they won't say who. Tell me, is it him?"

Riley would usually never disclose information about an ongoing investigation, but she needed to build rapport with the woman in case her husband's kidnapper reached out for a ransom. Riley needed to be her first call for help.

"No, it wasn't. The press is wrong—your husband wasn't being held hostage."

"Then where is he?" she asked.

"I'm still trying to find out. I'm doing everything I can to find him. If I learn anything, you'll be the first to know."

"Please, bring him home! I just—I just can't take this anymore."

"Like I said, I'll do everything I can. In the meantime, I suggest you stop watching the news. Get some rest, and try to remain positive. Your son Oliver will need you to be there for him."

"Okay. Okay, I will."

"All right. Goodbye, Mrs. Locke," Riley said, and hung up the phone. She turned back to Leeds and Kurt. "What about prints?"

Leeds shook his head. "Unfortunately, there were no prints on the body, or the box we received this morning."

"Not one?" Kurt asked. "Not even a hair fiber or other DNA?"

"No, I'm sorry. The body and box are clean."

She looked to a side table, where a pair of eyes rested next to the box she'd recovered from the *Chicago Wire* office. Both Locke's and Williams's eyes were blue, so there was no way to tell whose they were. "Do you have an ID on the eyes?"

"Not at this time. This morning we tried a swab test, but the eyes are covered in formaldehyde, hence the smell. So instead we cut off a piece of tissue and sent it to the lab for analyzing, but I stopped the process once the victim was brought in."

"Why would you do that?" she asked.

"We have a limited amount of resources to run DNA tests, and need to prioritize on a case-by-case basis. I stopped the test because I figured the eyes belonged to the victim. Is that a problem?"

"Yes." She pointed. "We need to know if those eyes belong to Williams as soon as possible. Is there a way you can see if the cuts on the eyes match the cuts on the victim?"

"Let me look." The doctor turned around and walked over to the side table. He leaned over and inspected each eye. "They appear to have been removed the same way as our victim, but there's no way to tell if the methodology was also used on someone else. I'm sorry about that, detectives. I'll have the lab expedite your request."

"Is there anything else we should know?" she asked.

"That's all I have for now. I'll let you know as soon as we have confirmation on the eyes."

"Thank you, Doctor," she said, and walked with Kurt through the doorway. They passed two gurneys, each covered in a black body bag, the second of which was half the size of the first.

"I need to get back to the station and review my notes," she said. "The only way we're going to catch this guy is if we figure out what he wants."

"I already told you, you can't understand crazy."

"He's not crazy."

"Then explain why he would take Officer Williams' eyes."

"It was a choice."

"How's that?"

"Our suspect could have killed Williams anytime he wanted, but he didn't. After taking his eyes, Williams was given a choice. Live the rest of your life in darkness, or die. He chose the latter."

THIRTY-ONE

Riley entered the station and approached the bullpen. Now that she knew the Black Snakes didn't kill Johnny, she needed to rethink her case from the ground up.

"Walker," Briggs called out, waving her over to his office.

She held up a hand and mouthed, "One second." Riley went to her desk and pulled open the side drawer to find it was empty. Reaching inside, she felt around to make sure. "It's missing."

"What?"

"My case file. It's gone. Did you take it?"

"I haven't touched it."

"Walker," Briggs called out from his office, waving her over.

She closed her desk drawer and walked across the room to the commander. "Someone has been through my desk."

"I know. Reyes forfeited everything we had to the feds as soon as they got here. You're needed in the conference room now."

"Why? The feds will—"

"Riley, the district attorney has been kidnapped. This is bigger than a local investigation. I need you to play nice on this one. Help the FBI with everything they need to get Locke back." Briggs checked his watch. "The chief is going to make a public announcement soon. You better get going."

Riley continued toward the conference room. "I can't believe she did that."

"I don't like this any more than you," Kurt said. "But a fresh pair of eyes might help us catch this guy."

She pulled open the conference room door and entered to find a thin man in a dark suit pinning a crime scene photograph from Johnny's house to a corkboard.

"You must be Detective Walker," he said, pinning another crime scene photograph of the *Chicago Wire* to the board. "I hope you don't mind me taking the liberty."

She crossed her arms. "I do mind. Just who do you think you are coming in here and taking my case notes?"

He finished pinning the photograph and turned around. He was clean cut with side-parted hair. "Agent Sam Harrison. I'm with the FBI's Behavioral Analysis Unit. Deputy Chief Reyes requested assistance in creating a psychological profile of your killer."

"What's all that?" Kurt asked.

He pointed to the left side of the corkboard, which was covered with autopsy reports for Johnny, Zeke, and Officer Williams—"Methodology." Then he pointed to the top of the corkboard, a timeline of photographs starting with Johnny's body. Each was covered in sticky notes with dates and times— "Chronology." Finally, he pointed to the right side of the board, where a grouping of prison records, driver's licenses, and personnel files were pinned together—"Known victims."

"How did you get Officer Williams's autopsy report?" Riley asked.

"I had the medical examiner send it over. Dr. Leeds is very thorough in his reporting."

Reyes entered through the doorway. "Good, everyone's here."

She took an aspirin and washed it down with a sip from her water bottle. "Maybe one of you can wake me up from this nightmare."

"Why isn't Violent Crimes on this?" Riley asked.

"They're busy with another case. The Bureau assured me that Agent Harrison is more than capable of helping us get Locke back and bringing this case to a close." She turned to him. "We have to make a press statement in a minute, do you have anything?"

"My analysis is still early, but given the methodology and the way the victims' bodies are displayed, all while leaving no evidence, I would classify our suspect as an organized killer."

"What's that mean?" Kurt asked.

"Well, for one, he's intelligent, strategic, socially adept, deliberate, cautious, and worst of all subtle. Organized killers are the most difficult to detect, because they could be anyone. A parent, a teacher, even a pillar of the community, but beneath those carefully crafted facades they're the apex predators of humanity. Ted Bundy, Zodiac, Dennis Rader, John Wayne Gacy—all organized killers."

"What about the messages he leaves at the crime scenes?" Riley asked.

"Think of each crime scene as a signature," Agent Harrison said, turning to the photographs. "Pretty macabre, to say the least. I did a keyword search online, but found no references to the phrase in any literature or theological text."

"Great, so we have a bogeyman on the loose with no way to narrow down who he is," Reyes said, then checked her watch. "We're late. I need you all to come with me to the press room now. The chief is going to make a statement and take questions. Keep a lid on this apex predator stuff. We don't need to cause a panic."

Riley, Kurt, and Harrison followed her into the hallway.

"How confident are you about your profile?" Riley asked.

"Our suspect has all the markers of an organized killer. I'd be surprised if he was anything else."

"I hope you're wrong," she said, and followed Reyes to the back door of the pressroom. The chief was waiting by the door, talking to Briggs. "Are they inside?"

"Yes," Briggs said. "Just waiting on you."

Chief Benedict shook his head. "What a mess."

"Chief, I'd like you to meet Agent Harrison," Reyes introduced. "He's with the FBI's BAU. He's going to aide our investigation."

Benedict shook Harrison's hand. "Pleased to meet you. Do us all a favor and catch the son of a bitch."

"I'll do my best, sir," Harrison said.

"Alright, then let's get this over with quickly." The chief held his keycard to the back door of the pressroom. At the same time, Riley's phone rang in her jacket pocket. She pulled it out and saw Holly Hart on her caller ID.

"I have to take this. Go on without me."

She stepped away from the door and answered. "Detective Walker."

"It's Holly. I just wanted to give you a heads-up that the *Wire* is going to post an article this afternoon about the eyes. I fought with our editors, but it's too big of a story."

"You can't," Riley said. "It will—"

"I know," Holly said. "But understand, if we don't go out with it, someone else will, whether it's the *Times* or the *Post*."

She thought about how best to minimize the damage to her case. If the *Wire* released the article, it might encourage a copycat or a flood of false confessions to jam up the station's phone lines. "Okay, if you must print the story, then keep the bloody message out of it. That will help us identify the real killer."

There was a long pause on the other end of the line. Holly must have been consulting with her editor. "We can do that."

"You know this is going to hinder our investigation. Maybe even cause someone to get hurt."

"We don't cause the actions of others, just report them."

"Sure you do," Riley said, and hung up the phone. The press room door was closed. She didn't want to interrupt the ongoing conference, so she walked around the bullpen to the front lobby, then crossed the floor to the press room. It was hot inside due to the amount of reporters crammed within.

"Do we know if this was an act of terrorism?" one reporter asked from the press pool.

"We have no reason to believe that is the case," Benedict said. "No one has come forth to claim responsibility for the kidnapping, and there has been no communication for demands of ransom." He pointed to another reporter. "Yes."

A man in a brown suit stood up from his chair. "What will happen to Robert Kane's prosecution now that the district attorney is missing?"

"That is an open investigation and I will not comment at this time. Anyone else?"

"Do you have any leads?" a reporter asked.

"We are actively pursuing several leads in partnership with the FBI."

"Will Mayor Cox appoint an interim district attorney?"

"You'll have to ask him. We will keep you all up to date as we move forward with our investigation. Thank you," Chief Benedict said, then walked off the stage. Riley turned around and backed out of the press room to beat the crowd to the lobby. What she had seen wasn't bad as far as press conferences go. The chief had provided enough cover for her to reexamine her case notes and find a lead. A case this big would make national news, and Riley would need all the time she could get.

She entered the lobby as a disheveled man pushed through the front door and limped to the center of the room. He was dripping wet, staring down at the floor. Riley glanced outside through the glass doors. It wasn't raining. His haggard suit jacket was frayed at the seams as if dragged across concrete. Blood leaked onto the tile floor from beneath his pant leg.

"Sir? Do you need any help?" the officer at the front desk asked. The man didn't respond. He stood with his damp hair hanging in front of his face. The knuckles on his right hand were covered in scabs above a gold owl signet ring. She walked around to face him. "Locke?"

He looked up at her with a bloodstained bandage wrapped over his eyes. "Stay back!"

She stumbled away from him. The front desk officer stood up from his chair. "Holy shit." He grabbed a radio from the table. "I need backup at the front entrance. All available officers."

The press room doors opened as a horde of reporters and cameramen entered the lobby. Riley held up her hand. "Everyone stay back! Don't come in here!"

The journalists stopped in their tracks. Several members of the group lifted their cameras and started recording.

"Locke, this is Detective Walker. You're safe now. Let me help you."

Locke shook his head. "No, I'm not. No one is safe."

A flood of officers entered the lobby through the rear door. Kurt, Reyes, and Harrison were among them.

"Oh my God," Reyes said.

Riley held up her hand. "Stay back! All of you!"

Locke's head swiveled from side to side, sensing the crowd of people filling the room. Everyone mumbled among themselves.

"It's going to be okay. We'll get you some help," she said.

"No. No, it won't," Locke said with a moan. "He'll never stop."

"Who did this to you?" she asked.

Locke dug his hand into his pants pocket. The surrounding officers raised their pistols.

"Get your hand out of your pocket!" one officer said.

"Put your hands up!" said another.

Locke raised his hands. In his left palm was a silver flip lighter. He thumbed open the cover and sparked a flame. "I have to do this. I have to or else he'll come after my family."

Riley extended her hand. "No!"

Locke dropped the lighter to the floor, engulfing his entire body in flames. He let out an ear-piercing scream.

"Put him out!" Riley said.

Locke dropped to his knees and fell forward in agony. The fire reflected in the wall of camera lenses from the press room doorway. One of the officers broke from the crowd and sprayed Locke with a fire extinguisher. By the time the smoke cleared, the district attorney's charred remains rested motionless on the floor.

THIRTY-TWO

After the lobby was cleared of press and police, the smell of scorched flesh lingered in the air. Riley stood behind the yellow police tape, watching Dr. Leeds's examination of Locke's body.

"I need to tell his wife," she said. "She deserves to know before the press release the footage."

"She's probably already aware," Harrison said. "It's all over the internet."

Riley turned away from the crime scene and Joan. The phone was answered on the fourth ring. "This is Detective Walker."

"We trusted you," Lori said. "You said you would bring him home. There are newspeople banging down Mrs. Locke's door. We had to disconnect the home phone."

"Is Mrs. Locke there? I'd like to speak with her."

A distant wailing came through the phone's receiver.

"You hear that?" Lori asked. "She's been hysterical since she saw the video."

"Tell her I'm sorry, and if she'd like to speak with me, I'm here."

Lori ended the call. Although she really didn't talk to Joan, the conversation left a sour taste in Riley's mouth. It was never easy calling a loved one of the deceased. In fact, she found it more difficult than looking at the body itself.

She returned to the crime scene to find Kurt arguing with Agent Harrison.

"Every instance will have variations, but the overall methodology will remain consistent."

"Oh yeah? Are you going to tell me my horoscope next?" Kurt said.

"What's going on?" Riley asked.

"He's full of it," Kurt said. "First it's signatures and subtlety, now this."

"It's a pattern," Harrison said. "This is consistent with all of his previous victims."

"Then explain it to me," Riley asked.

The agent turned to her. "First he stalks them, then subdues them and removes their eyes, then murders them either by his own hand or by forcing theirs. Johnny and Ezekiel were killed by our suspect, while Officer Williams killed himself. Locke's suicide is not unprecedented."

"That's the biggest load of—"

"Why don't you check the security footage," Riley said. "See if any of the exterior cameras caught a glimpse of our suspect."

Kurt looked back at the agent, then walked away.

"Never have to guess what's on his mind, huh?" Harrison said.

"He's not all bad."

"You'll want to see this," Dr. Leeds said.

Riley and Harrison ducked beneath the yellow police tape and approached Locke's scorched corpse. What was left of his skin was black and splotched red. His face was burned beyond recognition. Both sets of ears and lips were gone, leaving his mouth in a perpetual toothy grin. Bits of his collared shirt had melted into his shoulders and chest.

"There appears to be a foreign object inserted into the subject's left eye socket." The doctor removed a pair of splinter forceps from his breast pocket and reached into the mottled skull.

"What is it?" Harrison asked.

"I don't know. It appears to be stuck to the side, and I don't want to damage it."

Riley reached into her jacket and put on a pair of plastic gloves. Dr. Leeds pulled out a folded piece of paper and dropped it into her palm. The corners of the paper were singed black. She took her time to unfold each crease. Once it was open, she held it up to reveal a message written in blood.

CAN YOU SEE

"Get a shot of this," Riley said. She placed the note on the ground next to her, and someone took a photo. Agent Harrison reached into his pocket and pulled out a pair of plastic gloves. He kneeled down and lifted the note. "We might be able to get a print."

"We can dust it, but we won't get anything. He never leaves prints."

"What about the body?"

"The extent of his burns has masked any prints we could have lifted," Dr. Leeds said.

"Were his eyes taken like the others?" Riley asked.

The doctor looked down at Locke's face. "Yes. It appears his eyes were surgically removed like your previous victim."

"Was he tortured?" Harrison asked.

Leeds pointed to multiple gashes along Locke's seared torso. The skin around the cuts was swollen and bruised. "He was stabbed multiple times, but the wounds appear superficial. Same pattern as before. The killer appears to have missed every vital organ and major artery to cause a slow bleed." He pointed to Locke's right hand. All but his middle and ring fingers were burned off. "The ends of his fingernails are chipped. It looks like he was clawing at something."

"Could be from the arms of a chair if he were bound like Johnny," Riley said.

Harrison inspected the note. "Looks like it was written by hand. All capital letters. Makes it more difficult to detect a hand-writing style. What kind of paper is this?"

"What do you mean?" Riley asked.

He turned the note upright. "It's not lined, but it's too thick to be printer paper." He flipped the note over and looked at the back. Then he held it up to the overhead light. "It looks like there's some kind of marking here."

She stood next to him. "Where? I don't see anything."

Harrison lowered the paper and pointed with his index finger to the far left side. "Here, beneath the C."

Riley leaned in and squinted at the paper. She could make out small-typeface font in black ink. "It looks like the letters CHI, and beneath that the letter H. Or it could be an E, I'm not sure." She handed the paper to Dr. Leeds. "Can you make out what it is?"

He pushed his glasses up the bridge of his nose and glanced at the paper. "Might be some kind of watermark or scribblings."

She took the note back. "We need to get this over to FSD right away. They'll be able to show us what's beneath the blood."

"You might want to consult a botanist as well," one of the forensic members said. She was kneeling beside the open door-frame and scraping a clump of dirt into a small envelope. "There appear to be traces of soil that were stuck to the bottom of the victim's shoe."

Kurt burst into the lobby. "We got a hit on the van."

Riley handed the note to one of the forensic technicians, then crossed the lobby to Kurt. "Where is it?"

"Fortieth and Michigan. A patrol unit spotted it beneath an overpass."

They ran through the rear lobby door and passed the bullpen to the parking lot. The stone-gray evening sky was turning dark. Riley, Kurt, and Harrison entered her cruiser and drove out of the lot. She turned on her emergency lights and sped down the road.

"Our suspect wouldn't have left it in the open unless he wanted it to be found." Harrison asserted.

Kurt turned around in the passenger seat. "Or maybe we just caught a break. You ever think of that?"

"There have been four crime scenes. Four dead bodies. Have any of them yielded a single clue? I wouldn't underestimate who we're dealing with."

"He's just a man," Riley interjected. "People make mistakes."

"That's true, but more likely, he's been fantasizing about this for a long time."

"But why?" Riley asked. "Why do you think he's doing this?"

"Because he's a freak," Kurt proposed. "Case closed."

"Hard to say," said Harrison.

"Well, you must have some idea."

"Serial killers usually fall into one of four categories. Hedonistic killers do it for the thrill. Mission-oriented prey on minorities or any other group they perceive to be inferior. Visionary killers are compelled by hallucinations or voices they hear in their heads, and power-oriented killers do it to exert dominance and control over their victims."

"Doesn't seem that our suspect fits into any of those categories," Riley said.

"I know," Harrison agreed.

She drove down Michigan Avenue until she spotted a patrol

unit in the middle of the road. Its search lights beamed over the back of a white van with open rear doors. The cabin was empty save for a shotgun mounted over two metal poles that were bolted to the floor. A dead officer was lying on the pavement with half of his head blown off. Bits of skull and brain matter stained the asphalt. His partner was sitting on the curb, staring at the carnage.

Riley stepped out of her cruiser with the two men and approached.

"He—he was right there," the officer mumbled. "Fitzgerald . . . he was right there with me and now . . ."

Agent Harrison rested a hand over the officer's shoulder, "I know."

The officer lifted his radio. "715, 10-1 shots fired. Officer down at Fortieth and Michigan."

Riley approached the van and raised her flashlight. It reeked of formaldehyde. The sharp, nauseating odor made her eyes water. She wiped her face then looked over a strand of fishing line that was fastened around the shotgun's trigger. The other end attached to the rear door handle. The shotgun was rigged to fire as soon as it was opened. She leaned in closer. The shotgun's serial number had been filed off the side of the action.

"You were right," Kurt said to Harrison. "He left it here for us."

Riley walked to the open driver door and shined her flashlight over the empty seats. The back of the van was blocked by a partition. The officer's couldn't have known about the shotgun until it was too late. She beamed her light over the VIN, then pulled out her cell phone and called the station. "This is Detective Walker, I need to know the owner of a vehicle. I've got the VIN when you're ready."

"Go ahead, Detective."

She read the number and waited for a response.

"The vehicle belongs to a Mr. Ezekiel Rivers. Would you like his address?"

"That won't be necessary," she said, and hung up the phone. Once again, she was at a dead end with no suspects and no leads to follow. Riley sighed, then returned to the group to share the bad news.

THIRTY-THREE

The Forensic Services Division resided in the basement of the station. Riley, Kurt and Harrison exited the underground stairwell and continued down the hall, past the archives room and cold case office.

"Leaving the district attorney at the CPD's doorstep was reckless," Harrison said. "He's become more emboldened with every victim."

"And more likely to make a mistake," Kurt said.

"Yes, and when he does, that's when we'll capture him."

"But how many more people have to die until we do?" Riley asked.

"It's not a perfect world," said Harrison. "We can only do the best we can with what we have."

"Well, let's hope FSD pulls something from this note, otherwise we have nothing."

The Forensic Services Division's entrance was labeled with a stainless steel placard. Riley held her passkey to the door's sensor until it beeped. Then she crossed through the doorway and continued into the inner hallway. Glass walls divided the space into multiple compartmentalized offices. She continued to Sergeant Berns's office and opened the door.

Berns was standing over his desk, looking over a sheet of paper. He jerked his head up to look at her.

"Sorry, I didn't mean to startle you," she said.

"No problem. Sometimes it gets so quiet down here that any little noise becomes startling. Please come in, I was just going over the soil report from the sample recovered from the District Attorney's shoe. There appears to be a sizeable amount of mycelium within the dirt, which tell us he was being held in a place with a lot of fertilizer or an area with a lot of plant growth like a garden or greenhouse or forest."

"Or underground," said Harrison. "A single fungal organism can grow for miles."

"We'll keep that in mind." Riley rested the charred note on the sergeant's desk. It was covered in a clear plastic sleeve. "Right now, we need you to look over this paper."

Berns leaned forward and looked over the note. "You want me to dust it for prints?"

"Not at the moment. We know our suspect is too careful to leave anything like that. There appears to be ink written beneath the blood, and we want to know what it says."

He lifted the plastic-covered paper from his desk, looking at the front of the note then turning it over to the back. "Where did you get this?"

Riley paused to find the words.

"It was in the DA's skull," Kurt said. "Can you help us?"

Berns's eyes widened. "Yeah, I can help you, but it will take a minute." He led the group out of his office and down the hall. "Is this note from the same killer responsible for the Laflin Street murders?"

"Yes," Riley said. "Why do you ask?"

"That's quite the body count he's stacking up. What is it now, four?"

"Five," Agent Harrison said.

"That's a shame. We had a betting pool early on that this guy was a vigilante. I mean, who goes after a couple of local drug dealers like that?"

"How much did you lose?" Kurt asked.

"A couple bills and cleanup duty for the rest of the month, but I'll live." Berns removed a set of keys from his pocket and unlocked one of the office doors. "After you."

They entered the dim office space and waited. The sergeant closed the door behind them and turned on the lights. It was a cramped space, with a long table against the back of the room holding many computers, microscopes, and other scientific equipment that Riley didn't recognize. Berns walked across the room and placed the note on the table. He booted up the computer and logged in with his username and password.

"How long will this take?" Harrison asked.

"Depends on the lift and how it was imprinted. Either way, I should know if there's something to capture in a few minutes." He pulled a pair of plastic gloves from the dispensary box and snapped them over his wrists. Then he removed the charred note from its plastic sleeve and held it up to the light. "Where's the spot you wanted me to look at?"

Riley hovered her finger over the letter C. "Right there, at the top of the page. See that? There's black ink written beneath the blood."

The sergeant lowered his arms. "I see it."

He walked over to what appeared to be an oversized printer and opened a side compartment.

"What is that?" Riley asked.

"This is a Video Spectral Comparator, or VSC for short. It's an older model, but it should do the trick." Berns positioned the note so that the top of it was centered within the compartment. Then he closed the flap and powered on the machine. He clicked a program icon on his monitor, and after a moment, a high-fidelity image of the note was rendered on the screen.

"All right, let's see what we got here." He zoomed in on the image, focusing on the letter C. The black ink letters beneath the blood became more prominent. "Looks like the letters CHI, and beneath that looks like G or maybe another C. Not clear enough for me to make a distinction."

"Can you make out what type of writing it is?" Kurt asked.

Berns zoomed in on the letters again and repositioned the text so that it was centered on the monitor. He clicked an icon on the side of the screen. The lighting on the image shifted position. "It looks like it was printed. I don't see raised ink, and the penmanship is too concise to be handwritten. Yeah, this lettering definitely came through a printer."

He pressed an icon on the screen again, returning the lighting from the side of the note to overhead. Then he clicked a button on his keyboard, turning the coloring of the image pink and muting all color differentiators. The entire note became a solid pink square. Berns clicked the icon again, turning the note dark blue. The color of the blood became highlighted in a bright white.

"What are you doing?" Kurt asked.

"I'm trying to determine the quality of paper and its origin. Usually there's a watermark or indent of some sort that can be lifted, but I'm not seeing anything right now."

"Could it have been damaged in the fire?" Riley asked.

"It's possible. Either that or the liquid from the blood could have obscured it from detection." He clicked the icon again, turning the note a light green. The lettering of the blood and the text were a dark brown. "This doesn't seem to work. Let me try something else."

He clicked another icon on the program, and the image returned to normal. "If the ink is printed, that means it left an indent on the paper." Berns clicked another program icon, and the image turned a dark shade of purple. He cycled through three more settings before the image turned black and white. The blood had disappeared from view, as if removed from the note entirely. "There we go." He clicked on the zoom icon and enlarged the photo until the writing filled the screen. Then he reversed the colors so that the writing became a white text on a dark gray background.

"Here we go." Berns leaned toward the monitor. "It says, 'Chicago Wire, 233 S Wacker Dr., Chicago, IL 60606.' Beneath that it says 'Holly Hart.'"

The bloody note was written on stationary from Holly's desk at the *Chicago Wire* office. She should have realized it when the box of eyes was sent to her, "He's announcing his next target."

"I agree," Agent Harrison said.

Riley pulled her phone from her jacket pocket to call Holly, but her service was dead. "I don't have a signal down here."

She ran out of the lab room, through the FSD entrance and up the stairwell. When she reached ground level, she tried calling again.

Kurt and Harrison joined her on the main floor.

"Are you calling her?" Harrison asked.

"It's ringing. We sent a patrol unit home with her. Find out who that is." Kurt ran to Sergeant Hall's office at the back of the room. The phone rang until Holly's voicemail answered.

"Damn," she said, and tried calling again.

"No answer?" Harrison asked.

"Voicemail." She tried again. "She's not answering."

"Desk sergeant says the patrolman isn't answering his radio," Kurt said.

"When was his last check-in?" she asked.

"About an hour ago."

"We need to go now," Harrison said.

They ran out the back of the station to her cruiser. Riley started the ignition, turned on her emergency lights, and sped out of the parking lot.

THIRTY-FOUR

The cruiser roared into fourth gear down Interstate 290 toward South Western Avenue. Riley gripped the steering wheel with white knuckles, maneuvering through traffic.

"We're no good to her if we're dead. Slow down!" Kurt said, gripping the overhead handle. Riley veered into the far left lane, speeding past a dark sedan. She glanced at the speedometer, which held steady at eighty-five miles per hour. "Call her again."

"I called four times. She's not answering!"

Two upcoming vehicles rode parallel to each other, blocking her path ahead. She gritted her teeth and stomped on the gas pedal, careening across two lanes to pass them on the right. "Then try again!"

Kurt raised the phone to his ear. She rushed into the exit lane and merged onto Van Buren Street.

"She's still not answering," Kurt said.

"Keep trying."

The streetlight from the intersection ahead turned yellow. Riley sped up.

"You're not going to make it," Kurt said.

"I'm going to."

"You don't have enough time," Harrison warned from the back seat.

"I'm going to make it!"

The streetlight turned red as she entered the intersection and drifted left onto South Western Avenue. Her tires screeched against the cold pavement as the front of her cruiser dipped forward around the corner.

"Come on, come on, come on," she said, forcing the steering wheel into place. The cruiser straightened out on the long stretch of road, and she sped up again, pushing the cruiser's engine as hard as she could, flooring it down the road. Riley steered around a pot holes and weaved between cars. The upcoming intersection was busy with cross-traffic.

"Watch it!" Kurt said, pushing his hand against the ceiling. She eased off the gas pedal and glided toward the red light. Oncoming vehicles from both sides of the intersection skidded to a stop as she sped through the crossroads. Then she floored it down the road to West Taylor Street and turned right.

A patrol unit was parked in front of Holly's two-story townhouse. Riley parked behind the patrol vehicle. The back of the officer's head was visible in the driver's seat.

"Son of a bitch is just sitting there," Kurt said. "You think his radio is broken?"

Riley turned off the engine. "It better be."

They opened the car doors and stepped out of her cruiser. She approached the patrol unit and peered inside the driver's window. The officer was seated with his head slumped forward.

She knocked on the glass. "Hey, wake up."

The patrolman didn't respond. Riley pulled on the door handle, illuminating the vehicle's interior. The dashboard, steering wheel, and center console were covered in blood.

"Oh my God," she said, and opened the door. The officer was

sitting with his right hand clenched around his throat to stop the bleeding.

"What is it?" Kurt asked.

"He's been stabbed in the neck."

The officer looked up at her, wide-eyed. Blood oozed from his bubbling lips. She reached up to his neck to put pressure on the wound. His left arm had multiple lacerations on the shoulder and bicep. She glanced at the officer's name tag. Patterson.

Harrison ran up beside her. "Let me see."

Riley removed her hands and stood back.

"Call for help," he said.

She wiped the excess blood on her pant leg and radioed Dispatch. "5215, officer down. EMS needed at 2556 West Taylor Street."

"10-4, 5215. Sending emergency services to your location now."

She joined Harrison. "They're coming."

"I'll stay with him until help arrives," the agent said, keeping pressure on Officer Patterson's neck. "Be careful. This could be another trap."

"I will," she said, and removed her pistol from its holster. She walked around the patrol unit toward the front of Holly's building. Through the windows, she could see that all the lights within the house were turned off.

"I'll go around the back," Kurt said.

She ascended the front steps to the door. The lock above the handle was scratched with the same U-shaped markings she had seen before. Riley rubbed her thumb across the metallic etchings to be sure. She stepped to the side of the entryway to shield her body, then pushed open the door. The house inside was silent.

She peeked into the dark narrow hallway. "CPD! If anyone is in here, make yourself known!"

There was no response.

Riley removed her flashlight from her jacket pocket and beamed it into the empty hallway. "CPD, I'm coming inside! If anyone is in here, make yourself known!"

She inched her way into the hall, walking past framed photographs of Holly with her friends.

"Holly! This is Detective Walker. If you're here, let me know."

She continued to the end of the hallway at the base of the stairs and peeked around the corner. The living room was clean, save for a pair of lumpy throw pillows tossed over the couch. A flat-screen television rested on the wall above a media console. She looked around the living room and kitchen. Nothing appeared out of place. No signs of a disturbance, no signs of a struggle.

"Holly?" Riley called out again.

A knock came from the back of the room. Riley raised her flashlight to find Kurt standing on the back porch, pointing toward the door handle. Riley walked across the living room to the kitchen and let him in.

"Nothing back here," Kurt said. "You find her?"

"No."

A loud thud came from the ceiling above them.

"Come on," Riley said, and ran back to the staircase. She aimed her flashlight toward the second floor, "Holly! Are you home?"

"CPD!" Kurt said, into the house. There was no response. "I don't hear anything. Do you?"

"No," she said, climbing the staircase. "Holly? It's Detective Walker. If you're home, let me know."

She reached the second floor landing and peered down the hall. There were three doors along the walkway. Riley approached the first door and pushed it open. "CPD!"

Her flashlight shined over a white-tiled bathroom with an empty tub. She stepped inside to make sure no one was behind the door, then returned to the hallway. Kurt pushed open the next door and shined his flashlight into the room. "CPD!"

Riley followed him into a bedroom that had been converted into a home office with a desk, a laptop, a printer, and shelves full of books and magazines. The desk was covered in loose documents, sticky notes, and paper clips. On the wall next to it were several framed newspaper articles: "ELECTION BOARD MEMBERS RESIGN AFTER VOTER FRAUD SCANDAL," "CHICAGO SEX TRAFFICKING RING EXPOSED," "CHICAGO NEARS GRIM MILESTONE AFTER SPREE OF DEADLY SHOOTINGS," "GANG-LAND CHICAGO: A LOOK INSIDE THE CITY'S CRIMINAL UNDERWORLD."

One article stood out from the rest. It was much older, the paper yellowed. The headline read: "FOUR FAMILIES DEAD AFTER APARTMENT STRUCTURE FIRE." Riley recalled the burn mark on the back of Holly's hand. Was her family one of the four that were killed? She crossed the room and opened the closet door to find a filing cabinet, office supplies, and a vacuum. She returned to Kurt. "Nothing in there."

They went out into the hallway and continued to the last door at the end, standing on either side.

"Ready?" Kurt asked, grabbing the handle.

"Go," she nodded.

Kurt pushed the door open, and they beamed their flashlights into the room. Holly was swaying by her neck from an orange electrical cord tethered around a cross-support beam. A pool of blood had formed beneath her feet next to a toppled over stool. Riley ran to Holly and lifted her up to relieve the tension around her neck. Her wrists were handcuffed behind her back.

"Get it off!" she said.

Kurt ran up to Holly and unwrapped the cord from her neck. "Okay."

Riley and Kurt carried her to the bed and removed the duct tape from her mouth.

"Holly!" she said. "Breathe, Holly!"

Red and blue emergency lights pulsated through the bedroom window. Holly gasped for air and coughed.

"That's it," Riley said. "Breathe."

The side of the reporter's shirt and pants were drenched in blood. Riley lifted the bottom of her shirt to find a stab wound in her stomach.

"CPD!" someone called into the house from downstairs.

"Up here!" Riley said. "We need EMS!"

A gaggle of footsteps rushed up the stairs. Two EMTs carrying a stretcher and a handbag entered the room.

"We found her hanging from the ceiling. She's been stabbed," Riley said.

"Give us some space," one of the EMTs said. He leaned over the bed. "Miss? Miss, can you hear me?"

"Her name is Holly," Riley said.

"Holly, we are here to help. Don't move your head."

Riley turned around to find a large message on the wall, written in blood.

CAN YOU SEE

THIRTY-FIVE

Riley took another drag of her e-cigarette as she waited for the forensic team to finish sweeping Holly's house. Press crews had gathered at both ends of the street beyond the police tape. Their cameramen watched her every move like she was a caged animal.

Harrison joined her against the hood of her cruiser. "Officer Patterson didn't make it. He died on the way to the hospital. I'm sorry."

"And Holly?" she asked.

"She's in surgery, but they said she'll pull through."

"I should have known he would come for her. She could have died because of me."

"But she didn't," Harrison argued. "You saved her."

Riley took another drag and looked across the street to Kurt as he recounted the night's events to Reyes and Briggs. She too had been ruminating over what took place since the EMTs rushed Holly from the scene. More often than not, it was the details that would break a case, small inconsistencies that—once exposed—would unravel even the most convoluted of cases. And the one anomaly she had been focusing on was Holly.

"I didn't save her. She was spared," Riley said. "Officer Patterson's last check-in was an hour before we arrived. The killer had plenty of time to take her eyes, but he didn't. She's a break in his MO."

Harrison rubbed his chin in consideration. "I wouldn't call being stabbed and left for dead a break, but it is unusual he chose not to remove her eyes like the other victims. Do you have a theory as to why?"

Riley rose from the hood of the cruiser. "Not yet."

She walked toward the bloodstained asphalt where Officer Patterson had been carried out of his car and taken to the hospital. "In order for the killer to get to Holly, he first needed to neutralize the threat. He approached the car from his blind spot. By the time Officer Patterson saw the killer, he was already at the door."

She stopped at the open driver's door and looked at the empty seat within the police unit. "It was no longer than a moment. A quick stab to the neck and a couple strikes to the left shoulder was all it took to render Officer Patterson helpless. With only the use of his right hand, he wouldn't be calling for help or using his weapon. All he could do was clutch his neck to stop the bleeding. This allowed the killer to remove the handcuffs from his belt and proceed to the house."

"We should check the vehicle's dash cam to see if he walked across the front," Agent Harrison said.

"Dash cams only record when the officer activates their lights and sirens. His vehicle was off."

Riley continued up the front steps of Holly's building. "He entered through the front door by picking the lock, as he had with every previous location." She entered through the open doorway and walked to the end of the foyer, then stopped. "It was quiet."

In the living room, she looked at the lumpy throw pillows on the couch. "Holly had probably spent the evening watching the news, but decided to go to bed early."

She ascended the stairs to the second floor. The upper landing was crowded with forensic members detailing every inch of the hallway.

"Have you found anything?" she asked.

One pulled down his face mask. "We got a partial off the front door handle and a palm print from the staircase railing, but who knows. Both could be from the owner. Couldn't find any footprints coming in or out of the house and no blood traces outside the bedroom."

"Let us know if that changes," Agent Harrison said.

Riley walked down the hallway and entered Holly's bedroom. A couple of photographers were capturing the scene.

"About finished?" she asked.

"Just doing a second pass in case I missed anything. I already got plenty shots of the wall."

"Could we have the room for a minute?" Harrison asked.

"Sure," the photographer said, and walked out of the room. Riley stared at the pool of blood on the floor beneath the dangling extension cord. The image of Holly swaying from the support beam was seared in the back of her mind.

"You all right?" Harrison asked.

"Yeah. I'll be fine." Riley nodded.

She walked around the bloodstained floor and approached the bed. "She was sleeping when he attacked. He stood right here, watching her, taking in the moment before what came next."

"Did he use ketamine like the others?"

"No. It would have been too difficult to stand her up if she were unconscious. He moved her by force." Riley looked around the room. A space heater was toppled over in the far corner next to the closet. Walking to it, she pulled the electrical cord until she reached its end. She looked at the wall for an electrical outlet, but didn't see any. The closest outlet was on the opposite side of the room. "This is where the killer got the extension cord. The space heater wouldn't be able to reach otherwise. After the killer hand-cuffed Holly's wrists and duct-taped her mouth, he pulled the electrical cord from the wall and used it as a noose. He had her on the stool, bound and gagged. That's when he stabbed her and wrote the message."

Agent Harrison walked around the bloodstained floor. "He went through a lot of trouble to not kill her. No one goes to these lengths unless the act itself has meaning."

Riley looked around the room and at the bloodstained floor. Why let her live? Why give her a chance when so many other lives were taken? It didn't make sense, unless . . .

"This wasn't about Holly at all. It was about me."

"What do you mean?"

She looked at the message on the wall and walked toward it. "He could have killed her anytime he wanted, but he didn't. He stabbed her once so she would bleed out and slip on the stool. When I entered the house, I heard it topple over." She turned to face him. "The killer wanted me here just so I could watch her die."

Riley pulled a second chair so she could prop her legs on the seat. It was an uncomfortable position, but it was the best she could do with the limited space in the recovery room. She had been waiting for Holly to wake up while Kurt and Agent Harrison canvassed her neighborhood for witnesses and coordinated with the department on how to address the public.

"Riley?" a weak, groggy voice croaked behind her.

She turned around to face Holly. "Sorry, I didn't mean to wake you."

"Where am I?"

"You're at the hospital."

Holly laid her head back onto the pillow. "I never liked hospitals. When I was young, I spent a lot of time in them for the burns on my arm and back. My family's apartment building caught fire. I was so scared."

Riley leaned closer so she wouldn't have to strain her voice. "I know. I saw the news clipping in your office."

Holly raised her hand to feel the bandages around her neck. "Is he still out there?"

"Yes," Riley said.

Tears welled in the reporter's eyes.

Riley stood up. "I know this may be difficult, but you're our best hope of catching him and putting an end to this."

After a moment, Holly wiped the tears from her cheeks and nodded.

"Tell me what you remember."

"It was dark. Hard to see his face. I remember fragments. The way he grabbed me out of bed. The smell was awful. He never said anything to me. It was like . . ."

"I know this is hard, and you're doing great. You said there was a smell. Can you describe it to me?"

"Dead. Like a rotting animal. It was so strong."

"How big is he?"

"I don't know. It was dark, and it happened so fast."

"What color is he? Could you see his face?"

Holly nodded. "He's white. Too dark to make out any features."

"What was he wearing?"

"Dark. Dark clothes. A button-down shirt, maybe a work uniform. I can't remember. A lot is a blur."

"That's fine, Holly. Tell me what happened as best you can."

"I was sleeping when he grabbed me. He put my hands behind my back and cuffed them. When I screamed for the guard, he put tape over my mouth. I remember after that his hands went away, and I was too helpless to do anything." Holly stopped speaking as she got choked up. "I'm sorry."

"It's okay," Riley assured. "Keep going."

"He lifted me off the bed and wrapped the cord around my neck. He pulled until my feet were off the ground and I was kicking into nothing. I thought, this is it. This is how it ends. Then he put a stool beneath my feet, just enough so that my toes would reach. I had to keep my chin up to reach the stool. I couldn't see him, but it felt like he was just standing there, watching me struggle. When I found my footing, that's when he put his hand on me like he was feeling for something. Then I felt a sharp pain. It hurt so much. He patted my side a few times. I couldn't see what he was doing. After that, he walked out of the room. I felt the blood run down my side onto my feet. I held on for as long as I could."

"Is there anything else I should know?"

Holly thought for a moment, then shook her head. "No, that's all I remember."

"That's okay. Thank you, Holly. Get some rest," Riley said, and turned to walk out of the room.

"You said you want to put an end to this, but there is no end to this. Not for me." Holly's eyes were hollow. "Not after what he's done. It will be with me forever."

"I know," Riley said, hanging her head. The full weight of the burden rested on her shoulders. "I'm sorry."

THIRTY-SIX

Six pallbearers lifted an American flag off of Locke's casket and began folding it into a triangle. The enormous crowd surrounding the gravesite was full of familiar faces and some of Chicago's political and professional elite. Riley had been to dozens of funerals for slain officers and retired public servants, but none compared to this.

Joan stood beside her son Oliver at the front of the crowd and dabbed tears from her cheeks with a handkerchief. The sight was as cold as the wind chill against Riley's neck. Even in a crowd of mourners, they stood out with the heaviest of hearts.

Clouds darkened overhead as an elderly priest stood at the head of the casket and read from a worn bible. "But if I go to the east, he is not there; if I go to the west, I do not find him. When he is at work in the north, I do not see him; when he turns to the south, I catch no glimpse of him. But he knows the way that I take; when he has tested me, I will come forth as gold. My feet have closely followed his steps; I have kept to his way without turning aside. I have not departed from the commands of his lips; I have treasured the words of his mouth more than my daily bread. But he stands alone, and who can oppose him? He does whatever he pleases. He carries out his decree against me, and many such plans he still has in store. That is why I am terrified before him; when I think of all this, I fear him. God has made my heart faint; the Almighty has terrified me. Yet I am not silenced by the darkness, by the thick darkness that covers my face."

The pallbearers finished folding the flag and handed it to Mrs. Locke. She clenched it against her breast as if holding on to her late husband. After Locke's casket was lowered into the ground and the ceremony concluded, the crowd disbanded to their vehicles. The funeral left her with a festering rage in her gut. "He's been one step ahead of us this entire time. There must be another way to stop him."

"I don't like it either," Kurt said. "But Harrison is convinced it's only a matter of time before he makes a mistake, and when he does, that's when we'll catch him."

She shook her head. "We should be doing more than waiting around for another body to turn up."

"It's only been a few days, and besides, given the evidence, there isn't much else we can do."

As much as Riley hated hearing that, he was right. They were out of leads, and the case was getting colder by the day. Kurt turned to walk with the crowd. "You coming?"

She looked across the gravesite. "No. I'll catch up later."

"All right."

Riley walked around the gravesite and waited among the remaining crowd. A small cluster of people had formed around Joan, sharing their condolences for her late husband. Riley waited until there was an opening to speak with her. "I'm sorry for your loss."

The woman looked up to her with an anguished expression full of rage and sorrow. She said nothing, but she didn't need to. There was nothing to say that would bring her husband back.

Riley looked away and continued walking with the crowd toward their vehicles.

There have been five murders since this case began. Unlike Harrison, she didn't want to wait around for a sixth. Why was the killer going after these people? There was no discernible motive, no link tying the victims together. No matter how many times she reviewed the evidence, nothing made sense. She feared she would never know, and this case would go unsolved for years to come. Every retired detective she had met had one case that they still regretted, the proverbial one that got away. She didn't want this to be the case she obsessed over for the rest of her life.

When she reached the concrete pathway, Kurt was standing against the oncoming crowd, waiting for her. "Reyes wants to see you."

"About what?"

"I don't know, she asked me to come get you. I'm assuming it's about the case."

"Where is she?"

Kurt gestured to a grouping of trees, where Reyes was standing with Briggs, Harrison, and Benedict. They were several yards out of earshot from any of the other funeral attendees. Riley figured it was intentional. The deputy chief didn't want anyone to overhear their conversations and leak it to the press pool that was waiting outside the service.

She walked over to the group with Kurt and greeted each of them by rank. "Chief, Deputy, Commander."

"I've gone to more of these services than I care to count," Chief Benedict said. "And they never get any easier. I understand you both worked with Locke on this case. He was a good man, and I know he'll be missed by all of us."

"Have you seen the news this morning?"

"Not in particular."

"The papers have given our killer a name. They're calling him the Sandman. My guess it's because of the eyes. People are scared. Public confidence in the department is declining by the day. I have orders from up top to hand this case over to the federal authorities. Agent Harrison will lead the investigation from here on out."

This news sent a shock to Riley's core. She clenched her fists at her sides. "I have been on this case since the beginning," she said. "I was almost killed because of this case. We wouldn't have anything if it weren't for me. Kane, the Black Snakes, the drugs, none of it!"

"I know," Benedict assured her. "But the mayor wants us out of this investigation, and I'm inclined to agree with him. Too many people have died already."

"Please, just give me a couple more days. I can still—"

"I'm sorry. The decision is final."

Riley felt a tightness in her throat that made it difficult to swallow. She turned and walked away from the group. After everything she had done, how could they sideline her like this?

"Wait up," Kurt called out from behind her, but she didn't stop. She didn't want to talk to him, or anyone.

"I said wait up, damn it! I'm getting mud on my good boots."

She stopped and turned to him. "What?"

"We can't end it like this. There must be something we can do."

"You heard the chief—it's over. Besides, he's right. I've already let too many people die under my watch. I won't stand by and wait for more."

Kurt's lips tightened. "You don't mean that."

"I just need to be alone right now. I'll talk to you later," she said, and walked across the field. Most of the funeral attendees had already returned to their vehicles, but Joan was still standing at the gravesite with her son. Riley couldn't imagine how painful this must be for her. This case had been one tragedy after another, with each loss a greater burden on her soul.

More people were going to die unless she stopped this killer, but she couldn't do anything if the FBI was leading the investigation. She wandered the cemetery grounds until she stopped in front of her parent's tombstones.

David and Rachel Walker.

Rain began to fall as she looked down upon them. It had been years since she had last visited their graves. When Riley had been younger, she would sneak out of the orphanage just to be close to them. She had hoped the pain of their loss would fade with age, but it hadn't. That wound had always stayed with her.

An umbrella suddenly shielded her head from the rain. She looked over her shoulder to find Briggs standing beside her.

"There's not a day that goes by that I don't miss them," he said.

"Sometimes I wonder if what we do even matters. With the way things are . . . I don't know."

"The world has always been this way, but it doesn't mean we stop trying to make a difference. Your father taught me that a long time ago. I told the chief I've decided to stay on with the department. Seems that there's still some good this old man can do." Briggs rested his hand on her shoulder and smiled. "Your parents would be proud of you, Riley."

"Thank you."

He turned and walked away.

THIRTY-SEVEN

Riley was too conflicted to go home and sleep. She knew better than to turn in for the night when a case was weighing on her mind, so she stopped at the liquor store, then drove to Roy's townhouse. She turned right onto West Polk Street near the Jesse Brown Medical Center and parked her car against the sidewalk. It was a quiet neighborhood with green trees overhead and sprawling red brick buildings with large front living room windows.

She sat in her cruiser and smoked and watched Roy's home for a while. Riley wanted to clear her head before meeting him. The last thing she wanted to bring was any negativity into their relationship, even though Roy would be more understanding than most. He was good in that way.

She grabbed the bottle of wine from the passenger seat and walked up to his front door, then knocked three times and waited. After a minute of no response, she pressed the doorbell and knocked again.

"Who is it?" Roy asked from inside.

"It's Riley."

She heard the deadbolt unlock, and Roy cracked open the door. He peeked at her through the gap, then opened it wide. "Hey there, I wasn't expecting you."

"I know, but I was in the neighborhood and thought I'd come over." She raised the bottle and handed it to him. "I brought you a little something we could share."

He looked it over and smiled. "How thoughtful. Come in."

She entered his home, and he locked the door behind her. "I was just about to have dinner. Are you hungry?"

"I'm sorry, I didn't mean to—"

"It's no problem. Really. I always make more than I can eat. Saves me time on cooking again, and I can eat the leftovers for lunch. This wine would go perfect with the steaks I just made."

She followed him to the kitchen. "Sounds delicious."

"They are," he said, and walked around the counter. He pulled a pistol from the back of his pants and set it on the counter. She looked at the gun and then at him.

"You can never be too careful," he said. "I never answer the door at night without it." He opened a kitchen drawer and pulled out two sheets of tinfoil. "How do you like your steak?"

She took off her jacket and rested it over the back of a dining room chair. "Medium rare."

"Perfect, so do I." He covered the two steaks in foil over the wooden cutting board. "I let them sit after being cooked to let the meat soak in the juices." He grabbed a corkscrew and two glasses from the shelf and pierced the bottle. "Has Reyes given you a transfer date for the Violent Crimes Task Force yet?"

"No, not yet. I'm actually struggling with whether I should stay on my current case. The chief handed the reins to the feds today, and I don't know if I should fight back to see it through. If anything, I can push to stay on as an advisor."

Roy popped the cork and poured the wine into each of the

glasses. "It's easy to get caught up in our line of work, but you need to do what's best for you."

"I guess I'm still trying to figure out what that is."

Roy handed her a glass and leaned in. "Well then, here's to clarity."

They clinked glasses and drank. The wine was sweeter than she'd expected, a full body flavor with a hint of vanilla.

Riley rested her glass on the counter, and their eyes met. Roy pulled her close, wrapping his arm around her waist, and she pressed her lips against his. They kissed for a long moment before she led him by the hand to the bedroom upstairs. He embraced her from behind, kissing the nape of her neck. It sent a shiver through her body, allowing all of her concerns to fade away.

She turned around and pushed him against the edge of the bed and straddled his waist. Her breath became heavy, and she felt flushed. She leaned over and whispered in his ear, "I want you."

He unbuttoned her blouse from the bottom up, and Riley pressed herself against him in a warm embrace. She smelled the wine on his breath and felt his hands explore her body. They made love in the dark with a carnal intensity she didn't know she possessed. It was a heavy, bruising, physical act driven by lust and loss.

When they were finished, he held her under his arm while they lay in bed, looking up at the ceiling. She thought about things for a few minutes and decided that she was going to fight to stay on the case. She had invested too much time and effort to not see it through.

"I'm going to take a quick rinse in the shower," Roy said. "Want to join?"

She looked up at him. "Yeah, I just need a minute."

He leaned over and kissed her on the lips. "Well, don't be too long." Then he lifted his arm and rolled out of bed, heading to the bathroom and turning on the shower.

"I'm going to try and stay on the case," she called. "I'll meet with Reyes tomorrow morning to see what I can do."

"That's great," Roy said from the bathroom. "I knew you would."

She smiled and rolled over in the bed. Her bra strap had snagged on the knob of the nightstand drawer. She pulled it off, causing the drawer to slide open. Inside, she found a yellow plastic cell phone.

The same kind of burner phone she'd collected from the Black Snakes' warehouse.

"You coming?" Roy called to her from the shower.

She reached inside and pulled out the phone and turned it on. "Just a sec."

Riley scrolled through the contacts to see eight other phone numbers listed. Then she checked the phone's text messages and saw one sent from several days ago: "They're coming."

Roy must have warned the club about the raid on the farm.

Riley felt an empty flutter in her stomach that made her nauseous. She thought back to all of their conversations since she took on the case and realized she'd told him everything.

Roy turned off the shower. "What's going on?"

She collapsed the phone and slid the drawer back into place. Quickly gathering her clothes from the floor, she was putting on her shirt and underwear and pants as Roy stepped back into the bedroom. "Is something wrong?"

She hid the phone in her back pocket. "No, I just changed my mind. I can shower at my place."

"You don't need to do that," Roy said, and walked over to his dresser. She averted her eyes as he put on a T-shirt and boxer briefs. She couldn't stand to look at him now.

"I know. I just thought you might not want me around."

"Not want you around? Don't be ridiculous." He walked over to her and placed his hands over her arms. "I've been thinking about us for a while. When I went through my divorce, I lost everything. And now that I'm with you, I'm feeling things that I never thought I'd feel again. I know you feel it too."

She swallowed hard and looked up at him, trying not to cry. "I've been waiting a long time to hear you say that, but I never thought you felt the same way."

He rubbed a tear from her cheek, then leaned in and kissed her. She placed her hands on his chest. "Okay, I'll stay tonight, but first let me get some things from my car."

"That's great," he said, and let her go. She stepped around him and walked to the bedroom door.

"Riley?" he asked.

She stopped in the doorway and turned around to face him. "Yeah?"

He held up her bra. "Don't forget this."

"Thanks," she said, and walked back into the room. She grabbed the other end of it, but he didn't let go.

"I want my cell phone back too."

She glanced at the open nightstand drawer, then back at him. "I don't know what you're talking about."

He stepped forward and grabbed her wrist, pulling her close. "Yes, you do. And you're going to give it to me."

She kneed him in the groin as hard as she could, then ran out of the room and down the hall.

"Riley!" he screamed from the bedroom.

She ran down the stairs and grabbed her jacket off the dining room chair, which held her car keys and cell phone. His footsteps were approaching as she ran to the door and twisted the handle. It was locked. She turned the deadbolt and pulled open the door as Roy slammed into her from behind.

Riley dropped to the ground, and he pulled her back into the house by her hair. She screamed and kicked and clawed as he dragged her across the floor toward the kitchen.

Once inside, he let go of her head to grab the pistol off the counter. She rushed to her feet and grabbed his wrists as he fired two shots into the ceiling, then one into the wall. They struggled to the ground, causing the gun to slide across the floor.

He crawled on top of her and wrung his hands around her neck. She thrashed her arms, but his head was out of reach. Roy gritted his teeth and squeezed tighter until her consciousness faded into darkness.

Then a loud gunshot boomed above her head, and Roy fell back to the floor. Riley gasped for air as a pair of hands lifted her shoulders off the ground.

"Riley, are you okay?"

She looked up to Detective Hank Maloney and caught her breath. "I think so."

Roy was lying on the ground, holding his shoulder. Hank kicked his pistol away and took aim. "Get on your stomach, now! Hands outstretched to your sides, scumbag."

He rolled onto his stomach. Hank jammed his knee into Roy's lower back and cuffed his wrists together. "Don't give me a reason to put another one in you."

Hank rose to his feet and radioed dispatch. "1713, 10-1 shots fired. Officer down. I need an ambulance at West Polk and South Western." He kneeled beside her. "Help is on the way."

"How did you—why are you here?"

"A CI told me that during one of her drug pickups, she saw a detective that matched Roy's description. She said he was with some bikers. I logged her report in the system, but I left the detective part out. The next day, she was found strangled in her home."

"The girl you had on ice?"

"Yeah," Hank said, and extended his hand to lift her off the ground. "I'm not one to believe in conspiracies, but I don't believe in coincidences either. I've been shadowing Roy ever since. When I heard about your case and saw you two talking at the station, I couldn't tell if you were playing him or he was playing you."

"So that's why you interrupted our raid meeting. You wanted to know for sure."

"That's right."

"Why didn't you tell me?"

"Because I had no proof, but I hoped that you would eventually find the drugs and Roy's partners. And when you did, it would only be a matter of time before he slipped up. Even coldhearted bastards feel the heat."

"Thank you, Hank. I'm sorry to have suspected you."

"Don't mention it," he said, then crossed his arms and looked at Roy. "The way I see it, you were only doing what you were taught. Everyone is innocent..."

"But all of us are guilty," she concluded.

THIRTY-EIGHT

The next morning, Riley pulled into the station, sipping her cup of coffee. She'd only had a few hours of sleep after answering all of AID's questions about her relationship with Roy and the sequence of events that led to his shooting.

With Detective Maloney's testimony backing her own, it was easier to explain the situation. Their combined statements filled in any gaps internal affairs needed for their report and to clear her name. She knew no one in the department would speak about Roy or what happened to her. When a cop crossed the thin blue line, it gave them all a black eye.

She opened her car door and walked into the station. The bullpen was empty, as was Briggs's office. Desk phones were ringing, but no one was there to answer them. She entered the bullpen and looked around. At the end of the hall, there was a huddled mass of officers through the open conference room doorway. They were all facing the same direction, fixated on something across the room.

She moved around the outer walkway and approached the door to join them. Harrison darted from the conference room with his phone against his ear. "I need a tech team, ground support, and surveillance here as soon as possible."

"What's going on?" she asked.

He looked at her but didn't seem to recognize what she was saying. His disturbed expression made her heart race. "No. I don't have ninety minutes, I need them here now!"

"Harrison?"

He ignored her and walked toward the bullpen. "I don't care what other assignments they're on, this is our top priority."

Riley looked back at the conference room and entered through the crowded doorway. Once inside, she could see they were all watching the television, which was mounted to the wall. A news broadcast featured a live feed of Briggs. He was tied to a chair with a bleeding gash on his forehead and duct tape over his mouth. A digital clock with red numbers was counting down on the back wall above his head. 9:27:16 . . . 9:27:15 . . . 9:27:14 . . . 9:27:13 . . .

Riley dropped her coffee cup to the floor. A sudden shock of cold struck her core, leaving her breathless. The commander appeared to be in a dark room with industrial lighting overhead. The low-lighting picture grain made it difficult to tell if he was surrounded by dark walls or plastic tarp. He appeared conscious, although he wasn't looking around the room or at the camera. He seemed too afraid to look at whoever was standing in front of him, just beyond the frame.

A news reporter transitioned onto the left side of the screen and started talking, but the television was muted.

"Turn it up," Kurt said, from the side of the room. The volume on the television increased, along with the anchor's voice.

" . . . live feed we received this morning from the Sandman killer, responsible for the death of the late District Attorney Matthew Locke and several others. We are reluctantly showing you this footage at the behest of our network producers."

Deputy Chief Reyes barged into the room and stood next to Riley. She covered her mouth at the sight of the broadcast. "Oh my God."

"The Sandman's demands were clear," the news anchor said. "If we did not air the feed by 8 a.m. this morning, the man you are seeing on your screen would be executed. If at any time we cut away or end the transmission, he will be executed. If the police do not find him before the timer runs out, he will be executed. He has also demanded that we display a message, which we will now."

The news banner at the bottom of the screen changed.

CAN YOU SEE

Riley staggered out of the room in a daze and propped her hand against the wall to steady herself. A flush of adrenaline surged through her body. She squeezed her eyes, shaking her head in disbelief, trying to suppress all the dreadful thoughts of what might happen to Briggs.

"You okay?" a voice asked from beside her.

Riley opened her eyes to see Kurt. She pushed off the wall and stood up straight. "I'm fine."

Reyes entered the hallway. "Where's Agent Harrison?"

"He's in the bullpen," she said, and followed the deputy chief down the hall.

"I should have known something happened to him. He didn't come back after Locke's funeral. I thought he needed some time."

"None of us could have seen this coming," Kurt said.

Agent Harrison was pacing back and forth on his cell phone. "What else did the note say?" He listened for a response. "A federal agent will be there soon to collect it. Do not let anyone else touch it until they arrive. Is this a good number to call you back? Good, then keep this line open." He ended the call.

"What's happening?" Reyes asked, placing her hands on her hips.

"This morning, the network received a letter from the Sandman. It contained a note along with pictures of Briggs. I've contacted the Bureau to pull every available asset we have to get him back. A tech team should be here soon to help us trace the link of the live feed."

"How long does that take?" Riley asked.

"I don't know."

"Then we shouldn't rely on them," she warned, and turned to walk away.

"Where are you going?" Harrison asked.

"Rosehill Cemetery. That's where Briggs was last seen."

"Hold on, Detective."

She stopped, and Harrison walked up to her. "This is no longer your case. It's an FBI investigation."

"Briggs is like family. I'm not going to sit here and do nothing."

"I understand, but this killer is unpredictable. You may be walking into a trap."

"I can handle myself."

"No. It's just too risky."

"Then I'll go with her," Kurt offered.

Harrison contemplated for a moment. "Okay, but report what you find. Don't do anything else without my say."

"I will," she said, and walked with Kurt toward the back of the station and into the rear parking lot. They didn't share a word until they were alone in the car.

"I heard about last night," Kurt said. "I'm sorry about Roy."

"Me too," she said, and started the engine. She drove out of the parking lot and onto the interstate. Nothing about this case made sense. What was the motive? Why kill Johnny and the DA? Why take Briggs? Why taunt her with these messages? What was the connection? The longer she dwelled on the case, the more questions she had. "The night Holly was attacked. I think it was because of me, and I think this is too."

"What makes you say that?" Kurt asked.

"The Sandman could have killed Holly at any time, but he didn't. He only wounded her so that she would eventually slip on the stool and hang herself. I think he wanted me to see her die."

"Why would he want that?"

"I don't know."

"There was a case out in Texas," Kurt said slowly. "A mass shooting of twenty-six people, including an unborn child, during a Sunday prayer service. The church filmed their services so they can be broadcast over the internet. The gunman entered wearing tactical gear and a black mask to hide his face. He went from pew to pew, firing over seven hundred rounds for eleven minutes, pausing only to reload."

"What happened to him?"

"While leaving the church, he was confronted by a local resident who heard the shots from outside. The gunman was shot before fleeing the scene. He drove down the road and lost control of his vehicle before crashing it into a ditch. The gunman took his own life before he could be brought into custody." Kurt looked over at her from the passenger seat. "Sometimes there is no reason. No explanation. Just violence, for violence's sake. You should be ready for that possibility."

The clouds darkened overhead with a looming threat of rain. She took a drag of her e-cigarette. "You might be right, but regardless of his motivation, I'm not going to leave anything to chance. If there's a lead at the cemetery that will help me save Briggs, I'm going to find it."

THIRTY-NINE

Riley parked at Locke's gravesite and stepped out of her cruiser. The cemetery was empty save for a couple of mourning families across the field. She walked down the path to where Briggs's car would have been parked, looking for signs of blood or broken glass—anything that would indicate a struggle or a break-in. All she found was a crumpled carton of cigarettes, broken flowers, and an empty bottle of Jack Daniels.

"Doesn't look like there's anything to go on," Kurt said. "You'd think we'd see something. Tire marks, a dropped umbrella, something."

An icy breeze picked up, and Riley zipped her jacket. "There's nothing here. Let's go to the front. There should be a security office."

She got back into her cruiser with Kurt and drove to the front gate of the cemetery, which was surrounded by a two-story stone building wrapped in green vines and topped with medieval spires. She pulled over to the side of the road and parked in front of the customer center. The lights were on, and someone was inside.

When they entered the office, an overweight man in a fleece

sweater was on the phone. "Chuck, it's Paul. If you don't call me back, I'm going to have to let you go. This is your last warning." He hung up the phone and looked up at the detectives. "Sorry about that. I've got a groundskeeper that's been ducking my calls. How can I help you?"

"Yes, I'm Detective Walker with the Chicago Police Department. I noticed a security camera at the gate when I arrived. If you have recordings from the past twenty-four hours, I would like to see the footage."

The man crossed his arms. "I don't want any trouble, but the people that come here like their privacy. If you want to see the footage, you'll need a warrant."

"Is there a manager I can speak with?"

"I am the manager," he said, and leaned back in his seat. "What's this about, anyway?"

Kurt pulled out his cell phone and showed the manager the live newsfeed of Briggs tied to the chair. The countdown timer over his head had just dipped below eight hours and twenty minutes. "It's about this. You see that timer? Once it hits zero, he dies. He was last seen here, and you're obstructing our investigation. If you don't want trouble, I suggest you choose your next words carefully."

The man put his hands up. "Alright, alright, I get it. You don't have to tell me twice. The security office is on the other side of the building. Just head out the way you came in and go around. I'll radio Earl, our head of security, so he knows you're coming."

"Thank you," Riley said, and walked out of the office. She spotted another camera attached to the building, facing toward the cemetery. They walked across the road to the other side of the building, which had a door but no windows. She knocked twice, and a man with blond hair and a dark mustache answered. "Yes?"

"You Earl?" Kurt asked.

"Yes, come in." He led them inside to the small office space.

There were several monitors on the desk. Three of them were on, while two were off. "Paul said you want the footage of the front gate, right?"

"That's right. From the last twenty-four hours."

"No problem," Earl said, and sat in his desk chair. He turned on one of the monitors and logged on to the computer, opening a program which showed a grid of different security camera footage from all around the cemetery.

"How many cameras do you have?" she asked.

"Sixteen. Got a new system a couple years ago when vandals started tagging swastikas on Jewish tombstones."

Riley glanced at Kurt from the corner of her eye and saw his lips tighten into a frown.

"Are they all recording?"

"Yeah, they're all stored in this computer."

"How far back do they go?"

"A week. Then it starts to record over itself." Earl swiveled in his chair to face Riley. "What are you looking for?"

"There was a funeral for District Attorney Locke yesterday. I'd like to see the cars as they leave the cemetery."

"Shouldn't be a problem. We have one camera facing inside, on the front gate." Earl accessed the program and selected one of the live feeds, making it full screen. "What time was the funeral yesterday?"

"3:30, ended maybe around 5:00," she said.

Earl clicked a button on the screen, and the footage rewound. The screen grew dark as morning turned to night then brightened again. Riley saw a procession of cars leave the cemetery.

"That's it," she said. "Keep going to when they start to leave."

After the road became clear again, Earl hit the play button. The vehicles moved in real time. "What am I looking for?"

"A silver Cadillac sedan."

She let the feed play as groupings of vehicles left the cemetery, followed by a long, continuous line. After the flow slowed to a stop. Earl looked up from the monitor. "Well, that's it. I'm not seeing anything else."

"Just wait," she said. "I talked with him after the funeral. He should be coming soon." She waited several minutes before seeing another car, but it wasn't Briggs's silver Cadillac. It was a Ford SUV.

"You sure he drove out of here?" Earl asked.

"I was just up the road. His vehicle is no longer there. He left sometime after the funeral."

Just as she finished talking, the silver Cadillac came on the screen. She pointed to the monitor. "There, that's him."

Earl clicked a button on the program to rewind the feed. The Cadillac reversed back into the cemetery, and then he played the footage again. Riley waited until the camera had an unobstructed view of the vehicle. "Pause it."

Earl clicked the screen, and the image froze. She glanced at the timestamp: 5:13 p.m. Leaning forward, she inspected the image. The rain obscured the view, but she could clearly see Briggs's face in the driver's seat. "That's him." He was leaning forward with his head over the steering wheel. It appeared as if he were trying to get his face on camera. "Can you move the footage forward a couple of frames?"

"Sure," Earl said, and clicked a button on his keyboard. The car moved forward a couple feet. She leaned in again at Briggs's face. Why was he sitting like that? From what she could tell, he looked distressed. "Can you move it forward a couple more frames?"

Earl clicked his keyboard, and the vehicle came closer to the camera. A small object reflected in the light next to his head. "What is that?"

"I can't tell," Kurt said.

"Maybe it's the rear seatbelt?" Earl said.

"Move it forward again," Riley requested.

The vehicle moved closer to the camera, "I don't think it could go any further without him moving out of frame."

Riley placed her hand on the desk and inspected the screen. There was a dark silhouette in the back seat. She pointed at the monitor. "Can you enlarge the image?"

"Just a second," Earl responded, and clicked on the program. "The more I zoom in, the worse the quality will be."

He placed the cursor over Briggs's face and clicked. The image enlarged over that section. The details became blurred, but it was still clear enough to see. Someone in the back seat was holding a knife to the commander's head. The blade was reflecting in the windshield. She couldn't see their face, only their silhouette.

"Can you print this image?" she asked.

"Yeah, no problem," Earl said, and selected the print button on his keyboard.

"And can you zoom back out? I want to see something."

Earl reverted the screen to its original view. Riley radioed dispatch. "5215, I need a BOLO for a silver Cadillac sedan. License plate number: Two. Golf. Alpha. Tango. One, two, three."

"5215, 10-4. Putting out an APB for a silver Cadillac sedan. License plate number: Two. Golf. Alpha. Tango. One. Two. Three."

Earl handed her the printout. With the enlarged image, she could see more details in the car. Briggs was looking straight at the camera. He knew she would find the security footage once he had gone missing. She turned on a desk lamp and held the picture beneath the light. The hand holding the knife was pale. The rest of his body was hidden by the roof of the car. "You see that?"

"Yeah," Kurt said. "He must have broken into the back of Briggs's car during the funeral and ambushed him while he was leaving."

She looked at Earl. "Can you make a copy of this tape and all other feeds until two hours prior to the funeral?"

"Shouldn't be a problem, but it will take a while to download."

"How long?"

"Hard to say. It's a lot of footage you're asking for."

"We need it as soon as possible. We'll send someone to pick up," Riley said, then walked out of the security office with Kurt. She lifted her cell phone and called Harrison. The call rang twice, then went to his voicemail. He must have been busy on the other line. "This is Walker," she said. "I've got something. Call me back."

She hung up the phone and walked across the road back to her cruiser.

"Maybe we can use traffic cams to see where he went," Kurt said.

"Traffic cams only trigger for photos once a vehicle runs a red light. And even if they did record, it would be impossible to know which intersections to list on the warrant." Her cell phone rang in her jacket pocket, and she pulled it out. "Walker."

"It's Agent Harrison. I got your message. What did you find?"

"Briggs was ambushed in his car after the funeral. We have security footage of him leaving the cemetery with a knife to his throat. Looks like our killer is a white male."

"Could you see his face?"

"No, but I could see his hand holding the blade. He wasn't wearing gloves. I have a photo printout, and I'm having their head of security download the footage up to two hours before the funeral. It won't be ready for a while. Have the station send a unit to pick it up in an hour."

"What about you?"

"I want to check out Briggs's house. The killer stalks his victims before abducting them. I doubt taking Briggs at Locke's funeral was his first choice."

"All right. Just be careful, and call me if you find anything else."

"What's going on over there?"

"The tech team is setting up in the conference room. We tried pinging the commander's phone to the nearest cell tower, but it's turned off. We have the link to the live feed, and we're going to trace it soon. I've got to go. I have another call."

She hung up the phone and started the engine. "They're going to trace the live feed. Hopefully, they'll find out where he's broadcasting from and we can end this."

Riley drove through the front gate, looking up at the security camera as Briggs had. The thought of his desperate expression left a bad taste in her mouth.

FORTY

Riley turned onto West Fortieth Place in Brighton Park. The neighborhood was lined with single-family homes from the turn of the twentieth century. She drove past Briggs's address, a red brick two-story building with white-painted window frames.

"Wasn't that it?" Kurt asked.

"Yes, but I'm going to park down the road."

"Why?"

"There's been no hits on the APB I put out on Briggs's vehicle. That means his car is off the road. There's a chance it's parked in the garage out back and he's broadcasting from the home."

"Okay, how do you want to play it then?"

She drove to the end of the street, then turned left into a back alley between two buildings. The rear pathway led between the rows of homes and their detached garages. She pulled over and parked a few homes away from Briggs's property.

"We should call for backup," Kurt said.

"No. If the Sandman is in there, I don't want him to know we're coming. He might kill Briggs."

Kurt thought about it for a moment, then nodded. "Okay, then how do you want to play it?"

"We go in through the back. Check the garage first, and enter the house through the rear." Before he could respond, she got out of the cruiser and popped the trunk. Kurt joined her at the rear. "I still think we should call for backup. Things can get out of hand real quick. We don't know what he has planned, and we'd be alone."

"Every second that we spend arguing is another second wasted." She lifted a bulletproof vest from the trunk and offered it to him. "Now, are you going to help me or not?"

Kurt hesitated for a moment, then took the vest from her. "Okay, but I don't like it."

Riley removed her jacket, then lifted her vest over her head. Kurt did the same. Once they were ready, they walked down the pathway to Briggs's property. They rounded the side of his garage toward the backyard. The blinds on the first- and second-story windows were drawn shut.

"Okay, looks like we're good. Let's go," she said, and approached the garage door on the left side of the structure.

Kurt peeked through a small the window next to the door. "I see a car."

"Is it the Cadillac?"

"Looks like it," he said, and grabbed the door handle. "Ready?"

She nodded and raised her pistol. Kurt twisted the handle and pulled it open. Riley moved inside and scanned all sides of the garage. The room appeared empty. "Clear."

She holstered her pistol and approached the vehicle. Then she opened the driver's door and peered inside. There was nothing out of the ordinary. Everything appeared to be in place, with no signs of a struggle. Looking to the back seat, she didn't see anything. Riley climbed out of the car. "It's clean."

"Then he might not expect us yet," Kurt said. "He might still be in the house."

They walked out of the garage and across the backyard to the back door. Kurt reached for the handle, but Riley held out arm to stop him. "Wait."

"What?" He recoiled.

"I need to see something first," she said, and bent down to one knee. She leaned in and inspected the lock above the doorknob. There were numerous scratches in the metal, forming a U beneath the keyhole. She felt a churning in her stomach. There was nothing good on the other side of the door, but she needed to open it. She needed to save Briggs. "The lock has been picked. He was here. Ready?"

Kurt readied has pistol. "Yeah."

She twisted the handle and pushed through the door. They entered a narrow hallway that led to the kitchen and dining room. It was a stuffy space with low ceilings. Everything was enveloped in shadow, with a single window on the opposite end of the floor letting in gray light from outside. The house was silent, with no signs of life. Riley led the way through the house with her pistol aimed ahead of her.

Daylight reflected off a half-empty bottle of whiskey, which sat on a tray table next to a leather recliner. It was resting across from a large television and media cabinet. The room smelled of cigars and beer. She flipped on the light switch next to the doorway. No one.

Kurt tapped her shoulder from behind and motioned toward the stairs next to the front door. They continued through the room to the end of the stairwell. Riley crept up each step, trying to remain as quiet as possible. Her palms sweated against the grip of her pistol.

She ascended the stairs to the second story and aimed down both ends of the hall. The bedroom door was ajar, and she stepped inside. She looked around the room, but didn't see anyone. A double bed rested against the wall. Its sheets were tucked and neat. She crossed the room and opened the closet door. A rack of cheap suits and pre-knotted neck ties rested over wire hangers. She returned to the hall, where Kurt had remained. He pushed open the second bedroom door, and she followed him inside to find the guest bedroom was empty.

"Looks like no one's home," Kurt said, holstering his pistol.

"Then why would he break in through the back door?"

"Maybe he did it sometime earlier. He could have broken in days ago, but decided to take Briggs yesterday."

She walked down the stairs, considering his theory. The Sandman had stalked each of his victims before abducting them. It was more than likely that he'd broken into Briggs's house while the commander was at work. "Then why not take him from here? Why wait until Locke's funeral and risk the exposure?"

She entered the living room and looked at an old photo of Briggs in military fatigues. He must have been eighteen years old when the photo was taken. She looked at the next framed photograph on the shelf. Briggs was a little older, grinning from ear to ear with his arm wrapped around a beautiful woman with striking green eyes.

"That his wife?" Kurt asked.

"Rhonda. She passed away eight years ago. Cancer."

"That's rough. Any kids?"

"No," she said, and looked to the third photograph on the shelf. It was a picture of Briggs in a patrolman's uniform standing next to her father, David. They looked happy in the way some partners can be after years of serving together. She noticed they were carrying revolvers. This photo must have been taken when .38 Special was department-approved ammunition.

Kurt leaned in beside her. "Who is that?"

"My father," she said, and turned away from the photo. They

walked down the hall and out of the house. "I think I know why Briggs was abducted at the funeral and not from his home."

They continued across the backyard and entered the detached garage. Riley went into the Cadillac and reached across to the passenger glove box. Briggs's revolver was resting there. "He carried this everywhere he went. It would have been too risky to ambush him at home. He left it in the glove box before attending Locke's funeral. That's how the killer knew Briggs would be unarmed."

She rested the gun on the dashboard and radioed the station, canceling the APB order and requesting a forensic team to come to Briggs's address. The Sandman wasn't wearing gloves in the security image she'd collected from the cemetery, so his fingerprints must have been on the back seat of the car.

Riley called Harrison, and this time he answered on the second ring.

"Harrison, it's Walker. I'm at Briggs's house."

"Did you find anything?"

"I did. His vehicle is parked in the garage. It looks like the Sandman had him drive home before switching vehicles. Forensics are on their way to dust it for prints."

"Was there anything inside the house?"

"No. The house is empty. I didn't see any signs of a disturbance."

"What about messages?"

"None."

"All right. Come back to the station when you're done. Maybe we can figure something else out."

"What about the trace? Any progress on that?"

"The team found out he's using an overlay network to anonymize the source of the feed. They're trying to narrow it down, but it will take time."

"How much time?"

"I can't say for certain. They're still unpacking the amount of relays. The signal is bouncing through hundreds of servers all over the country."

She felt a dull ache in her chest. "Will they be able to find him in time?"

"They're doing all they can. I'll call you back if anything changes."

Riley hung up the phone and explained the situation to Kurt. He shared her pessimism. "There must be something else we can do. They'll never track down the source in time."

"There's nothing else we can do. We'll just have to wait for forensics to get here." She smoked her e-cigarette and ruminated about the case. How long had he been planning this, and to what end? What did he have to gain by causing so much suffering?

These questions and many more plagued her mind for the next hour until the team arrived. Sergeant Berns stood in the garage's doorway, carrying a plastic case. "Is that the car?"

"Yes, it is," Riley said, pocketing her e-cigarette. "I need you to dust for prints in the back seat."

Berns set the case down next to the car and opened it. "No problem."

"Is it just you?" Kurt asked.

"No, Rahul should be here in a minute to take photos." He retrieved a jar of black latent print powder and a fiber brush. "What side was he sitting on?"

"Left side, behind the driver."

The sergeant dusted the left passenger door handle. Rahul entered the garage with his camera draped around his neck. He walked past Kurt and begin taking photos of the vehicle. "Did you find the gun on the dashboard?"

"No," she said. "It was in the glove box."

"I'll have to note that in my report," Rahul acknowledged out loud. "Did you move anything else?"

"No."

He leaned over the windshield and took a photo of Briggs's revolver.

"I'm not getting anything off the door handle," Berns said. "It looks like he wiped it down before he left. I'll try inside." He reached into his kit and grabbed another jar of white latent powder. This would make fingerprints stand out against the dark leather interior. He opened the rear passenger door and began dusting the inside handle and back seat. Rahul continued walking around the car, taking photos.

"There are markings on the lock to the back door of the house. You should capture that as well," she said.

"Thanks. I'll get to it after the car." Sergeant Berns stopped dusting. "Are you sure he wasn't wearing gloves?"

Riley pulled the security image from her pocket and showed it to him. "Yes, I'm certain."

"Okay, let me try one more thing," he said, and grabbed another jar of fluorescent powder and a portable UV light. He leaned into the car and dusted everything again. Then he shined the light over the back seat. "I don't believe this."

"What?" she asked.

"See for yourself."

Riley looked into the car's interior as Sergeant Berns held the light. There were dozens of hand impressions on the backseat— all of which contained outer ridges, but none with a core. There were no traces of arches, loops, or whorls. It was as if the skin had been peeled off the center of each finger.

"How is that possible?" Kurt asked.

"I don't know," Berns admitted. "I've never seen anything like it before."

FORTY-ONE

Five unmarked black SUVs with government plates occupied the front of the station's parking lot.

"Looks like they've brought an entire squad," Kurt said. Riley took a drag of her e-cigarette. "Let's just hope they've found more than we did."

She stepped out of her cruiser and walked across the parking lot to the station. A rustling of foot traffic filled the hall as twenty FBI agents in matching blue windbreakers moved about the department. They had occupied half of the desks within the bullpen and put them together into clusters of two and four. All department computers had been replaced with their own military-spec workstations that were built into protective cases. They created a network of cables that connected to a central hub in the middle of the room.

Riley walked around the edge of the bullpen through a herd of federal agents to the conference room. It had been converted into a command center, with groups manning the desks and coordinating their efforts to find Briggs. Harrison was at the edge of the room watching the television screen. The commander was still bound in the chair. The red digital clock was almost down to four and a half hours.

She walked over to him. "Anything new?"

"Not yet. They're still trying to narrow down the location. What about you?"

Riley handed Harrison the security image she recovered from the cemetery, "We got the car, but no prints. Did you get the footage from the cemetery?"

"It was dropped off a half hour ago. We have a couple agents going through it in the other room. It's a lot of footage to comb through."

"Then I'll help them out," Kurt said, and walked out of the conference room. Riley looked up at the screen and shuddered. Watching the clock tick down was like waiting for an execution.

"I hate this."

"We're doing everything we can to get him back."

"I know you are. I'm just afraid it won't be enough," she said, and walked back to her desk in the bullpen. She pulled open her drawer to review her case file, but remembered it had been taken by Agent Harrison and the FBI. She closed the drawer, then logged on to her computer and searched the department's database for keywords relating to her case.

She typed in "eyes" and "mutilated" into the search bar. A list of police reports filled her screen, hundreds of cases dating back to the 1970s. She selected the first link in the catalogue, titled "Jane Doe: September 12, 2018."

The screen loaded a digitized police report, including a crime scene photograph of an unidentified young blonde girl. Her body had washed up against the creek bed of the Des Plaines River. Cause of death was drowning, although the circumstances of her death remain unknown. The medical examiner concluded that her eyes, ears, and tongue had been eaten by aquatic life prior to recovery. Riley shifted in her seat, then returned to the list.

She skimmed through the catalogue until she found one titled "Father John Blackwell: February 12, 2004." She clicked on the link. A photograph showed Father Blackwell standing behind three young altar boys. The next photograph showed the father's disfigured corpse abandoned in a dumpster. The report stated that during a neighborhood barbecue, the boys had confessed to being molested by Blackwell. That same night, their three dads had kidnapped Blackwell and tortured him until sunrise. His wounds included eye gouging, castration, and third-degree burns from a blowtorch. They were each convicted of murder in the first degree.

Riley returned to the list and reviewed each case one by one: Domestic abuse, armed drug store robbery, drive-by shooting, animal cruelty, fatal carjacking, police raid gone awry, infant found in gutter, homeless woman attack, kidnapping victim, rape victim, gang killing, home burglary and assault. She until her eyes hurt from looking at the screen. Each report was more depraved than the one before, and none appeared to be connected to her case.

Leaning back in her chair, Riley combed her fingers through her hair. The worst part about these reports was the aftermaths. Most cases were unsolved, with no follow-up or closure for the victims. The database was an accumulation of tragic events to be indexed and filed away until the end of time.

"Walker," a voice called out to her.

She sat up and looked towards Briggs's office to find Reyes standing in the doorway. Riley rose from her seat and walked over.

"Come in," the deputy chief said, and closed the door behind her. "Take a seat."

Riley sat in one of the armchairs across from Briggs's desk. Reyes pulled a bottle of bourbon and two glasses from a side drawer. She poured into each of the glasses and offered one to Riley. "You look like you could use a drink."

She took the glass and finished it in one gulp. "Thanks."

Reyes did the same, then wiped her mouth. "I know you and Briggs have history. He's a good man and an even better commander. He understands the importance of what we're doing here."

Riley looked up to her. "Yeah? And what's that?"

Reyes took Riley's glass and refilled it. "Chaos is the law of nature. Has been since the beginning of time. We maintain order." She handed the glass back. "I see a lot of potential in you, Riley. You're smart, persistent. I know you want to rejoin the Violent Crimes Task Force, but you could do so much more. Someone with your determination could end up running the department one day—with the right guidance, of course."

"You mean from someone like you?"

"Yes, and I can make it happen, but first I need to know you can toe the line. I can't have anyone going rogue under my watch."

"What do you need?"

"This investigation belongs to the FBI. I want you to stay out of it. When it fails, I want the department to distance itself from the fallout."

"It's not going to fail. We still have time."

"There's only two hours left, and the FBI's technicians are no closer to finding Briggs than when they started. I know you don't want to hear this, but it's the truth."

Riley looked down. She had lost track of time while researching the other cases on the CPD database.

"We can do great things together. I've had conversations with Ryan Baum's campaign team. If Mayor Cox loses this election, there's going to be a lot of changes around here."

Riley stood up and handed back her glass. "Thanks for the drink, but I'll pass."

"You're making a big mistake." Reyes scowled.

"Maybe, but I'll be damned if I don't do everything I can to save him."

She turned away and walked out of the office to the conference room. Harrison was standing behind an FBI tech, looking over his shoulder.

"How's the search going?" she asked.

"The team is getting close. We think the feed is coming from somewhere near the Lower West Side." She looked at the monitor screen. There was a map of Chicago with a large green circle over the bottom left-hand region. "Looks like the Heart of Chicago, Little Village, or McKinley Park. There are hundreds of buildings he could be in. How much longer do they need until they have an address?"

"I can't say for sure, but they're going as fast as they can. Just give them time."

"We don't have time!"

Everyone in the room stopped what they were doing and looked at her. Agent Harrison placed his hands on his hips. "I think it's time for you to go."

She walked out of the room and down the hallway toward the bullpen. Reyes was right—they were never going to reach Briggs in time. Riley felt a flutter in her chest that made her skin crawl. Her cell phone vibrated in her pocket. She pulled it out and answered it. "Detective Walker."

She waited for a response, but heard only breathing on the other end of the line.

"Who is this?"

The breathing morphed into a low crackle. "Can you see?"

She stopped in her tracks with a sudden shock that left her breathless. A flush of adrenaline surged through her body, and she turned away from the commotion within the bullpen. "What do you want?"

"Damen Silos. Come alone."

"And if I don't?"

"He dies."

The call ended. She looked at her phone's screen for the call-back number, but it was blocked. He must have taken her contact information from Briggs's cell phone.

Riley went to the bullpen and removed her jacket from the back of her chair. Kurt walked up to her. "We've been through the footage twice. No sign of our guy. He must have entered the cemetery sooner than two hours before the funeral." He paused, noticing what she was doing. "Where are you going?"

She put on her jacket. "The FBI has narrowed down the signal to the Lower West Side. I'm heading out so once they have an address, I'll already be down there."

"Want me to come with you?"

"No. Reyes and the FBI don't want me involved. I need you to tell me the address once they have it."

"All right then," he said.

"If anything else happens, call me," she said, and continued to the back of the station. She walked across the parking lot and entered her cruiser. Gripping the steering wheel, she looked back at the station, considering whether to tell Kurt where she was going and the danger she was putting herself in.

No, it was too risky. Riley needed to do this on her own. She started her cruiser and drove out of the parking lot toward the Damen Silos.

FORTY-TWO

Riley parked her cruiser on West Twenty-Ninth Street, just beyond the gate surrounding the abandoned silos. The two-centuries-old, dilapidated buildings were surrounded by a barren field of concrete rubble and decaying warehouses. She considered calling Kurt again, but decided against it. The Sandman had told her to come alone, and she didn't want to jeopardize Briggs's life. She stepped out of the cruiser and gathered her bulletproof vest and flashlight from the trunk. When she was ready, she approached the front entrance, where the two fences were held together by a rusted padlock and chain, then squeezed through the gap.

Each of the concrete silo buildings were over eight stories tall and bridged to a tower that was even larger. She approached the closest building and looked for an entrance with her flashlight. The cement walls were covered in layers of graffiti and reddish-brown water stains. She walked around the perimeter of the building, but there was no entrance in sight. When she crossed the dirt road between the structures, her cell phone rang in her jacket pocket. "Detective Walker."

"They found Briggs's location," Kurt said. "He's at a warehouse near the corner of Forty-Seventh and St. Louis."

She looked toward the south. The intersection was several minutes away from her location. "Are you sure?"

"Yeah, the FBI techs were able to pinpoint the source of the live feed. We have a SWAT team and police units on their way now."

If Briggs was at a different location, then why would the Sandman lead her here? She looked ahead to the next building and saw a large opening in one of the concrete silos. Above it was the horrible, familiar message, written in blood.

"Keep me updated," Riley said, and approached the opening. She shined her flashlight into a large, circular room that was seven feet below ground. The floor was littered with trash and dirt, and the walls were covered with graffiti. She ducked through the opening and leaped inside.

The ceiling was made up of a rusted grain silo which funneled to the center of the room. Across from her was a dark corridor that extended hundreds of feet throughout the length of the building. She raised her pistol and followed it to the next silo room. Broken glass crunched beneath her boots. The floor had a grimy, sewer-like odor. She scanned the room from side to side and continued farther into the corridor. The temperature dropped with each step.

Riley entered the third silo room, and a pair of rats scurried from her light beam into a heap of plastic tubing.

"Can you see?" someone said from the darkness. His voice echoed in all directions.

Riley glanced back to make sure he wasn't behind her, then crept forward to the next silo room. She struggled to hold her gun steady as her heart pounded against her chest. He could be anywhere, waiting for her. Rusted pipes and chains extended from the damaged funnel, its slats hanging suspended in the air. She looked back again to make sure he wasn't behind her. The opening she had entered through was now hidden beyond her flashlight's beam. Proceeding around the pipes, Riley went through the next doorway.

The fifth silo room was cluttered with scrap metal, flattened cardboard boxes, and plastic bags. She scanned the room, then continued. The corridor led to a large room with ventilator shafts and exposed rebar from where the ceiling had caved in. A pile of rubble sloped up to a crevice on the roof that was large enough for a small animal to crawl through. She beamed her light across the room to another open doorway.

"I'll show you," the Sandman invited from within.

She followed his voice through the doorway to a staircase that descended farther underground into a black chasm. She crept down the rickety metal steps one by one to the bottom level, which was flooded with brown, murky water. The underground passage was connected to a series of parallel tunnels along the left wall. Water dripped from cracks in the ceiling where the building had settled. She entered the passageway and aimed down each of the tunnels she crossed. Empty spray cans and bits of wood floated over the water. Her flashlight began to flicker. She stopped and shook it until the beam steadied.

"Do you know why I take the eyes?"

The tunnels rumbled with his voice. She turned around, then turned back and waited for the sound to fade. It was impossible to hear where his voice originated from. She continued through the passageway and neared a tunnel with a raised walkway. Decrepit trolly cart tracks led farther into the darkness.

"You will," he said.

She followed the tracks while trying to remain as quiet as possible. The tunnel was full of rusted pipes, broken planks, and trash. The cold cement walls were slimy with mold and algae. Cobwebs dangled above her head. Riley passed several discarded pallets and a rotting mattress, then proceeded farther into the dark cavern.

She stopped beneath another silo funnel and found a pathway that led across each of the tunnels. Her flashlight began to flicker, then shut off. Everything became pitch-black. She shook her flashlight, but it didn't turn on.

"I'll show you the world for what it truly is," the man whispered in front of her.

She took a step back and aimed her pistol into the darkness. Her arm swayed from left to right as she listened for movement. The eerie silence made her skin crawl. A putrid smell of rotten meat lingered all around her. He was coming closer—she could feel it. Her grip tightened, and she took another step back against the concrete wall.

Without knowing where he was, there was nowhere she could run. Riley clenched her jaw to steady her breathing, smacking the flashlight against her thigh until it flickered back to life. She raised the beam and caught a glimpse of him moving across the pathway three tunnels ahead of her.

Riley chased after him and aimed her pistol into the tunnel. He ran the front of the corridor, then continued up the flooded passageway. She followed his path to a second staircase that led up to the base of the silo tower. Moonlight streamed into the L-shaped stairwell from the upper levels. Looking up, she saw him rush into a doorway on the eighth floor.

Riley pulled out her cell phone and called the station. "This is Detective Walker. I'm in pursuit of a homicide suspect. Send backup to the Damen Silos on West Twenty-Ninth Street."

"Dispatching all available units to your location now."

She pocketed her cell phone and climbed the steps while aiming her pistol up the stairwell. When she rounded the fifth-floor platform, one step gave out beneath her. She grabbed the handrail to stop herself from falling through. The broken step crashed against the lower levels, then landed on the concrete floor. Riley regained her balance on the next step, then continued up to the eighth floor.

A greenish-blue glow emanated from within the doorway. She leaned against the wall, then peeked down a long hallway that extended over each of the silos. Blown-out windows on both sides of the floor gave a sweeping view of the city below. The man was facing two computer monitors at a makeshift table in the center of the room. She entered the doorway and took aim.

"Hands up! Step away from the computer!"

He raised his hands and stepped back. A red digital clock on the table was counting down from two minutes. She closed the gap between them. "Get down on your knees! Hands on your head."

The man lowered himself to the ground and interlocked his fingers with slow, fluid movements. Bloodstains covered the sleeves of his dark gray jumpsuit. She unclipped the handcuffs from her belt and secured his wrists behind his back. He reeked of death and chemicals. She patted his sides and pulled a bloody folding knife from his pocket. An icy chill coursed through her veins as she gazed upon his gaunt face. Dark, bullet-sized pupils marked her for death. "You're running out of time."

She placed the knife on the table and looked at the two monitors. The left showed the live feed of Briggs strapped to the chair, and the right showed a group of five SWAT officers trapped in a small room. They pounded against a steel door as another digital clock counted down above their heads. 00:01:26 . . . 00:01:25 . . . 00:01:24 . . . An illuminated toggle switch rested beneath each monitor. They were both wired to a laptop and transmitter that was powered by a suitcase-sized portable generator under the table.

"What is this?" she said.

"You've known it your whole life, you just couldn't see."

She turned around to face him. "Where's Briggs?"

He stared up at her with a predatory smile. "He's close, but you'll never find him in time. The only way you're going to save any of them is by making a choice. Stop one bomb, and the other will detonate. Do nothing, and everyone dies."

She returned to the table in a panic. The digital clock was almost down to one minute. There had to be some other way, but nothing came to mind. She opened the laptop, but the screen was password protected. Emergency lights flashed on the road below. Two police units pulled up to the fence surrounding the property. She watched the monitors as Briggs struggled to get out of his seat. The SWAT members started shooting at the steel door, but to no avail. She turned around and grabbed him by the collar. "Tell me how to stop it!"

"Stop it?" he asked. "What's the point of a bomb if it doesn't explode?"

She drew her pistol and aimed at his head. "Tell me!"

He pressed his face against the barrel. "They're going to die, and there's nothing you can do to stop it."

She pulled away and pistol-whipped him across the jaw. He fell back against the floor and spat out a rotten tooth. Blood dripped from his lips as he laughed. "That's it, let it out. Now you'll see, everything leads to ruin."

She looked at the monitors and trembled. Thirty seconds. A tightness in her chest made it difficult to breathe. Waves of heat and adrenalin surged through her body. She placed both hands on the table to steady herself. He was right, there was nothing she could do. By choosing to save one, she would condemn the other to death. It would be murder.

Riley looked at the clock above Briggs's head. Twenty seconds. She yanked every cable attached to the laptop and smashed the transmitter on the ground. Each of the monitors cut to black. She ran to the broken windowsill and peered out to the city.

A thunderous explosion erupted in the distance, followed by a second detonation in the warehouse below the silo tower. It mushroomed into a fireball toward the sky. The heat of the blast caused her to step back from the window. Everything was engulfed in flame, and the Sandman's cries of laughter turned manic.

FORTY-THREE

A grouping of police vehicles, ambulances, and fire trucks surrounded the entrance of the Damen Silos as Riley led the Sandman out of the building by the arm. He hadn't uttered a word since the bombs exploded. Several news vans approached the scene and parked beyond the yellow police tape that blocked off the end of the street. Riley guided him across the lot to the nearest police unit and placed him in the back seat. She slammed the door shut and ordered an officer to take him to the station for processing. The Sandman stared at her from the back seat, smiling as they drove away.

Riley turned around and watched the flames consume the warehouse. Tiny flakes of ash fell all around her. She drew near the burning inferno and felt a sudden ache in her heart that quickly turned to tears down her cheeks.

Dropping to her knees, she wept for Briggs. She had failed him. She had failed all of them. Everyone was dead because of her, and there was nothing she could do to make it right. Riley leaned forward with quaking shoulders and wailed. Her body shook with the force of her anguished cries as she watched the firefighters, half-hidden in smoke and dust, try to extinguish the raging flames.

An EMT lifted her off the ground. "Are you hurt?"

"No," Riley said, and trudged back to her cruiser. She collapsed into the driver's seat and wiped the tears from her hot, gummy eyelids. She wished she'd had the strength to make a different choice. Emergency personnel approached her cruiser, but she waved each of them away. She took a drag, but the flashing red light at the end of the stick indicated it was out of juice. Riley leaned forward and retrieved her emergency cigarette carton from beneath the driver's seat. Her hand trembled as she stuck one between her lips. She thumbed the lighter's wheel, but the spark didn't catch.

"Damn it!"

Riley threw the lighter against the dashboard, then pounded the steering wheel over and over until her fist bruised. Tears streamed down her cheeks as she fell back against her seat and wept. She recalled the fateful night when her parents were murdered and she was left frightened in the dark. The closet door opened, and Briggs reached down to lift her into the light.

"Don't be scared," he said. "You're safe now."

There was a knock on the driver's window. She wiped the tears from her face and looked up to see Harrison, Reyes, and Kurt. She opened the door and stepped out of the cruiser to join them.

"Is it true?" the deputy chief asked. "Has the Sandman been arrested?"

"Yes," she said, with a sore throat. "I sent him away in one of the units to be processed."

"What happened?" Harrison asked.

"He called my cell phone and told me to come alone, otherwise he'd kill Briggs."

"When?"

"Before I left the station," she admitted.

290

"You could have told us," Reyes fumed. "You put this entire investigation—"

Harrison raised a hand to interject. This was his inquiry, and he wasn't going to let her derail it. Reyes stopped talking, then backed off. The agent looked at Riley. "Go on."

She hesitated to proceed. Any information she gave could be used against her by Reyes. "I found an opening on one of the silos. Once inside, I followed a corridor that led deeper underground. There's a series of tunnels beneath us that connect between the two silo buildings. He was there, waiting for me."

"Then what happened?"

"I pursued him through the tunnels and up the tower. I cornered him on the upper level, but by the time I arrested him, it was too late. There was nothing I could do to stop it."

Kurt's eyes narrowed, but he didn't say anything. Harrison crossed his arms, "Did he give a reason why he contacted you?"

Riley wiped her cheeks again and sniffled. "He said he wanted to show me the world for what it truly is. Then the bombs went off."

"So you know about the SWAT team?" Harrison asked.

"On the upper floor of the tower he had a laptop and a couple of monitors on a table. I saw everything."

"Is Briggs . . . gone?" Reyes asked.

Riley nodded to confirm. She couldn't bring herself to say it.

"Did he say anything else or give any indication of other bombs?" Harrison asked.

"No," she nodded. "That's it."

"I'll have FSD comb through the laptop," Reyes said. "If anything is on there, they'll find it."

"This is still a federal investigation," Harrison contended. "All evidence will be collected by the Bureau."

"Of course," the deputy chief said.

The FBI agent stepped closer to Riley and looked her in the

eye. "I know this is difficult for you, but we need to know everything we can to be sure this is over. A lot of people have died already, and there could be others in danger that we don't know about yet."

"He didn't say anything."

"All right then." He nodded, and rested a hand on her shoulder. "I know it doesn't feel like it right now, but you did good. You collared him—that's what matters."

She glanced over to eight firefighters as they sprayed the warehouse flames, "You're right, it doesn't feel like it."

"Give it some time and it will. I promise," Harrison said, then signaled for several FBI agents to investigate the silo tower. He grouped together with them and entered the building.

Reyes approached Riley, glaring. "There's nothing more you can do here. Go back to the station and draft your statement. Be sure not to skimp on any details. I have to discuss this with the chief, and the department will need to make a press statement first thing tomorrow morning."

"I will."

Reyes leaned in close to her. "I don't care what the feds say. The moment your call ended, you should have informed us what was going on. You may have caught him, but I won't forget this."

She pulled out her cell phone and walked away to make a call. Riley felt a sudden chill and crossed her arms. "You were right about him. The Sandman is insane."

"I'm not so sure anymore," Kurt said, placing his hands on his hips.

She turned to him. "What do you mean?"

"It could have been us in that warehouse tonight. If he wanted us dead, we would be. But instead, he contacted you. After all I've seen with Locke, Williams and Holly, I don't think the Sandman does anything unless it's planned."

"What are you suggesting?"

"That there's more to what happened here than you're letting on."

"I told you everything."

"You're a terrible liar," Kurt said, then stepped closer to her. "Reyes and Harrison might buy that, but I don't. He didn't call you and bring you all the way out here just to watch everyone die."

"I'm telling you, there isn't."

"The Sandman hasn't left so much as a fingerprint at any crime scene we've investigated. Why would he expose himself to capture now unless he had something to gain?"

There was a long pause as she considered how to respond, "I . . . I don't know." She turned away from him to get back into her cruiser.

Kurt grabbed her by the arm and pulled her toward him. "Why won't you tell me?"

"Because it's my fault!"

He let go of her and took a step back. "What do you mean?"

"He gave me a choice. Save Briggs or save the other officers. Whichever I chose, the other would die. That's why he called me here. To turn me into a murderer." She felt tears run down her cheeks again. "But I couldn't do it. I couldn't make that choice, and now they're all dead because of me."

Kurt ran his finger through his hair and took a moment to process what she had admitted. "It didn't have to be that way. You could have told me. I asked you at the station if you wanted me to come with you, and you said no."

"It's not that simple. If anyone showed up other than me, Briggs would have been killed. There was nothing I could do."

Kurt frowned and shook his head. "That's not true, and you know it. We could have worked together. We could have figured something out, but you decided to go alone."

She hung her head. "Are you going to tell the others?"

"No," he said. "But I can't work with someone who only trusts themselves. If you still have an opportunity to join the Violent Crimes Task Force once this is finished, I suggest you take it."

"I understand."

Kurt turned away from her and joined the crowd of emergency responders. Riley wiped another tear from her cheek, then entered the cruiser to drive back to the station alone.

FORTY-FOUR

Hushed conversations filled the bullpen as Riley drafted her report of the Sandman's arrest. She looked up from her desk to see a couple of FBI agents looking at her from the next row. They turned away and continued watching the live news coverage of the bombings on their computer screens.

Word of her involvement had traveled through the ranks and spread to every officer and agent in the building. Riley rubbed her throat and returned to writing her account of the night's events. Her mind was plagued with haunting recollections. Briggs's frightened face, the Sandman's shrieking laughter, and the burning warehouse. She wanted to forget all of it, but knew she never would.

Reyes approached her desk. "I need you to come with me."

"Is everything all right?"

"I'll tell you on the way."

She rose from her desk and followed the deputy chief out of the bullpen and down the hall of interview rooms. "What's going on?"

Reyes handed her a fingerprint sheet. The individual markers were smeared with black ink blotches. "He chemically burned the surface of his hands and feet. That's why he never left a print."

"What about clothing?"

"FSD has it now. His worker's uniform appears secondhand. The lengths of the sleeves and pant legs were short on him. There was a name patch sewn onto the left breast pocket—'Charles.' Mean anything to you?"

Riley thought for a moment, then shook her head. "No."

Reyes frowned. "Agent Harrison has been with him for the last hour, but he didn't say a word until five minutes ago."

"He ask for a lawyer?"

"No, he asked for you." Reyes opened the viewing room door. Chief Benedict and Kurt were standing in front of the two-way mirror observing the next room. Riley entered and looked through the glass. The Sandman was seated in the middle of the room with his wrists shackled to the table. The short sleeves of his detainee shirt revealed dozens of scars along each of his arms.

"Someone do that to him?" she asked.

"He has markings like that all over his body. The booking nurse said they're self-inflicted. He's been cutting himself for years."

"Why does he want to talk to me?"

The chief turned to her. "He offered to give a confession, but he'll only talk to you."

"No," she blurted. "I won't do it. We have plenty of evidence already. We don't need his confession."

"Yes, we do," Reyes objected. "Look at him. Without a confession, a defense attorney could easily bargain an insanity plea."

"This is ridiculous," Kurt said. "He's toying with us."

"You might be right," Reyes said. "But a confession is the only way we can guarantee he gets locked away for good."

"I'll take my chances," Riley said.

"If not for yourself, then do it for Frank," Benedict said. "I know he meant a lot to you. He meant a lot to me too. We came up together. Please, don't let him off easy."

She thought about Briggs struggling to free himself from the chair. She clenched her fists as her heart began to race. "All right, I'll do it."

The chief pressed an intercom button on the wall. Agent Harrison lifted the case file from the interview table and exited the room. The Sandman didn't lift his gaze from the table.

Riley lifted her gun from its holster and set it on a side table. "Has he been like that the whole time?"

"Hasn't moved a muscle. Just sat there staring at his hands," Kurt informed.

Agent Harrison entered the viewing room. "I can't get a read on him. Are you going in there?"

"Yeah," she confirmed.

"I don't know what kind of game he's playing, but he asked to speak with you for a reason. Don't give him anything. Just stick to his confession."

"I will," Riley said, and walked out of the viewing room. She approached the two guards standing on either side of the next doorway.

"If you need us, just call," one guard offered. "We'll be right here."

Riley entered the interview room and closed the door behind her. The Sandman's gaze rose from the table, and his busted lips curled into a twisted grin. "Hello, Detective."

"Why are you doing this?"

"If you have to ask, then you still can't see."

She glanced at the two-way mirror, then took her seat across from him, "Then help me understand. I get why you would kill

297

Johnny and Zeke, but going after Locke, Williams, Holly? What's the point?"

"The point is, there is no point. Look around. Police corrupt justice, press distort facts, politicians betray trust, priests pervert morals, leaders become cowards, and we descend further and further every day."

Riley clasped her hands together over the table. "People can make a difference. It's monsters like you that deserve to die in a six-by-nine cell. They're going to bury you under the prison."

He let out a high-pitched cackle. "Of all the lies we tell ourselves, you think you're making the world a better place? You're like Sisyphus, endlessly rolling a rock up a hill just to watch it fall down again. And you know what they say about insanity?" He leaned forward, chains rattling against the steel table. "How many more people need to die before you see that in this world, nothing is sacred and no one is saved?"

"You're right." Riley nodded. "It is a foul world, full of pain and suffering. I gaze into that abyss with every victim I come across, but the difference between me and you is, when the abyss gazed back, I didn't flinch."

"You think you know suffering?" he growled. "I have so much in store for you."

She rose from her seat and walked toward the door. "I doubt you'll be doing much of anything now. You're finished."

"That's funny, the old man said the same thing . . ."

Riley stopped.

"He had such high hopes you would save him."

She turned around, and felt her fists clench at her sides.

"He struggled at first, of course, but like the others, it didn't take long for him to break. We got to know each other really well." He tilted his head to the side. "Poor little Riley, all alone again. Does it haunt you? All those lives you could have saved. Do you see their faces? Can you hear their screams?"

She lunged across the room and grabbed him by the shirt. She cracked her fist against his face, pummeling him again and again. "You sick freak!"

Between blows, he started laughing. The two guards burst into the room, followed by Reyes, Harrison, and Kurt. They grabbed each of her arms and dragged her across the room. "I'll kill you!"

The Sandman smiled with a mouth full of blood. "I'm already dead."

The guards dragged her into the hallway and pinned her against the wall. She thrashed to break free of their grip. "Let me go!"

"That's enough!" Reyes ordered. "Stop resisting, or I'll have you detained."

Riley's pulse was pounding in her ears. The deputy chief glared at her. She took several deep breaths to steady herself. "I'm good."

Reyes nodded for the guards to release her, and they did. She rubbed her wrists and caught her breath.

"Any chance we can still use his confession?" Kurt asked.

"Even if we edit the video, the court will want to see the whole thing," Chief Benedict replied.

"It was a mistake to have you go in there," Agent Harrison said. "I'm sorry."

"Me too," she said, rubbing the blood from her trembling knuckles. He had gotten under her skin and clawed his way to the bone. It wasn't just a momentary lapse of judgment—she had lost herself.

Kurt leaned against the wall next to her. "The good thing about bringing in a roughed-up scumbag is no one's going to question a few more bruises. Lord knows it's the least I would have done to him. You good?"

"I'm fine."

"What do you want to do with him?" Reyes asked Benedict.

"Hold him overnight. First thing in the morning, we'll have a press conference and file charges. I don't want him talking to anyone else until then."

"That won't be a problem," Reyes assured, then looked at Riley. "Is your statement ready?"

"It's in the system."

"Good," she said. "We'll handle it from here. Why don't you go home and get some rest? Be back here tomorrow morning for the conference."

Riley walked to the end of the hall and through the rear exit.

"Hey," a voice called out to her. She turned around to find Harrison coming towards her. He extended his arm and handed back her pistol. "You don't want to forget this."

She took it and added it to her belt. "Thanks."

"Those things you said in there,—did you mean them?"

"I did."

He put his hands in his pockets. "There's a story about a group of rabbis that put God on trial during the holocaust. Because of all the horrors they endured in Auschwitz, they charged God with breaking his covenant and forsaking his chosen people. Arguments from both sides were scrutinized and debated at length for three days. By the end of the hearing, the rabbis found him guilty, and afterwards they left together to pray." He looked her in the eye. "I know that darkness you carry. It's the price we pay for making things right. It never goes away, but you don't need to fight it alone."

She nodded. "Are you going to stay for the press conference?"

"No," he said, checking his watch. "I'm needed back in DC. I have to catch the red-eye tonight."

"Why so soon?"

"There are a lot of monsters in the world. It was nice to meet you, Riley. Take care of yourself out there."

"You too."

He started walking back.

"Why do you do it?" she called out. "Why fight?"

"Because I hate evil," Harrison said, then entered the station.

Riley slid into her white Mustang and drove out of the parking lot.

FORTY-FIVE

Streetlights blurred through the streaks of rain on her windshield. Riley turned on the car's wipers and examined the back of her hand. Dry blood surrounded the cuts on her knuckles. She was too shaken by the night's events to feel anything, but knew the pain would set in soon. Leaning her elbow on the driver's door, Riley propped her head against her hand. Thoughts of Briggs crept up from the recesses of her mind and clung to her like a shadow.

She recalled seeing him bound to the chair, helpless and afraid. He didn't deserve to die like that. Not at the mercy of that psycho. Briggs was a good man, and she'd never forgive herself for letting it happen. She was responsible for all of them: Briggs, Patterson, Locke, Williams, Fitzgerald, and the five brave SWAT officers. Her breath became shallow. Every death weighed on her like a judgment. Her eyes welled up. She took a deep breath, and the streetlights blurred again in a haze of tears.

She sobbed all the way back to her apartment building, where she sat in the parking garage, lamenting the loss of everyone she couldn't save. Tears streamed down her cheeks with her shaky breaths. When the thoughts subsided, she wiped her face and stepped out of her Mustang. The cold, howling wind echoed throughout the garage. She shut her car door, then took the elevator up to her apartment.

Once inside, she turned on the light and removed her boots, dropping her jacket to the floor. She turned on the sink to let the warm water run over her knuckles. Purple-and-green bruising marked the lengths of her forearms from the climb up the silos. Each injury was tender to the touch.

Riley turned off the water and dried her hands before opening the refrigerator. A shelf full of condiments, two beer bottles, and a moldy block of cheese was all there was inside. She threw the cheese in the trash, then reached in and grabbed a beer. The cool glass soothed her sore knuckles. She rested the bottle against the edge of the counter and slammed her palm against the lid, causing it to pop off. Then she raised the drink to her lips and gulped it down. The contents were as unsatisfying as they were filling.

Setting the bottle on the counter, Riley stared at the crack in her living room floor where the snake had been beheaded. Scuff marks along the baseboards. A string of cobwebs on the ceiling. A layer of dust covering the air conditioner. The silence left her with a lonely ache in her throat. For the first time, she realized how empty her apartment was. A fridge with no food. A living room with no furniture. All she had were boxes of case files scattered across the floor.

Riley removed her pistol and walked into the living room, where she sat in front of a three-layer stack. She pulled the top box from the pile and took off the lid. The folders within smelled like damp newspaper. She thumbed through the files one by one until she reached the end, then returned the lid and pushed the box aside. She leaned forward and pulled the next box from the stack and repeated this process four more times until she found the black file.

Its edges had worn with age, and one corner had dogeared with a crease. It had been years since she looked at it, but there was a time when it was her obsession. In her free time after work and during days off, she would reexamine every detail of the case, sifting through the evidence and memorizing critical information.

She scooted back a couple feet to give herself space on the floor, then set the file down in front of her. She licked her thumb and opened it to find the report of her parents' murder. The file was full of field reports, evidence sheets, witness statements, and autopsy findings.

Riley flipped to the back of the file, where the crime scene photographs were held. The first image showed her father David shot dead in the driveway. His body—still steaming with heat—was lying facedown in the bloody snow. He had come home after a twelve-hour shift and been ambushed from behind with one gunshot to the back.

Next, she turned to the next photograph of her mother Rachel, lying on her back near the front walkway. Her wide eyes stared up at the night sky. Riley never understood why she ran out of the house. Perhaps she saw David in the snow but didn't see his killer until it was too late. The coroners found the bullet lodged in her heart. She was dead before she hit the ground.

Then there was the photograph of Briggs holding her over his shoulder while carrying her infant brother Michael in the other arm. They were surrounded by several emergency vehicles in the street outside her home with a couple of police officers taping off the scene in the background. There was so much sorrow on his face. The perpetual frown she had become accustomed to as an officer. He had just lost a partner and a dear friend. From the photographs Briggs kept in his home, she believed he never got over her father's death.

Then Riley holding Michael at the police station. She was covered in a thick wool blanket and sitting on a chair in one of the interview rooms. The look of her petrified gaze within the image made her heart ache. The police had interviewed her several times throughout the night, as she was the closest witness to the scene and the victims. She remembered being too afraid to sleep. All she wanted to do was hold on to her little brother for fear of losing him too. She was just a child, but couldn't help feeling that a piece of her died that night as well.

Riley turned to the next image, of Michael with his new parents, a middle-class couple with a small brown dog. The Cook County Children's home gave her the photograph a month after the adoption, and it was the last image she had of him. She looked at the three of them sitting on a carpeted living room floor in front of a fireplace. He was smiling from ear to ear. The couple had offered to adopt Michael two weeks after her parents' murder, but only him—and she was given a choice—have Michael stay with her to be raised by the Cook County Children's Home, or let him live with them.

For years, she told herself that she let Michael go because they would provide him a better life, but now she realized that was a lie. She let him go out of fear that she couldn't protect him, the same way she couldn't protect Briggs. She was so afraid to lose him, she pushed him away and had done the same to everyone else in her life since. Tears ran down her cheeks as she traced her finger over the photograph.

Riley closed the file and placed it back in the box. The Sandman was right. She was alone—and it was her fault.

FORTY-SIX

"Step inside, facing the wall," the pig with too much cologne said. "You move and I'll break something."

The Sandman entered the vacant cell and waited for the door to be sealed behind him. Once it clanked shut, he reached back to have his handcuffs removed. The chain was yanked toward the bars, and his braces were squeezed tight around his wrists. "The guard will be right over, freak. Don't give me a reason to come back."

The pig removed the cuffs and walked down the hall to join the two other wastes of life in the observation room.

It was a mistake to bring him here unmasked. He now knew the officers in charge of the cellblock carried tasers instead of guns, and the one behind the console was obese, which meant he would be the last through the door—and the last alive. The overcompensating pig with the cologne and the pathetic threats kept his keys on his right hip and would most likely attack from that side. As for the guard, he wouldn't have a chance. It was intoxicating to think about the mayhem that would occur in the next few minutes, like a loaded gun waiting to go off.

He tongued his lips to taste the blood and felt himself getting hard. He'd be with her soon enough. That was the thing about darkness—it came for everyone. Walking to the far cement wall, he sat on the ground beside the seatless toilet. It wouldn't be long now. He raised his wrist to his mouth and bit into a thick scar that ran along his forearm. Blood trickled from the crook of his elbow and dripped onto the floor. He spat the scar tissue and bit into his arm again, teething through the blood until he plucked out a three-inch nail. He made a fist with his other hand and tucked the nail between his middle and ring finger, then concealed it beneath his leg. If only they knew what they had invited.

He relaxed his arm and watched the blood spread across the cell floor. Perhaps the blood loss would take its toll and he'd drift into nothingness. One could hope, if there was anything to hope for. The observation room door buzzed open, and a pair of footsteps came down the hall. He closed his eyes and leaned his back against the wall. The footsteps drew closer and stopped outside his cell.

"Hey, I need help over here!"

Keys jingle from the guard's belt as he unlocked the cell. The observation room door buzzed open again, and another pair of footsteps came running down the hall. "What happened?"

"He cut himself. There's blood everywhere."

The guard entered the cell and kneeled beside him. Two fingers rested upon his neck. "I've got a pulse."

He opened his eyes and plunged the nail deep into the guard's neck. They stared at each other as the pig entered the doorway. "Get away from him!"

He stabbed the guard two more times, leaving the nail embedded in his neck. Blood gushed everywhere from his ruptured carotid artery. The guard fell back as the pig ran into the cell and swung at him with his right fist. The Sandman dodged the blow and jabbed the pig in the throat, collapsing his trachea. The pig dropped to his knees, eyes wide, unable to breathe.

The Sandman wiped the mask of blood from his face and rose to his feet. The choking gasps echoed off the cell walls before the pig grasped his throat and fell to the ground.

The observation room door buzzed open again, and another pair of heavy footsteps came down the hall. "Tucker? Marcus? You guys all right?"

He reached down and retrieved the taser from the guard's belt, stepping out of the cell.

"Oh shit!" the fat officer said, then ran back toward the observation room, causing his hat to fall off. The Sandman followed, leaving a trail of bloody footsteps. Why did they always run? Couldn't they see it was inevitable?

The fat officer pulled the observation room door, but it was locked. The Sandman raised his bloody arm and aimed the taser. The officer glanced back in horror before collapsing to the ground with twelve hundred volts coursing through his body.

The Sandman peered through the window of the observation room door. No one else was in sight. A halo of blood began to pool around the fat officer's temple as he lifted his legs and dragged him back to his cell at the end of the hall. All three bodies lay motionless on the ground. He stood over them, savoring the moment. Darkness had come for them. His darkness. And soon, she'd understand the depths of his darkness too. They'd all see.

Like the shedding of old skin, he removed his blood-splattered clothing and tossed it onto the floor. He ripped the guard's shirt and wrapped his wound before putting on the pig's uniform. In the pockets were a set of car keys, mints, and a wallet. A short walk to the rear parking lot, and it would be like he was never there. He removed the fat officer's keys and attached them to his belt, then washed his face in the sink above the toilet.

The Sandman walked out of the cell and lifted the officer's hat from the floor. The neighboring cell was empty, but the next one had a man with an anchor tattoo cowering against the back wall. He winked to the man, then continued to the next cell, where Robert Kane stood behind the bars. He stopped on the opposite side of the door and stared at him.

"Who sent you?" Kane asked.

The Sandman extended the pull string from his belt and sorted through the ring of keys. They were numbered one through six to correspond with each cell. He lifted key number three from the bundle and inserted it into the lock.

"Listen, whatever they're paying you, I can double it. Triple it! I'll pay you more money than you know what to do with."

He unlocked the cell door and opened it.

Kane took a step back. "A person like me only gets where he is through loyalty. I know who runs the prisons. The Big Five have nothing to fear from me. I'll honor our deal. On my life, I promise I won't say a word."

The Sandman entered the cell.

"Do you know who I am! Do you have any idea the people that will come for you?"

He took another step closer, and Kane took another step back. "You can have my operation. It's yours, take it. You can have whatever you want!"

Another step. Kane backed against the wall, then dropped to his knees. "Why are you doing this?"

He looked down at Kane, placing a hand on each side of his face. "Why not?"

Then he plunged his thumbs deep into Kane's eye sockets, causing the man to wail in agony. Blood oozed down the sides of his cheeks as he collapsed to the ground.

FORTY-SEVEN

A loud buzzing roused Riley from sleep. She lifted her head off the pillow to find her cell phone vibrating against the nightstand table. It was a call from the station. She sat up in bed and rubbed her groggy eyes before answering it. "Walker."

A flurry of distressed yelling came through the phone. She pulled it away from her ear, then brought it back. "Slow down. I can't understand you."

"He escaped!" Reyes shouted. "The Sandman is gone!"

Her heart skipped a beat. "What are you talking about? How is that possible?"

"I don't know. We're pulling the surveillance footage. The midnight shift found the guard and two officers dead in his cell. It's a goddamn bloodbath."

A thousand questions percolated in her mind, but she was at a loss for words.

"We put out a BOLO and called in extra patrols to search the area. Agent Harrison is already on a plane back to DC. I need you down here now."

"I'm on my way," she said.

"There's one more thing you should know. Kane is dead. I'm sorry."

The news knocked the wind out of her. With Kane gone, so was any chance of taking down the Big Five. She placed a hand over her face. "Me too."

"Every minute counts. I'll see you soon."

She hung up the phone and rose from her bed in a cold sweat. With only two hours of sleep, her movements were sluggish, but this wasn't the time to be soft. The Sandman was out there, and Riley needed to stop him before he hurt anyone else.

As she finished putting on her clothes, she punched in the code to her gun safe. She holstered her Glock, then hurried into the living room, where she slid on her boots and lifted her jacket from the floor. After locking her apartment, Riley took the elevator down to the parking garage and rushed across the lot to her white Mustang. She slid into the driver's seat and started the engine. Her car rumbled to life as a cold piece of metal pressed against her neck.

"Turn off the car," a guttural voice said from the back seat. She peered into the rearview mirror to see the Sandman's unblinking eyes staring back at her. His hands and police uniform were stained with blood. A flush of adrenaline left her breathless.

"Do it!" he said.

Riley inched her arm toward the keys and shut off the engine. He pressed the metal harder into her neck. "Now lock the doors."

His breath was sickening. If she pressed that button, her chances of escape would plummet. "We have patrols looking for you all over the city. There's nowhere you can hide where they won't find you."

He chuckled to himself. "Find me? They wouldn't even know where to start. Take yourself, for instance. I've been following you this whole time. Thirsty, city hall, the hospital, the plant, the cemetery. Sometimes, I lie beneath your bed and listen to you sleep. All those terrible nightmares you have. Makes me want to reach up and smother them away."

She looked away and shuddered. He twisted the metal against her neck. "Don't make me ask twice."

She reached for the driver's door and pressed the auto lock button. It wouldn't be long before Reyes and Kurt took notice of her absence. Her best hope of survival was to stall him for as long as possible. "How did you escape? There must have been two guards watching your cell."

"Three actually, but none of that matters now. Not for you. Not anymore. Put your hands on the wheel."

It was in her best interest to comply. If he wanted her dead, she would be. Riley reached forward and placed both hands on the steering wheel.

"Where's your gun?"

"My hip."

"Remove it with your right hand. Slowly."

She hesitated for a moment. If she fired her gun, would anyone hear it?

"That metal you feel against your neck is a taser I took from one of the guards. You'll never get a shot off, so don't try it."

She reached to her side and lifted the gun from its holster, keeping the barrel pointed toward the dashboard. A sudden wave of hyperventilating panic screamed through her. She knew what was coming. First he did it to Locke, then to Williams. All the other killings were out of necessity. This was his true modus operandi.

"Shh, shh-shh. Breathe, Riley. Everything is going to be all right."

Her hand trembled as she took a deep breath, then exhaled. Her heart pounded in her ears.

"That's right. Take another one. In and out. You're safe here. Close your eyes. No one is going to disturb us."

His voice had slowed to a soft monotone. She took another deep, cleansing breath until her lungs filled with air, then exhaled. Her pulse began to relax. She closed her eyes and sank deeper into the driver's seat.

"That's good, Riley. Really good. Take another deep breath, in and out. Let all your worries fade away. Nothing matters now. Think about your parents. How happy they'll be to see you. Can you see them? Can you see their smiling faces?"

She took another deep breath and envisioned her mother and father smiling at her the way they had so many years ago. Riley missed them so much. She thought about all the things she wished to say.

"Yes," she said.

"And Briggs, he'll be there too. He was so proud of you. Such a good detective you've become, just like your father. You'll be reunited with all of them, Riley. You'll never be alone again. Not like here. They don't want you to be in pain, do they?"

Tears ran down her cheeks. She sniffled and nodded. "No."

"That's right. No more pain. No more nightmares. No more fear. Think of their happy faces smiling. Smiling at you. Feel the warmth of their embrace. They're love. They're waiting for you, Riley. All you have to do is pull the trigger."

The weight of her burden lifted from her shoulders as she raised the barrel against her head.

"That's right. Leave it all behind. It doesn't matter now. Let everything fade away . . ."

She opened her eyes and found herself surrounded by light. Everything was brighter. Warmer. Her parents stood before her, smiling with open arms. They were waiting for her. Waiting to take her far away. She moved through the infinite light and wrapped her arms around them. She breathed in her mother's floral perfume and felt her father's stubbled cheek. That warmth radiated through her with a sense of peace. Riley was weightless.

All sense of time had faded away. She was ready to go with them. Ready to move beyond, but within that reverie of light and love, something awful bubbled up from the depths.

Tar-like arms clawed onto her legs and dragged her down into the cold, vile muck. Her parents slipped through her grasp, and they watched her descent into the black abyss. Riley thrashed and kicked against their grip, but the arms pulled her deeper and deeper into the great below until she was surrounded by hordes of lost souls. The victims that waited dormant within the stacks of case files on her living room floor. They stared at her, longing for the final word. They needed her. She was their voice, their advocate, their keeper. She couldn't leave them now. Not when there was so much left unanswered. Not while evil reigned free.

Riley opened her eyes and lowered the gun from her head. "No. I won't do it."

"Such a waste," the Sandman said. "Roll down the window. Throw it outside."

She lowered the driver's window and tossed her gun into the neighboring parking space. It slid across the pavement and thumped against the concrete block.

"Now your cell phone and radio."

She reached into her jacket pocket, wishing she still had her knife.

"Don't test me," he said.

She threw them out the window.

"Close it," he said. "Then put your hands back on the wheel."

Riley shut the driver's window, then rested both hands on the steering wheel. She gazed into the rearview mirror. "You won't get away with this."

He smiled a big toothy grin. "I already have—since the moment I left the anonymous tip that led you to Johnny."

A sudden chill struck her core. "This was about Kane. You knew I wouldn't stop until I brought him in."

"Now that Kane is dead, the gangs will go to war. Police tensions will escalate, fanning the flames of public discontent. Civil unrest will erupt into disorder. Neighbor will turn against neighbor, and this city will tear itself apart. Everyone will see just how far we can fall." He leaned forward and whispered in her ear. "You think I cower before the darkness? You're wrong. I am the darkness."

A burning shock from the taser surged through her body. She screamed as all of her muscles tightened. The Sandman gripped the back of her head, then slammed her face into the steering wheel.

FORTY-EIGHT

CAN YOU SEE

The bloody words were marked on the cement wall above Kane's eyeless corpse. Kurt entered the cell and crouched beside his body. How the hell could this have happened? Three officers dead, including one suspect in police custody. All those hard-earned days of putting the case together, gone in a single night. He wanted a drink but knew that would have to wait—he needed to keep his edge for this.

Unlike previous victims, the skin around Kane's eye sockets was intact, which meant he hadn't used a knife. He doubted the Sandman could have smuggled one past the guards anyway. There were no defensive wounds on his arms or hands. No ligature marks around his wrists and no stab wounds on his torso. It was possible the Sandman could have attacked Kane while he was sleeping.

Kurt turned around and looked at the blood trail leading from the observation room door to the end of the hall. No, there would have been too much noise for that. So what then? Kane must have seen the events play out between the guards, then watched the Sandman come for him. That was why his body was lying here at the back of the cell and not by the door. He didn't try to escape. He didn't even fight back. After all that talk about power, in the end he was just a coward.

Kurt rose to his feet and walked out of the cell to join Reyes in the hallway. She had been pacing between the cells, cross-armed. "Well, what do you think?"

"Can't know for sure until the ME takes a look, but it appears the Sandman did this with his bare hands."

"How the hell am I supposed to explain this to the chief? Avery is going to be furious. Where's Riley? She should have been here already."

"I don't know," he said, and walked with her to the next cell. Roy was sitting on his bed with his back against the wall. "Has he said anything?"

"He's refusing to talk to us."

Kurt stepped toward the bars. "You sure that's how you want to play this, chief? Where you're going, I'd be begging for an out."

"What are you offering?"

"Nothing right now, but if you play ball, perhaps we can get you into PC."

Roy looked down at the floor, lost in thought. Kurt had cast the line and gotten a bite. Now it was time to reel him in. He leaned his arms through the bars. "We both know they're going to eat you alive in gen pop. Come on, what harm could it do?"

Roy stood up from the bed. "I want a guarantee. Get it in writing, or I'm not saying anything."

"No time. This is the best I can do. It's now or never."

Roy stepped closer to the bars as Kurt pulled his arms back. "You scared?"

"If I got my hands on you, I wouldn't be able to stop myself," Kurt said.

"What happened between me and Riley was never personal."

"I'm sure she feels the same way."

"This job took everything from me. My wife, my daughter. I lost everything!"

Kurt's eyes narrowed. "You want forgiveness? Save it for the prison chaplain. Last chance."

Roy turned away, then sat back on his bed.

"Your funeral," Kurt said, then followed the trail of bloody footprints to the end of the hall. Three bodies rested in a pool of blood in the center of the last cell. They weren't staged in any particular way, more like trash discarded on the side of the road. He hadn't known any of them on a personal level, but had seen them around the station at one time or another.

"All three were on guard tonight?" he asked Reyes.

"No, just Officer Watts and Officer Smith." She pointed to the third officer, who was stripped down to his T-shirt and underwear. "Officer Jackson was responsible for transferring the Sandman from the interview room to here."

"Have their families been notified? Better to hear it from us than a group of reporters on their front doorstep tomorrow morning."

"They will be," Reyes said. "As soon as we understand what happened here."

Kurt flashed her a smile, but it didn't sit right with him. Some things should take precedence over politics and vanity, even if the news was uglier than sin. He walked around the perimeter of the cell so that he didn't disturb the crime scene. Blood stains covered the walls, the bed, the toilet and the bars. He couldn't touch any of the bodies since forensics hadn't captured the scene, but he didn't need to. Their wounds were visible for all to see.

He stepped over the bodies to the back of the cell, where Officer Watts was lying on his left shoulder. Kurt placed his hand against the wall to balance himself over the body. A piece of metal was embedded in the right side of his neck next to two other puncture wounds—the Sandman was left-hand dominant. He looked at the thin, wavy line of arterial spray, just above knee height. Officer Watts had been crouching when the Sandman punctured his carotid artery. Kurt pushed off the wall. "This one bled out in seconds. The Sandman ruptured his carotid with a piece of metal."

"A knife?" Reyes asked.

"No, looks more like a sliver of something."

"He was searched when we brought him in. How did he get it past the guards?"

"I don't know. He might have broken it off the interview room table." He looked around the cell. "Or maybe from something in here. The ME will have to determine what it is."

"I'll have both rooms inspected after forensics takes their photographs."

Kurt rounded the cluster of bodies to Officer Smith. The blood trail that started at the observation room door ended at the side of his head. What had caused him to fall like that? Blunt force trauma from behind? Kurt bent down to look at him from another angle. There were no stab wounds, and no other signs of a struggle. How could that be?

"Do the guards carry guns?"

"No," Reyes said. "They're not allowed in the cell block."

"What about Officer Jackson? He's not a guard."

"He would have been disarmed before entering the area."

Kurt turned back to her. "Jackson led him to the cell unarmed?"

She crossed her arms. "The Sandman was restrained, and both of the guards have tasers."

Kurt looked at Officer Watts's belt. The holster for his taser was empty. "He took Watts's taser after stabbing him to death, then used it against Officer Smith. That's why he fell to the floor and hit his head."

He continued moving around the cell to Officer Jackson. The man was lying on his back with both eyes staring at the ceiling. The Sandman's blood-soaked clothing was on the floor next to him. There were no signs of stab wounds, bruising, or ligature marks; blood stained his skin, but that came from Officer Watts. Heart attacks from taser shocks were rare, but not unheard of.

He kneeled down to take a closer look. No skin under his fingernails, no defensive wounds, and no missing organs. He had to be missing something.

Kurt looked over the body one more time, then rose to his feet. He would have to wait for the medical examiner's report to determine a cause of death. The whole scene left a bitter taste in his mouth. Something had caused Watts and Jackson to enter the Sandman's cell, and it had cost them everything. Kurt walked out of the kill room to join Reyes in the hall.

"Did Officer Jackson have access to a vehicle?"

"He brought the Sandman in from the Damen Silos. Why?"

Kurt's heart raced. He pulled out his cell phone and started dialing. "The Sandman used Jackson's uniform as a disguise to escape the station. His keys would have been in his pocket. We need to find his vehicle now!" He radioed Dispatch. "5239, I need the location of a squad car belonging to an Officer Jackson. I don't have the unit number." The dispatcher requested Jackson's first name, and he got the information from Reyes. "Carl, his name is Carl."

He waited as the dispatcher searched the location of the vehicle. A pair of forensic members entered the hallway, each carrying an equipment case under their arm. Reyes motioned for them to examine Kane's cell. The dispatcher came back on the phone. "The vehicle is currently in Hyde Park on South Cornell Avenue between East Fifty-Fifth and Fifty-Sixth."

Kurt. clenched his fist. "Send all available units to that location now! The vehicle was stolen by a homicide suspect. He's armed and dangerous."

"5239, 10-4. Sending all available units to that location now."

He hung up the phone and started running down the hall. "He's going after Riley! Send me her address."

FORTY-NINE

Riley awoke with a head-throbbing groan. She was lying faceup with her right forearm wedged beneath the small of her back. There was a dampness in the air, a cold, palpable stillness. Where was she? The lost sense of time and place was unnerving. The last thing she remembered was her head hitting the steering wheel. If the Sandman had wanted her dead, she would have been. So why was she still alive?

She recalled his threat from the interview room. *You think you know suffering? I have so much in store for you.* She pinched her lips together to keep her chin from trembling. This had been his plan all along.

Riley listened for movement, but all she could hear was the sound of her breathing. The floor beneath her was firm and cold. After a few minutes, she worked up the nerve to slip the dead weight of her arm out from under her.

Clenching her fist to regain sensation, she felt her pinky finger rub up against a wall. Then she ran her hand along the wooden surface. Its finish was uneven and rutted with cracks. She returned her hand to the floor and remained still. If he was nearby, she didn't want to him to know she was awake. How long had she been unconscious? Since she'd never arrived at the station, Reyes and Kurt had to know something is wrong. Every patrol unit in the city should have been looking for her.

Clearly, she had been resting here for a while. The numbness in her arms and legs faded the more she moved them. She inched her toes downward until the edges of her feet pushed against another wall. Her limbs were unrestrained. She had to be lying in some sort of small room. There was a chance of escape if she waited for the right moment. As long as she was still breathing, there was hope.

Riley crept her fingers around her pockets. Her cell phone and pistol were gone. She would have to use whatever she could find as a weapon against him. Reaching out to the wall again, she tested its durability. The wood was solid and thick. She returned her hand to the floor and felt the same material. A horrifying thought emerged in the back of her mind, but she repressed it like a bad memory.

From the deafening silence around her, she got the sense that she was alone. He could be back any minute, and she needed to be ready to fight. After a few minutes, she decided to risk sneaking a peek at her surroundings. She opened her eyes to a squint, but saw nothing. Then she opened them all the way—still nothing.

"No," she trembled.

A sudden chill swept through her body. What had he done? Everything was consumed by darkness, a black emptiness so oppressive it had weight. It couldn't be. Her heart began to race, an awful dread in the pit of her stomach. Riley looked all around, but couldn't see anything. She shook her head back and forth. No, this couldn't be happening. She reached up to her face and felt her elbows bump against walls on either side of her. Tucking in her arms, she rubbed her eyes. Everywhere she looked, she saw nothing but infinite black.

Riley tried to sit up, but only banged her forehead against the ceiling six inches above her. She pushed her palms against it and felt the same wood material. Her breath became heavy. The lid was weighed down from the other side. This wasn't just a wooden box, it was a coffin. She had been buried alive.

Riley pounded her fist against the ceiling. "Let me out!"

She leaned to the side and pressed her body against the walls, but nothing budged. She stomped against the floor again and again, but couldn't see if she was making a dent. There wasn't enough room to kick the ceiling, and the more energy she exerted, the more air she would lose. She banged against the lid until her arm gave out from exhaustion. It was no use. Nothing she did could break through. She fell back and covered her mouth. Her chin trembled with a painful lump in her throat. Tears streamed down the sides of her face and into her hair. "No, please. No."

Her voice broke in a strangled cry of desperation. She would do anything to feel the sun against her face or take one last fresh breath. She would relive her worst day again, just to have another.

Riley rolled onto her side and lay still for what felt like hours. How long had she been in here? Even if Kurt and Reyes were looking for her, they'd never find her in time.

She closed her eyes and thought about all the victims she had seen over the years. Hundreds of faces gazing into that final abyss. She liked to believe that behind their eyes was a sense of peace. Now she'd be one of them. A sliver among the vast heap of case files—if she was ever found. All she had to do was slip into an endless sleep.

"No," she said, and rolled onto her back. The Sandman might take her life, but she refused to go willingly. She would fight for life with every breath until her last. One last darkness before oblivion.

FIFTY

Rain poured over the cruiser's windshield as Kurt barreled down State Street. Riley's address wasn't far, but every minute counted. He should have known something was wrong. She never missed a call.

He stomped on the gas pedal, causing the engine to roar. The tachometer pushed to the redline, then shifted into gear. He weaved in and out of traffic, emergency lights flashing.

The cruiser hydroplaned through a puddle, but he didn't slow down. Nothing was going to stop him. An intersection was fast approaching. Cars pulled over to the side of the road, giving him a clear path ahead. Kurt let off the gas and made a hard left onto East Garfield Boulevard.

"Come on," he said.

The cruiser over-steered around the turn, whipping the back end out of control. Kurt wrestled against the steering wheel until the car straightened a couple feet from the curb. He floored it again and sped down the three-lane road toward Morgan Drive. He veered right around Washington Park and continued onto East

Fifty-Fifth Street. From there, it was a five-minute straight shot to South Cornell Avenue.

He turned right onto the street and continued down the road until he saw two flashing police units barricading the middle of the road. He pulled up behind the pair of officers with their guns drawn and stepped out of the cruiser.

"Get back in your vehicle!" one officer said.

Kurt flashed his badge. "CPD, homicide." He looked past the officers to the police unit parked on the side of the road. "Is that it?"

"Yeah, we got here a few minutes ago. Doesn't look like anyone is inside."

Kurt drew his pistol. "Cover me."

He walked past the barricade and approached the vehicle. Its lights were off, and there was no steam coming from the exhaust. The vehicle's interior was too dark to see, and his vision was obscured by the rain. He aimed at the windshield and crept up to the driver's door. The two officers were following on either side of his shoulder.

Aiming into the driver's window, Kurt saw that the seat was empty. He looked into the back seat, then opened the door. There were drops of blood on the steering wheel and seat, but the vehicle was empty.

He holstered his pistol and turned to the officers. "There's no one inside. One of you, check the trunk. The other come with me." He ran across the street into the apartment lobby and pressed the elevator button several times.

"Is it true? Has the Sandman escaped?" the officer asked.

"Yeah," Kurt said, pressing the elevator button again.

"I heard he takes the victim's eyes. What's he do with 'em?"

"I don't know, but if you get a shot at him, take it."

He pulled open the stairwell door and ran up three flights to Riley's floor. The hallway was empty. He rushed to her apartment to find that the door was shut. There were several metallic scratches on the deadbolt lock above the handle. The Sandman was here. He pulled his pistol from its holster and grabbed the door handle. It was locked. He banged on the door three times,

"Riley, are you in there?"

There was no response. He banged three more times. "Riley! It's Kurt, I'm coming in."

The officer aimed his pistol toward the door.

"Step back," Kurt said, then kicked the door. Chunks of wood broke from the doorframe and slid across the floor. Kurt aimed his pistol and stepped inside the dark apartment. He didn't sense any movement. The officer turned on his flashlight and beamed it across the room.

There was no one in sight. The living room was close to empty. No furniture, no pictures on the walls, just stacks of brown cardboard boxes scattered across the floor. Did she just move in? Kurt reached against the wall and turned on the light. Upon a second glance, it became clear that the room was too lived-in to be new. This was how it always was.

He aimed around the corner to the walk-in kitchen. A half-finished beer bottle rested on the counter. Kurt rubbed the glass with two fingers. The bottle was still sweating. "Riley! Are you in here?"

He crossed the barren living room to the bedroom door, which was cracked open. His breathing became shallow as his footsteps creaked along the floor.

"Riley?" he called into the room, pushing the door with his foot. The officer beamed his flashlight against the back wall. Kurt scanned the room but didn't see anyone. He turned on the bedroom light as the officer entered the bathroom. The bedsheets were ruffled. She had been disturbed from sleep, same as him. Another stack of cardboard boxes rested beneath the window.

"It's all clear," the officer said as he returned to the bedroom. "Anything else?"

"No, that's all."

The officer left him at the foot of Riley's bed. The gun safe on her nightstand table was open. He looked around the room. If the Sandman had taken her from here, there'd be signs of a struggle. Blood on the floor, knocked-over furniture, gunshots. But nothing appeared out of place.

"He didn't take her from here. He needed someplace more secluded."

Kurt walked out of the apartment and into the hallway. The officer was standing opposite of a neighbor in a bathrobe. "Who do you people think you are? I have to be up at five in the morning!"

"Sir, I need you to calm down."

Kurt rushed down the hall and took the stairwell to the underground parking garage. The lot was full of vehicles. He hurried along the pathway, looking for her white Mustang. In the middle of the second row, a gun was lying against a cement parking block.

He lifted it off the ground. It was a loaded Glock 19. Same as Riley's. He looked around the lot, then called her number. A cell phone rang beneath a car in the neighboring parking space. He lifted it off the asphalt and looked at the caller ID to confirm.

Kurt looked around for her vehicle again, but didn't see it anywhere. He ended the call and dialed Reyes's number. She answered on the second ring,

"What have you found?"

"He took her. Riley's gone."

"Are you sure?" she asked.

"I found her service pistol and phone in the parking garage of her building. It looks like he ditched the police unit and took her vehicle. You need to change the BOLO to a white Mustang coupe. Late model."

"Any idea where they might have gone?"

"No." He frowned.

"Our best bet is to keep searching the area. I'll have CDOT pull traffic cam footage from the last hour. I'll call you if they find anything."

"All right," he said, and hung up the phone. He tucked Riley's gun in the back of his pants and pocketed her phone. He looked around the parking garage again. "Come on, Riley, where did he take you?"

She must have dropped her phone and pistol when he took her. How did he do it? He could have attacked while she was entering her car, the same way he did to Locke, but something in his gut told him that wasn't true. She would have expected him after hearing of his escape. So what then?

He looked at the empty parking space next to him. The Sandman didn't attack her next to the car. He was already inside —just like he had been with Briggs.

Kurt's face became flushed, his fists tight. The pounding in his ears was deafening. He reached into his coat pocket and unscrewed the cap of his flask, pulling the container to his lips, but it was empty. He lifted the spout above his mouth. Two drops of whiskey fell to the ground. Chucking the flask against the wall, he let out a frustrated groan.

He fell back against the wall and slid to the ground. There was no way to find her. Kurt removed his badge and thumbed the city seal. He didn't deserve to wear it. He was a fake. It was foolish to think otherwise. He was about to throw the badge away when a thought appeared in the back of his mind. He paused for a moment, then called Reyes.

"We don't have anything yet," she said. "We're still putting in our request."

"I'm not calling about the footage. What did the name patch on the Sandman's uniform say?"

"Charles. Why?"

He remembered the Rosehill Cemetery manager saying the groundskeeper Chuck had been missing his calls.

That was why the security footage never showed the Sandman entering the cemetery. He was already inside.

"Just a hunch. I'll call you back if anything changes."

Kurt rose from the ground and put on his badge. It was a long shot, but it was the only one he had.

FIFTY-ONE

Kurt drove up to the Rosehill Cemetery entrance. Through the streaks of the cruiser's windshield wipers, it was clear the iron gate was sealed with a padlock and chain. He backed up thirty yards, then skidded to a stop. There was no time to waste. He shifted into drive and floored the gas pedal. The tires peeled out against the wet asphalt, then took off toward the gate, bursting it wide open. He followed the road deeper into the cemetery. "Where are you?"

The cruiser's headlights illuminated a roundabout with a towering statue of a soldier. He swerved around the structure and continued down the narrow road. The hard rain pelted his windshield as he sped past numerous mausoleums, obelisks, and tombstones. He veered around a small pond and continued up the road until he found Riley's white Mustang parked in front of an old stone chapel. The gothic building was crowned with a Celtic cross standing tall over a red-tiled roof. He slowed to a stop and radioed dispatch. "5239, need backup at 5800 North Ravenswood Avenue. Homicide suspect on the premises."

"5239, 10-4. Sending a unit to your location now."

He collected his flashlight and stepped into the pouring rain. The road was empty in all directions. Kurt peered into Riley's car. The front and back seats were empty. He ran across the road to the chapel and pushed through the double-door entrance. Inside, it was dark and silent. Rain trickled down the stained-glass windows, casting shadows all around him.

He scanned his flashlight across the room. The walls and floor were covered in handcrafted tile. Oak archways curved along the ceiling to a glass pendant that hung over the main gallery. Kurt crept down the aisle of pews, searching every row, then continued toward an oversized wooden door at the back of the room. Wet blood smears covered the brass handle.

As Kurt pushed against the thick, heavy door, it creaked open into a mortuary with seven skylights overhead. He beamed his flashlight across a wall of white cadaver cabinets. A table full of medical equipment rested in the corner, collecting dust. He walked down the cement steps to an open crematorium. Small mounds of chalky remains were scattered within. The silence was broken by a low, moaning wind coming from a dark archway across the room. The entrance was sealed by a wrought-iron gate. He approached the mouth of the passage and shone his light down into an underground cavern.

Everything beyond his flashlight was pitch-black. His grip tightened over the pistol as he opened the gate and descended into the crypt.

At the bottom of the stairs was an enormous expanse with twenty-four stone support columns. Each of the outer walls had a dark corridor that led deeper underground. A low gust of wind echoed all around. He scanned his beam around the room and found an arched wooden door next to the stairs. Crusted blood smears streaked the frame above the metal latch. He looked over his shoulder, then opened the door into a small, damp room that smelled like rotten meat.

A corpse was slumped over in a wooden chair. The man's decaying green flesh was infested with maggots. Black flies buzzed around the open wounds on his back. Kurt covered his mouth and walked around the chair. The man's wrists and ankles were bound by rope. Multiple stab wounds to his abdomen were leaking pus and bile. He crouched down to look at his face. Bloodstains trickled from the man's hollow eye sockets and pooled on the floor.

Kurt backed out of the room and closed the door behind him. He spat on the ground and tried not to vomit. The placement of the restraints matched the ligature marks on Johnny Stone's corpse. This was where the Sandman had killed him.

He scanned his flashlight across the four rows of stone columns, then crept through them toward the back of the room. A rustle of quick footsteps blindsided him. Kurt turned toward the noise as something struck his arms. Kurt fired his gun and dropped his flashlight to the floor. He aimed into the darkness, but didn't see anyone. Where did he go?

He reached down to lift the flashlight. Blood dripped from the edge of his sleeve onto the ground. A large gash had been cut into his forearm. He picked up the flashlight and aimed at the surrounding columns. His heart pounded against his chest. The Sandman could be anywhere.

Cautiously, Kurt crept forward. The high-pitched ringing in his ears made it difficult to hear, but he could sense the Sandman lurking just out of sight. Kurt turned around and aimed toward the back of the room.

The monster lunged from the darkness and slashed the back of his leg. He dropped to his knees with a painful scream and fired three shots. The bullets ricocheted off a stone column, sparking. He rose to his feet with a grunt. Warm blood trickled down his calf and pooled in his shoe. He remembered Johnny's autopsy report. The medical examiner had said he was stabbed multiple times, for a slow bleed. The Sandman was toying with him.

He limped to the next row.

"Can you feel it?" the Sandman asked from the darkness. "The slow erosion deep inside? No one is coming to save you. Drop your gun, and I'll make it quick."

Kurt gritted his teeth. He scanned the next row of columns, then hobbled toward them. A sharp pain stabbed his side. "Ahh!"

He spun around and fired two more shots, but the Sandman had vanished. Kurt gripped his ribs and felt winded. He leaned back against a stone column and slid down to the cold, hard earth. His arms felt weak. The flashlight rolled from his fingertips and flickered on the ground. The room became quiet again. He could hear the Sandman's footsteps echoing in the dark, but all he could do was sit and wait in the shadows.

After a minute, the Sandman appeared from the darkness and stopped in front of the flashlight. He looked down at the trickle of blood, which led to an empty space in front of a stone column. Kurt stepped out from the darkness and pressed his gun to the back of the Sandman's head. "Drop the knife."

The blade clinked against the ground, and Kurt slid it away with the sole of his shoe. He kicked the back of the Sandman's legs, dropping him to his knees. "Where is she?"

"You're too late."

Kurt fired at the ground, then jammed the burning muzzle against his neck. "Tell me!"

He winced at the pain, then laughed. Kurt pulled the gun away and kicked him to the ground. The Sandman rolled onto his back. "If you ever want to see her again, you'll have to let me go."

A festering rage boiled in Kurt's gut. He clenched his teeth, then lowered his gun. "Where is she?"

The Sandman grinned and pointed toward a dark corridor across the room. "Down there, at the end of the hall."

Kurt lifted the flashlight off the ground and limped toward the passageway.

"See you around, Detective," the Sandman said.

"You better hope not," Kurt said and continued limping into the corridor. His flashlight shone over dozens of gray metal plaques embedded in the walls. Each was inscribed with the names of the deceased.

"Riley! Riley! Can you hear me?"

Kurt rounded the corner and continued down the path to a dead end. He looked to the walls for another entrance, but there was nothing. It didn't make sense. He looked down at the loose patch of dirt and shovel resting next to his feet.

"Oh God."

He dropped the flashlight, and began digging. By the time he was waist deep into the hole, his palms had blistered, but he continued digging through the pain until the tip of his shovel banged against something solid. "Riley! Hold on!"

He scraped the excess dirt from the coffin and used the tip of the shovel to pry open the lid. Removing the wood panel, he found her lying unconscious within. Her skin was pale and her lips were blue. Kurt lifted her out of the hole and placed her on the ground. He checked her neck for a pulse, but felt nothing.

"Come on, Riley!"

He clasped his hands together and pressed against her chest. He blew into her mouth then continued his chest compressions. "Breathe Riley, breathe!"

Kurt continued, but she was unresponsive. Sitting up, he pumped harder. "Come back to me. Wake up."

Beads of sweat dripped down his brow. He leaned over again and breathed into her mouth once more. Her body remained still. He pounded his fist against her chest three times, then fell back against the wall, out of breath. There was nothing else he could do. Riley was gone. He looked at her motionless corpse again, then hung his head. His body shuddered with a falling sensation in his gut. Kurt clenched a fist against his trembling chin. It was all his fault.

Riley gasped for air. She rolled onto her side, coughing into the dirt. Kurt crawled to her and lifted her shoulders off the ground. She caught her breath and looked up at him. Her wide eyes were full of fear. Riley pulled him close and sobbed into his chest. Kurt wrapped his bloody arms around her back and told her she wasn't alone.

FIFTY-TWO

Riley sat on the rear fender of an ambulance, watching dozens of police officers search the burial fields. The rain from the previous night had washed away all trace of the Sandman's escape. FBI agents had closed off the entire cemetery for investigation. It wasn't long before news vans circled the perimeter like vultures, trying to capture whatever footage they could. Someone from the department must have tipped them off.

Reyes didn't seem too concerned with the press. She was preoccupied with a group of three feds at the entrance of the chapel. Riley figured they were heading the investigation in Agent Harrison's stead. A pair of coroners wheeled a body through the chapel doors. The sight left her with a chill down her neck. She pulled the thermal blanket tight around her shoulders.

"You're hard to kill," Kurt said, stepping down from the back of the ambulance. His bandaged arm was wrapped in a sling.

She lowered the oxygen mask from her face. "So are you."

He took his time to lean against the seat next to her. "Yeah, I've been banged up worse before."

"You saved my life," she said. "I would still be down there if it weren't for you."

He cracked a smile and nodded. "Then let's call us even."

Reyes broke from her conversation with the three FBI agents and approached them. "The feds have called in every available asset to help our search. We set up a twelve-mile perimeter with checkpoints on all major roads." Reyes crossed her arms and looked Riley in the eye. "I want you to know that no matter how this pans out, I'll keep my word. You'll be reinstated to the Violent Crimes Task Force. I've already connected with Agent Welles, and she's agreed to have you back."

"Thank you," Riley said. "But I'm staying with Kurt."

"Riley?" he said.

"Are you sure?" Reyes asked.

"Kane's death will leave a power vacuum for the gangs. There's no telling how bad things will get." She looked at him. "And I'll need a partner I can trust."

"I understand." Reyes nodded, then turned to walk away. "Get some rest," she called over her shoulder. "You're going to need it."

The sun broke over the horizon, casting everything in a bright, glowing haze. "If they haven't found the Sandman by now . . ." Kurt said, rubbing the back of his neck. "You know he'll be back. Sooner or later."

"I do," Riley said. "And when he returns, we'll face him —together."

FIFTY-THREE

Riley's thoughts returned to that moment when she was lost in darkness. Through the terror of her final breaths, a calming peace had emerged from within. She realized that the struggle against evil was not hers alone to bear, but a calling for every generation. That in this dark world of murder and madness, there will always be those who carry the light.

THANK YOU

Dear Reader,

Thank you for choosing Of Murder and Madness as your thrilling journey into a world of mystery and suspense. If you enjoyed this book, please leave a review.

Your feedback not only means the world to me, but also helps other readers discover this heart-pounding thriller. Thank you for helping me spread the excitement to others.

You can sign up for the mailing list at **mylesschulman.com** to join a community of thriller fanatics and can also receive:

Limited-Time Offers: Promotions and special discounts you can't get anywhere else.

Exclusive Content: Journey deeper into darkness with additional stories from Riley's past, present, and future. Available only to members!

Thrilling Updates: Prepare for even more twisted thrillers with sneak peeks and first looks into future releases.

I look forward to sharing more thrilling reads with you.

Thank you,

Myles Schulman

ACKNOWLEDGMENTS

The author would like to thank many people for their help with the creation of this novel. First, a great debt of thanks to his parents who have given him everything and still find ways to give more.

Secondly, he would like to thank his brother Avery, without whom there would be no novel. The author would also like the thank LAPD Officer Samantha Chapman for her insight into police procedure. This is a work of fiction. Any errors or exaggerations in the law or its practice are wholly those of the author.

The author is also deeply appreciative of Jan Schulman, Phil Schulman, Brad Schulman and Patricia Wagner for their early reads of the work in progress. Their feedback was invaluable. Lastly, the author's appreciation goes to Stuart Bach for his beautiful cover design and Dylan Garity for editing an unwieldy story. Many thanks to all who helped.

ABOUT THE AUTHOR

Myles Schulman was born and raised outside the city of Los Angeles, California. He graduated from California State University Northridge with a degree in cinema television arts. While working as a Hollywood assistant, he began writing OF MURDER AND MADNESS.

For more information about Myles Schulman, please visit his website at www.mylesschulman.com. Follow him on social media!

FREE DIGITAL COPY!

Thank you for choosing Of Murder and Madness for your thrilling journey into a world of mystery and suspense. To celebrate, I'm offering you a FREE digital copy of this book!

Get your limited-time complimentary ebook and join an exclusive community of thriller fanatics by signing up for the mailing list at the link below. I looking forward to sharing more captivating reads with you!

Of Murder and Madness digital book link:
BookHip.com/DWDZRHJ

Printed in the USA
CPSIA information can be obtained
at www.ICGtesting.com
LVHW051645091123
763431LV00010B/16/J